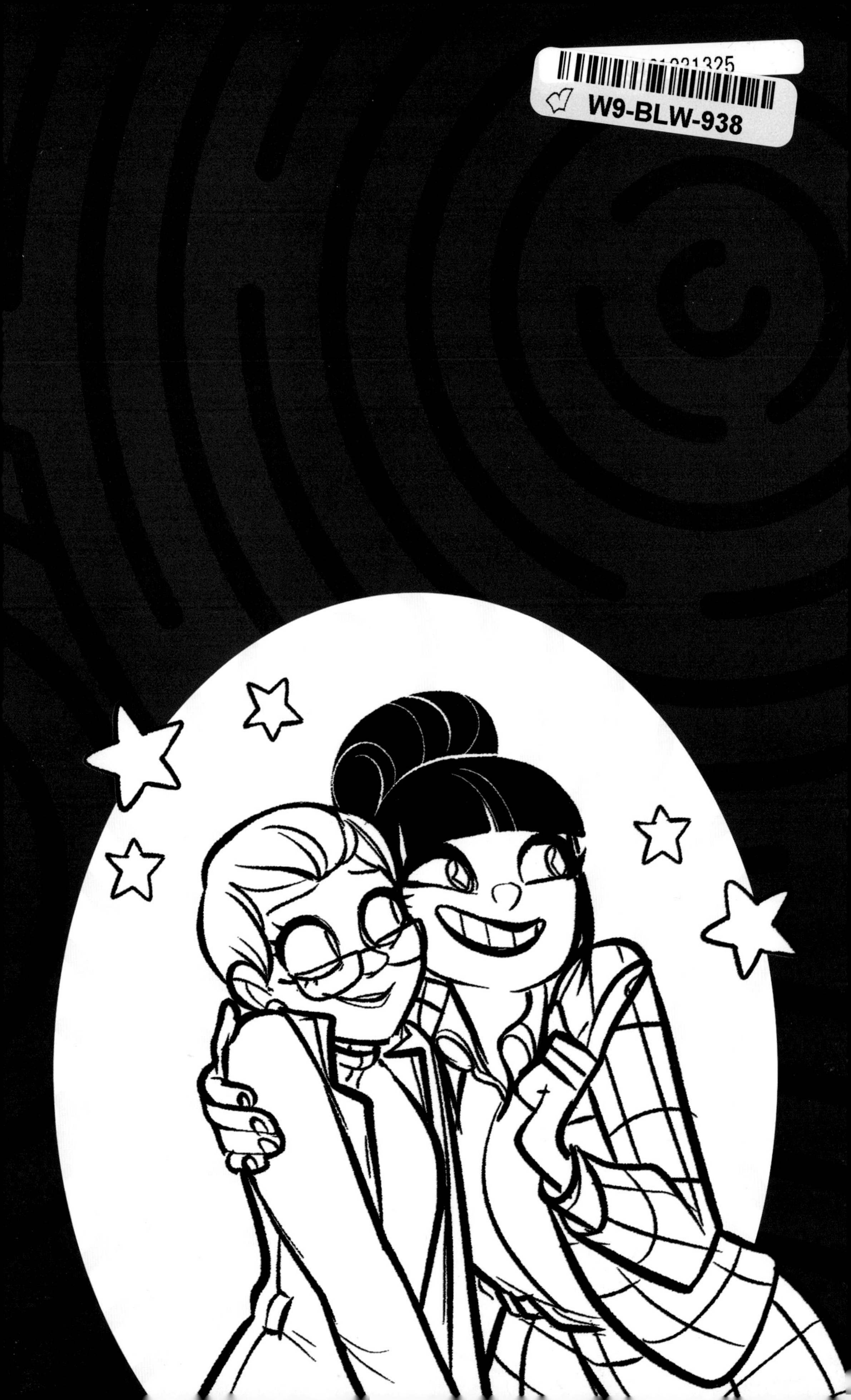

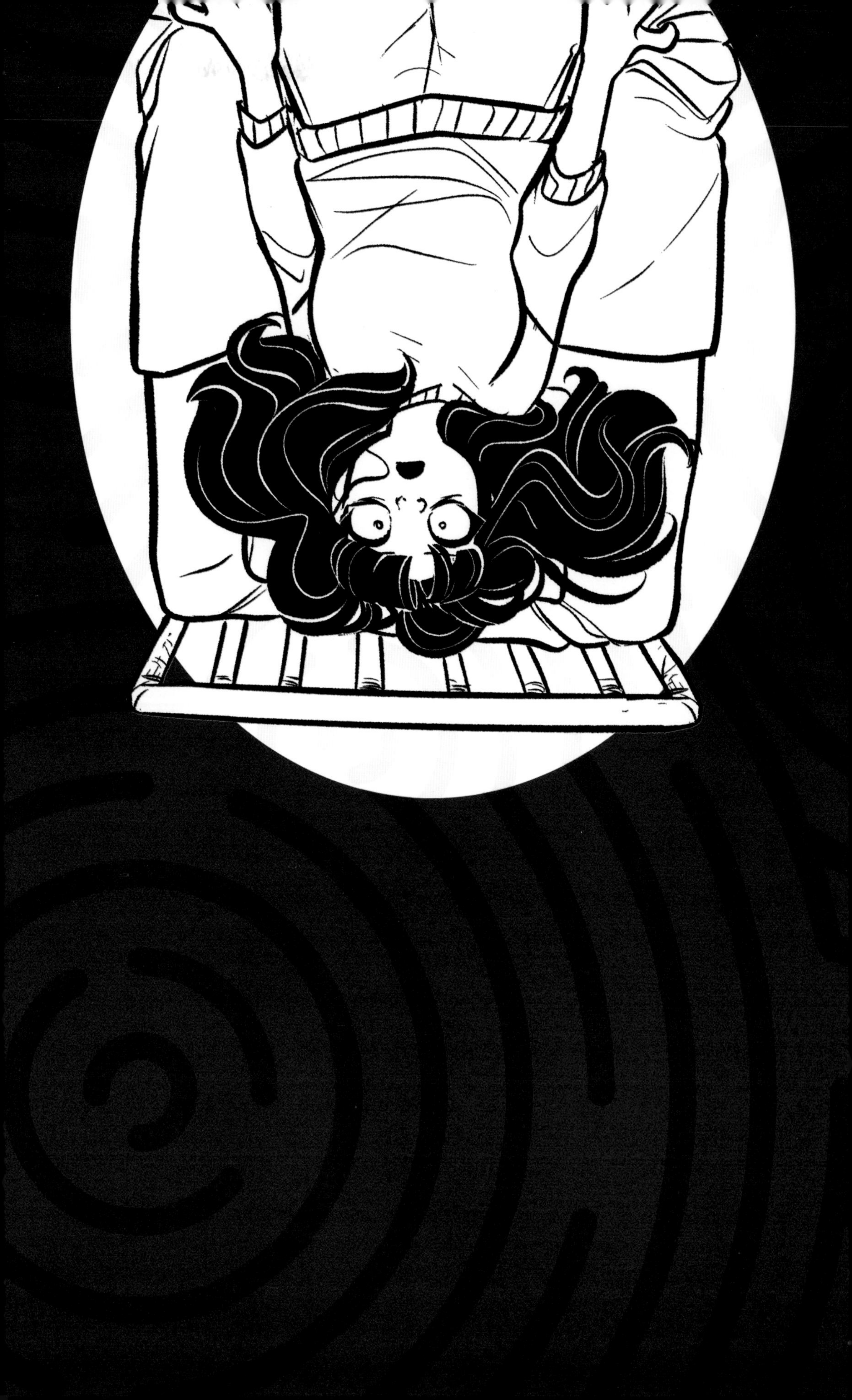

# WICKED THINGS ™

CREATED & WRITTEN BY
## JOHN ALLISON

ART BY
## MAX SARIN

COLORS BY
## WHITNEY COGAR

LETTERS BY
## JIM CAMPBELL

COVER BY
## MAX SARIN

CHAPTER BREAK ART BY
## MAX SARIN

SERIES DESIGNER
**MICHELLE ANKLEY**

ASSOCIATE EDITOR
**SOPHIE PHILIPS-ROBERTS**

COLLECTION DESIGNER
**MARIE KRUPINA**

EDITOR
**SHANNON WATTERS**

# CHAPTER ONE

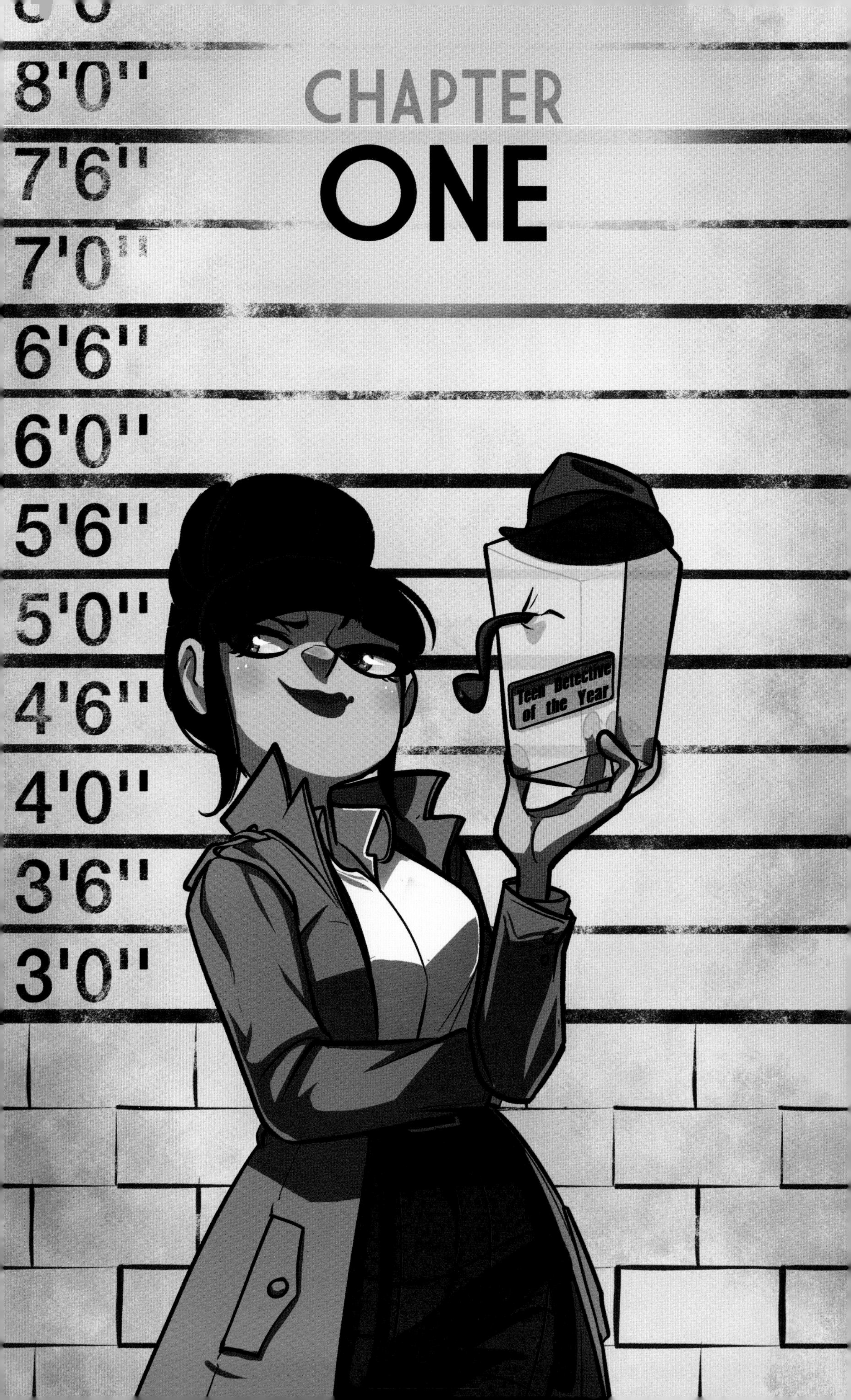
8'0''
7'6''
7'0''
6'6''
6'0''
5'6''
5'0''
4'6''
4'0''
3'6''
3'0''
Teen Detective of the Year

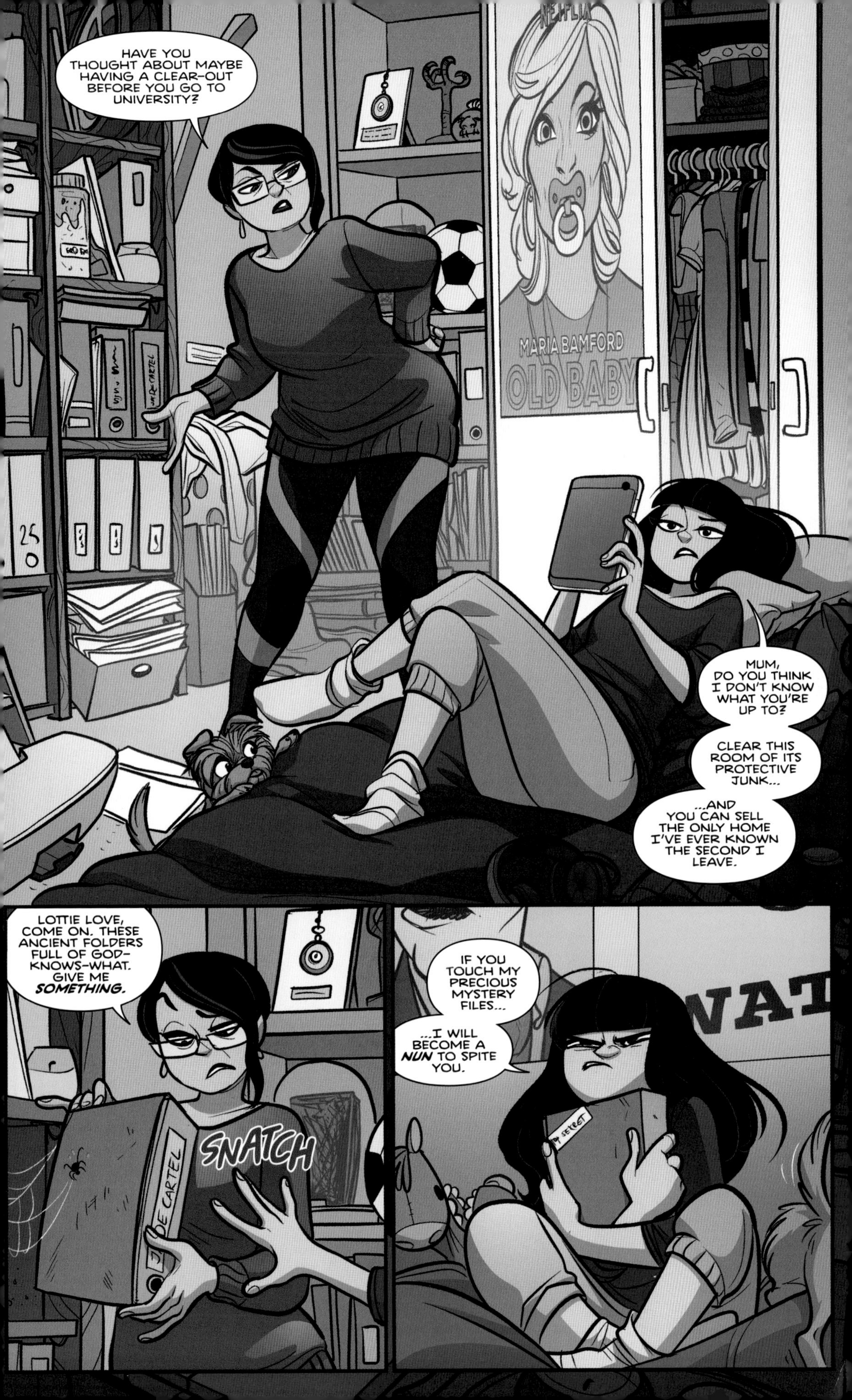
HAVE YOU THOUGHT ABOUT MAYBE HAVING A CLEAR-OUT BEFORE YOU GO TO UNIVERSITY?
MARIA BAMFORD
OLD BABY
MUM, DO YOU THINK I DON'T KNOW WHAT YOU'RE UP TO?
CLEAR THIS ROOM OF ITS PROTECTIVE JUNK...
...AND YOU CAN SELL THE ONLY HOME I'VE EVER KNOWN THE SECOND I LEAVE.
LOTTIE LOVE, COME ON. THESE ANCIENT FOLDERS FULL OF GOD-KNOWS-WHAT. GIVE ME *SOMETHING.*
SNATCH
DE CARTEL
IF YOU TOUCH MY PRECIOUS MYSTERY FILES...
...I WILL BECOME A *NUN* TO SPITE YOU.

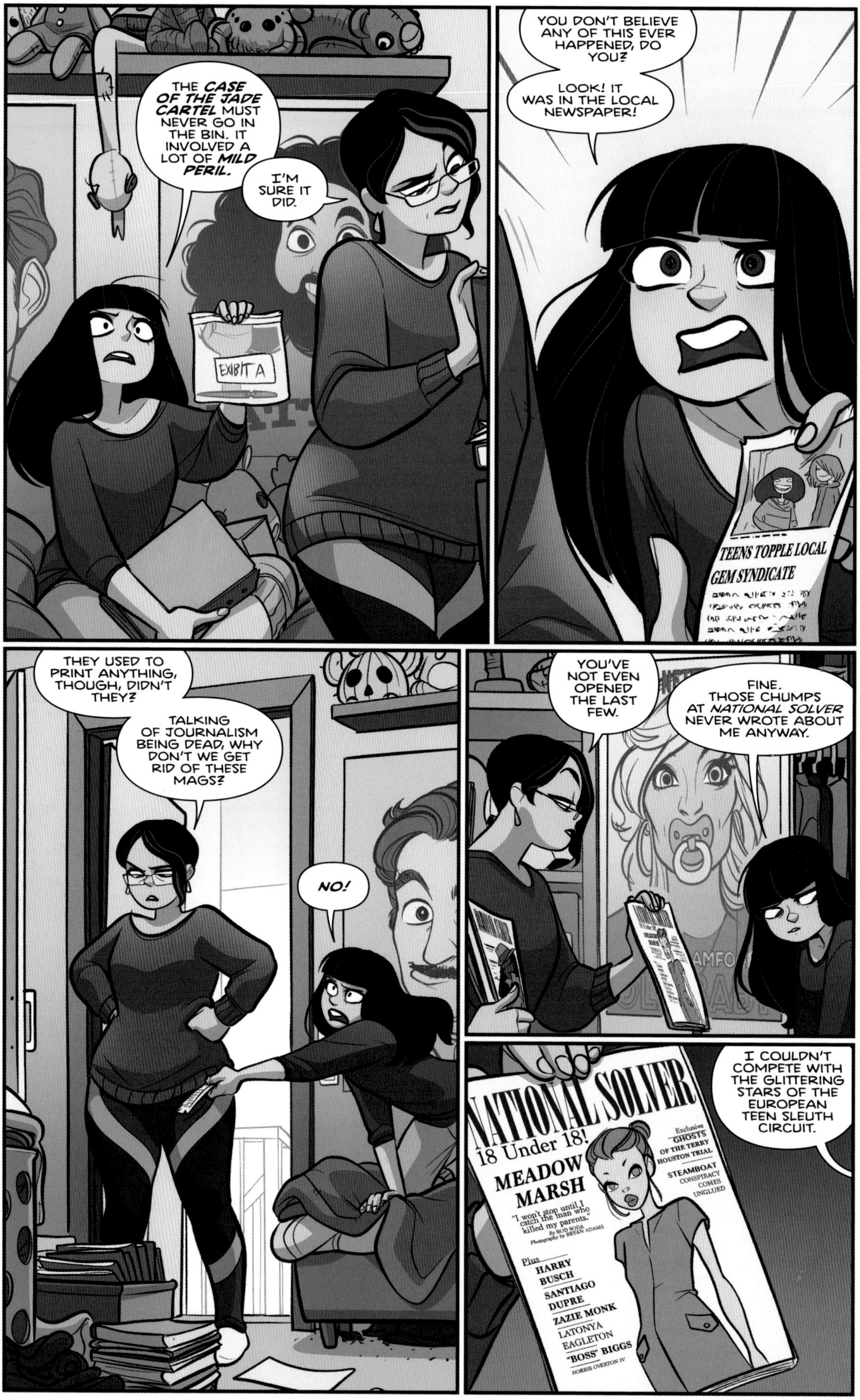
THE *CASE OF THE JADE CARTEL* MUST NEVER GO IN THE BIN. IT INVOLVED A LOT OF *MILD PERIL.*
I'M SURE IT DID.
EXIBIT A
YOU DON'T BELIEVE ANY OF THIS EVER HAPPENED, DO YOU?
LOOK! IT WAS IN THE LOCAL NEWSPAPER!
TEENS TOPPLE LOCAL GEM SYNDICATE
THEY USED TO PRINT ANYTHING, THOUGH, DIDN'T THEY?
TALKING OF JOURNALISM BEING DEAD, WHY DON'T WE GET RID OF THESE MAGS?
NO!
YOU'VE NOT EVEN OPENED THE LAST FEW.
FINE. THOSE CHUMPS AT *NATIONAL SOLVER* NEVER WROTE ABOUT ME ANYWAY.
NATIONAL SOLVER
18 Under 18!
MEADOW MARSH
"I won't stop until I catch the man who killed my parents."
By ROD SODA
Photography by BRYAN ADAMS
Exclusive GHOSTS OF THE TERRY HOUSTON TRIAL
STEAMBOAT CONSPIRACY COMES UNGLUED
Plus
HARRY BUSCH
SANTIAGO DUPRE
ZAZIE MONK
LATONYA EAGLETON
"BOSS" BIGGS
NORRIS OVERTON IV
I COULDN'T COMPETE WITH THE GLITTERING STARS OF THE EUROPEAN TEEN SLEUTH CIRCUIT.

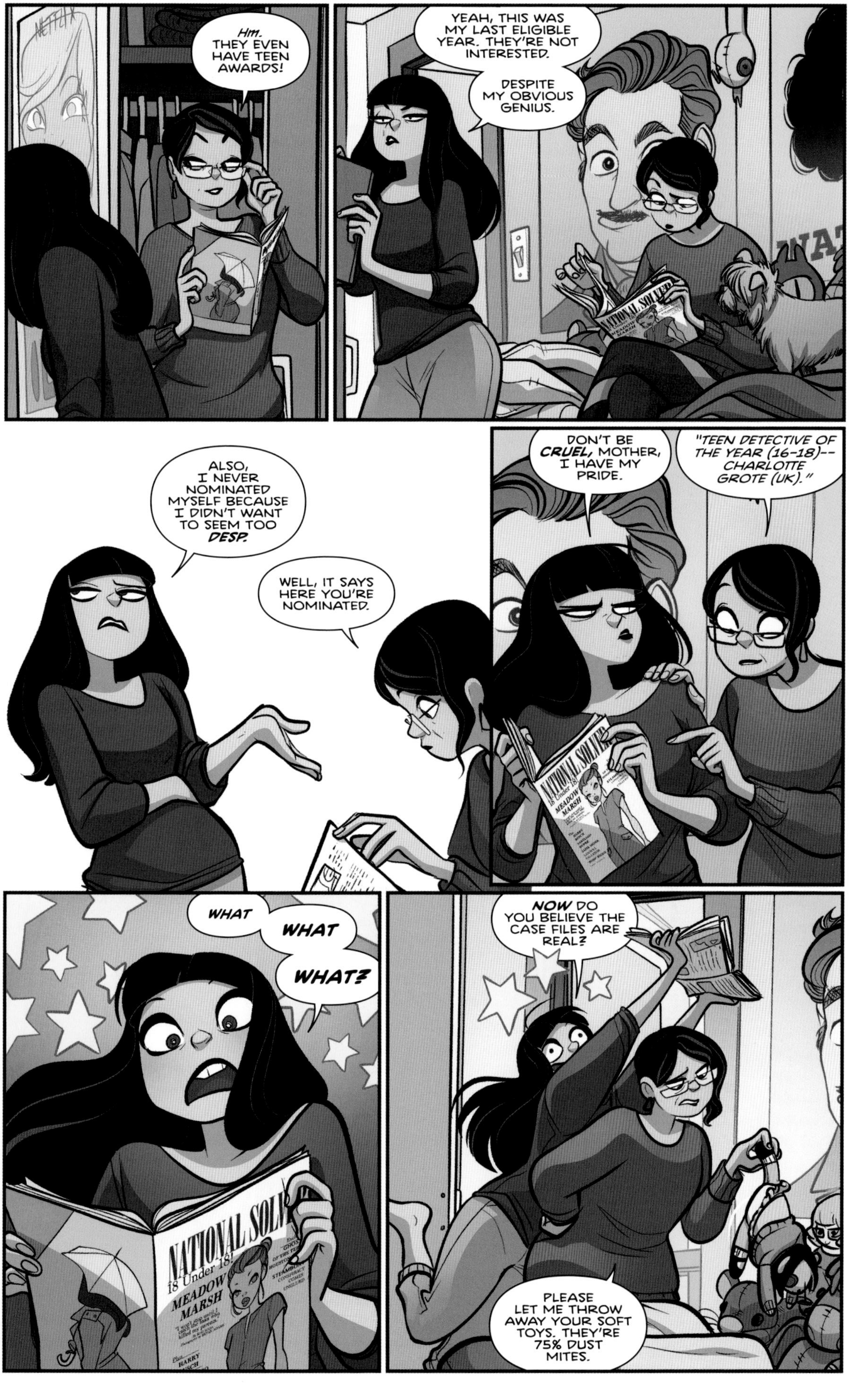

*Hm.* THEY EVEN HAVE TEEN AWARDS!
YEAH, THIS WAS MY LAST ELIGIBLE YEAR. THEY'RE NOT INTERESTED.
DESPITE MY OBVIOUS GENIUS.
ALSO, I NEVER NOMINATED MYSELF BECAUSE I DIDN'T WANT TO SEEM TOO ***DESP.***
WELL, IT SAYS HERE YOU'RE NOMINATED.
DON'T BE ***CRUEL,*** MOTHER, I HAVE MY PRIDE.
*"TEEN DETECTIVE OF THE YEAR (16-18)-- CHARLOTTE GROTE (UK)."*
***WHAT***
***WHAT***
***WHAT?***
NATIONAL SOLV
18 Under 18!
MEADOW MARSH
***NOW*** DO YOU BELIEVE THE CASE FILES ARE REAL?
PLEASE LET ME THROW AWAY YOUR SOFT TOYS. THEY'RE 75% DUST MITES.

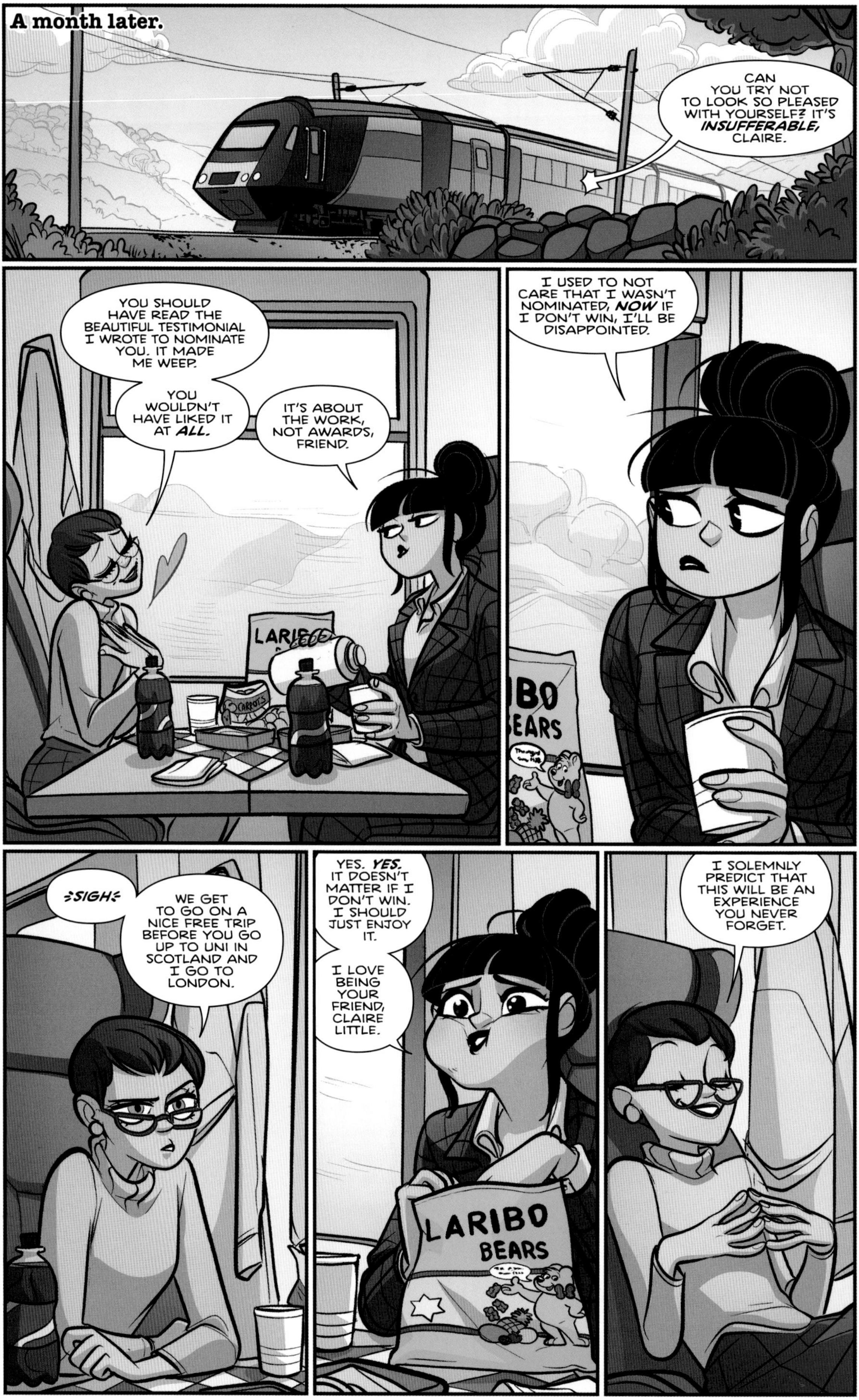
A month later.
CAN YOU TRY NOT TO LOOK SO PLEASED WITH YOURSELF? IT'S INSUFFERABLE, CLAIRE.
YOU SHOULD HAVE READ THE BEAUTIFUL TESTIMONIAL I WROTE TO NOMINATE YOU. IT MADE ME WEEP.
YOU WOULDN'T HAVE LIKED IT AT ALL.
IT'S ABOUT THE WORK, NOT AWARDS, FRIEND.
I USED TO NOT CARE THAT I WASN'T NOMINATED, NOW IF I DON'T WIN, I'LL BE DISAPPOINTED.
SIGH
WE GET TO GO ON A NICE FREE TRIP BEFORE YOU GO UP TO UNI IN SCOTLAND AND I GO TO LONDON.
YES. YES. IT DOESN'T MATTER IF I DON'T WIN. I SHOULD JUST ENJOY IT.
I LOVE BEING YOUR FRIEND, CLAIRE LITTLE.
LARIBO BEARS
I SOLEMNLY PREDICT THAT THIS WILL BE AN EXPERIENCE YOU NEVER FORGET.

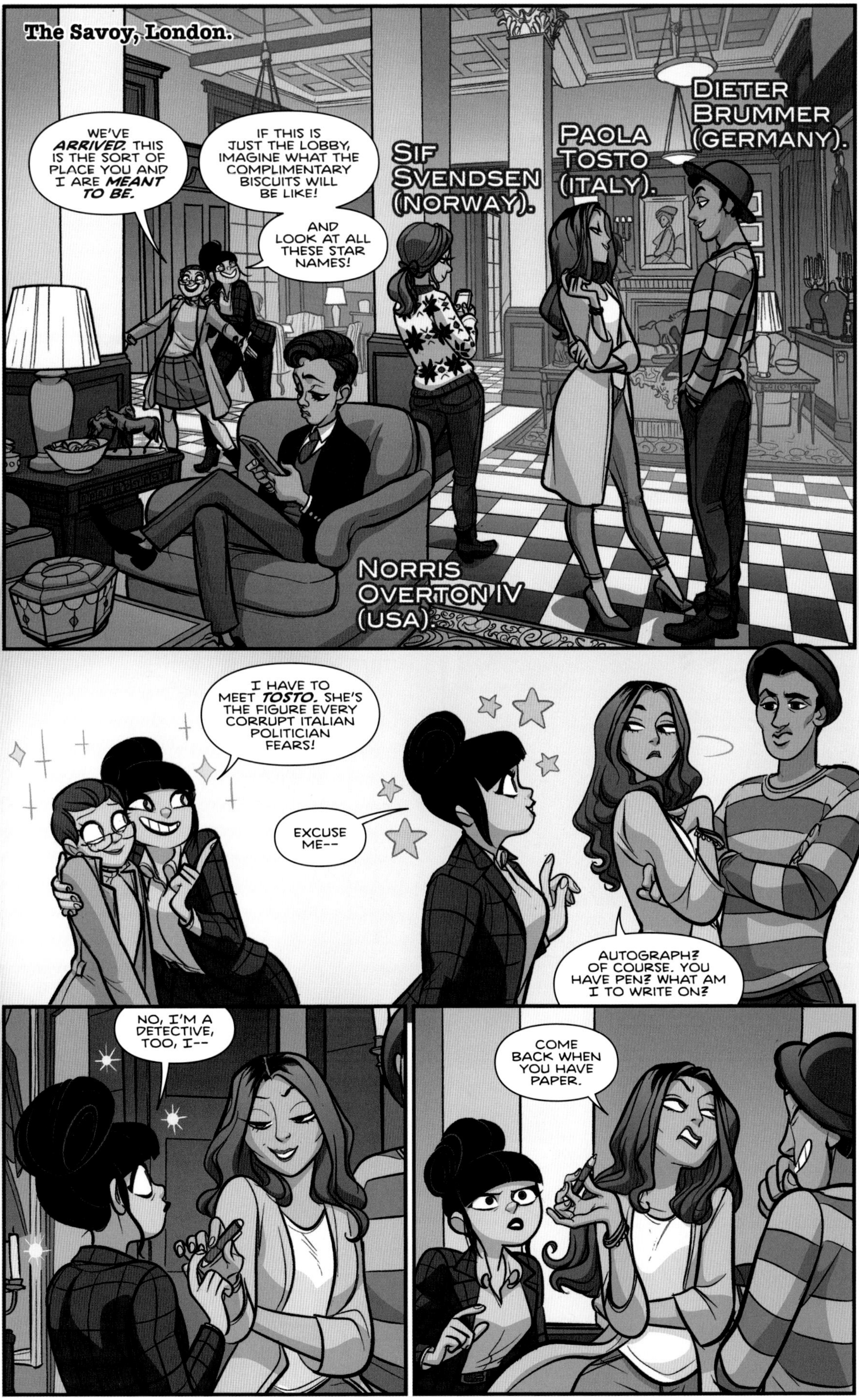

The Savoy, London.
WE'VE ARRIVED. THIS IS THE SORT OF PLACE YOU AND I ARE MEANT TO BE.
IF THIS IS JUST THE LOBBY, IMAGINE WHAT THE COMPLIMENTARY BISCUITS WILL BE LIKE!
AND LOOK AT ALL THESE STAR NAMES!
SIF SVENDSEN (NORWAY).
PAOLA TOSTO (ITALY).
DIETER BRUMMER (GERMANY).
NORRIS OVERTON IV (USA).
I HAVE TO MEET TOSTO. SHE'S THE FIGURE EVERY CORRUPT ITALIAN POLITICIAN FEARS!
EXCUSE ME--
AUTOGRAPH? OF COURSE. YOU HAVE PEN? WHAT AM I TO WRITE ON?
NO, I'M A DETECTIVE, TOO, I--
COME BACK WHEN YOU HAVE PAPER.

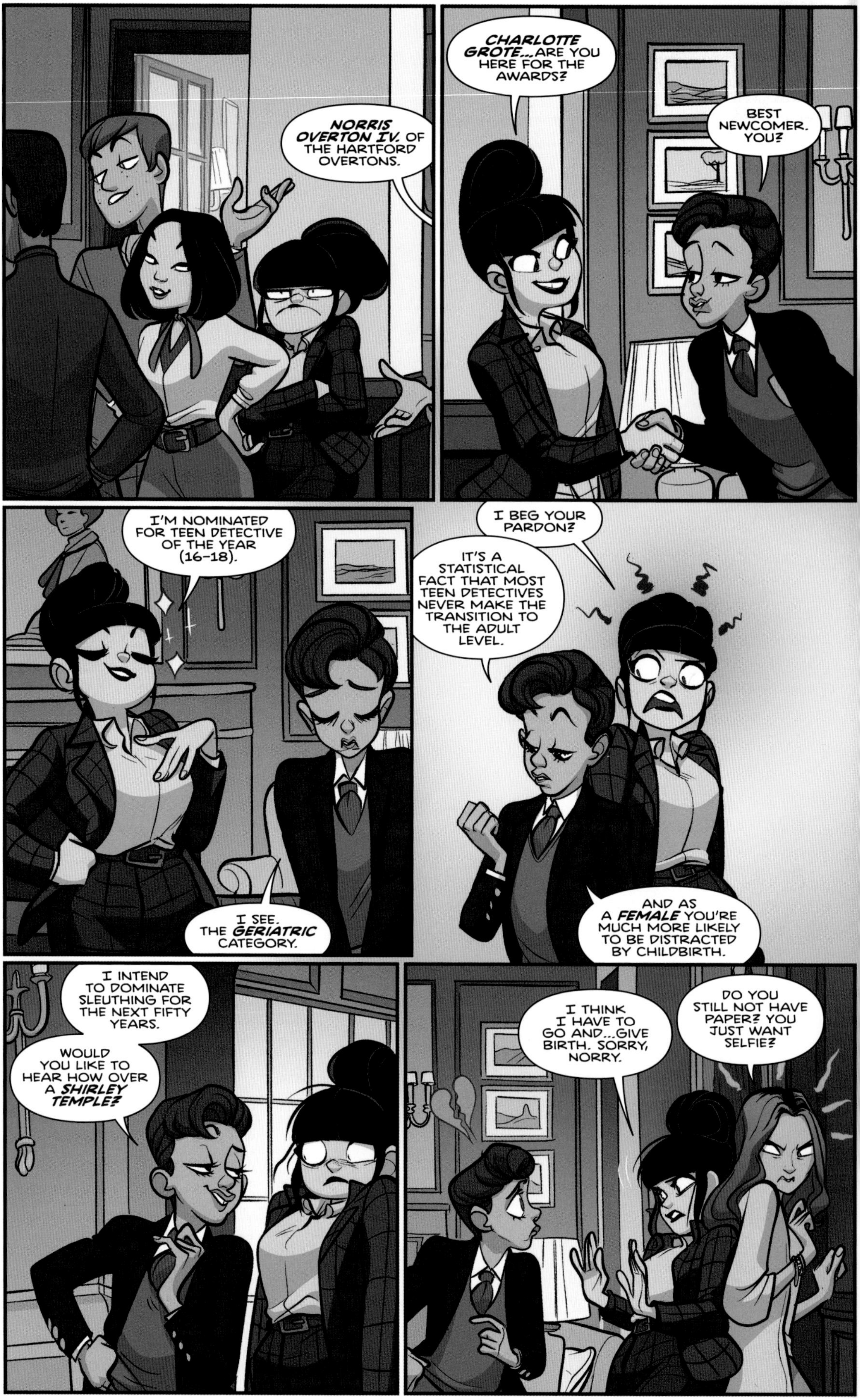
NORRIS OVERTON IV. OF THE HARTFORD OVERTONS.
CHARLOTTE GROTE... ARE YOU HERE FOR THE AWARDS?
BEST NEWCOMER. YOU?
I'M NOMINATED FOR TEEN DETECTIVE OF THE YEAR (16-18).
I SEE. THE GERIATRIC CATEGORY.
I BEG YOUR PARDON?
IT'S A STATISTICAL FACT THAT MOST TEEN DETECTIVES NEVER MAKE THE TRANSITION TO THE ADULT LEVEL.
AND AS A FEMALE YOU'RE MUCH MORE LIKELY TO BE DISTRACTED BY CHILDBIRTH.
I INTEND TO DOMINATE SLEUTHING FOR THE NEXT FIFTY YEARS.
WOULD YOU LIKE TO HEAR HOW OVER A SHIRLEY TEMPLE?
I THINK I HAVE TO GO AND...GIVE BIRTH. SORRY, NORRY.
DO YOU STILL NOT HAVE PAPER? YOU JUST WANT SELFIE?

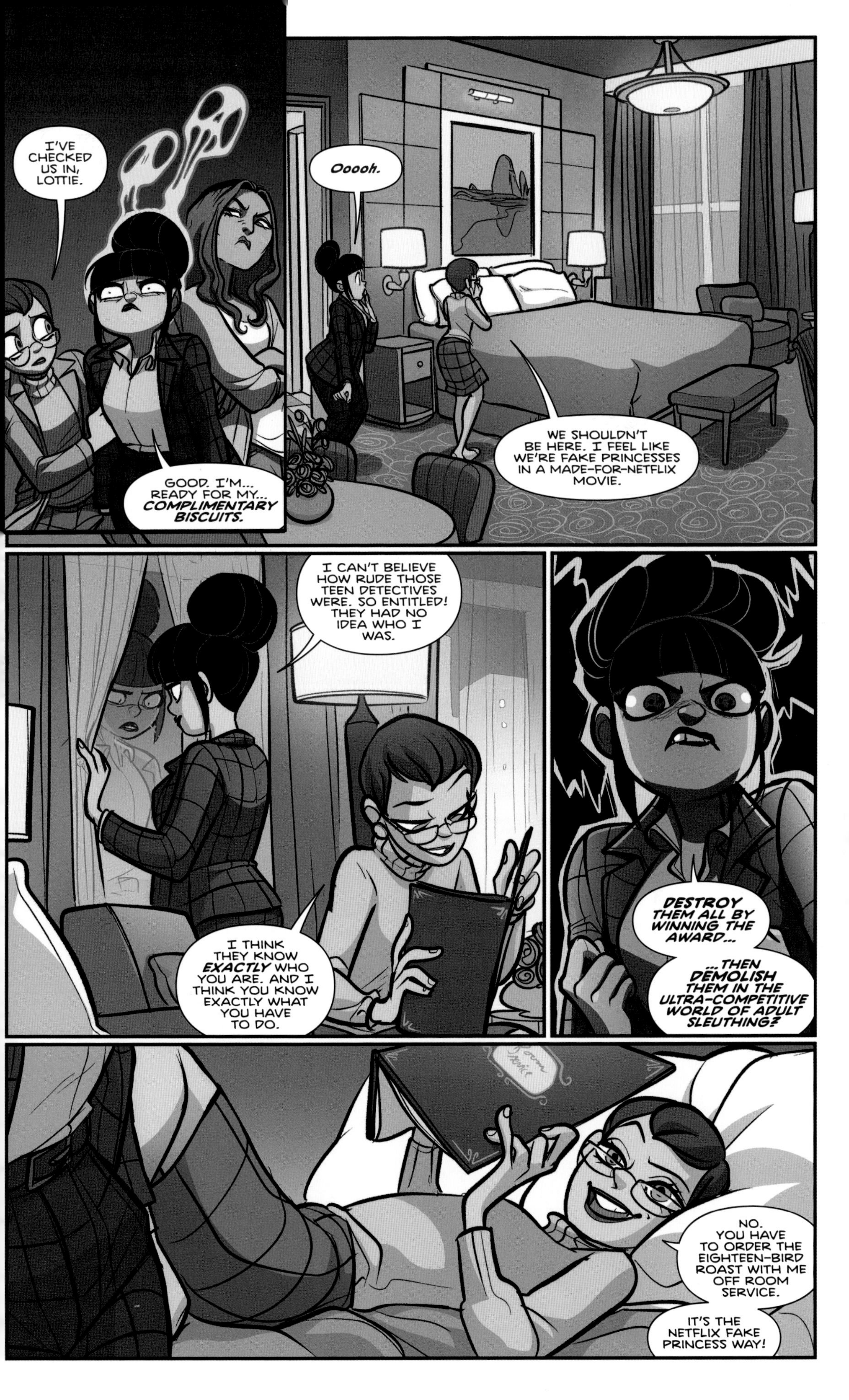
I'VE CHECKED US IN, LOTTIE.
GOOD. I'M... READY FOR MY... COMPLIMENTARY BISCUITS.
Ooooh.
WE SHOULDN'T BE HERE. I FEEL LIKE WE'RE FAKE PRINCESSES IN A MADE-FOR-NETFLIX MOVIE.
I CAN'T BELIEVE HOW RUDE THOSE TEEN DETECTIVES WERE. SO ENTITLED! THEY HAD NO IDEA WHO I WAS.
I THINK THEY KNOW EXACTLY WHO YOU ARE. AND I THINK YOU KNOW EXACTLY WHAT YOU HAVE TO DO.
DESTROY THEM ALL BY WINNING THE AWARD...
...THEN DEMOLISH THEM IN THE ULTRA-COMPETITIVE WORLD OF ADULT SLEUTHING?
NO. YOU HAVE TO ORDER THE EIGHTEEN-BIRD ROAST WITH ME OFF ROOM SERVICE.
IT'S THE NETFLIX FAKE PRINCESS WAY!

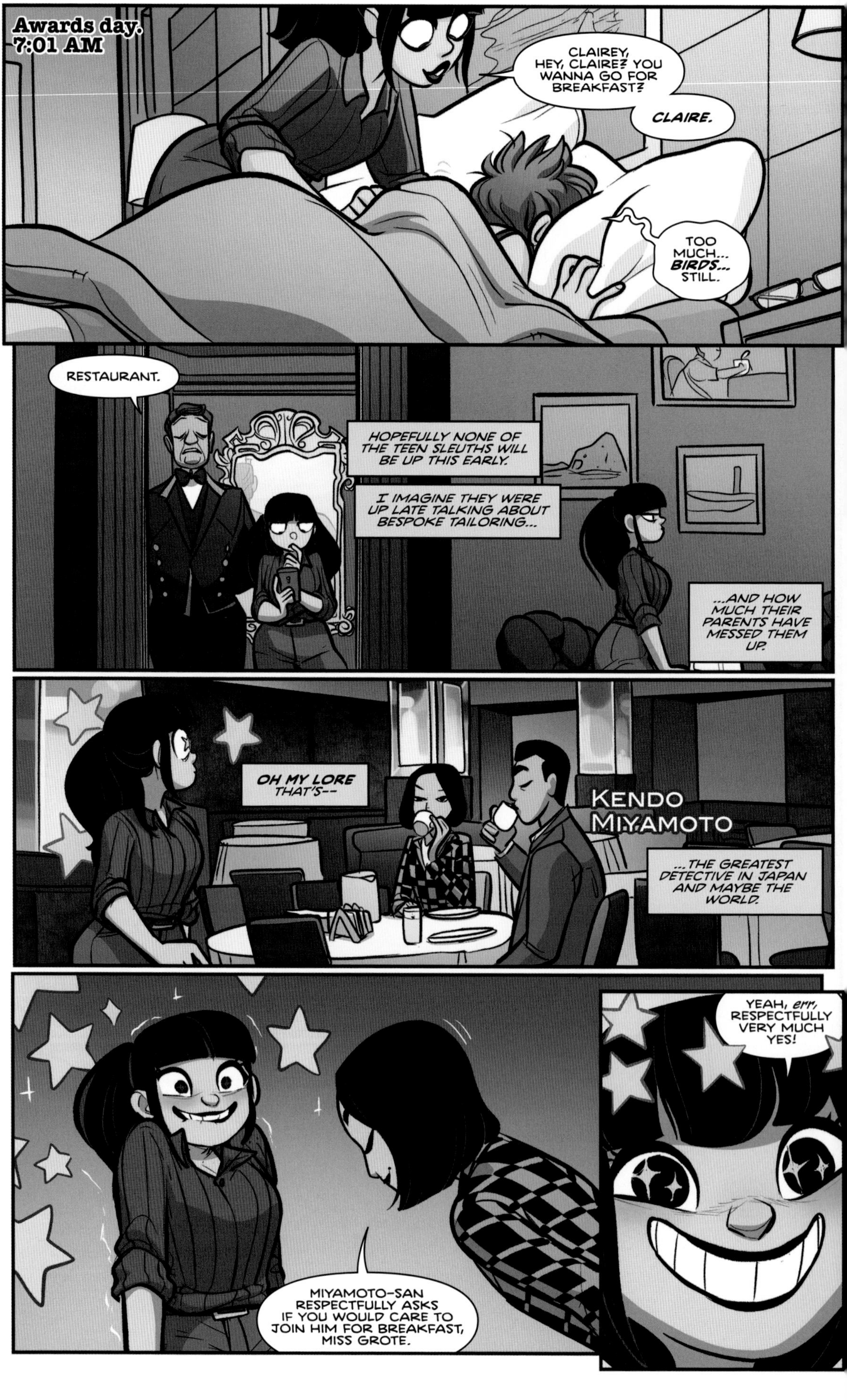
Awards day.
7:01 AM
CLAIREY, HEY, CLAIRE? YOU WANNA GO FOR BREAKFAST?
CLAIRE.
TOO MUCH... BIRDS... STILL.
RESTAURANT.
HOPEFULLY NONE OF THE TEEN SLEUTHS WILL BE UP THIS EARLY.
I IMAGINE THEY WERE UP LATE TALKING ABOUT BESPOKE TAILORING...
...AND HOW MUCH THEIR PARENTS HAVE MESSED THEM UP.
OH MY LORE THAT'S--
KENDO MIYAMOTO
...THE GREATEST DETECTIVE IN JAPAN AND MAYBE THE WORLD.
MIYAMOTO-SAN RESPECTFULLY ASKS IF YOU WOULD CARE TO JOIN HIM FOR BREAKFAST, MISS GROTE.
YEAH, err, RESPECTFULLY VERY MUCH YES!

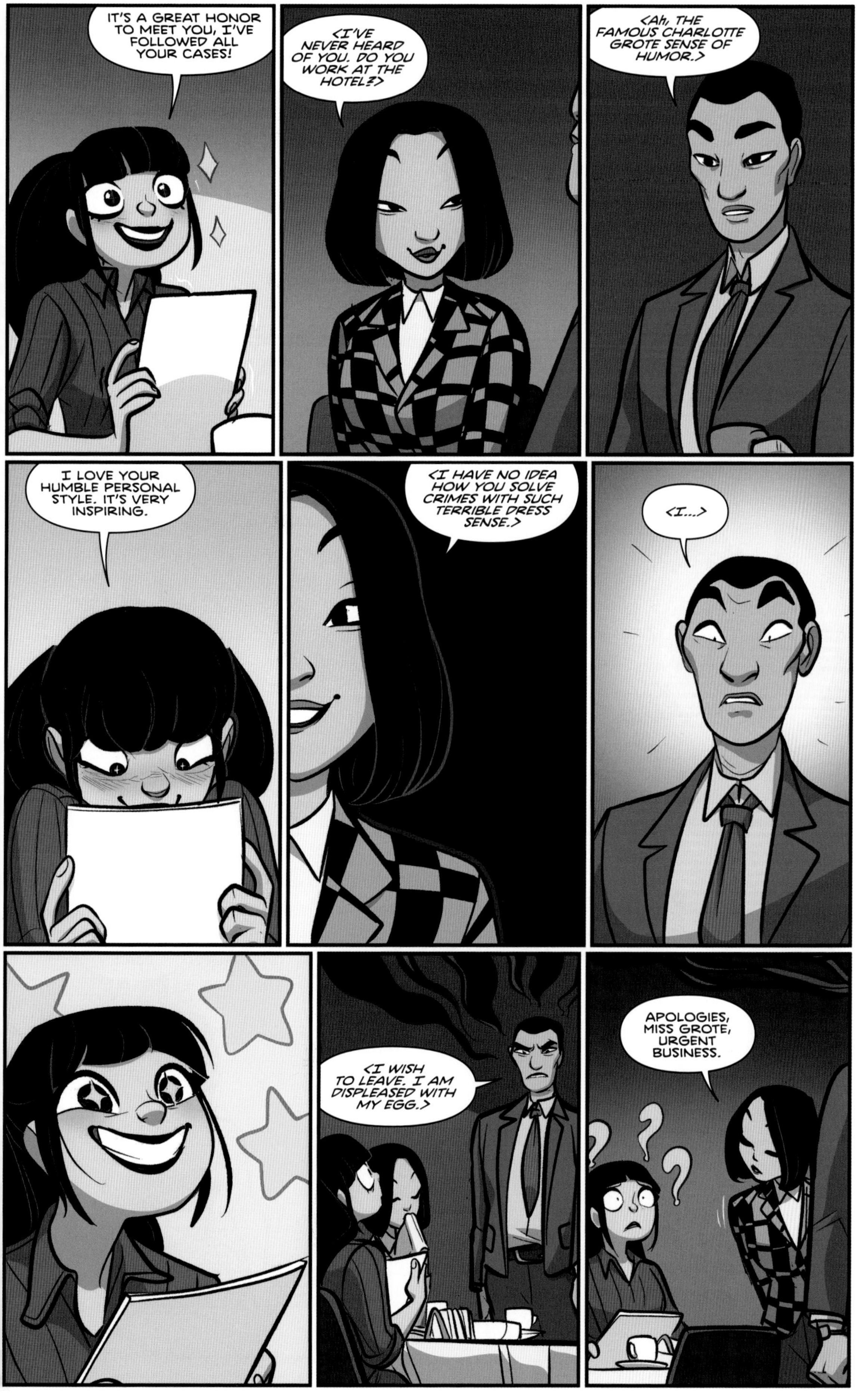
IT'S A GREAT HONOR TO MEET YOU, I'VE FOLLOWED ALL YOUR CASES!
<I'VE NEVER HEARD OF YOU. DO YOU WORK AT THE HOTEL?>
<Ah, THE FAMOUS CHARLOTTE GROTE SENSE OF HUMOR.>
I LOVE YOUR HUMBLE PERSONAL STYLE. IT'S VERY INSPIRING.
<I HAVE NO IDEA HOW YOU SOLVE CRIMES WITH SUCH TERRIBLE DRESS SENSE.>
<I...>
<I WISH TO LEAVE. I AM DISPLEASED WITH MY EGG.>
APOLOGIES, MISS GROTE, URGENT BUSINESS.

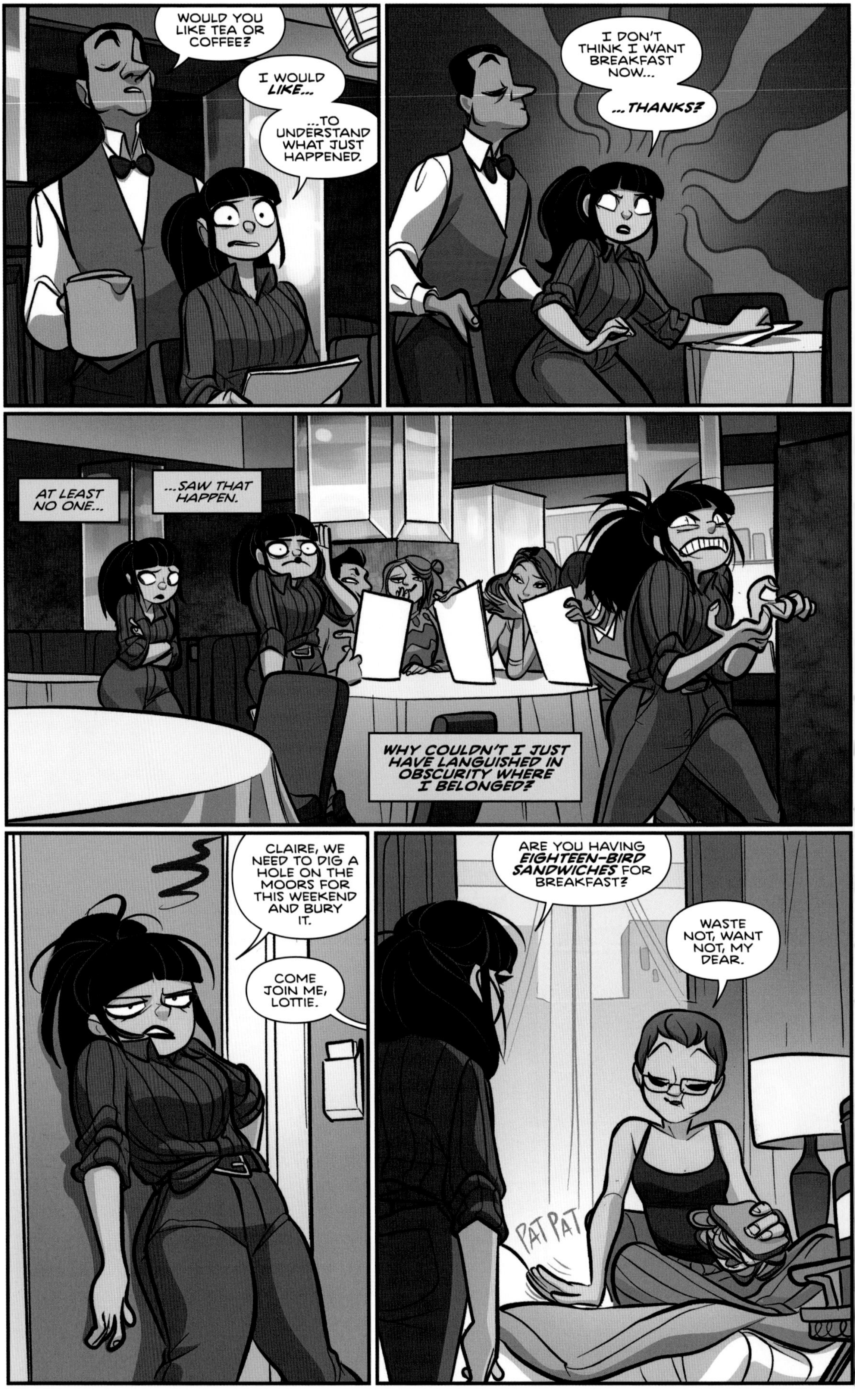
WOULD YOU LIKE TEA OR COFFEE?
I WOULD *LIKE...*
...TO UNDERSTAND WHAT JUST HAPPENED.
I DON'T THINK I WANT BREAKFAST NOW...
*...THANKS?*
*AT LEAST NO ONE...*
*...SAW THAT HAPPEN.*
*WHY COULDN'T I JUST HAVE LANGUISHED IN OBSCURITY WHERE I BELONGED?*
CLAIRE, WE NEED TO DIG A HOLE ON THE MOORS FOR THIS WEEKEND AND BURY IT.
COME JOIN ME, LOTTIE.
ARE YOU HAVING ***EIGHTEEN-BIRD SANDWICHES*** FOR BREAKFAST?
WASTE NOT, WANT NOT, MY DEAR.
PAT PAT

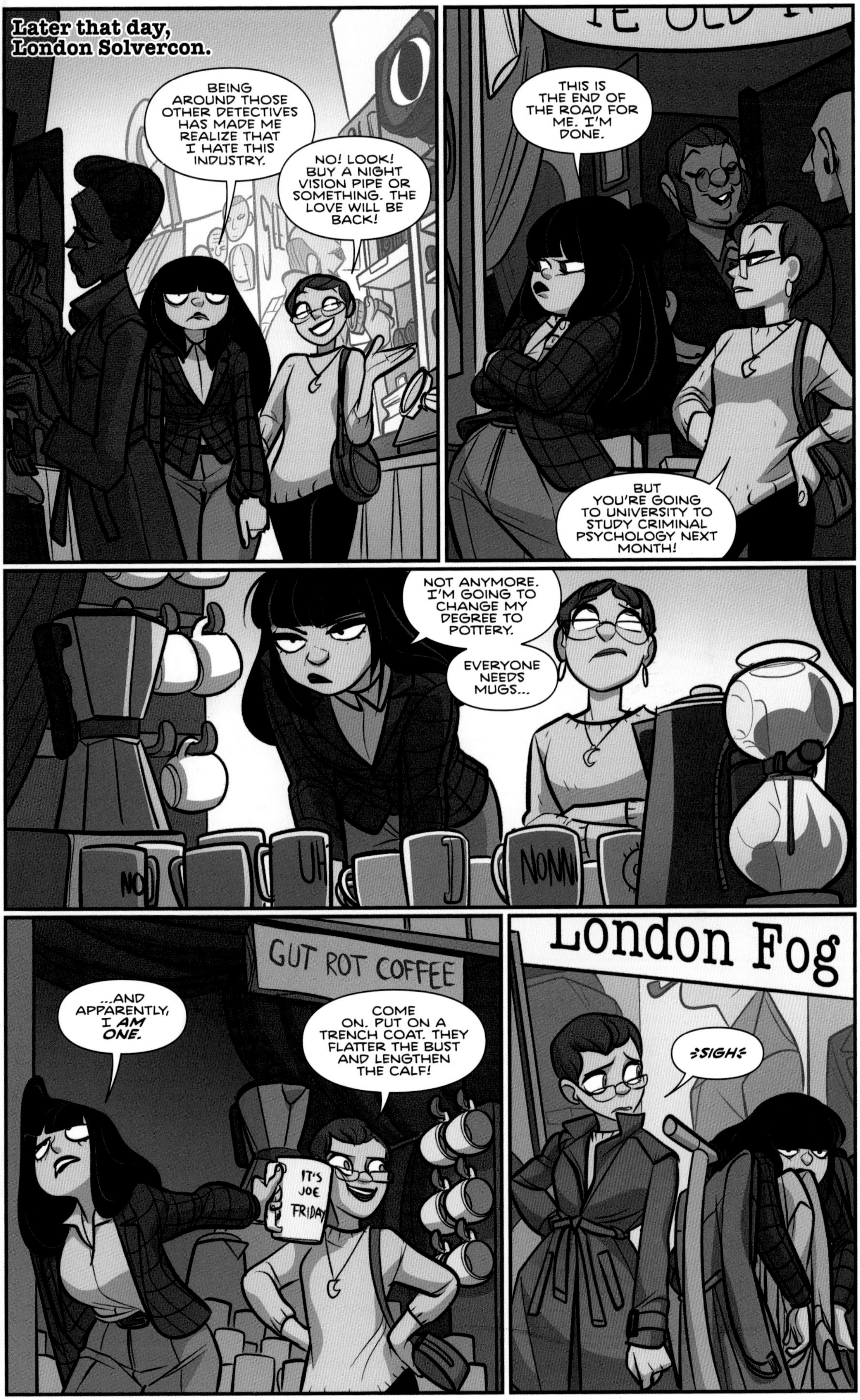
Later that day, London Solvercon.
BEING AROUND THOSE OTHER DETECTIVES HAS MADE ME REALIZE THAT I HATE THIS INDUSTRY.
NO! LOOK! BUY A NIGHT VISION PIPE OR SOMETHING. THE LOVE WILL BE BACK!
THIS IS THE END OF THE ROAD FOR ME. I'M DONE.
BUT YOU'RE GOING TO UNIVERSITY TO STUDY CRIMINAL PSYCHOLOGY NEXT MONTH!
NOT ANYMORE. I'M GOING TO CHANGE MY DEGREE TO POTTERY.
EVERYONE NEEDS MUGS...
GUT ROT COFFEE
...AND APPARENTLY, I *AM ONE.*
COME ON. PUT ON A TRENCH COAT. THEY FLATTER THE BUST AND LENGTHEN THE CALF!
IT'S JOE FRIDAY
London Fog
*SIGH*

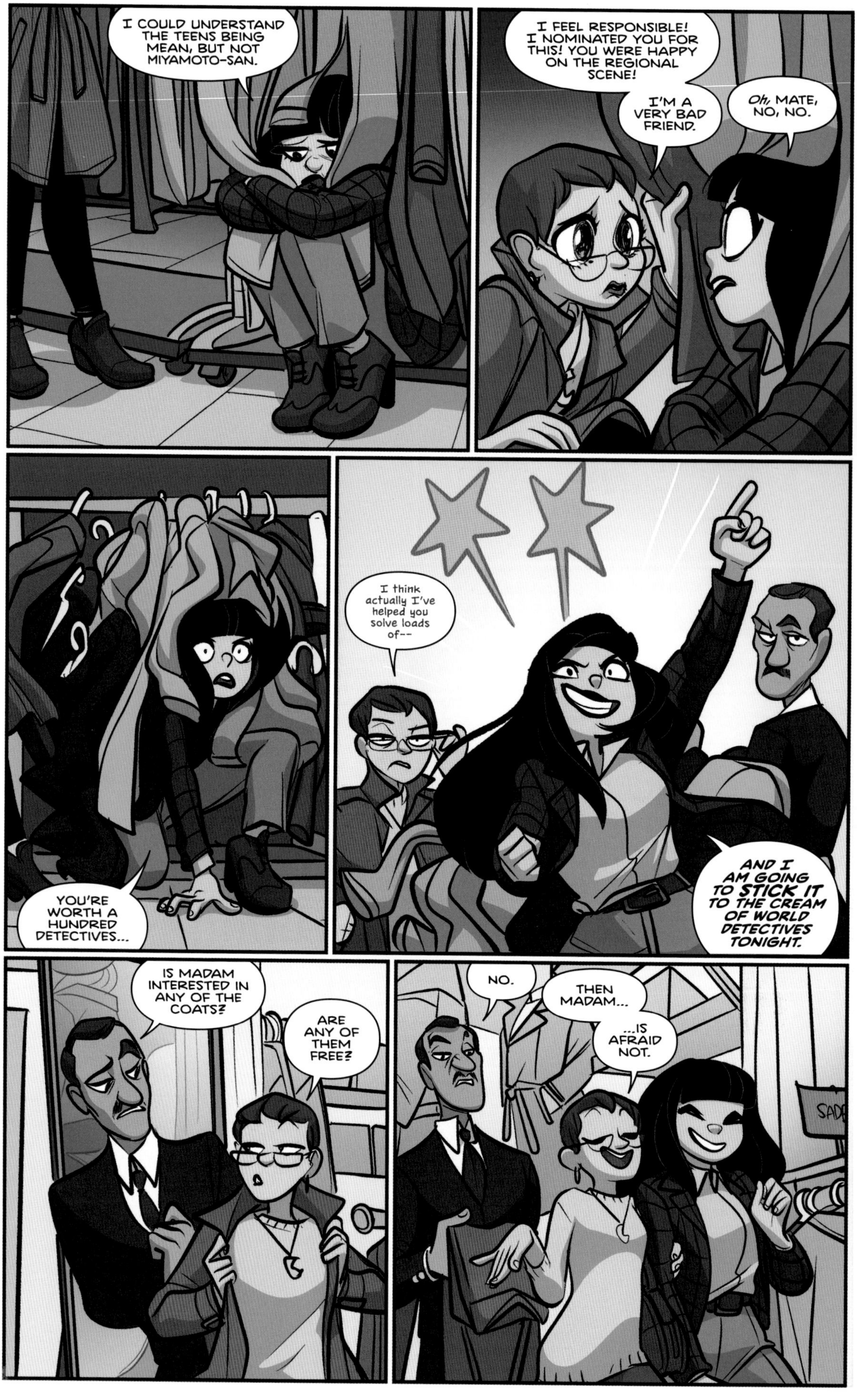
I COULD UNDERSTAND THE TEENS BEING MEAN, BUT NOT MIYAMOTO-SAN.
I FEEL RESPONSIBLE! I NOMINATED YOU FOR THIS! YOU WERE HAPPY ON THE REGIONAL SCENE!
I'M A VERY BAD FRIEND.
Oh, MATE, NO, NO.
YOU'RE WORTH A HUNDRED DETECTIVES...
I think actually I've helped you solve loads of--
AND I AM GOING TO STICK IT TO THE CREAM OF WORLD DETECTIVES TONIGHT.
IS MADAM INTERESTED IN ANY OF THE COATS?
ARE ANY OF THEM FREE?
NO.
THEN MADAM...
...IS AFRAID NOT.

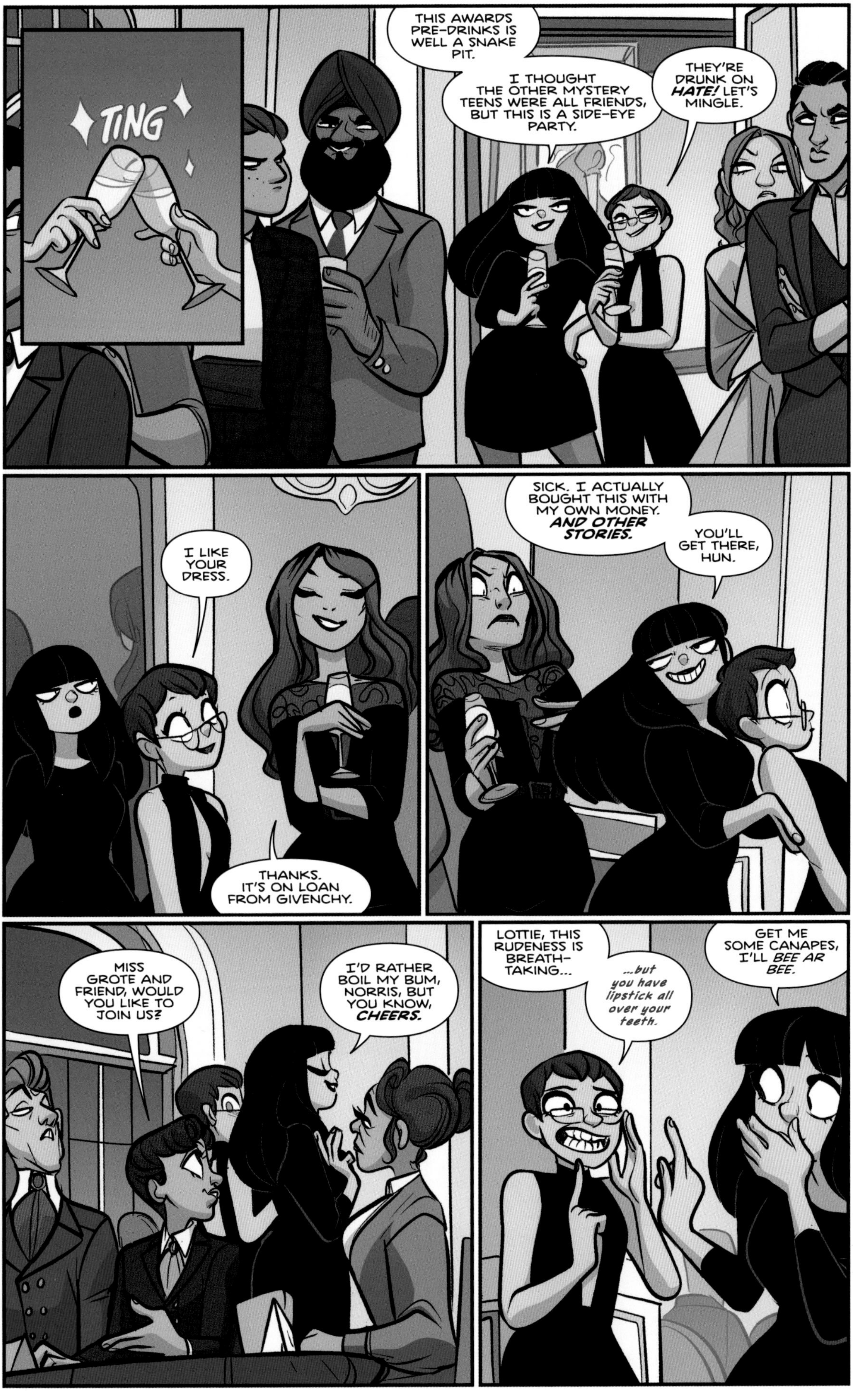
TING
THIS AWARDS PRE-DRINKS IS WELL A SNAKE PIT.
I THOUGHT THE OTHER MYSTERY TEENS WERE ALL FRIENDS, BUT THIS IS A SIDE-EYE PARTY.
THEY'RE DRUNK ON HATE! LET'S MINGLE.
I LIKE YOUR DRESS.
THANKS. IT'S ON LOAN FROM GIVENCHY.
SICK. I ACTUALLY BOUGHT THIS WITH MY OWN MONEY. AND OTHER STORIES.
YOU'LL GET THERE, HUN.
MISS GROTE AND FRIEND, WOULD YOU LIKE TO JOIN US?
I'D RATHER BOIL MY BUM, NORRIS, BUT YOU KNOW, CHEERS.
LOTTIE, THIS RUDENESS IS BREATH-TAKING...
...but you have lipstick all over your teeth.
GET ME SOME CANAPES, I'LL BEE AR BEE.

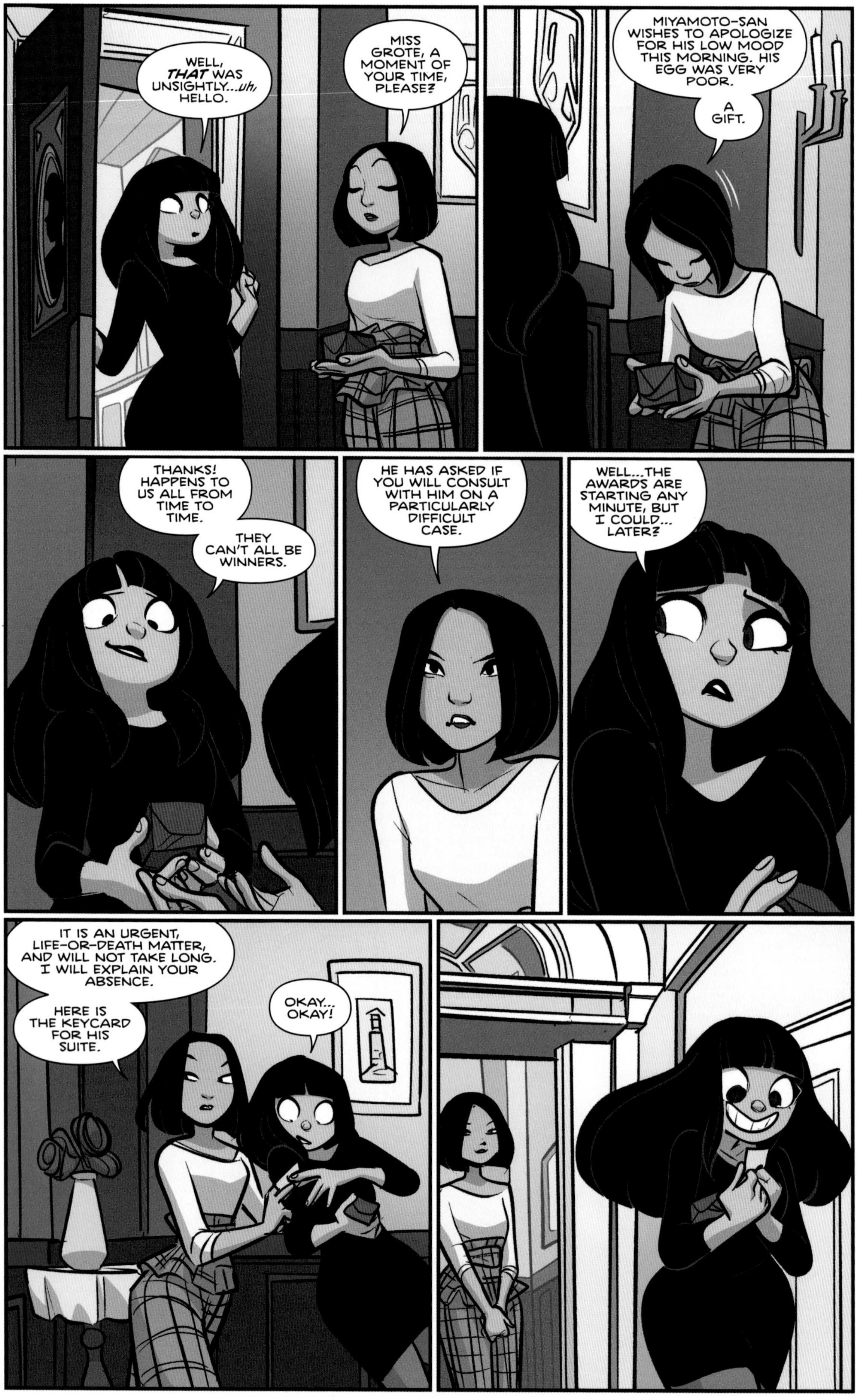
WELL, THAT WAS UNSIGHTLY...uh, HELLO.
MISS GROTE, A MOMENT OF YOUR TIME, PLEASE?
MIYAMOTO-SAN WISHES TO APOLOGIZE FOR HIS LOW MOOD THIS MORNING. HIS EGG WAS VERY POOR.
A GIFT.
THANKS! HAPPENS TO US ALL FROM TIME TO TIME.
THEY CAN'T ALL BE WINNERS.
HE HAS ASKED IF YOU WILL CONSULT WITH HIM ON A PARTICULARLY DIFFICULT CASE.
WELL...THE AWARDS ARE STARTING ANY MINUTE, BUT I COULD... LATER?
IT IS AN URGENT, LIFE-OR-DEATH MATTER, AND WILL NOT TAKE LONG. I WILL EXPLAIN YOUR ABSENCE.
HERE IS THE KEYCARD FOR HIS SUITE.
OKAY... OKAY!

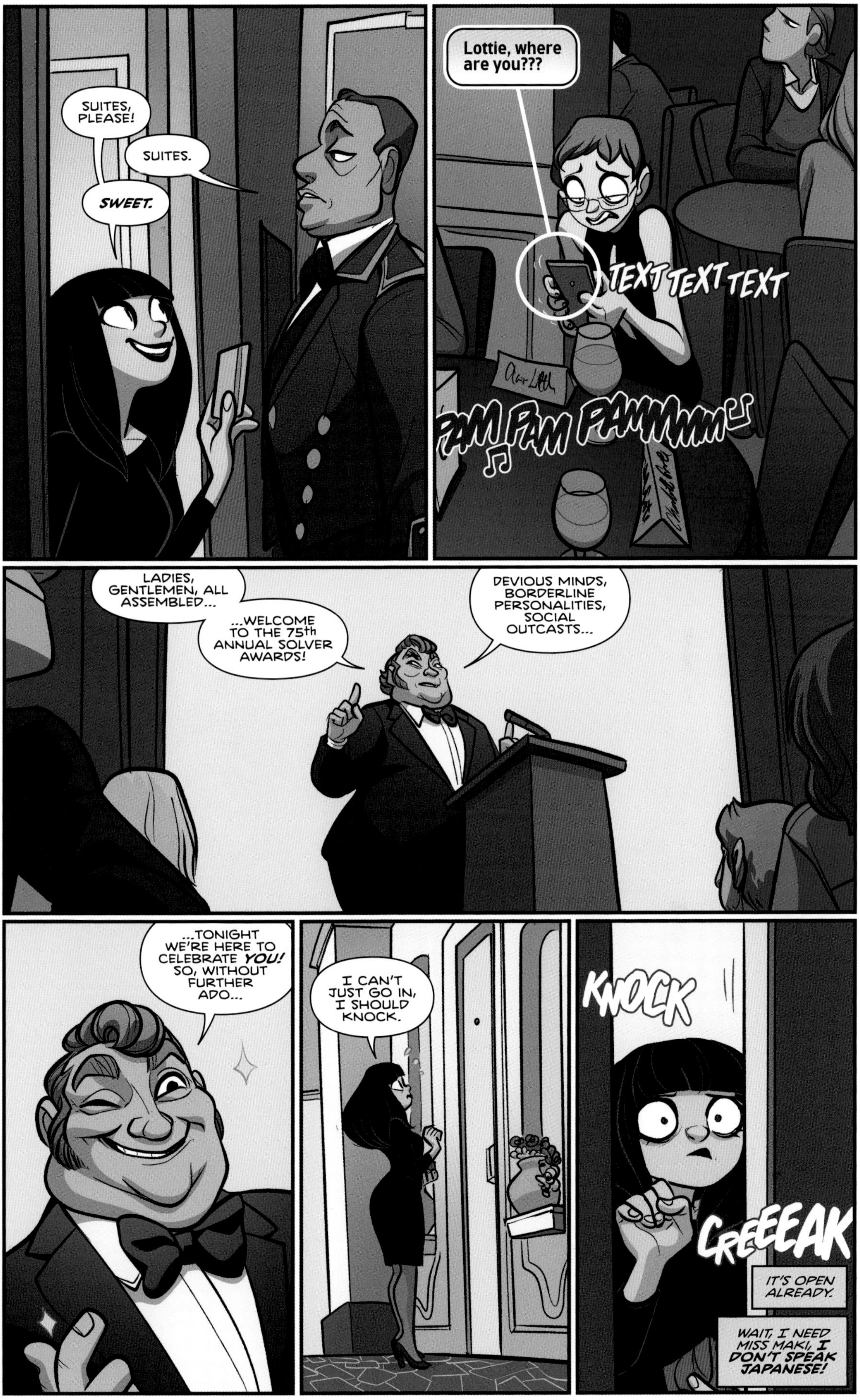
SUITES, PLEASE!
SUITES.
SWEET.
Lottie, where are you???
TEXT TEXT TEXT
PAM PAM PAMMMM
LADIES, GENTLEMEN, ALL ASSEMBLED...
...WELCOME TO THE 75th ANNUAL SOLVER AWARDS!
DEVIOUS MINDS, BORDERLINE PERSONALITIES, SOCIAL OUTCASTS...
...TONIGHT WE'RE HERE TO CELEBRATE YOU! SO, WITHOUT FURTHER ADO...
I CAN'T JUST GO IN, I SHOULD KNOCK.
KNOCK
CREEEAK
IT'S OPEN ALREADY.
WAIT, I NEED MISS MAKI, I DON'T SPEAK JAPANESE!

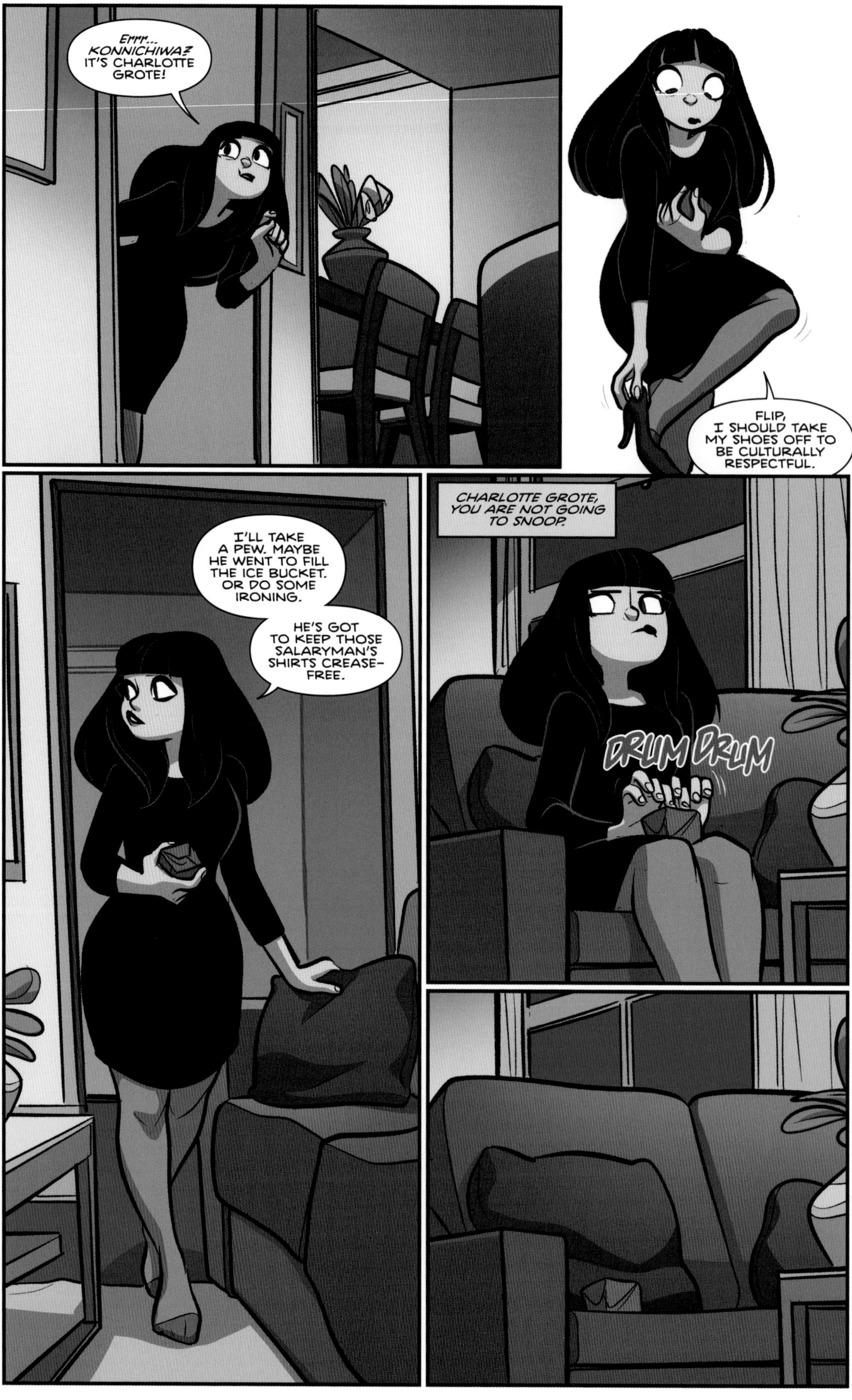
Errr... KONNICHIWA? IT'S CHARLOTTE GROTE!
FLIP, I SHOULD TAKE MY SHOES OFF TO BE CULTURALLY RESPECTFUL.
I'LL TAKE A PEW. MAYBE HE WENT TO FILL THE ICE BUCKET. OR DO SOME IRONING.
HE'S GOT TO KEEP THOSE SALARYMAN'S SHIRTS CREASE-FREE.
CHARLOTTE GROTE, YOU ARE NOT GOING TO SNOOP.
DRUM DRUM

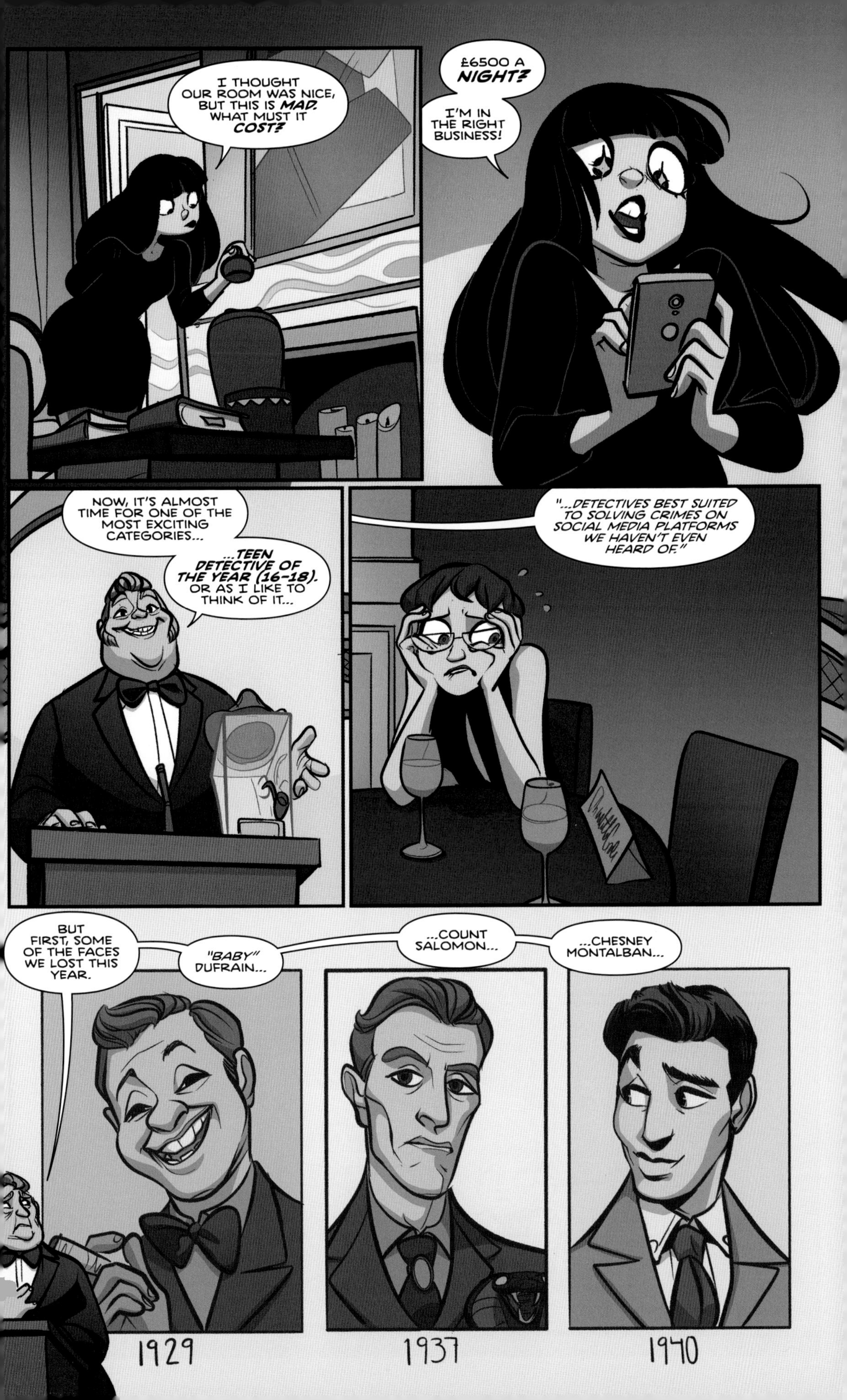

I THOUGHT OUR ROOM WAS NICE, BUT THIS IS MAD. WHAT MUST IT COST?
£6500 A NIGHT?
I'M IN THE RIGHT BUSINESS!
NOW, IT'S ALMOST TIME FOR ONE OF THE MOST EXCITING CATEGORIES...
...TEEN DETECTIVE OF THE YEAR (16-18). OR AS I LIKE TO THINK OF IT...
"...DETECTIVES BEST SUITED TO SOLVING CRIMES ON SOCIAL MEDIA PLATFORMS WE HAVEN'T EVEN HEARD OF."
BUT FIRST, SOME OF THE FACES WE LOST THIS YEAR.
"BABY" DUFRAIN...
...COUNT SALOMON...
...CHESNEY MONTALBAN...
1929
1937
1940

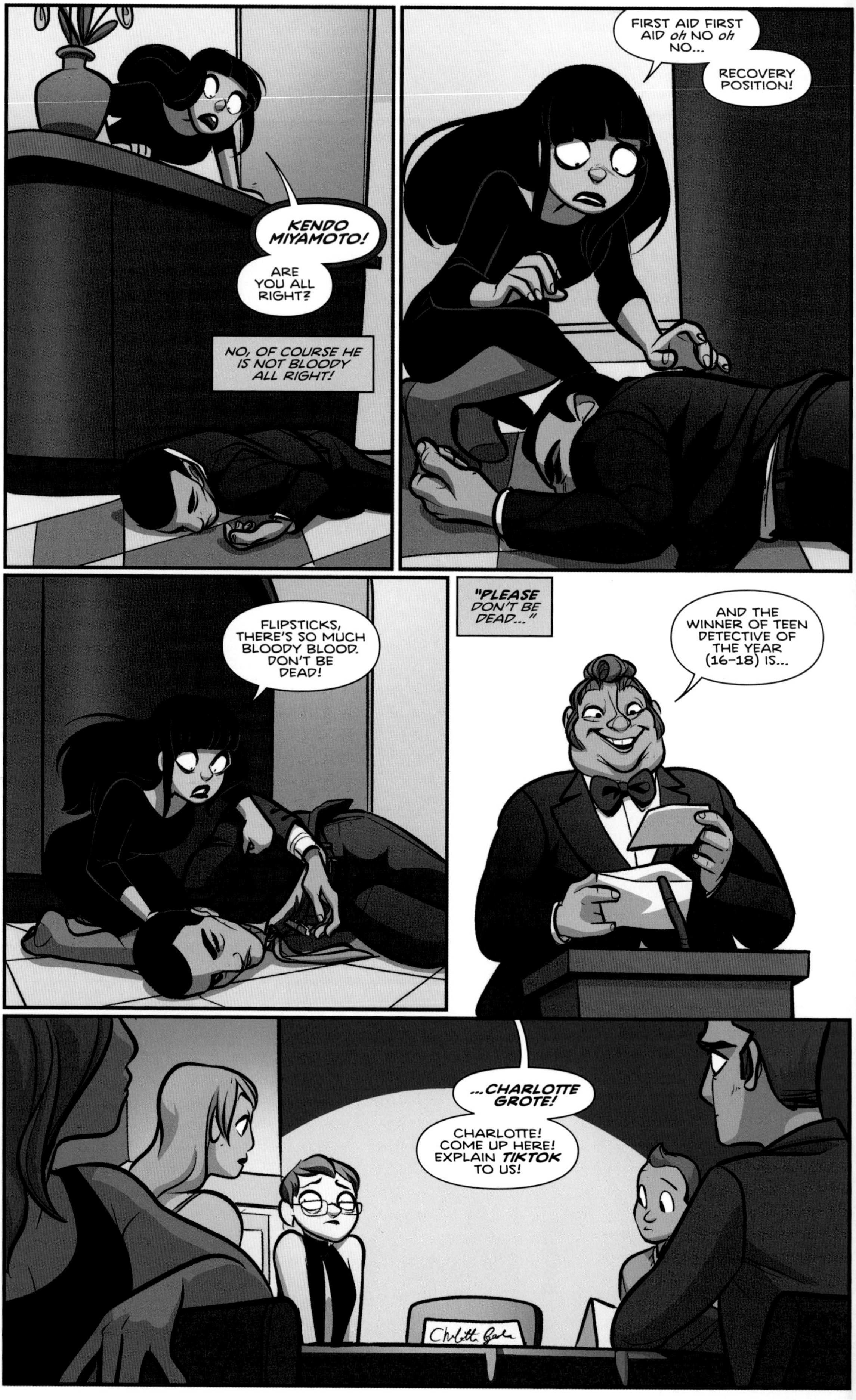
KENDO MIYAMOTO!
ARE YOU ALL RIGHT?
NO, OF COURSE HE IS NOT BLOODY ALL RIGHT!
FIRST AID FIRST AID oh NO oh NO...
RECOVERY POSITION!
FLIPSTICKS, THERE'S SO MUCH BLOODY BLOOD. DON'T BE DEAD!
"PLEASE DON'T BE DEAD..."
AND THE WINNER OF TEEN DETECTIVE OF THE YEAR (16-18) IS...
...CHARLOTTE GROTE!
CHARLOTTE! COME UP HERE! EXPLAIN TIKTOK TO US!

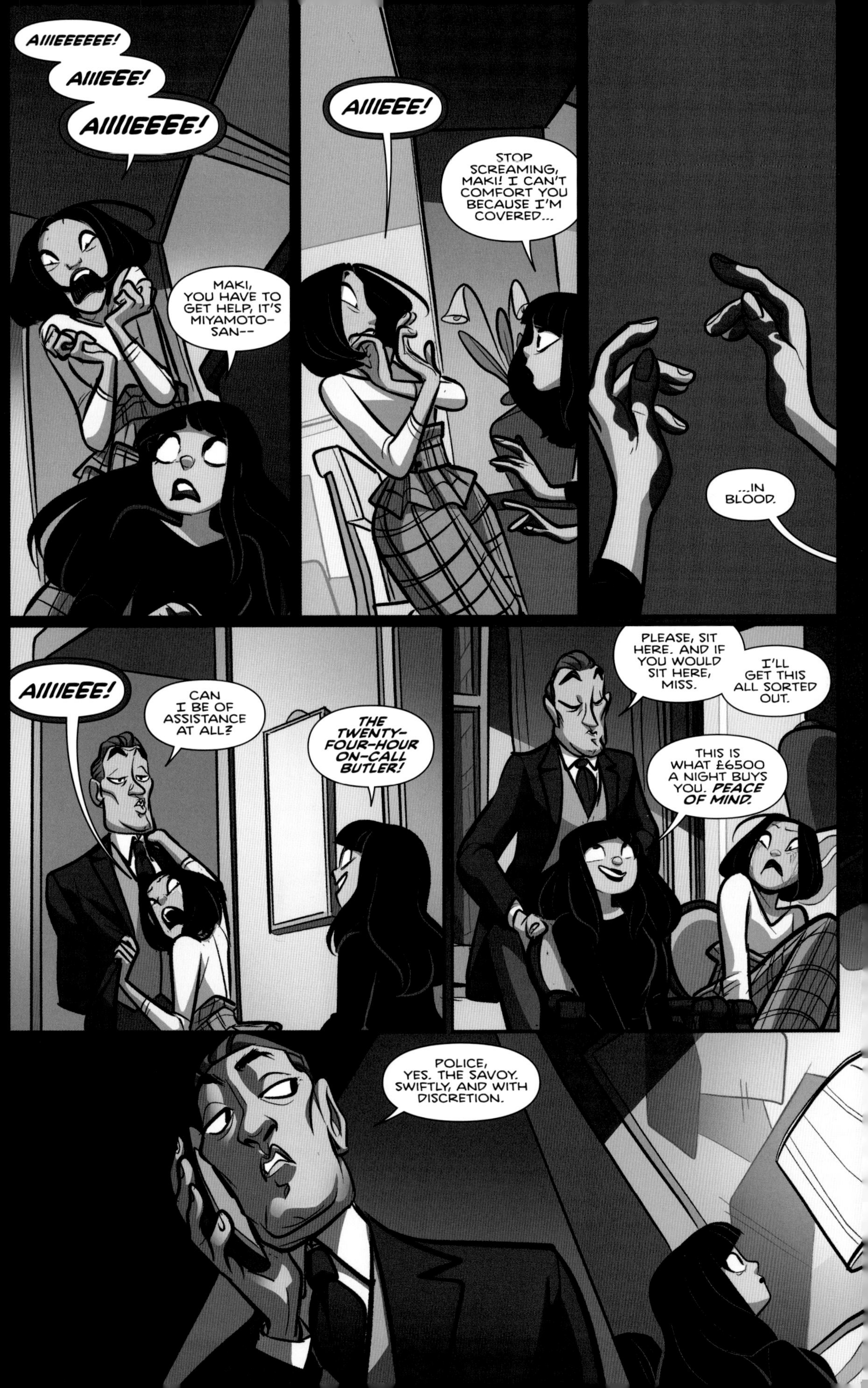
AIIIEEEEEE!
AIIIEEE!
AIIIIEEEEE!
MAKI, YOU HAVE TO GET HELP, IT'S MIYAMOTO-SAN--
AIIIEEE!
STOP SCREAMING, MAKI! I CAN'T COMFORT YOU BECAUSE I'M COVERED...
...IN BLOOD.
AIIIIEEE!
CAN I BE OF ASSISTANCE AT ALL?
THE TWENTY-FOUR-HOUR ON-CALL BUTLER!
PLEASE, SIT HERE. AND IF YOU WOULD SIT HERE, MISS.
I'LL GET THIS ALL SORTED OUT.
THIS IS WHAT £6500 A NIGHT BUYS YOU. PEACE OF MIND.
POLICE, YES. THE SAVOY. SWIFTLY, AND WITH DISCRETION.

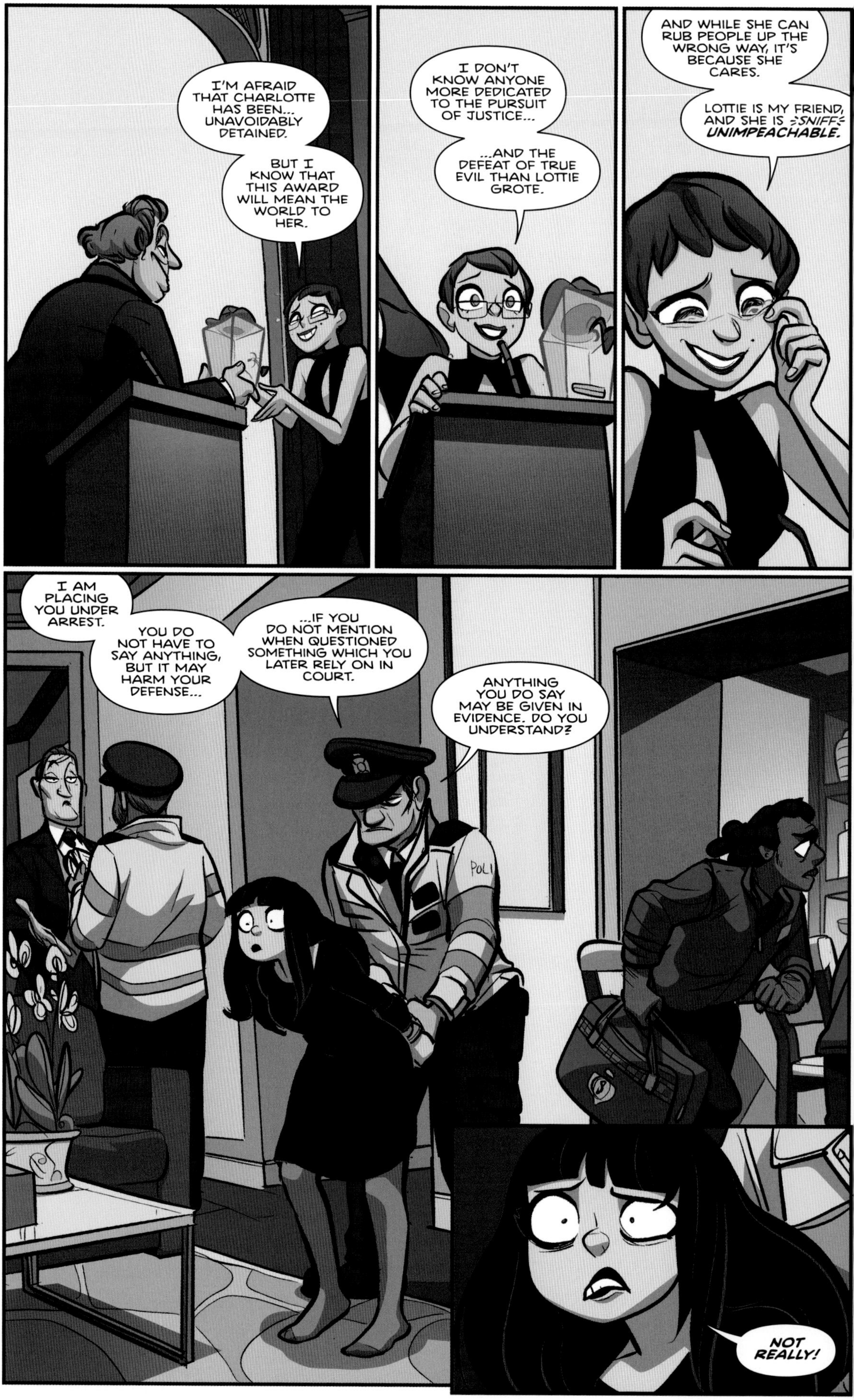
I'M AFRAID THAT CHARLOTTE HAS BEEN... UNAVOIDABLY DETAINED.
BUT I KNOW THAT THIS AWARD WILL MEAN THE WORLD TO HER.
I DON'T KNOW ANYONE MORE DEDICATED TO THE PURSUIT OF JUSTICE...
...AND THE DEFEAT OF TRUE EVIL THAN LOTTIE GROTE.
AND WHILE SHE CAN RUB PEOPLE UP THE WRONG WAY, IT'S BECAUSE SHE CARES.
LOTTIE IS MY FRIEND, AND SHE IS *SNIFF* **UNIMPEACHABLE.**
I AM PLACING YOU UNDER ARREST.
YOU DO NOT HAVE TO SAY ANYTHING, BUT IT MAY HARM YOUR DEFENSE...
...IF YOU DO NOT MENTION WHEN QUESTIONED SOMETHING WHICH YOU LATER RELY ON IN COURT.
ANYTHING YOU DO SAY MAY BE GIVEN IN EVIDENCE. DO YOU UNDERSTAND?
POLI
***NOT REALLY!***

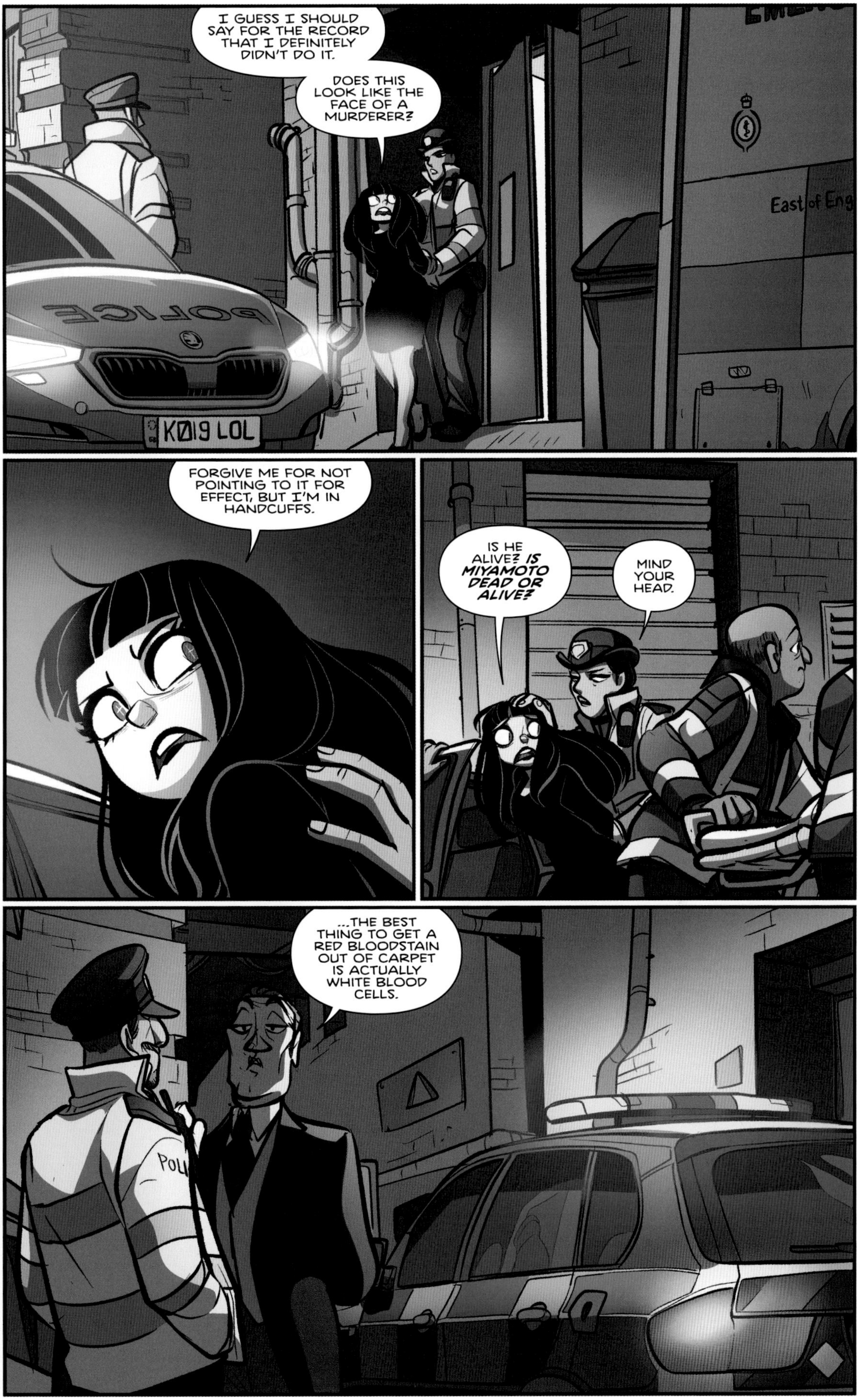
I GUESS I SHOULD SAY FOR THE RECORD THAT I DEFINITELY DIDN'T DO IT.
DOES THIS LOOK LIKE THE FACE OF A MURDERER?
POLICE
K019 LOL
East of Eng
FORGIVE ME FOR NOT POINTING TO IT FOR EFFECT, BUT I'M IN HANDCUFFS.
IS HE ALIVE? *IS MIYAMOTO DEAD OR ALIVE?*
MIND YOUR HEAD.
...THE BEST THING TO GET A RED BLOODSTAIN OUT OF CARPET IS ACTUALLY WHITE BLOOD CELLS.
POLI

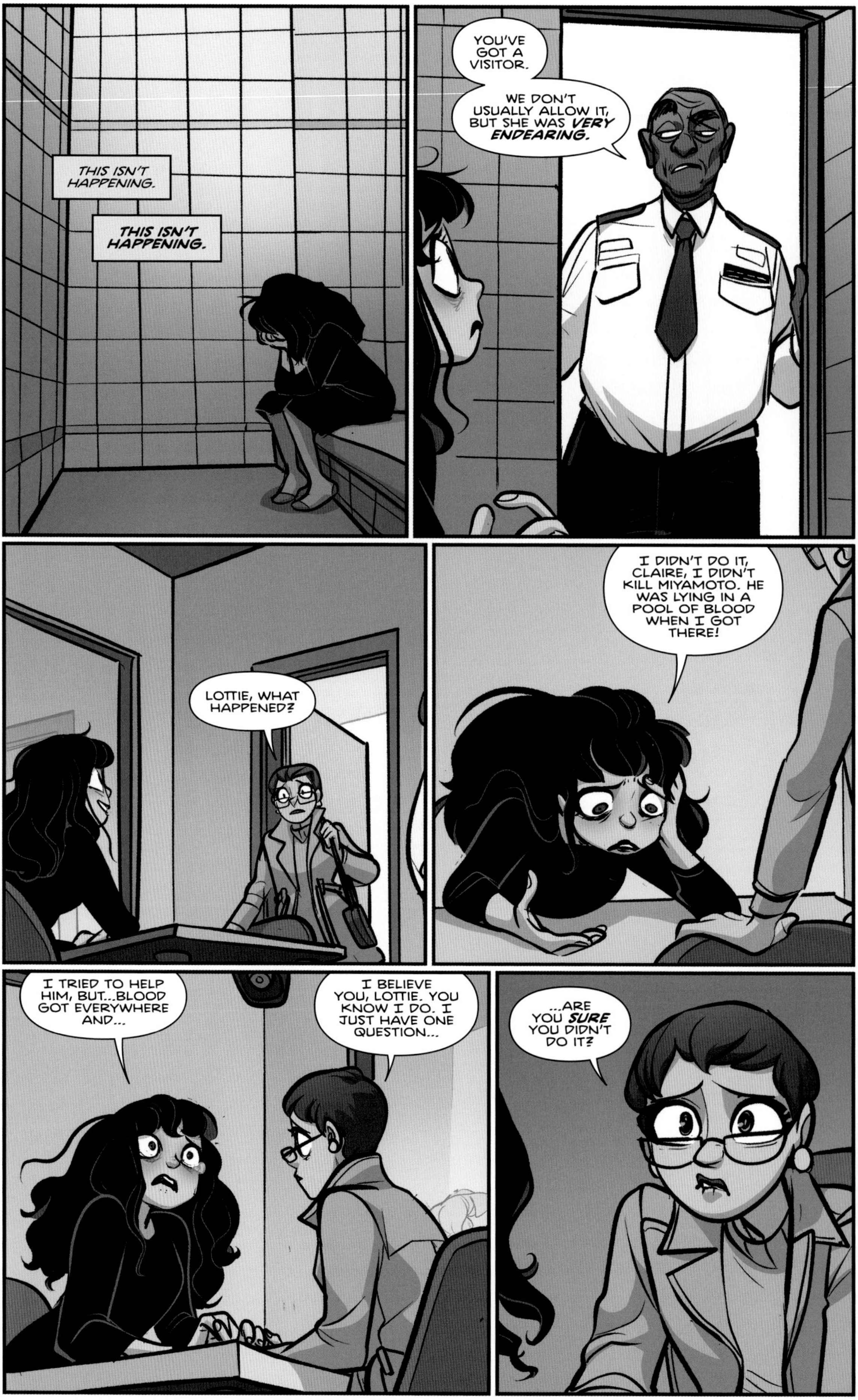
THIS ISN'T HAPPENING.
THIS ISN'T HAPPENING.
YOU'VE GOT A VISITOR.
WE DON'T USUALLY ALLOW IT, BUT SHE WAS VERY ENDEARING.
LOTTIE, WHAT HAPPENED?
I DIDN'T DO IT, CLAIRE, I DIDN'T KILL MIYAMOTO. HE WAS LYING IN A POOL OF BLOOD WHEN I GOT THERE!
I TRIED TO HELP HIM, BUT...BLOOD GOT EVERYWHERE AND...
I BELIEVE YOU, LOTTIE. YOU KNOW I DO. I JUST HAVE ONE QUESTION...
...ARE YOU SURE YOU DIDN'T DO IT?

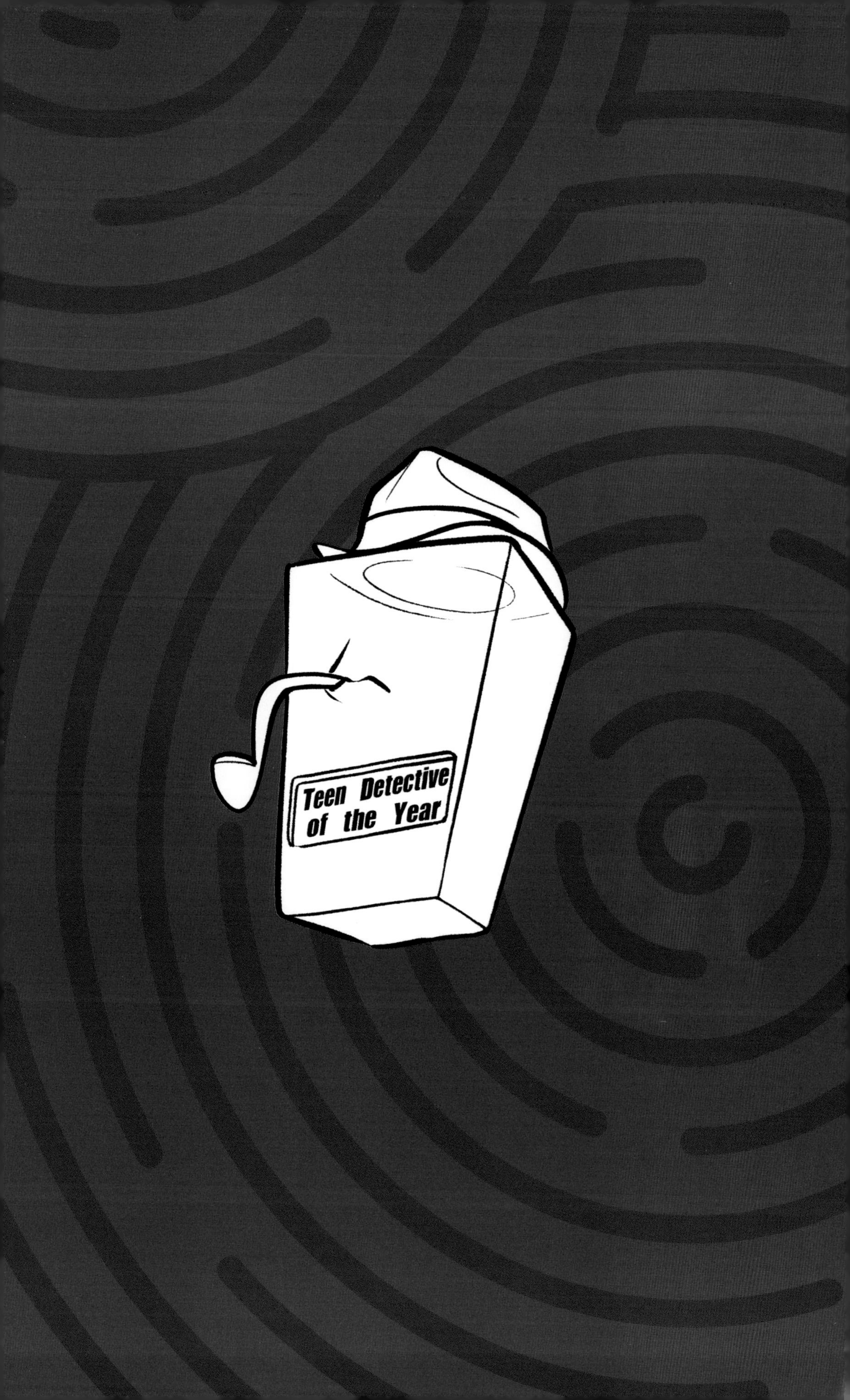
Teen Detective
of the Year

# CHAPTER TWO

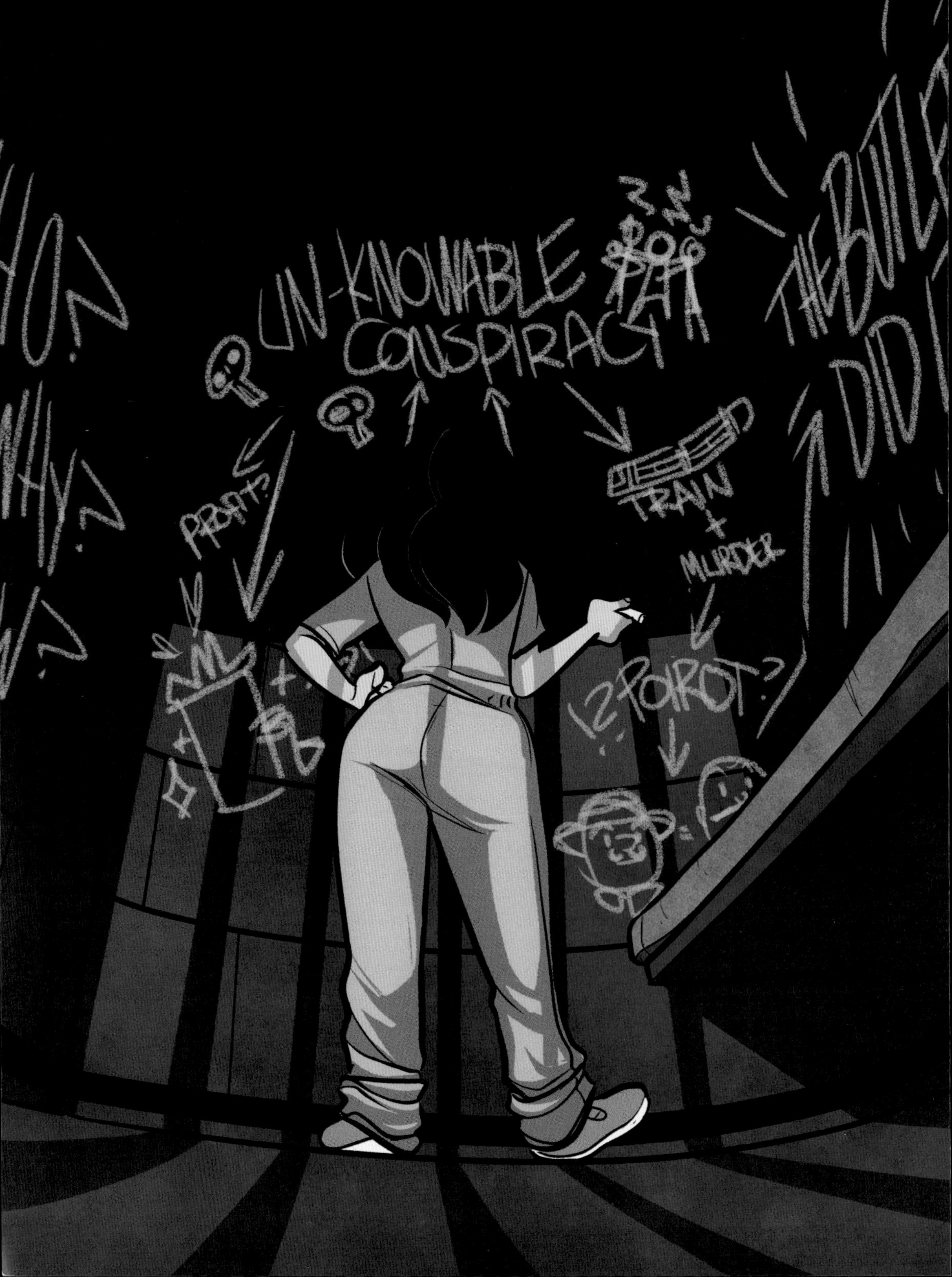
UN-KNOWABLE CONSPIRACY
PROFIT?
TRAIN + MURDER
POIROT?

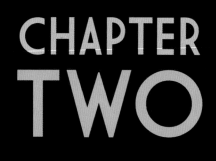

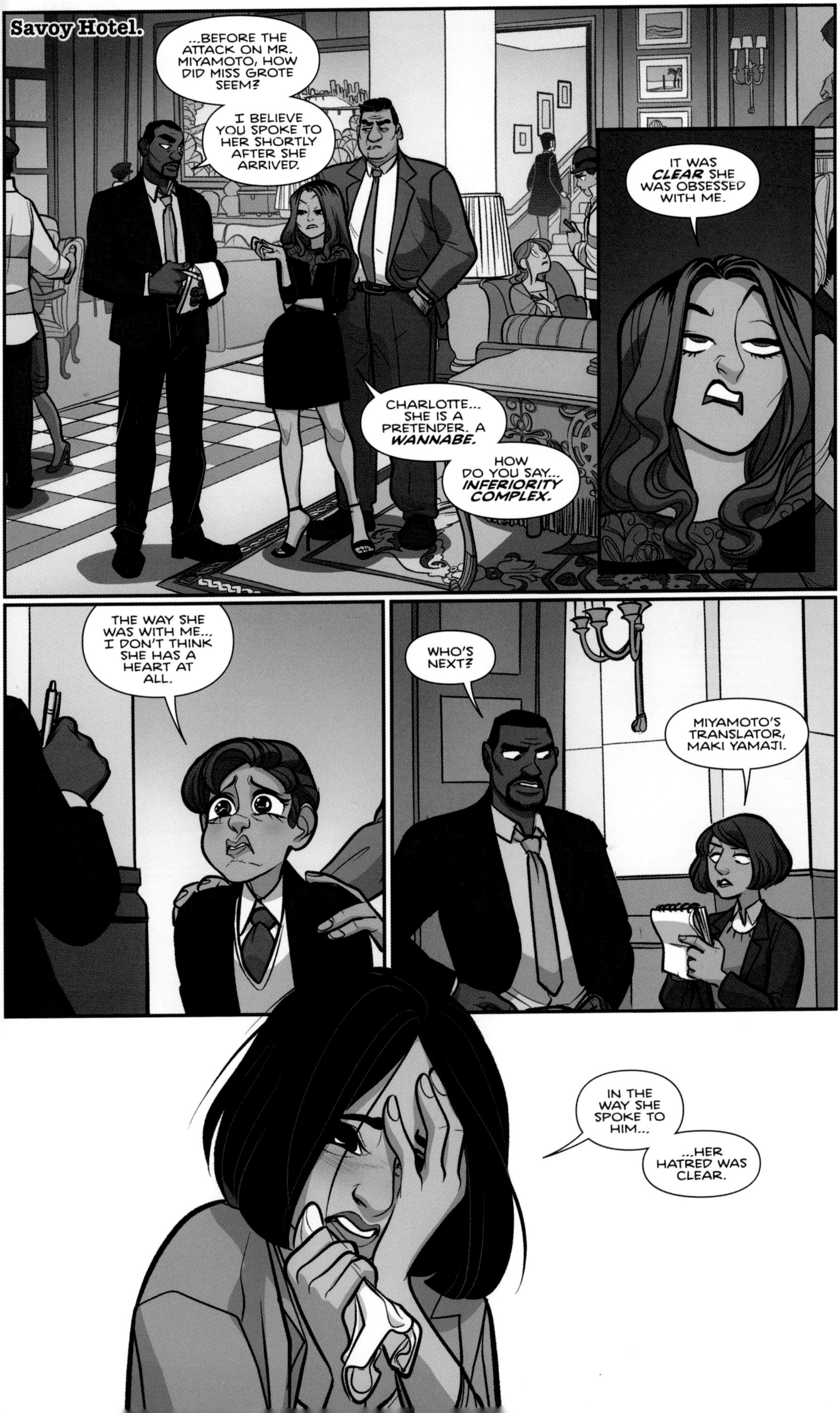
Savoy Hotel.
...BEFORE THE ATTACK ON MR. MIYAMOTO, HOW DID MISS GROTE SEEM?
I BELIEVE YOU SPOKE TO HER SHORTLY AFTER SHE ARRIVED.
IT WAS CLEAR SHE WAS OBSESSED WITH ME.
CHARLOTTE... SHE IS A PRETENDER. A WANNABE.
HOW DO YOU SAY... INFERIORITY COMPLEX.
THE WAY SHE WAS WITH ME... I DON'T THINK SHE HAS A HEART AT ALL.
WHO'S NEXT?
MIYAMOTO'S TRANSLATOR, MAKI YAMAJI.
IN THE WAY SHE SPOKE TO HIM...
...HER HATRED WAS CLEAR.

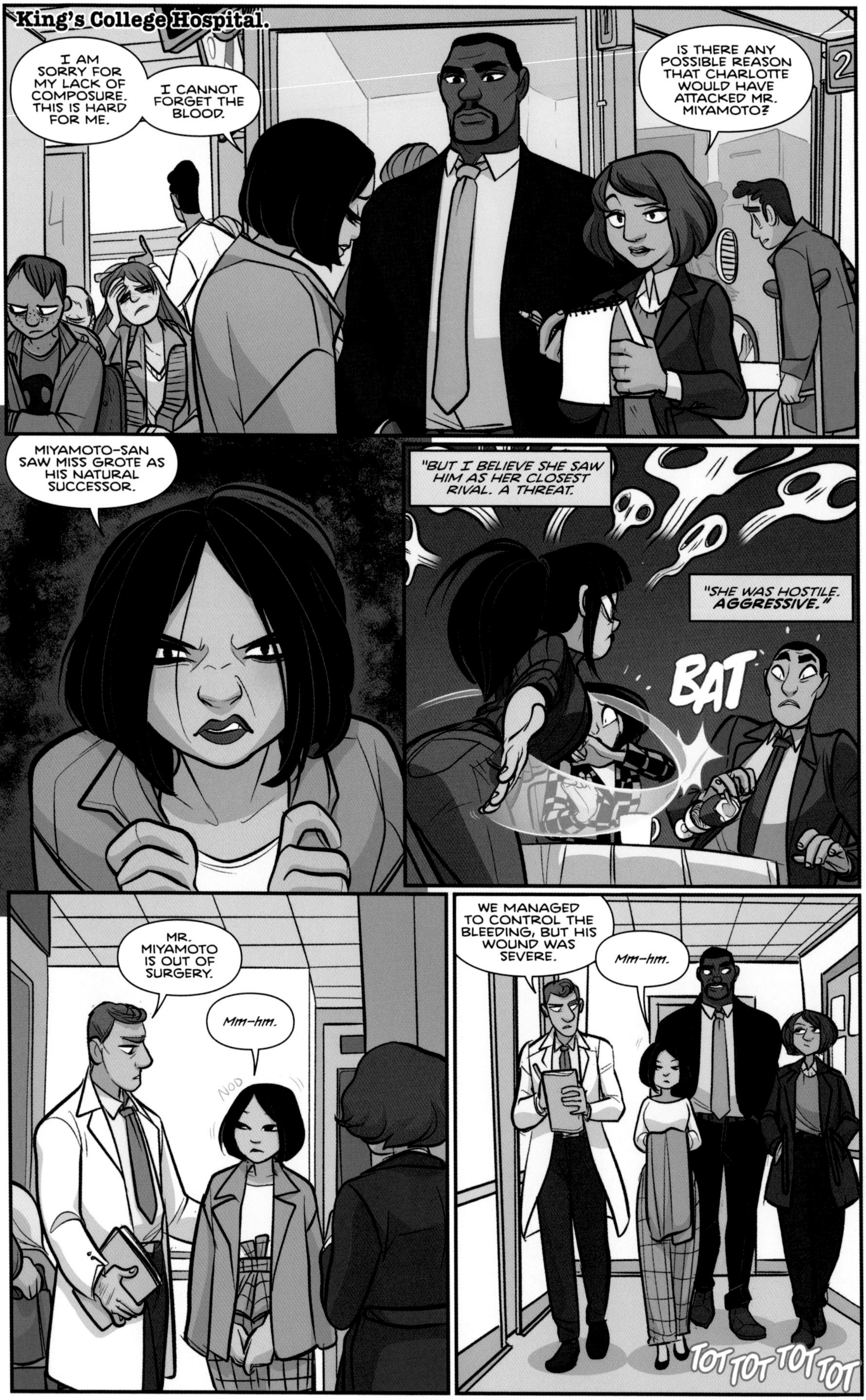
King's College Hospital.
I AM SORRY FOR MY LACK OF COMPOSURE. THIS IS HARD FOR ME.
I CANNOT FORGET THE BLOOD.
IS THERE ANY POSSIBLE REASON THAT CHARLOTTE WOULD HAVE ATTACKED MR. MIYAMOTO?
MIYAMOTO-SAN SAW MISS GROTE AS HIS NATURAL SUCCESSOR.
"BUT I BELIEVE SHE SAW HIM AS HER CLOSEST RIVAL. A THREAT.
"SHE WAS HOSTILE. AGGRESSIVE."
BAT
MR. MIYAMOTO IS OUT OF SURGERY.
Mm-hm.
NOD
WE MANAGED TO CONTROL THE BLEEDING, BUT HIS WOUND WAS SEVERE.
Mm-hm.
TOT TOT TOT TOT

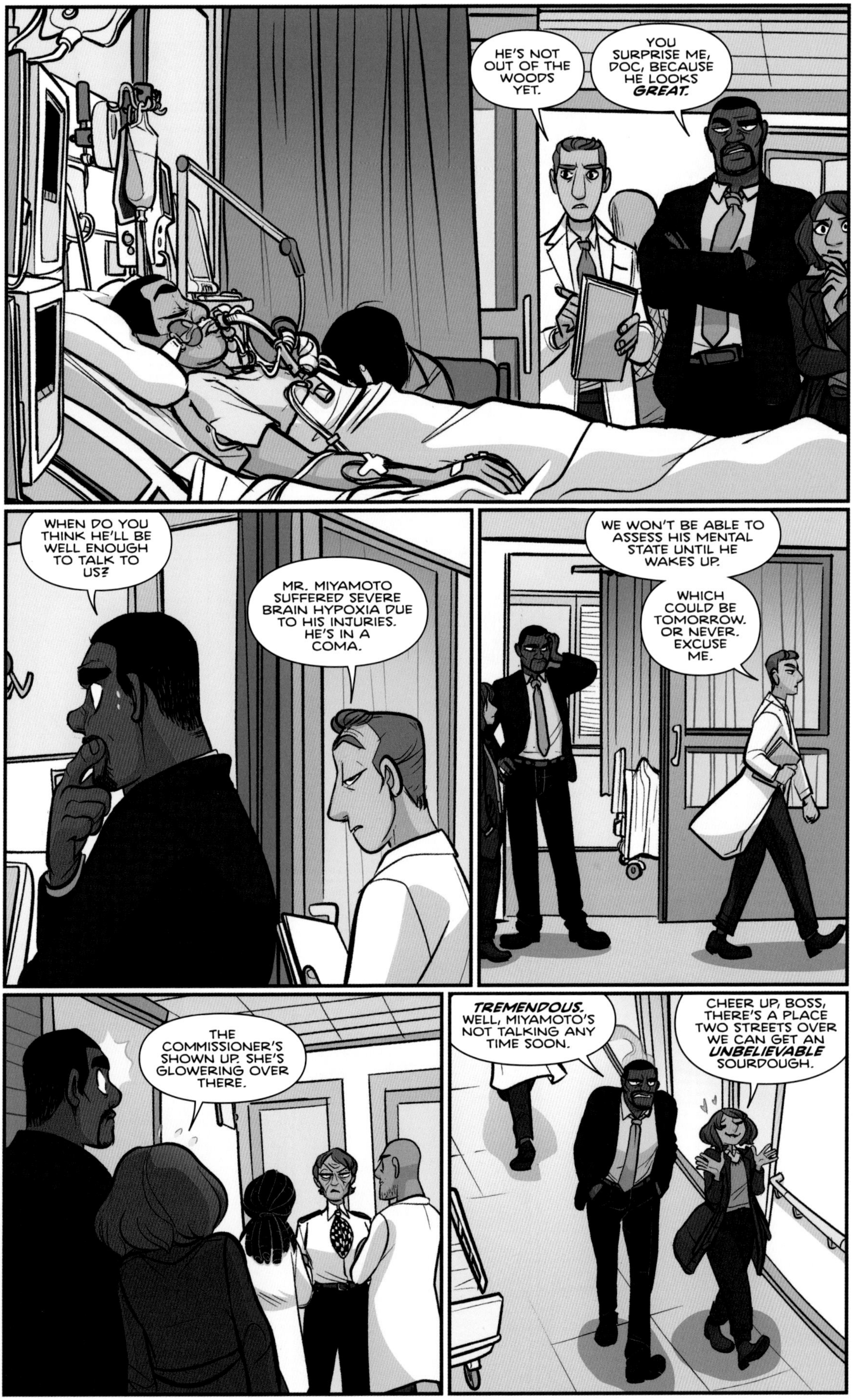
HE'S NOT OUT OF THE WOODS YET.
YOU SURPRISE ME, DOC, BECAUSE HE LOOKS *GREAT.*
WHEN DO YOU THINK HE'LL BE WELL ENOUGH TO TALK TO US?
MR. MIYAMOTO SUFFERED SEVERE BRAIN HYPOXIA DUE TO HIS INJURIES. HE'S IN A COMA.
WE WON'T BE ABLE TO ASSESS HIS MENTAL STATE UNTIL HE WAKES UP.
WHICH COULD BE TOMORROW. OR NEVER. EXCUSE ME.
THE COMMISSIONER'S SHOWN UP. SHE'S GLOWERING OVER THERE.
*TREMENDOUS.* WELL, MIYAMOTO'S NOT TALKING ANY TIME SOON.
CHEER UP, BOSS, THERE'S A PLACE TWO STREETS OVER WE CAN GET AN *UNBELIEVABLE* SOURDOUGH.

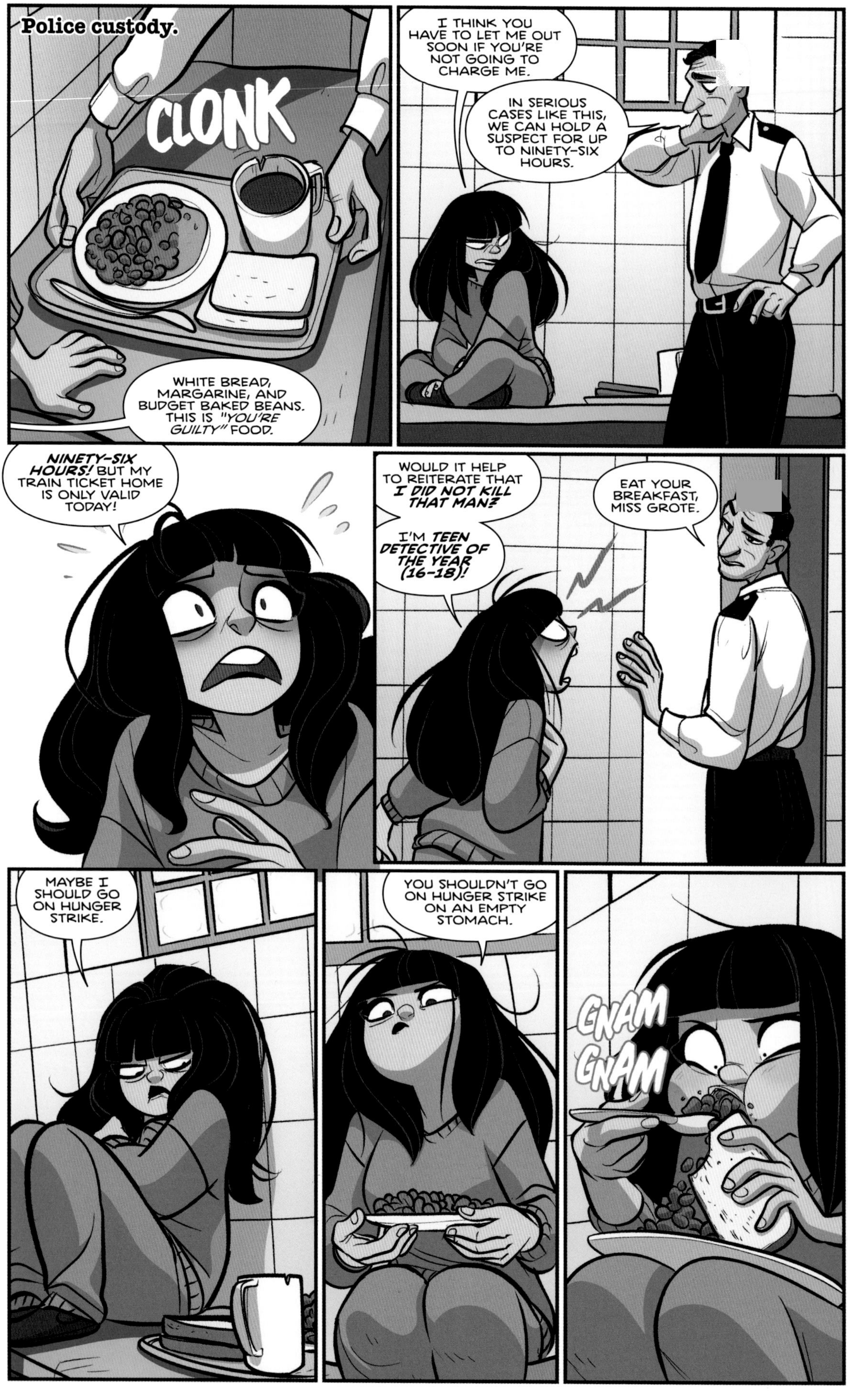
Police custody.
CLONK
WHITE BREAD, MARGARINE, AND BUDGET BAKED BEANS. THIS IS "YOU'RE GUILTY" FOOD.
I THINK YOU HAVE TO LET ME OUT SOON IF YOU'RE NOT GOING TO CHARGE ME.
IN SERIOUS CASES LIKE THIS, WE CAN HOLD A SUSPECT FOR UP TO NINETY-SIX HOURS.
NINETY-SIX HOURS! BUT MY TRAIN TICKET HOME IS ONLY VALID TODAY!
WOULD IT HELP TO REITERATE THAT I DID NOT KILL THAT MAN?
I'M TEEN DETECTIVE OF THE YEAR (16-18)!
EAT YOUR BREAKFAST, MISS GROTE.
MAYBE I SHOULD GO ON HUNGER STRIKE.
YOU SHOULDN'T GO ON HUNGER STRIKE ON AN EMPTY STOMACH.
GNAM GNAM

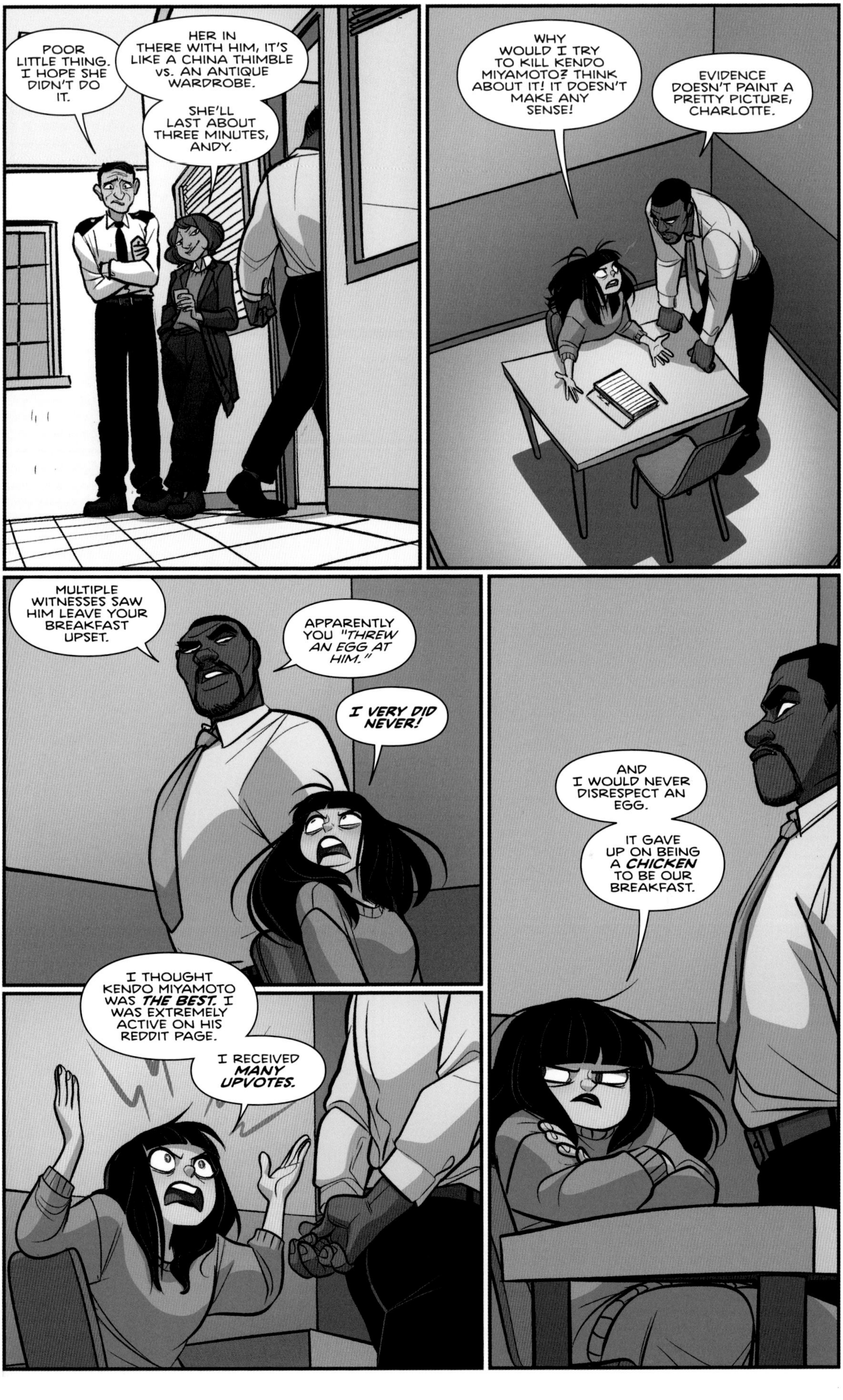
POOR LITTLE THING. I HOPE SHE DIDN'T DO IT.
HER IN THERE WITH HIM, IT'S LIKE A CHINA THIMBLE VS. AN ANTIQUE WARDROBE.
SHE'LL LAST ABOUT THREE MINUTES, ANDY.
WHY WOULD I TRY TO KILL KENDO MIYAMOTO? THINK ABOUT IT! IT DOESN'T MAKE ANY SENSE!
EVIDENCE DOESN'T PAINT A PRETTY PICTURE, CHARLOTTE.
MULTIPLE WITNESSES SAW HIM LEAVE YOUR BREAKFAST UPSET.
APPARENTLY YOU "THREW AN EGG AT HIM."
I VERY DID NEVER!
AND I WOULD NEVER DISRESPECT AN EGG.
IT GAVE UP ON BEING A CHICKEN TO BE OUR BREAKFAST.
I THOUGHT KENDO MIYAMOTO WAS THE BEST. I WAS EXTREMELY ACTIVE ON HIS REDDIT PAGE.
I RECEIVED MANY UPVOTES.

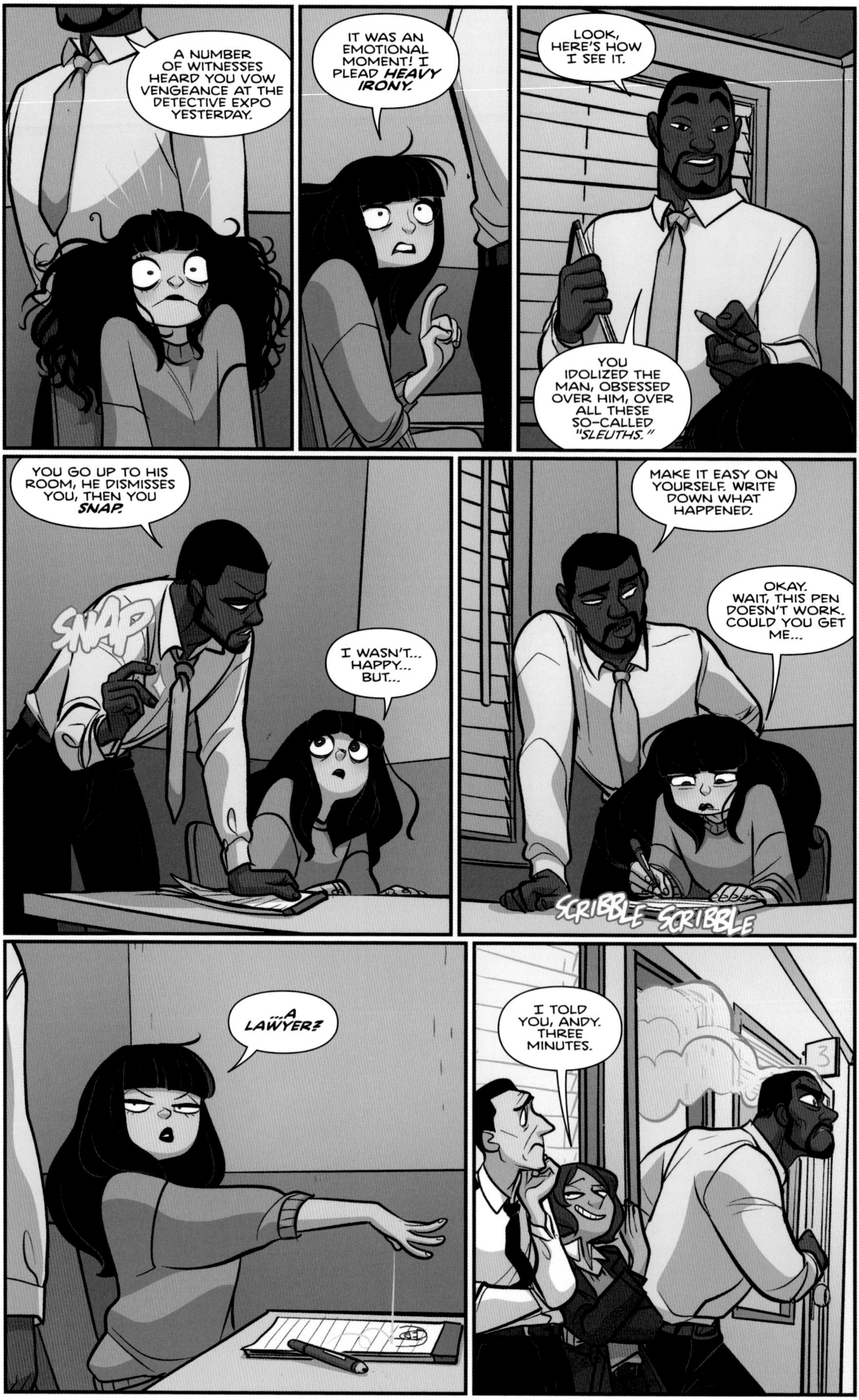
A NUMBER OF WITNESSES HEARD YOU VOW VENGEANCE AT THE DETECTIVE EXPO YESTERDAY.
IT WAS AN EMOTIONAL MOMENT! I PLEAD HEAVY IRONY.
LOOK, HERE'S HOW I SEE IT.
YOU IDOLIZED THE MAN, OBSESSED OVER HIM, OVER ALL THESE SO-CALLED "SLEUTHS."
YOU GO UP TO HIS ROOM, HE DISMISSES YOU, THEN YOU SNAP.
SNAP
I WASN'T... HAPPY... BUT...
MAKE IT EASY ON YOURSELF. WRITE DOWN WHAT HAPPENED.
OKAY. WAIT, THIS PEN DOESN'T WORK. COULD YOU GET ME...
SCRIBBLE SCRIBBLE
...A LAWYER?
I TOLD YOU, ANDY. THREE MINUTES.
3

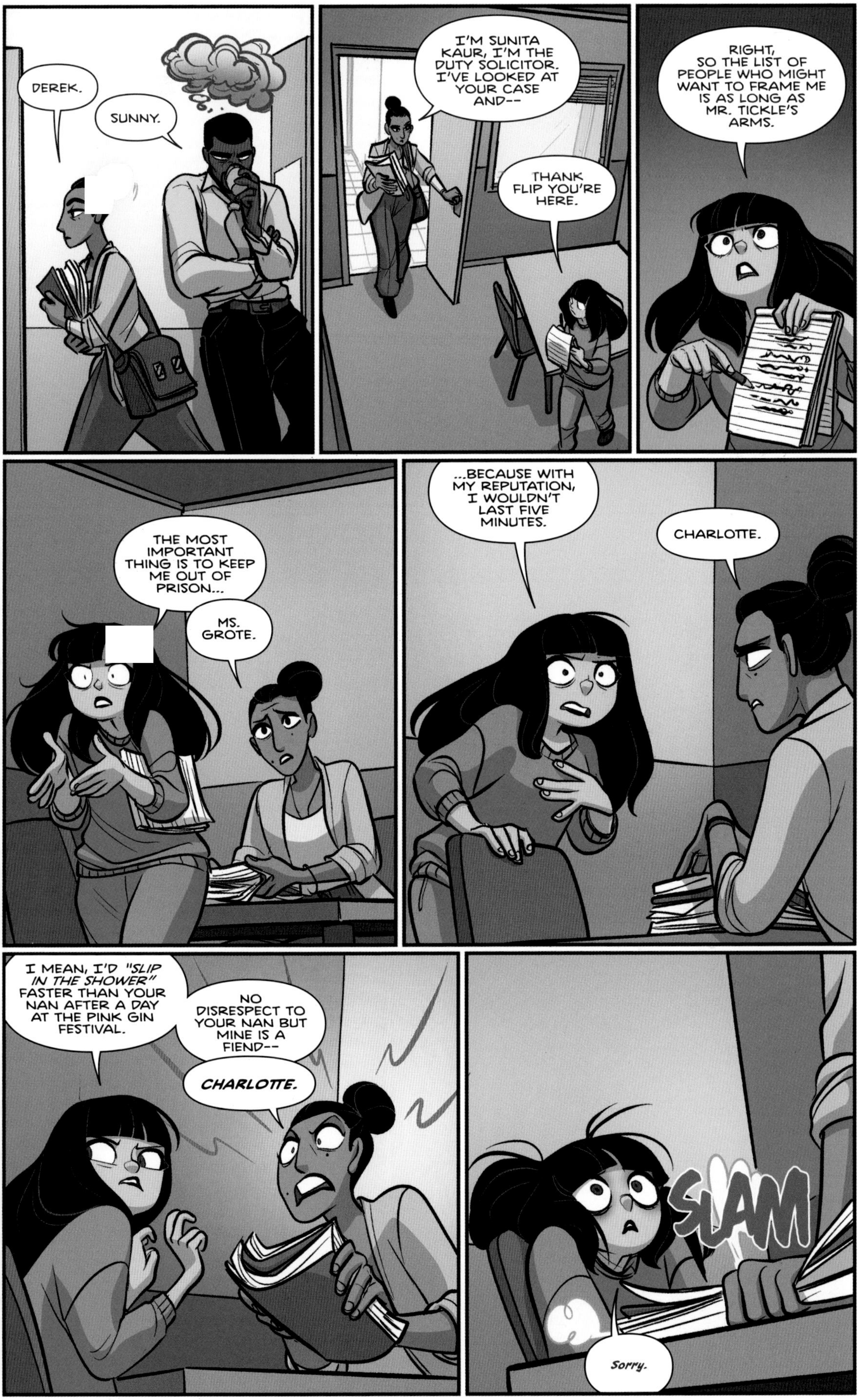

DEREK.
SUNNY.
I'M SUNITA KAUR, I'M THE DUTY SOLICITOR. I'VE LOOKED AT YOUR CASE AND--
THANK FLIP YOU'RE HERE.
RIGHT, SO THE LIST OF PEOPLE WHO MIGHT WANT TO FRAME ME IS AS LONG AS MR. TICKLE'S ARMS.
THE MOST IMPORTANT THING IS TO KEEP ME OUT OF PRISON...
MS. GROTE.
...BECAUSE WITH MY REPUTATION, I WOULDN'T LAST FIVE MINUTES.
CHARLOTTE.
I MEAN, I'D *"SLIP IN THE SHOWER"* FASTER THAN YOUR NAN AFTER A DAY AT THE PINK GIN FESTIVAL.
NO DISRESPECT TO YOUR NAN BUT MINE IS A FIEND--
***CHARLOTTE.***
SLAM
*Sorry.*

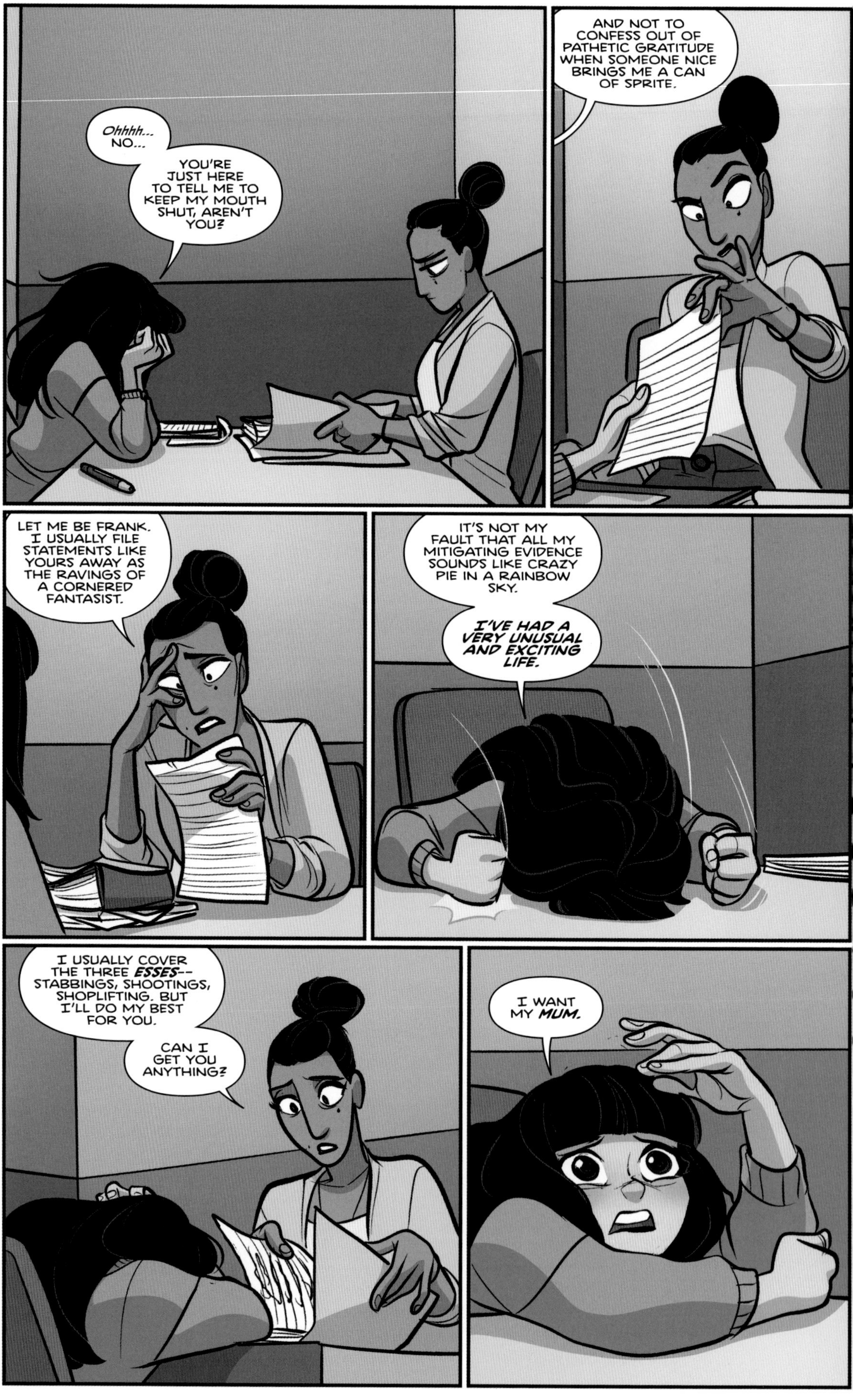
Ohhhh... NO...
YOU'RE JUST HERE TO TELL ME TO KEEP MY MOUTH SHUT, AREN'T YOU?
AND NOT TO CONFESS OUT OF PATHETIC GRATITUDE WHEN SOMEONE NICE BRINGS ME A CAN OF SPRITE.
LET ME BE FRANK. I USUALLY FILE STATEMENTS LIKE YOURS AWAY AS THE RAVINGS OF A CORNERED FANTASIST.
IT'S NOT MY FAULT THAT ALL MY MITIGATING EVIDENCE SOUNDS LIKE CRAZY PIE IN A RAINBOW SKY.
I'VE HAD A VERY UNUSUAL AND EXCITING LIFE.
I USUALLY COVER THE THREE ESSES--STABBINGS, SHOOTINGS, SHOPLIFTING. BUT I'LL DO MY BEST FOR YOU.
CAN I GET YOU ANYTHING?
I WANT MY MUM.

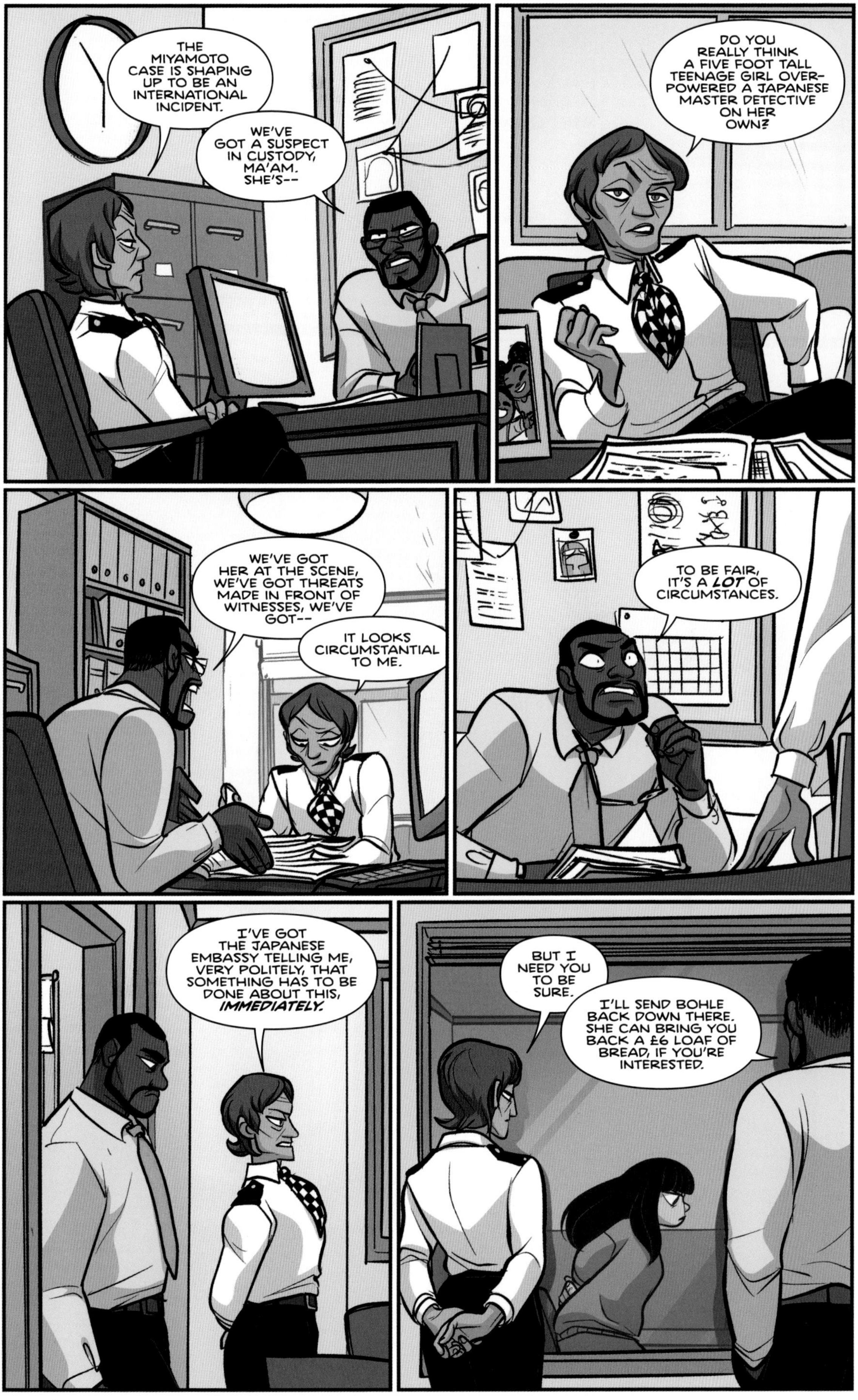
THE MIYAMOTO CASE IS SHAPING UP TO BE AN INTERNATIONAL INCIDENT.
WE'VE GOT A SUSPECT IN CUSTODY, MA'AM. SHE'S--
DO YOU REALLY THINK A FIVE FOOT TALL TEENAGE GIRL OVER-POWERED A JAPANESE MASTER DETECTIVE ON HER OWN?
WE'VE GOT HER AT THE SCENE, WE'VE GOT THREATS MADE IN FRONT OF WITNESSES, WE'VE GOT--
IT LOOKS CIRCUMSTANTIAL TO ME.
TO BE FAIR, IT'S A *LOT* OF CIRCUMSTANCES.
I'VE GOT THE JAPANESE EMBASSY TELLING ME, VERY POLITELY, THAT SOMETHING HAS TO BE DONE ABOUT THIS, *IMMEDIATELY.*
BUT I NEED YOU TO BE SURE.
I'LL SEND BOHLE BACK DOWN THERE. SHE CAN BRING YOU BACK A £6 LOAF OF BREAD, IF YOU'RE INTERESTED.

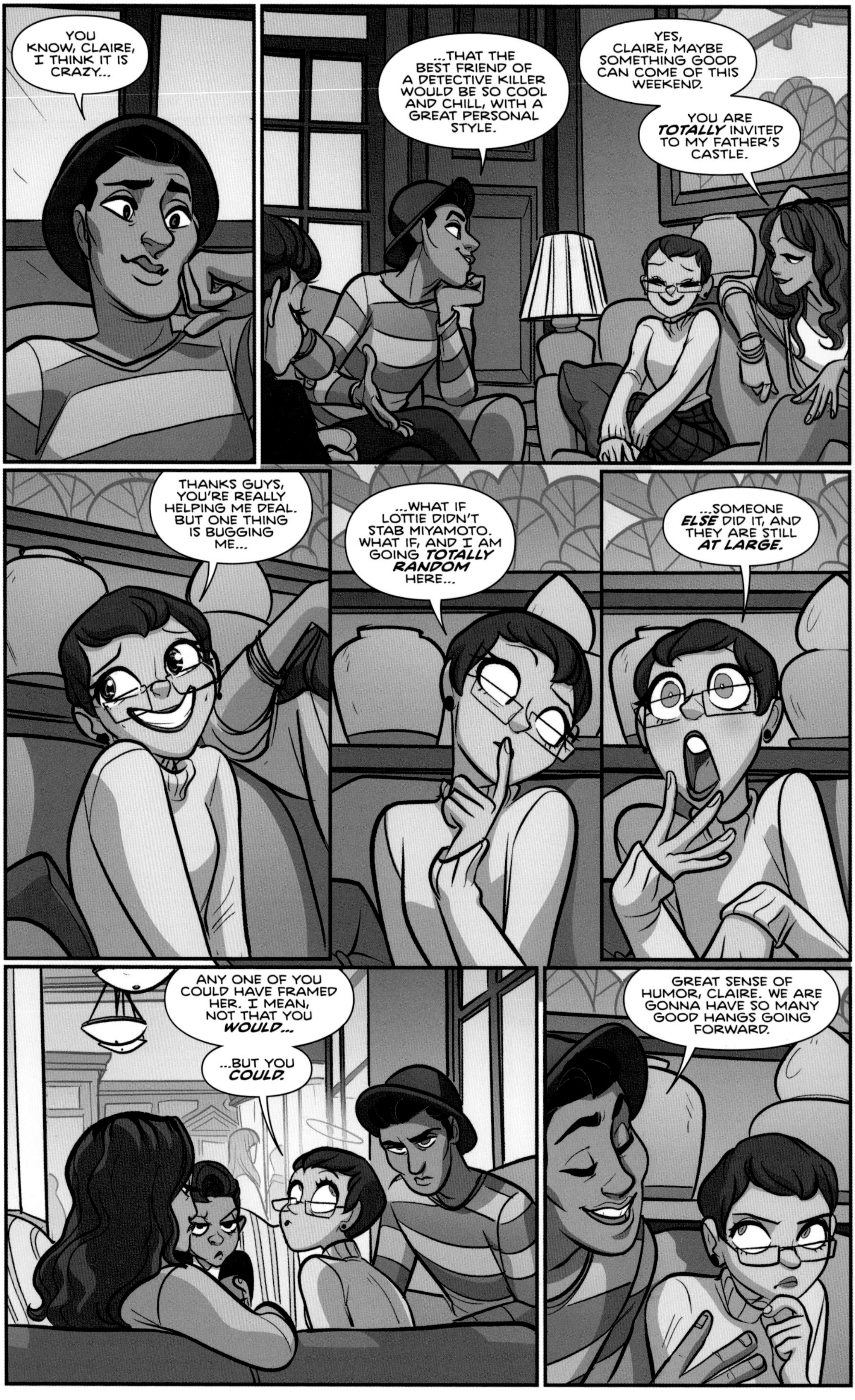
YOU KNOW, CLAIRE, I THINK IT IS CRAZY...
...THAT THE BEST FRIEND OF A DETECTIVE KILLER WOULD BE SO COOL AND CHILL, WITH A GREAT PERSONAL STYLE.
YES, CLAIRE, MAYBE SOMETHING GOOD CAN COME OF THIS WEEKEND.
YOU ARE *TOTALLY* INVITED TO MY FATHER'S CASTLE.
THANKS GUYS, YOU'RE REALLY HELPING ME DEAL. BUT ONE THING IS BUGGING ME...
...WHAT IF LOTTIE DIDN'T STAB MIYAMOTO. WHAT IF, AND I AM GOING *TOTALLY RANDOM* HERE...
...SOMEONE *ELSE* DID IT, AND THEY ARE STILL *AT LARGE.*
ANY ONE OF YOU COULD HAVE FRAMED HER. I MEAN, NOT THAT YOU *WOULD...*
...BUT YOU *COULD.*
GREAT SENSE OF HUMOR, CLAIRE. WE ARE GONNA HAVE SO MANY GOOD HANGS GOING FORWARD.

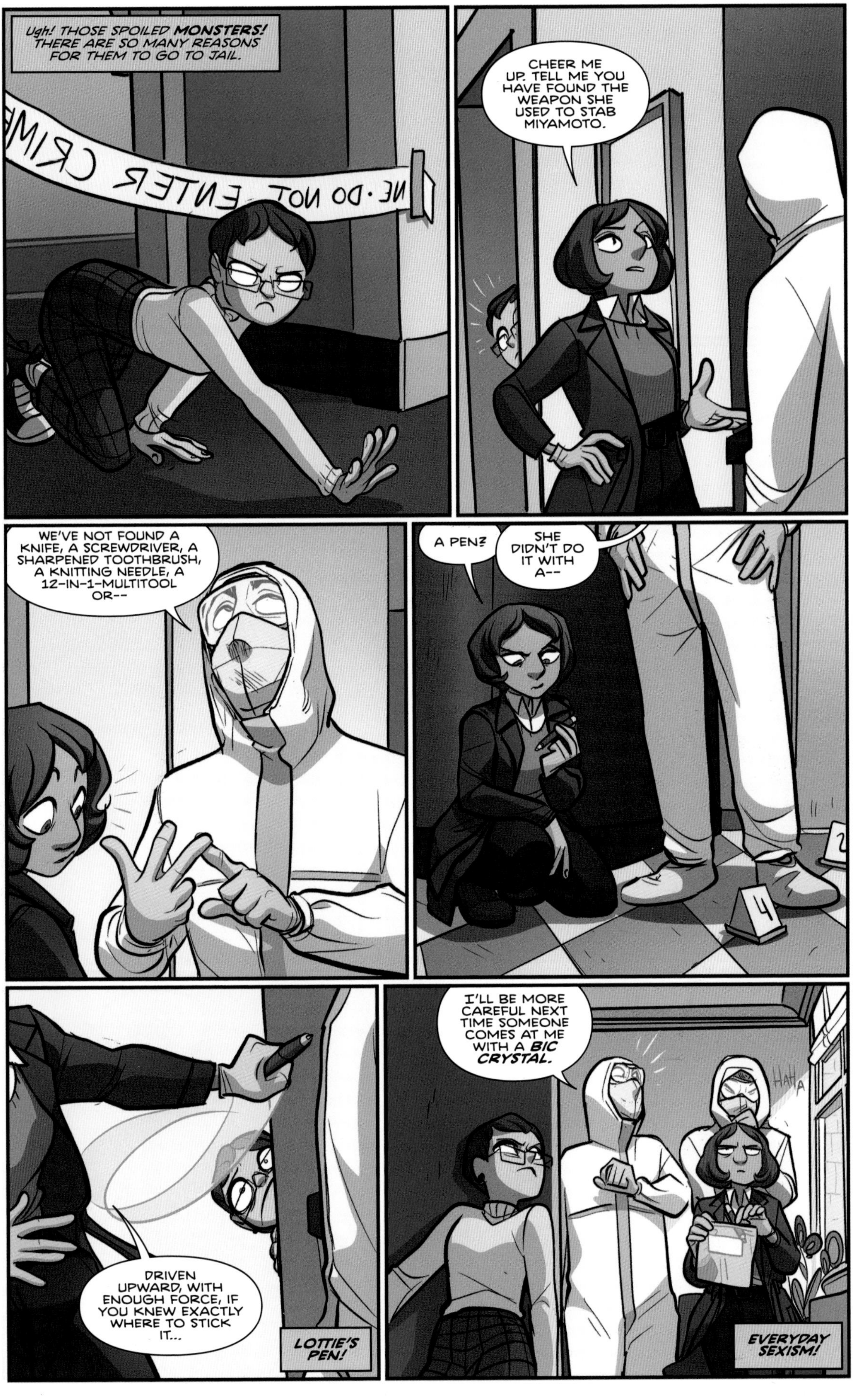

Ugh! THOSE SPOILED MONSTERS! THERE ARE SO MANY REASONS FOR THEM TO GO TO JAIL.
NE · DO NOT ENTER CRIME
CHEER ME UP. TELL ME YOU HAVE FOUND THE WEAPON SHE USED TO STAB MIYAMOTO.
WE'VE NOT FOUND A KNIFE, A SCREWDRIVER, A SHARPENED TOOTHBRUSH, A KNITTING NEEDLE, A 12-IN-1-MULTITOOL OR--
A PEN?
SHE DIDN'T DO IT WITH A--
DRIVEN UPWARD, WITH ENOUGH FORCE, IF YOU KNEW EXACTLY WHERE TO STICK IT...
LOTTIE'S PEN!
I'LL BE MORE CAREFUL NEXT TIME SOMEONE COMES AT ME WITH A BIC CRYSTAL.
HAH HA
EVERYDAY SEXISM!

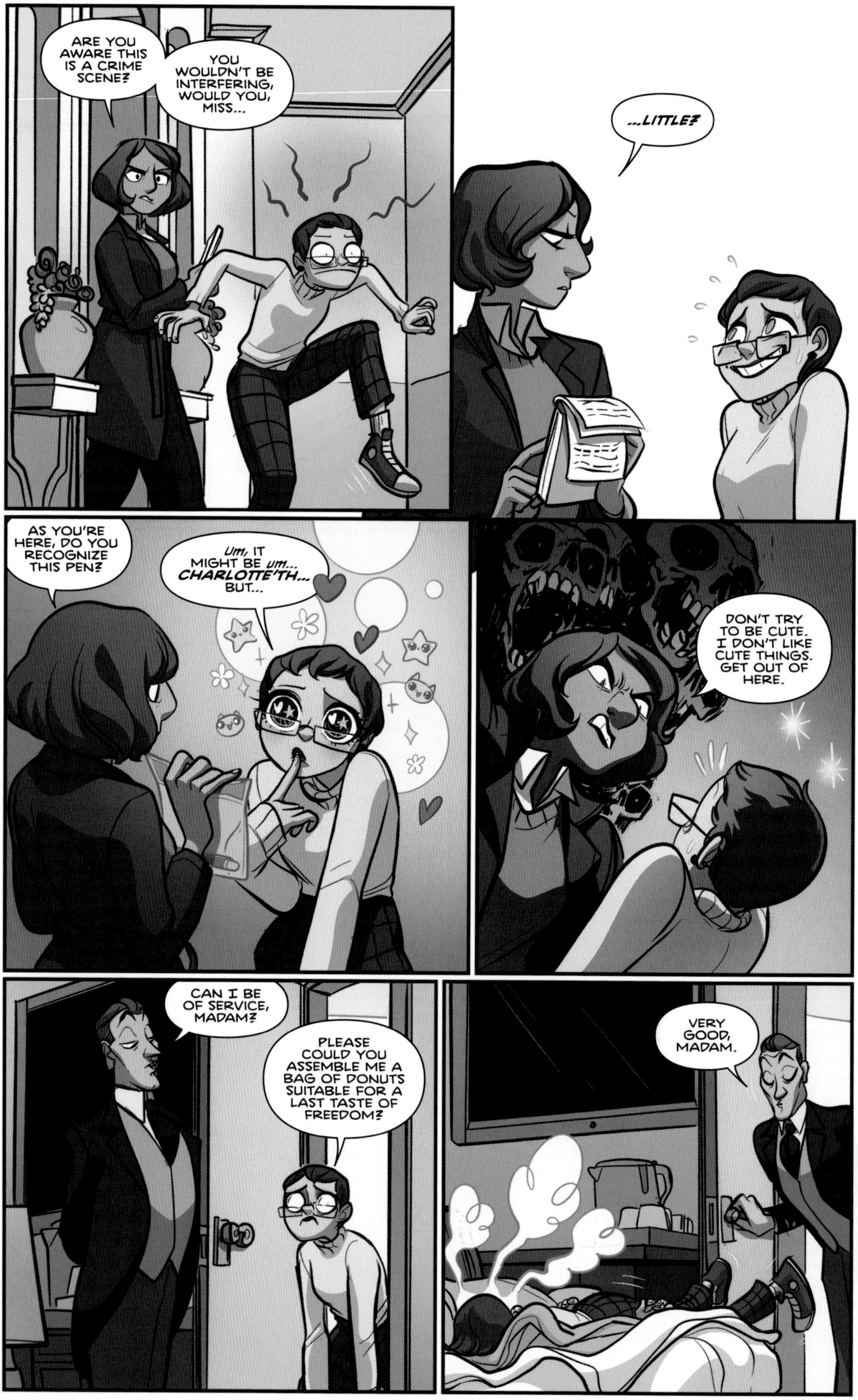
ARE YOU AWARE THIS IS A CRIME SCENE?
YOU WOULDN'T BE INTERFERING, WOULD YOU, MISS...
...LITTLE?
AS YOU'RE HERE, DO YOU RECOGNIZE THIS PEN?
UM, IT MIGHT BE UM... CHARLOTTE'TH... BUT...
DON'T TRY TO BE CUTE. I DON'T LIKE CUTE THINGS. GET OUT OF HERE.
CAN I BE OF SERVICE, MADAM?
PLEASE COULD YOU ASSEMBLE ME A BAG OF DONUTS SUITABLE FOR A LAST TASTE OF FREEDOM?
VERY GOOD, MADAM.

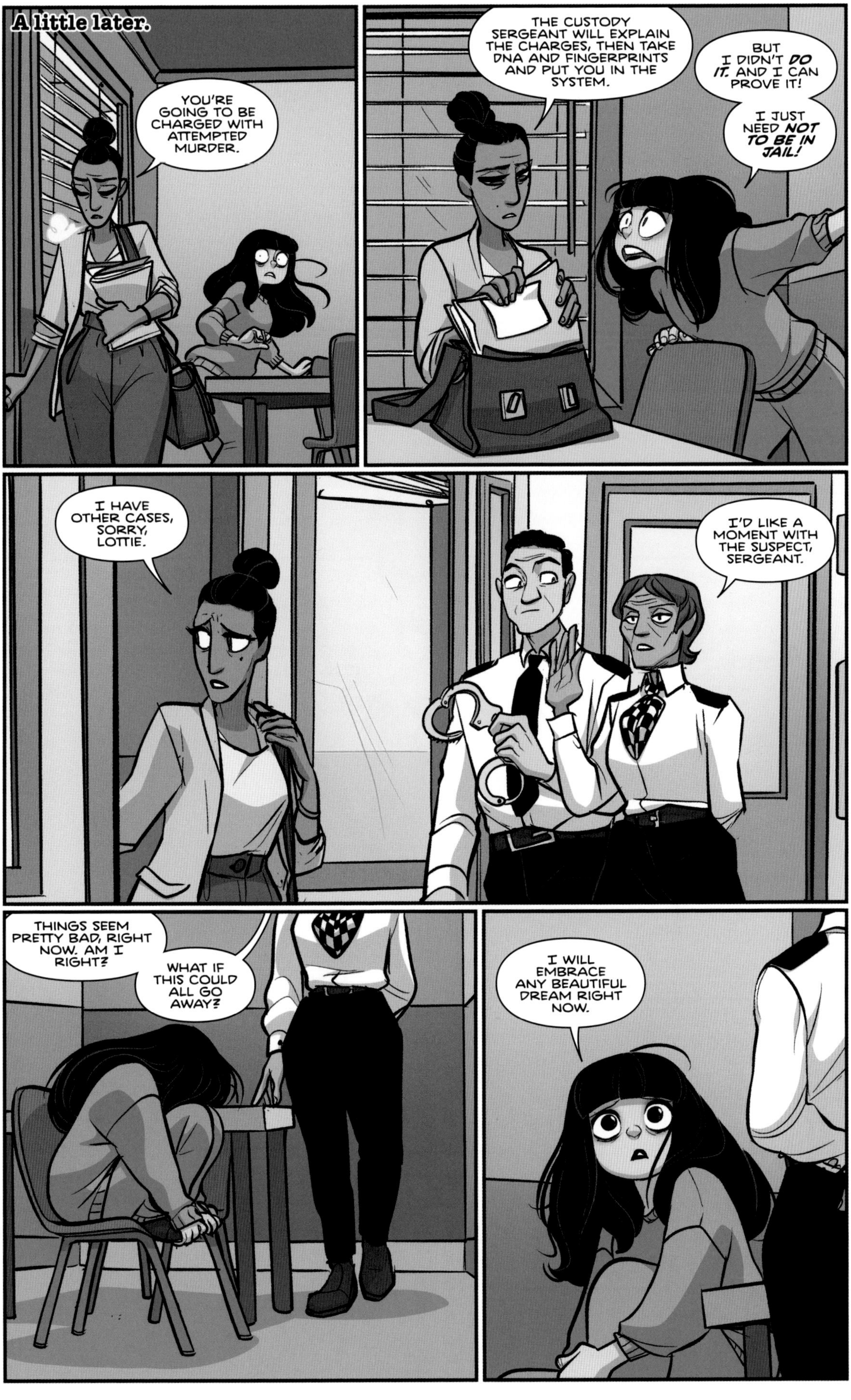
A little later.
YOU'RE GOING TO BE CHARGED WITH ATTEMPTED MURDER.
THE CUSTODY SERGEANT WILL EXPLAIN THE CHARGES, THEN TAKE DNA AND FINGERPRINTS AND PUT YOU IN THE SYSTEM.
BUT I DIDN'T *DO IT.* AND I CAN PROVE IT!
I JUST NEED ***NOT TO BE IN JAIL!***
I HAVE OTHER CASES, SORRY, LOTTIE.
I'D LIKE A MOMENT WITH THE SUSPECT, SERGEANT.
THINGS SEEM PRETTY BAD, RIGHT NOW. AM I RIGHT?
WHAT IF THIS COULD ALL GO AWAY?
I WILL EMBRACE ANY BEAUTIFUL DREAM RIGHT NOW.

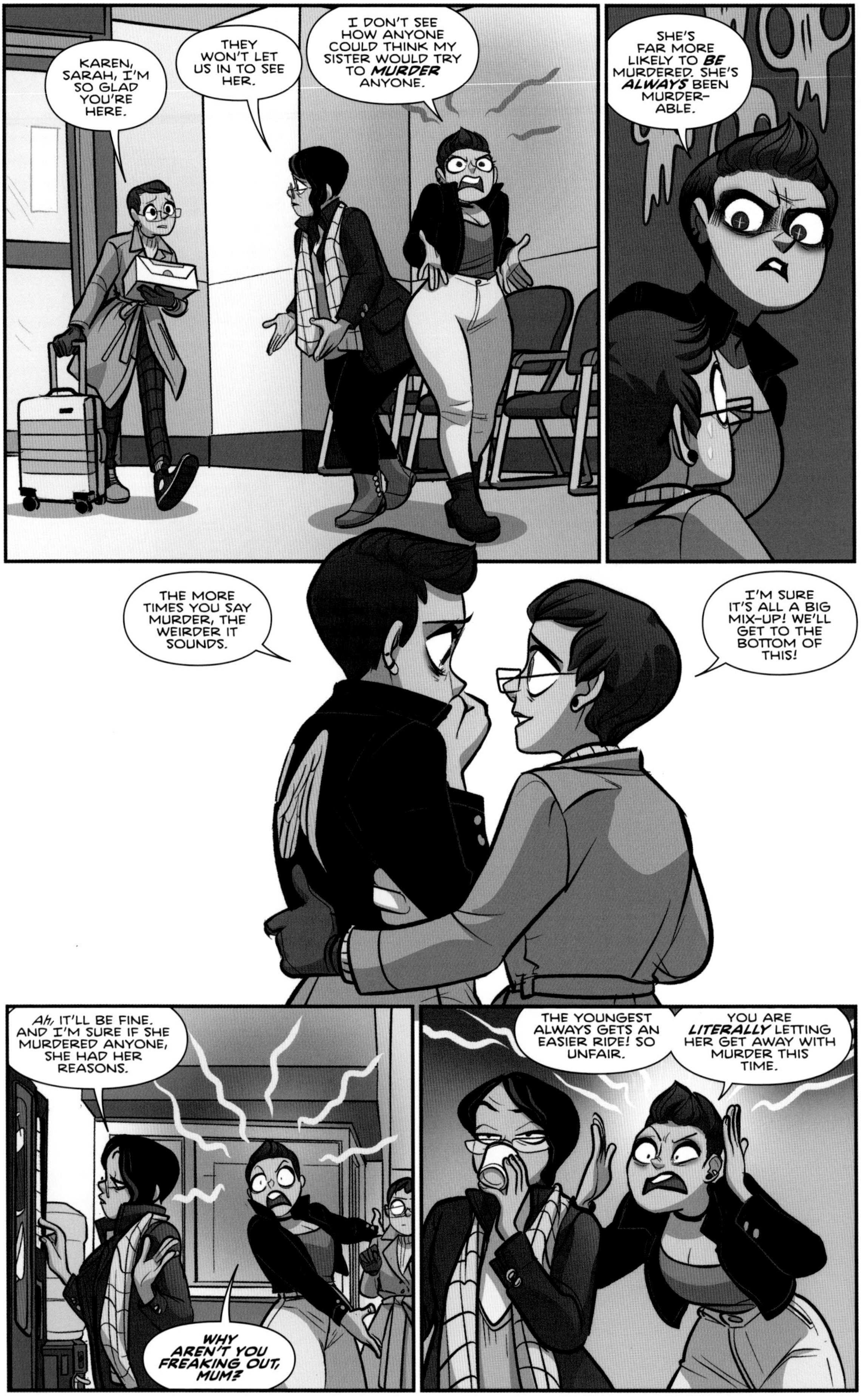
KAREN, SARAH, I'M SO GLAD YOU'RE HERE.
THEY WON'T LET US IN TO SEE HER.
I DON'T SEE HOW ANYONE COULD THINK MY SISTER WOULD TRY TO *MURDER* ANYONE.
SHE'S FAR MORE LIKELY TO *BE* MURDERED. SHE'S *ALWAYS* BEEN MURDER-ABLE.
THE MORE TIMES YOU SAY MURDER, THE WEIRDER IT SOUNDS.
I'M SURE IT'S ALL A BIG MIX-UP! WE'LL GET TO THE BOTTOM OF THIS!
*Ah,* IT'LL BE FINE. AND I'M SURE IF SHE MURDERED ANYONE, SHE HAD HER REASONS.
*WHY AREN'T YOU FREAKING OUT, MUM?*
THE YOUNGEST ALWAYS GETS AN EASIER RIDE! SO UNFAIR.
YOU ARE *LITERALLY* LETTING HER GET AWAY WITH MURDER THIS TIME.

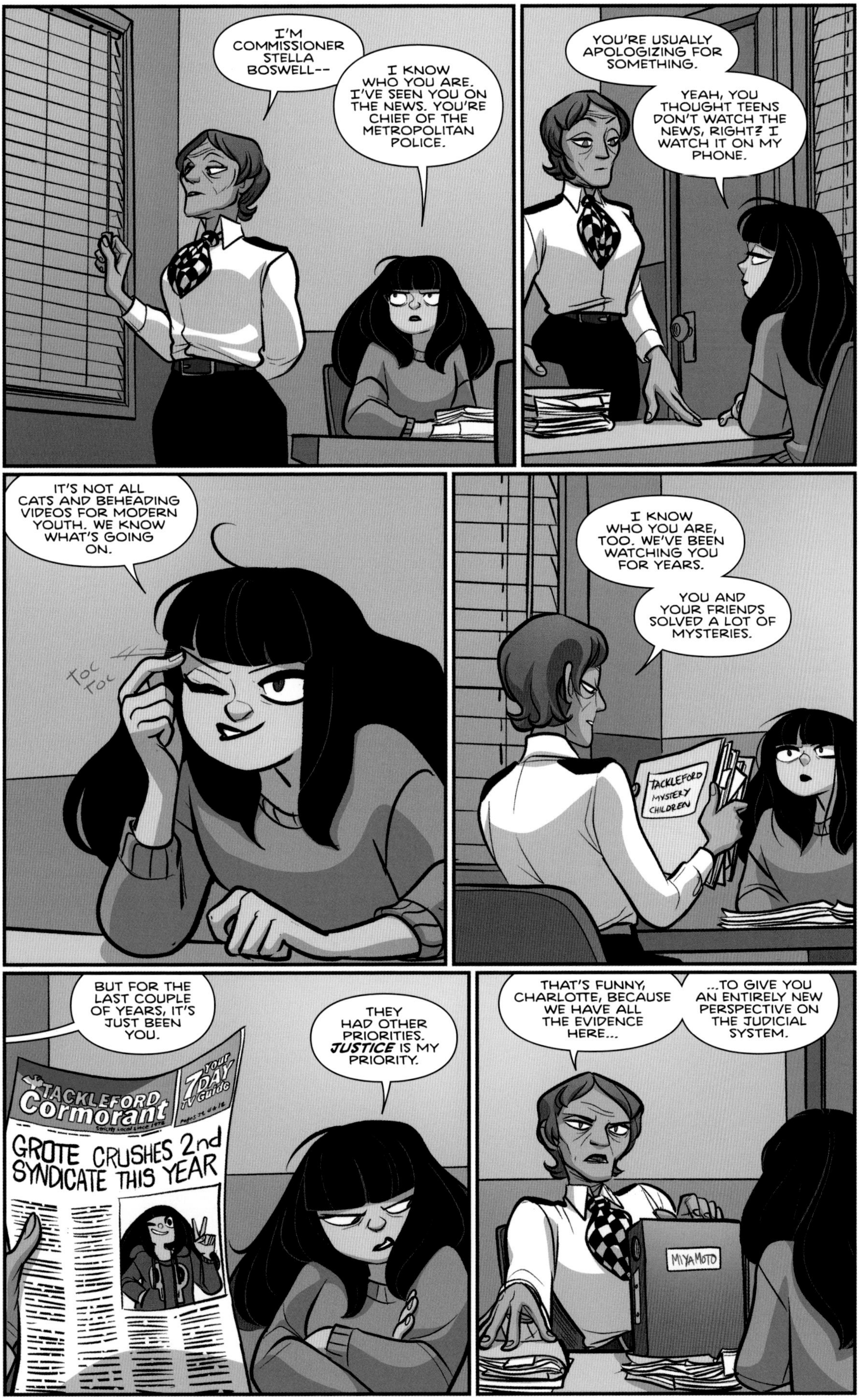
I'M COMMISSIONER STELLA BOSWELL--
I KNOW WHO YOU ARE. I'VE SEEN YOU ON THE NEWS. YOU'RE CHIEF OF THE METROPOLITAN POLICE.
YOU'RE USUALLY APOLOGIZING FOR SOMETHING.
YEAH, YOU THOUGHT TEENS DON'T WATCH THE NEWS, RIGHT? I WATCH IT ON MY PHONE.
IT'S NOT ALL CATS AND BEHEADING VIDEOS FOR MODERN YOUTH. WE KNOW WHAT'S GOING ON.
TOC TOC
I KNOW WHO YOU ARE, TOO. WE'VE BEEN WATCHING YOU FOR YEARS.
YOU AND YOUR FRIENDS SOLVED A LOT OF MYSTERIES.
TACKLEFORD MYSTERY CHILDREN
BUT FOR THE LAST COUPLE OF YEARS, IT'S JUST BEEN YOU.
TACKLEFORD Cormorant
Your 7DAY TV Guide
GROTE CRUSHES 2nd SYNDICATE THIS YEAR
THEY HAD OTHER PRIORITIES. JUSTICE IS MY PRIORITY.
THAT'S FUNNY, CHARLOTTE, BECAUSE WE HAVE ALL THE EVIDENCE HERE...
...TO GIVE YOU AN ENTIRELY NEW PERSPECTIVE ON THE JUDICIAL SYSTEM.
MIYAMOTO

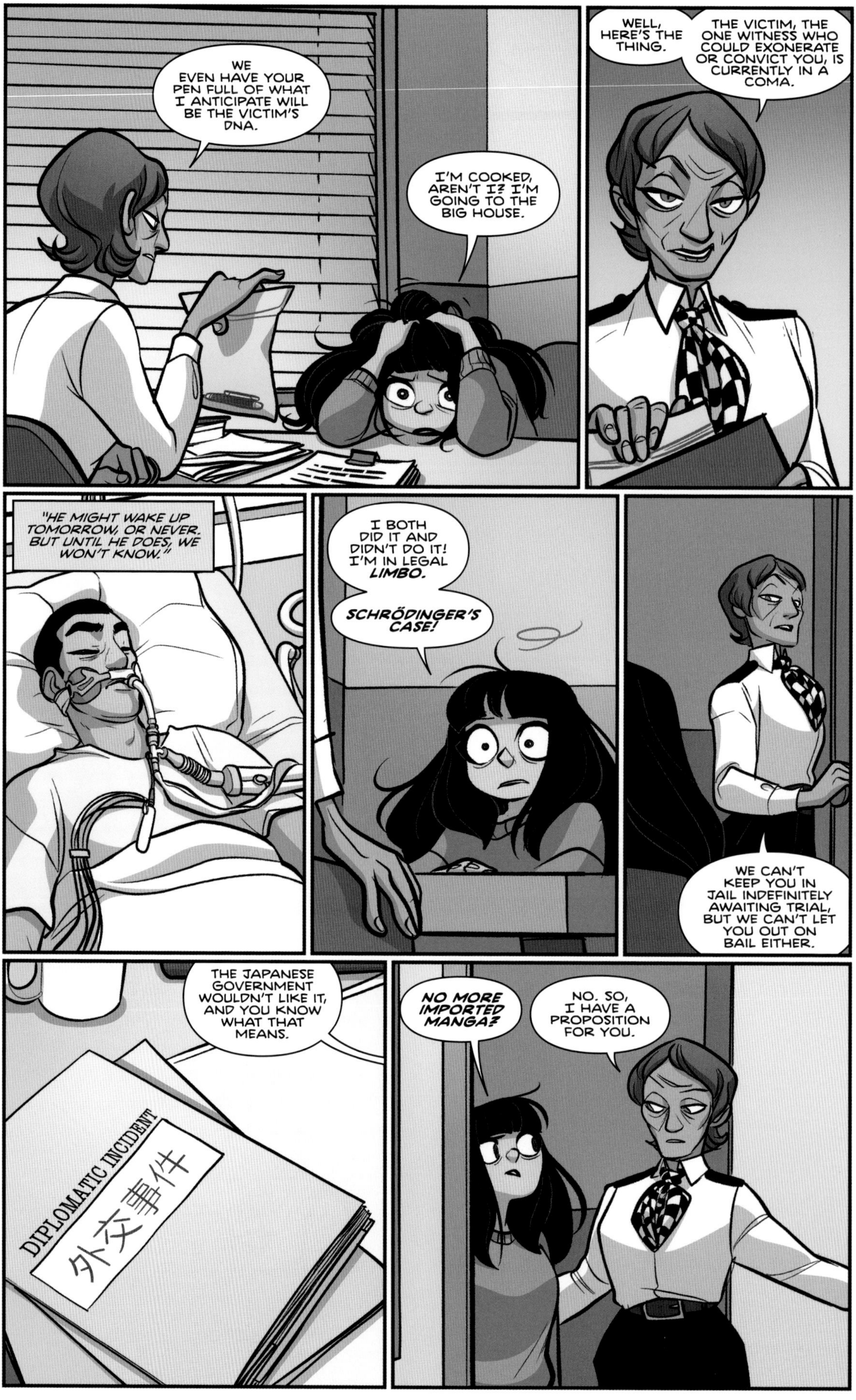
WE EVEN HAVE YOUR PEN FULL OF WHAT I ANTICIPATE WILL BE THE VICTIM'S DNA.
I'M COOKED, AREN'T I? I'M GOING TO THE BIG HOUSE.
WELL, HERE'S THE THING.
THE VICTIM, THE ONE WITNESS WHO COULD EXONERATE OR CONVICT YOU, IS CURRENTLY IN A COMA.
"HE MIGHT WAKE UP TOMORROW, OR NEVER. BUT UNTIL HE DOES, WE WON'T KNOW."
I BOTH DID IT AND DIDN'T DO IT! I'M IN LEGAL LIMBO.
SCHRÖDINGER'S CASE!
WE CAN'T KEEP YOU IN JAIL INDEFINITELY AWAITING TRIAL, BUT WE CAN'T LET YOU OUT ON BAIL EITHER.
THE JAPANESE GOVERNMENT WOULDN'T LIKE IT, AND YOU KNOW WHAT THAT MEANS.
DIPLOMATIC INCIDENT
外交事件
NO MORE IMPORTED MANGA?
NO. SO, I HAVE A PROPOSITION FOR YOU.

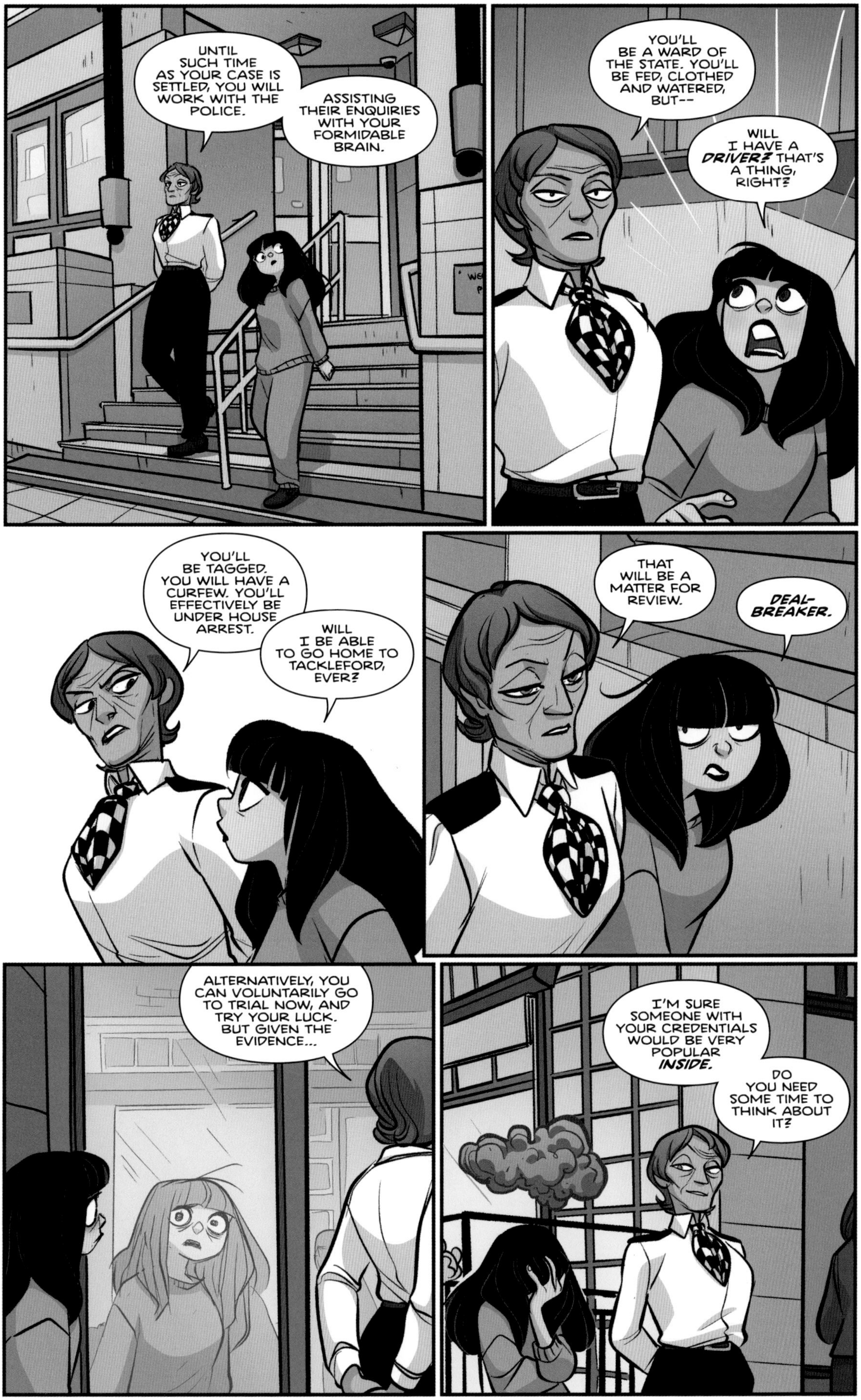
UNTIL SUCH TIME AS YOUR CASE IS SETTLED, YOU WILL WORK WITH THE POLICE.
ASSISTING THEIR ENQUIRIES WITH YOUR FORMIDABLE BRAIN.
YOU'LL BE A WARD OF THE STATE. YOU'LL BE FED, CLOTHED AND WATERED, BUT--
WILL I HAVE A DRIVER? THAT'S A THING, RIGHT?
YOU'LL BE TAGGED. YOU WILL HAVE A CURFEW. YOU'LL EFFECTIVELY BE UNDER HOUSE ARREST.
WILL I BE ABLE TO GO HOME TO TACKLEFORD, EVER?
THAT WILL BE A MATTER FOR REVIEW.
DEAL-BREAKER.
ALTERNATIVELY, YOU CAN VOLUNTARILY GO TO TRIAL NOW, AND TRY YOUR LUCK. BUT GIVEN THE EVIDENCE...
I'M SURE SOMEONE WITH YOUR CREDENTIALS WOULD BE VERY POPULAR INSIDE.
DO YOU NEED SOME TIME TO THINK ABOUT IT?

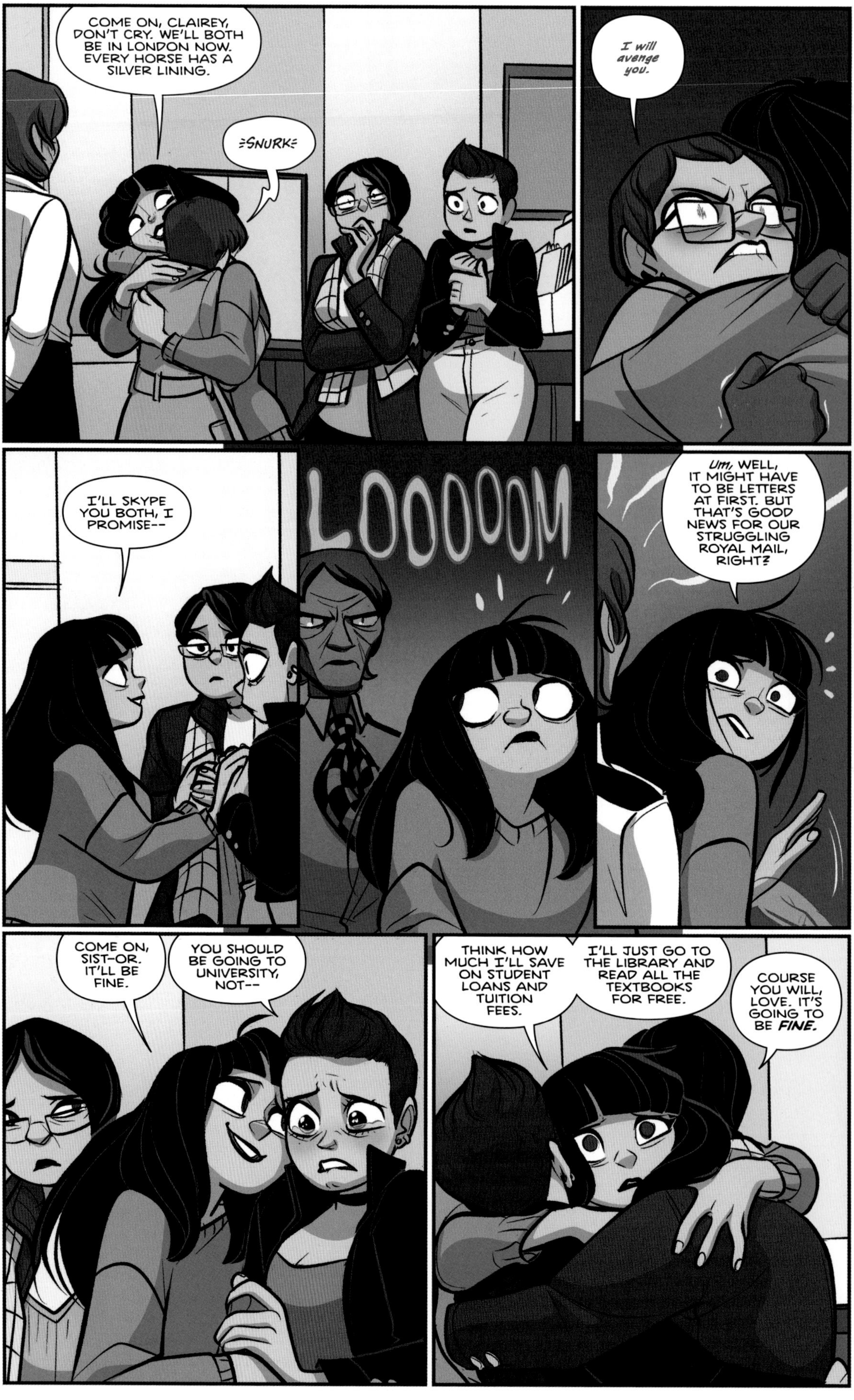
COME ON, CLAIREY, DON'T CRY. WE'LL BOTH BE IN LONDON NOW. EVERY HORSE HAS A SILVER LINING.
=SNURK=
I will avenge you.
I'LL SKYPE YOU BOTH, I PROMISE--
LOOOOOM
Um, WELL, IT MIGHT HAVE TO BE LETTERS AT FIRST. BUT THAT'S GOOD NEWS FOR OUR STRUGGLING ROYAL MAIL, RIGHT?
COME ON, SIST-OR. IT'LL BE FINE.
YOU SHOULD BE GOING TO UNIVERSITY, NOT--
THINK HOW MUCH I'LL SAVE ON STUDENT LOANS AND TUITION FEES.
I'LL JUST GO TO THE LIBRARY AND READ ALL THE TEXTBOOKS FOR FREE.
COURSE YOU WILL, LOVE. IT'S GOING TO BE FINE.

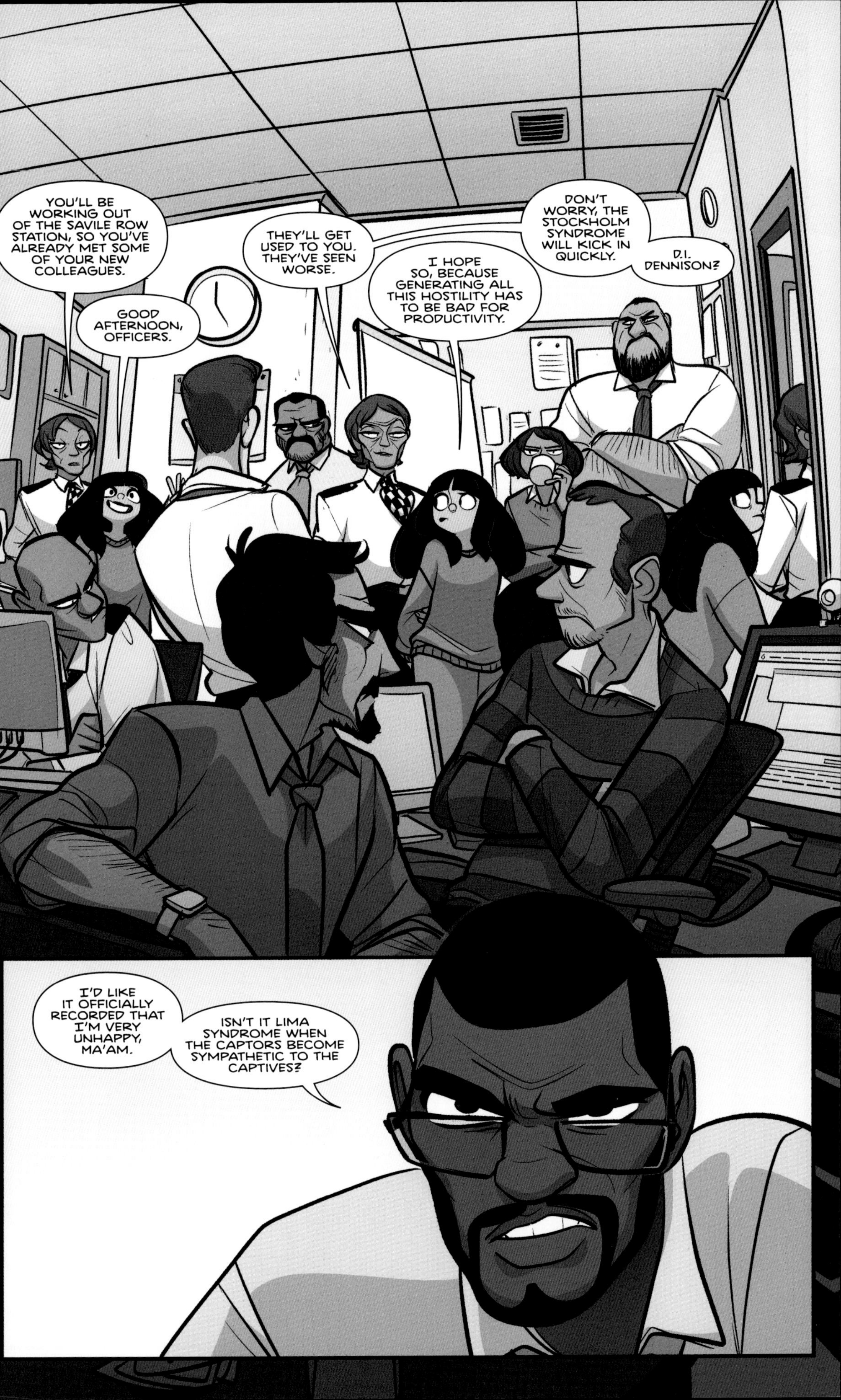
YOU'LL BE WORKING OUT OF THE SAVILE ROW STATION, SO YOU'VE ALREADY MET SOME OF YOUR NEW COLLEAGUES.
GOOD AFTERNOON, OFFICERS.
THEY'LL GET USED TO YOU. THEY'VE SEEN WORSE.
I HOPE SO, BECAUSE GENERATING ALL THIS HOSTILITY HAS TO BE BAD FOR PRODUCTIVITY.
DON'T WORRY, THE STOCKHOLM SYNDROME WILL KICK IN QUICKLY.
D.I. DENNISON?
I'D LIKE IT OFFICIALLY RECORDED THAT I'M VERY UNHAPPY, MA'AM.
ISN'T IT LIMA SYNDROME WHEN THE CAPTORS BECOME SYMPATHETIC TO THE CAPTIVES?

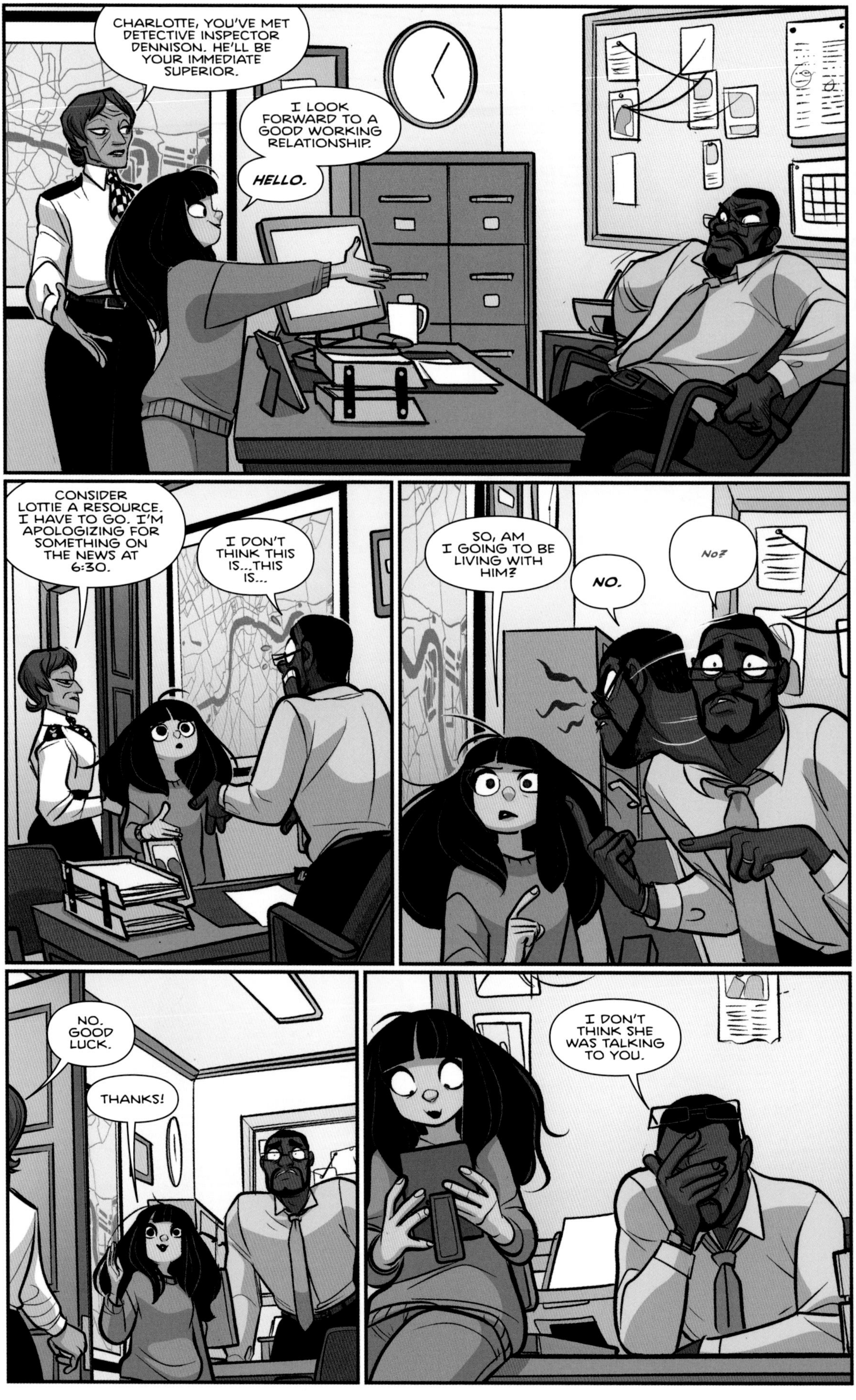
CHARLOTTE, YOU'VE MET DETECTIVE INSPECTOR DENNISON. HE'LL BE YOUR IMMEDIATE SUPERIOR.
I LOOK FORWARD TO A GOOD WORKING RELATIONSHIP.
HELLO.
CONSIDER LOTTIE A RESOURCE. I HAVE TO GO. I'M APOLOGIZING FOR SOMETHING ON THE NEWS AT 6:30.
I DON'T THINK THIS IS... THIS IS...
SO, AM I GOING TO BE LIVING WITH HIM?
NO.
No?
NO. GOOD LUCK.
THANKS!
I DON'T THINK SHE WAS TALKING TO YOU.

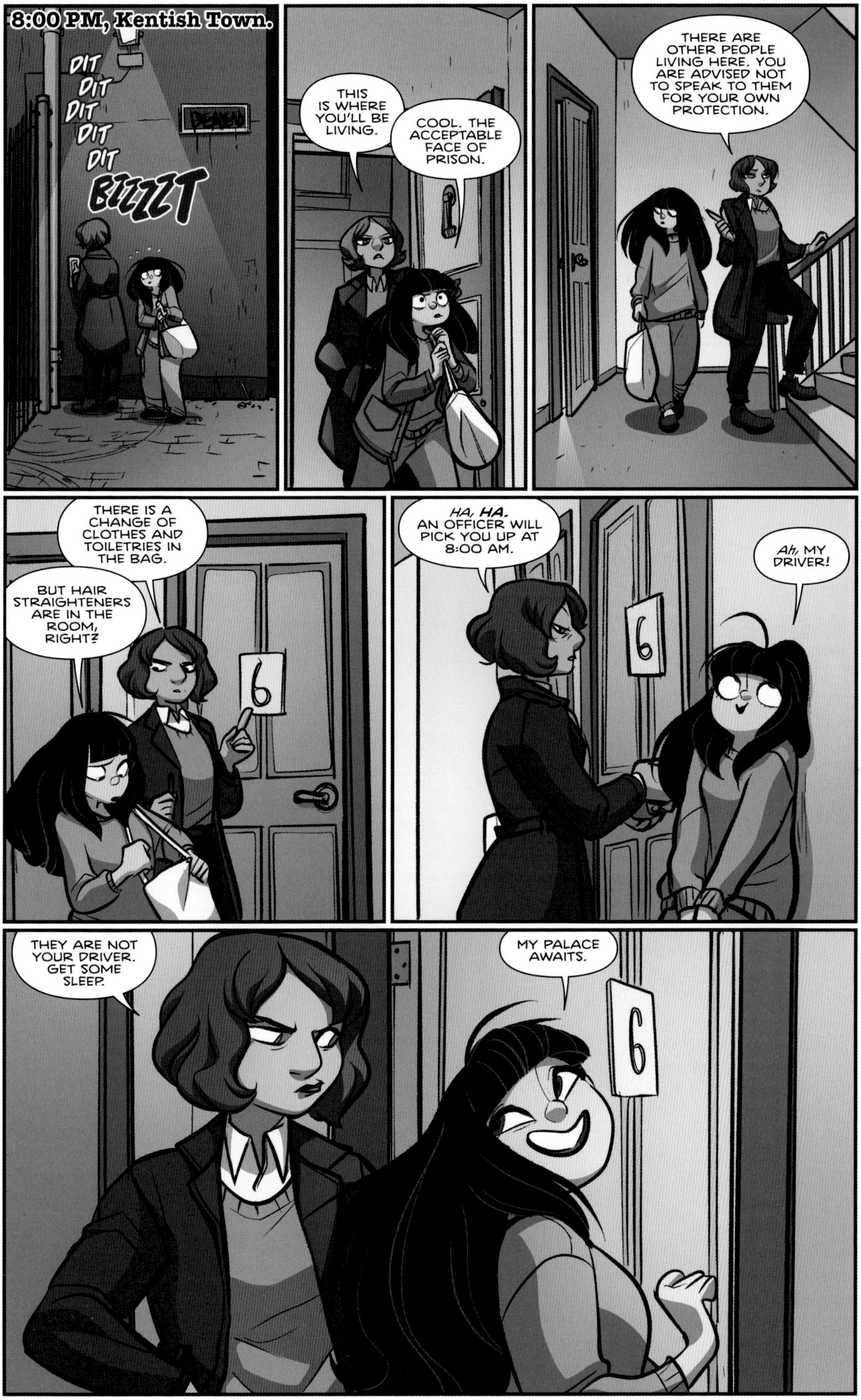
8:00 PM, Kentish Town.
DIT DIT DIT DIT DIT BZZZZT
THIS IS WHERE YOU'LL BE LIVING.
COOL. THE ACCEPTABLE FACE OF PRISON.
THERE ARE OTHER PEOPLE LIVING HERE. YOU ARE ADVISED NOT TO SPEAK TO THEM FOR YOUR OWN PROTECTION.
THERE IS A CHANGE OF CLOTHES AND TOILETRIES IN THE BAG.
BUT HAIR STRAIGHTENERS ARE IN THE ROOM, RIGHT?
HA, HA. AN OFFICER WILL PICK YOU UP AT 8:00 AM.
Ah, MY DRIVER!
6
THEY ARE NOT YOUR DRIVER. GET SOME SLEEP.
MY PALACE AWAITS.
6

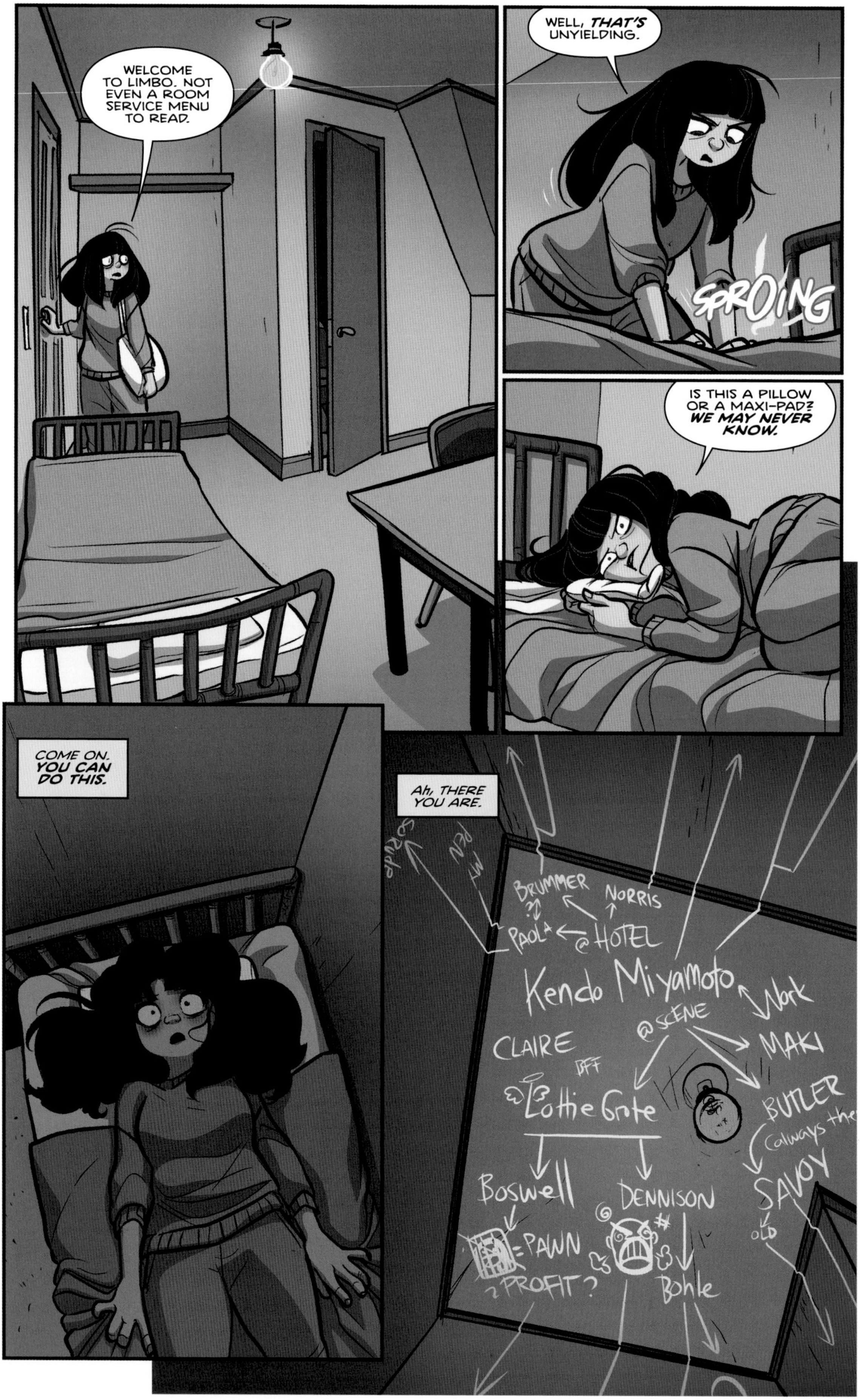
WELCOME TO LIMBO. NOT EVEN A ROOM SERVICE MENU TO READ.
WELL, THAT'S UNYIELDING.
SPROING
IS THIS A PILLOW OR A MAXI-PAD? WE MAY NEVER KNOW.
COME ON. YOU CAN DO THIS.
Ah, THERE YOU ARE.
BRUMMER
NORRIS
PAOLA
@ HOTEL
Kendo Miyamoto
Work
@ SCENE
CLAIRE
BFF
MAKI
Lottie Grote
BUTLER
(always the
SAVOY
Boswell
DENNISON
= PAWN
? PROFIT ?
OLD
Bohle

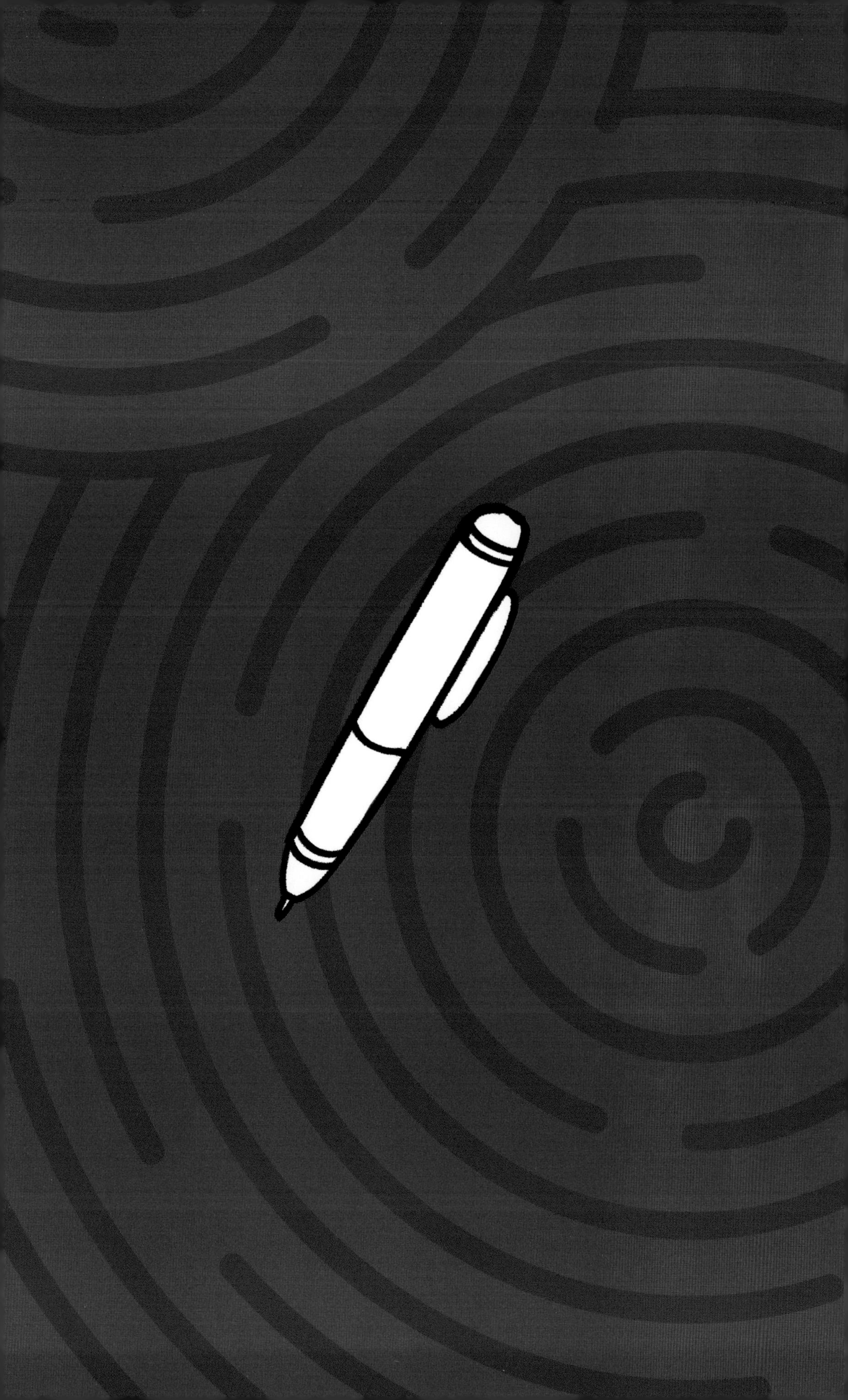

# CHAPTER
# THREE

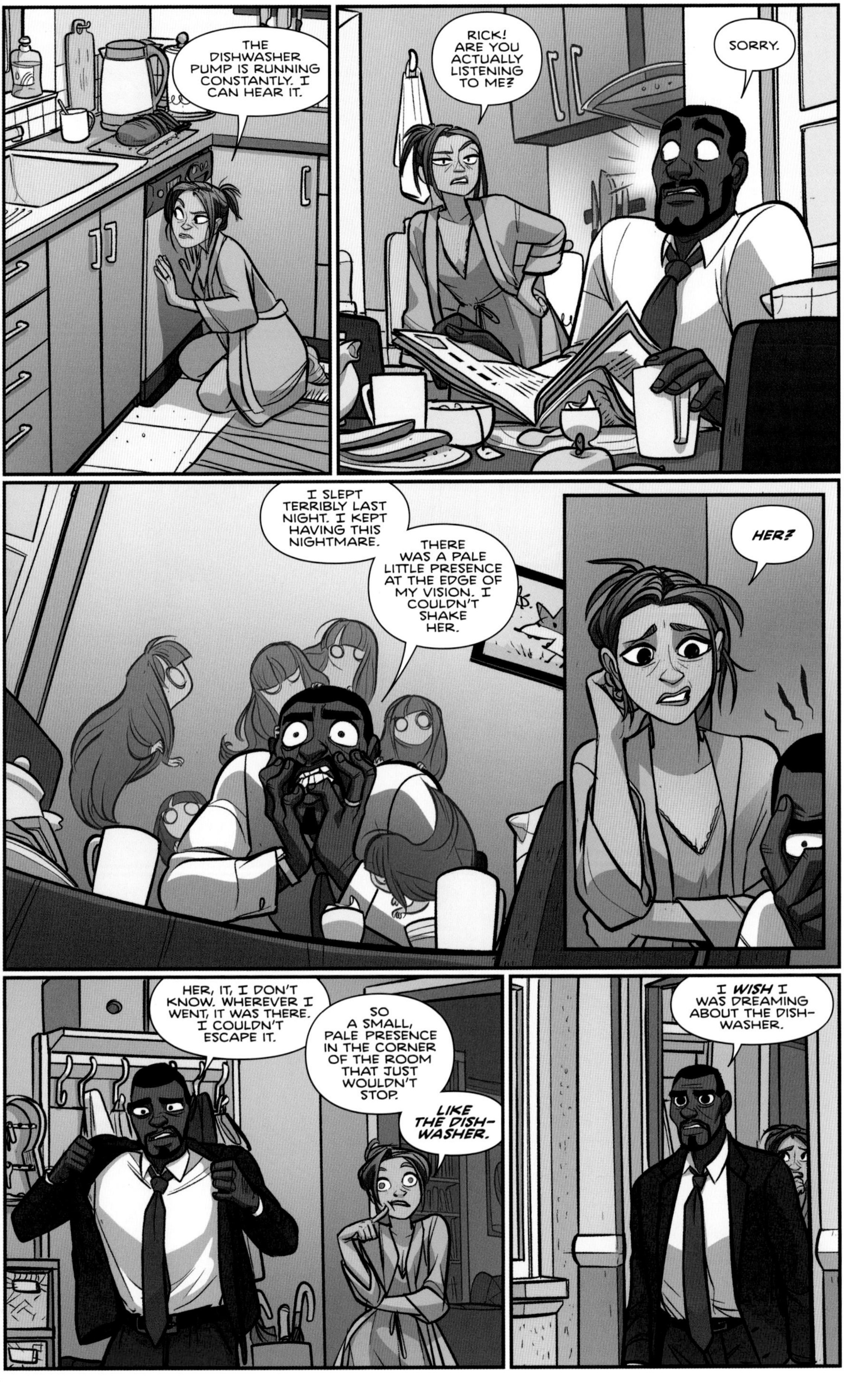
THE DISHWASHER PUMP IS RUNNING CONSTANTLY. I CAN HEAR IT.
RICK! ARE YOU ACTUALLY LISTENING TO ME?
SORRY.
I SLEPT TERRIBLY LAST NIGHT. I KEPT HAVING THIS NIGHTMARE.
THERE WAS A PALE LITTLE PRESENCE AT THE EDGE OF MY VISION. I COULDN'T SHAKE HER.
HER?
HER, IT, I DON'T KNOW. WHEREVER I WENT, IT WAS THERE. I COULDN'T ESCAPE IT.
SO A SMALL, PALE PRESENCE IN THE CORNER OF THE ROOM THAT JUST WOULDN'T STOP.
LIKE THE DISH-WASHER.
I WISH I WAS DREAMING ABOUT THE DISH-WASHER.

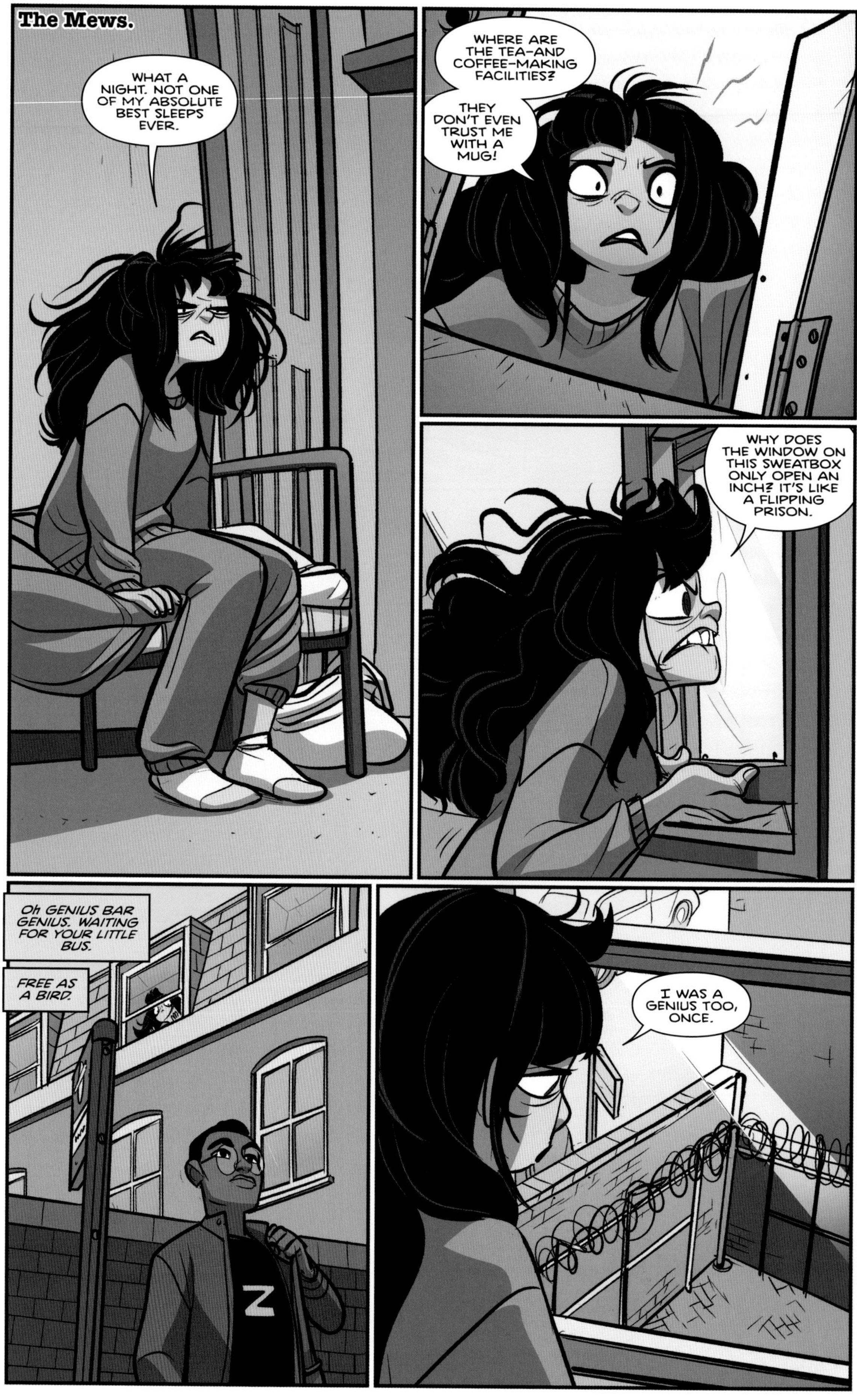
The Mews.
WHAT A NIGHT. NOT ONE OF MY ABSOLUTE BEST SLEEPS EVER.
WHERE ARE THE TEA-AND COFFEE-MAKING FACILITIES?
THEY DON'T EVEN TRUST ME WITH A MUG!
WHY DOES THE WINDOW ON THIS SWEATBOX ONLY OPEN AN INCH? IT'S LIKE A FLIPPING PRISON.
Oh GENIUS BAR GENIUS. WAITING FOR YOUR LITTLE BUS.
FREE AS A BIRD.
Z
I WAS A GENIUS TOO, ONCE.

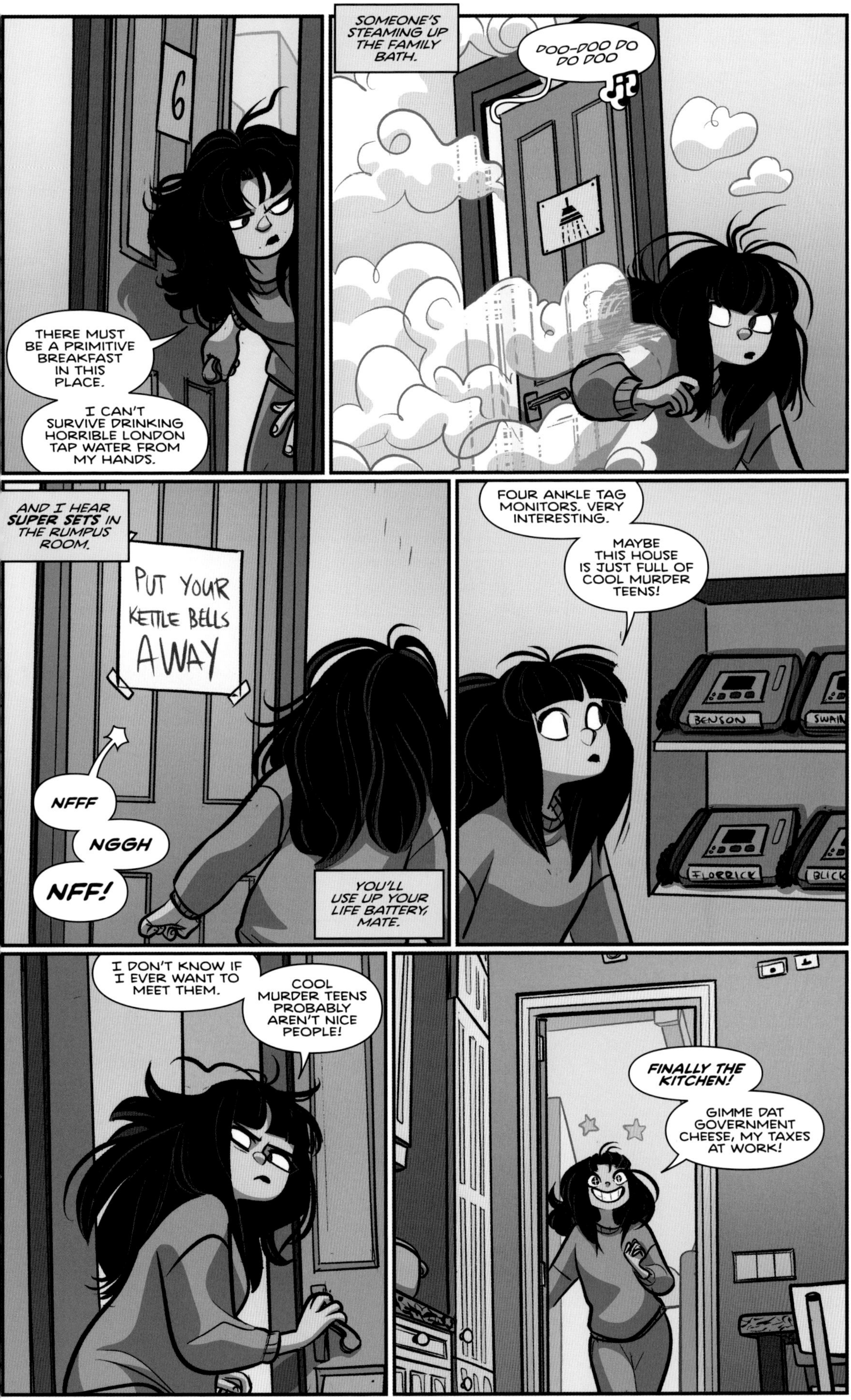
6
THERE MUST BE A PRIMITIVE BREAKFAST IN THIS PLACE.
I CAN'T SURVIVE DRINKING HORRIBLE LONDON TAP WATER FROM MY HANDS.
SOMEONE'S STEAMING UP THE FAMILY BATH.
DOO-DOO DO DO DOO
AND I HEAR SUPER SETS IN THE RUMPUS ROOM.
PUT YOUR KETTLE BELLS AWAY
NFFF
NGGH
NFF!
YOU'LL USE UP YOUR LIFE BATTERY, MATE.
FOUR ANKLE TAG MONITORS. VERY INTERESTING.
MAYBE THIS HOUSE IS JUST FULL OF COOL MURDER TEENS!
BENSON
FLORRICK
I DON'T KNOW IF I EVER WANT TO MEET THEM.
COOL MURDER TEENS PROBABLY AREN'T NICE PEOPLE!
FINALLY THE KITCHEN!
GIMME DAT GOVERNMENT CHEESE, MY TAXES AT WORK!

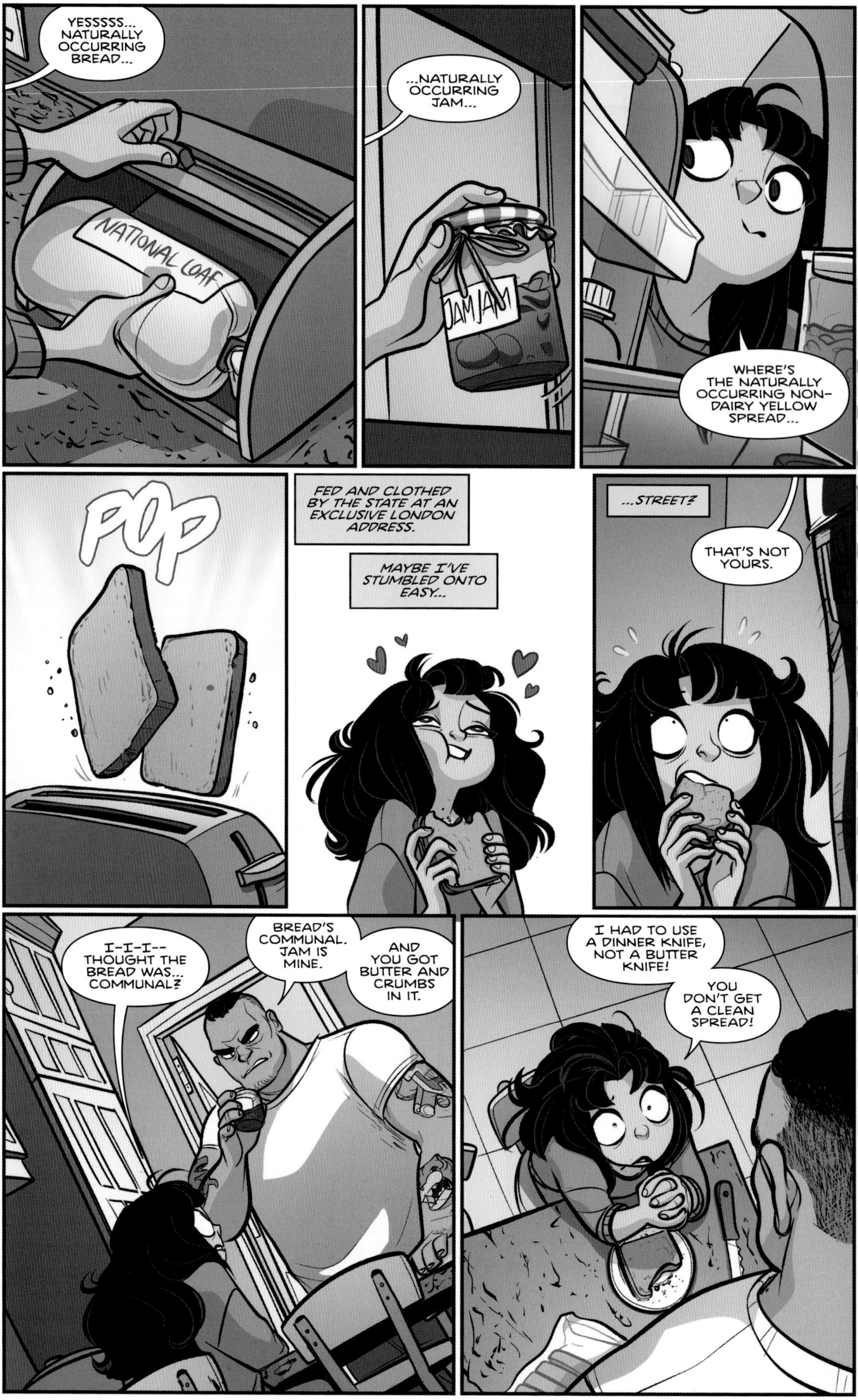
YESSSSS... NATURALLY OCCURRING BREAD...
NATIONAL LOAF
...NATURALLY OCCURRING JAM...
JAM JAM
WHERE'S THE NATURALLY OCCURRING NON-DAIRY YELLOW SPREAD...
POP
FED AND CLOTHED BY THE STATE AT AN EXCLUSIVE LONDON ADDRESS.
MAYBE I'VE STUMBLED ONTO EASY...
...STREET?
THAT'S NOT YOURS.
I-I-I-- THOUGHT THE BREAD WAS... COMMUNAL?
BREAD'S COMMUNAL. JAM IS MINE.
AND YOU GOT BUTTER AND CRUMBS IN IT.
I HAD TO USE A DINNER KNIFE, NOT A BUTTER KNIFE!
YOU DON'T GET A CLEAN SPREAD!

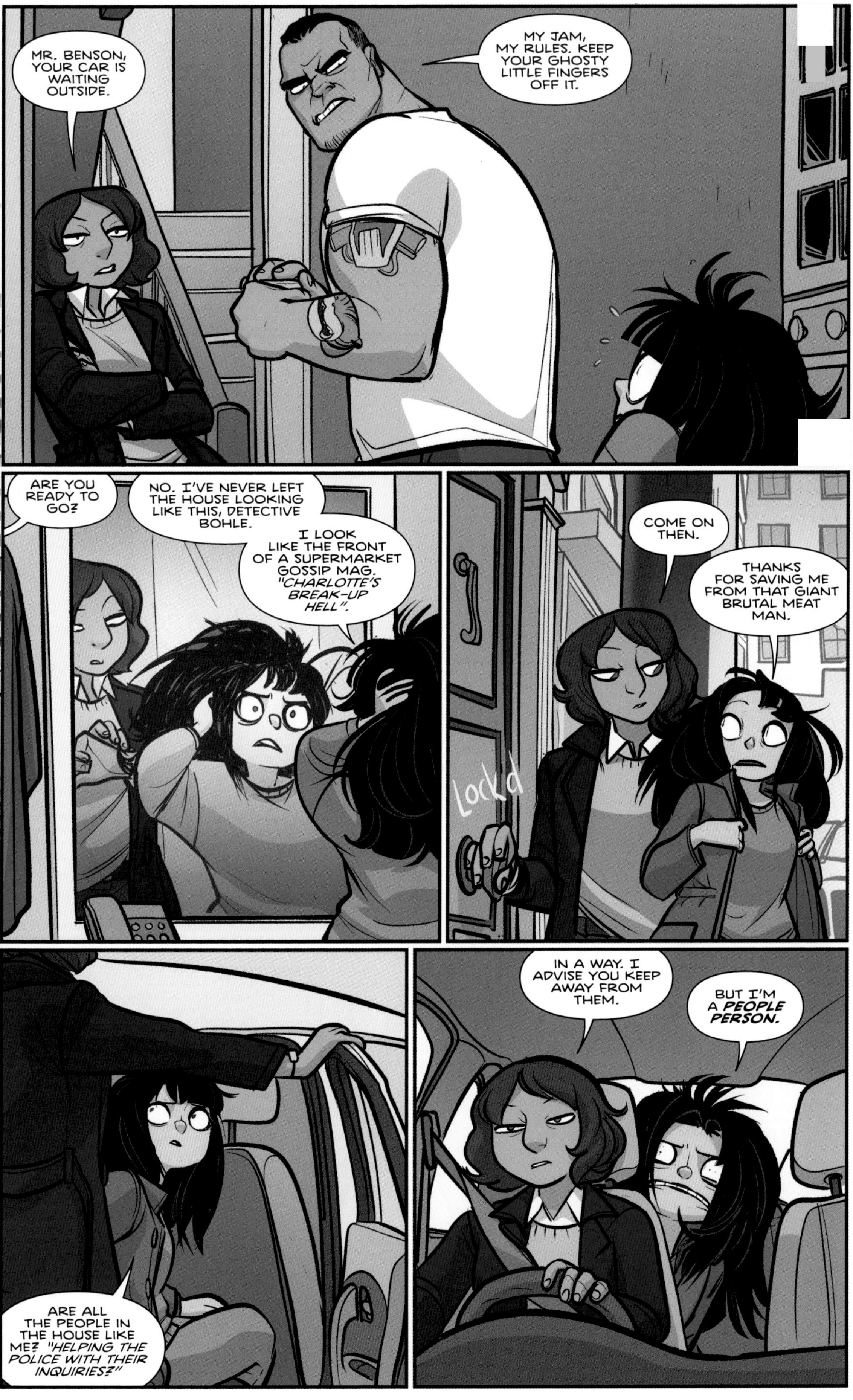
MR. BENSON, YOUR CAR IS WAITING OUTSIDE.
MY JAM, MY RULES. KEEP YOUR GHOSTY LITTLE FINGERS OFF IT.
ARE YOU READY TO GO?
NO. I'VE NEVER LEFT THE HOUSE LOOKING LIKE THIS, DETECTIVE BOHLE.
I LOOK LIKE THE FRONT OF A SUPERMARKET GOSSIP MAG. "CHARLOTTE'S BREAK-UP HELL".
COME ON THEN.
THANKS FOR SAVING ME FROM THAT GIANT BRUTAL MEAT MAN.
Lock'd
ARE ALL THE PEOPLE IN THE HOUSE LIKE ME? "HELPING THE POLICE WITH THEIR INQUIRIES?"
IN A WAY. I ADVISE YOU KEEP AWAY FROM THEM.
BUT I'M A PEOPLE PERSON.

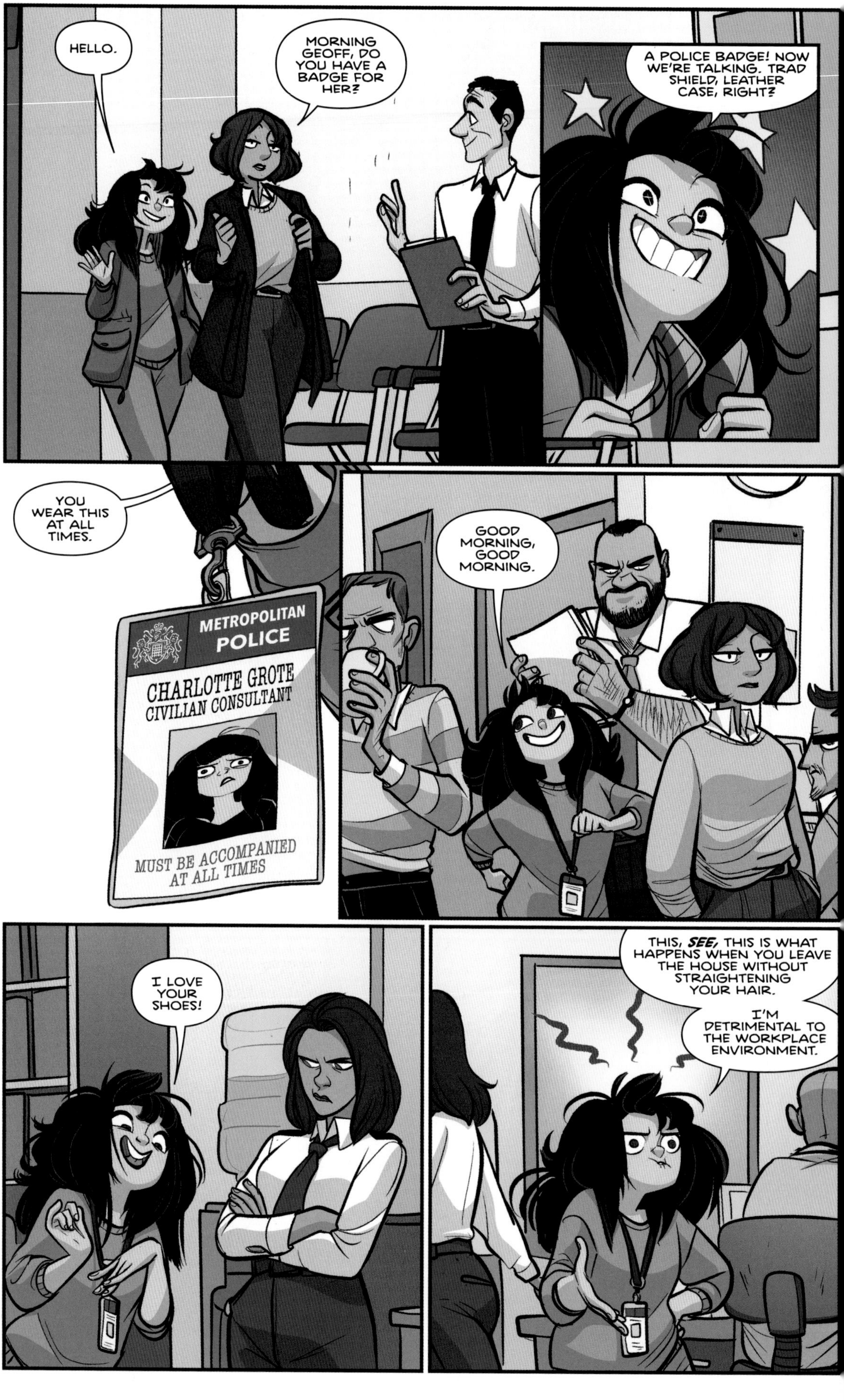
HELLO.
MORNING GEOFF, DO YOU HAVE A BADGE FOR HER?
A POLICE BADGE! NOW WE'RE TALKING. TRAD SHIELD, LEATHER CASE, RIGHT?
YOU WEAR THIS AT ALL TIMES.
METROPOLITAN POLICE
CHARLOTTE GROTE
CIVILIAN CONSULTANT
MUST BE ACCOMPANIED AT ALL TIMES
GOOD MORNING, GOOD MORNING.
I LOVE YOUR SHOES!
THIS, SEE, THIS IS WHAT HAPPENS WHEN YOU LEAVE THE HOUSE WITHOUT STRAIGHTENING YOUR HAIR.
I'M DETRIMENTAL TO THE WORKPLACE ENVIRONMENT.

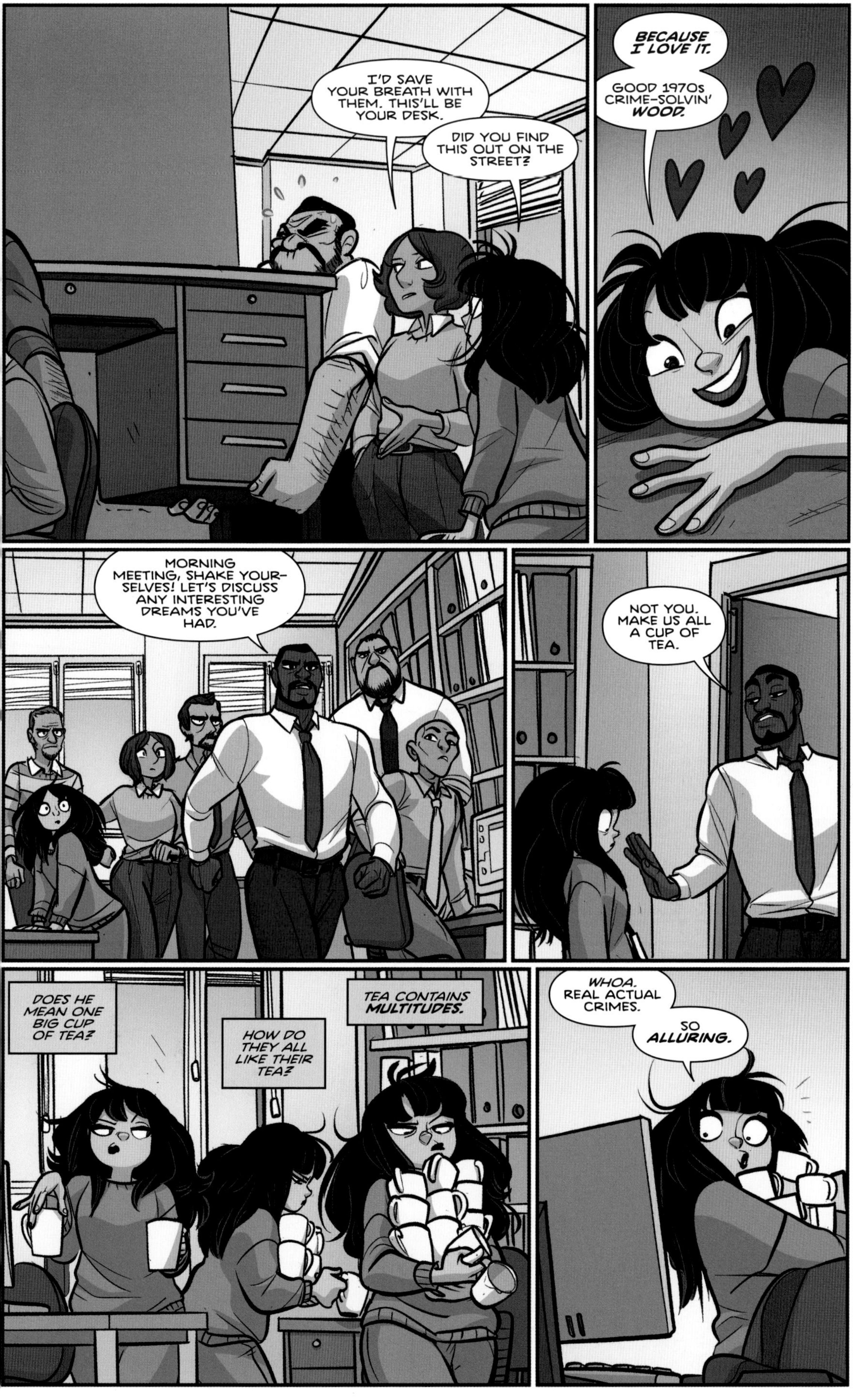
I'D SAVE YOUR BREATH WITH THEM. THIS'LL BE YOUR DESK.
DID YOU FIND THIS OUT ON THE STREET?
BECAUSE I LOVE IT.
GOOD 1970s CRIME-SOLVIN' WOOD.
MORNING MEETING, SHAKE YOURSELVES! LET'S DISCUSS ANY INTERESTING DREAMS YOU'VE HAD.
NOT YOU. MAKE US ALL A CUP OF TEA.
DOES HE MEAN ONE BIG CUP OF TEA?
HOW DO THEY ALL LIKE THEIR TEA?
TEA CONTAINS MULTITUDES.
WHOA. REAL ACTUAL CRIMES.
SO ALLURING.

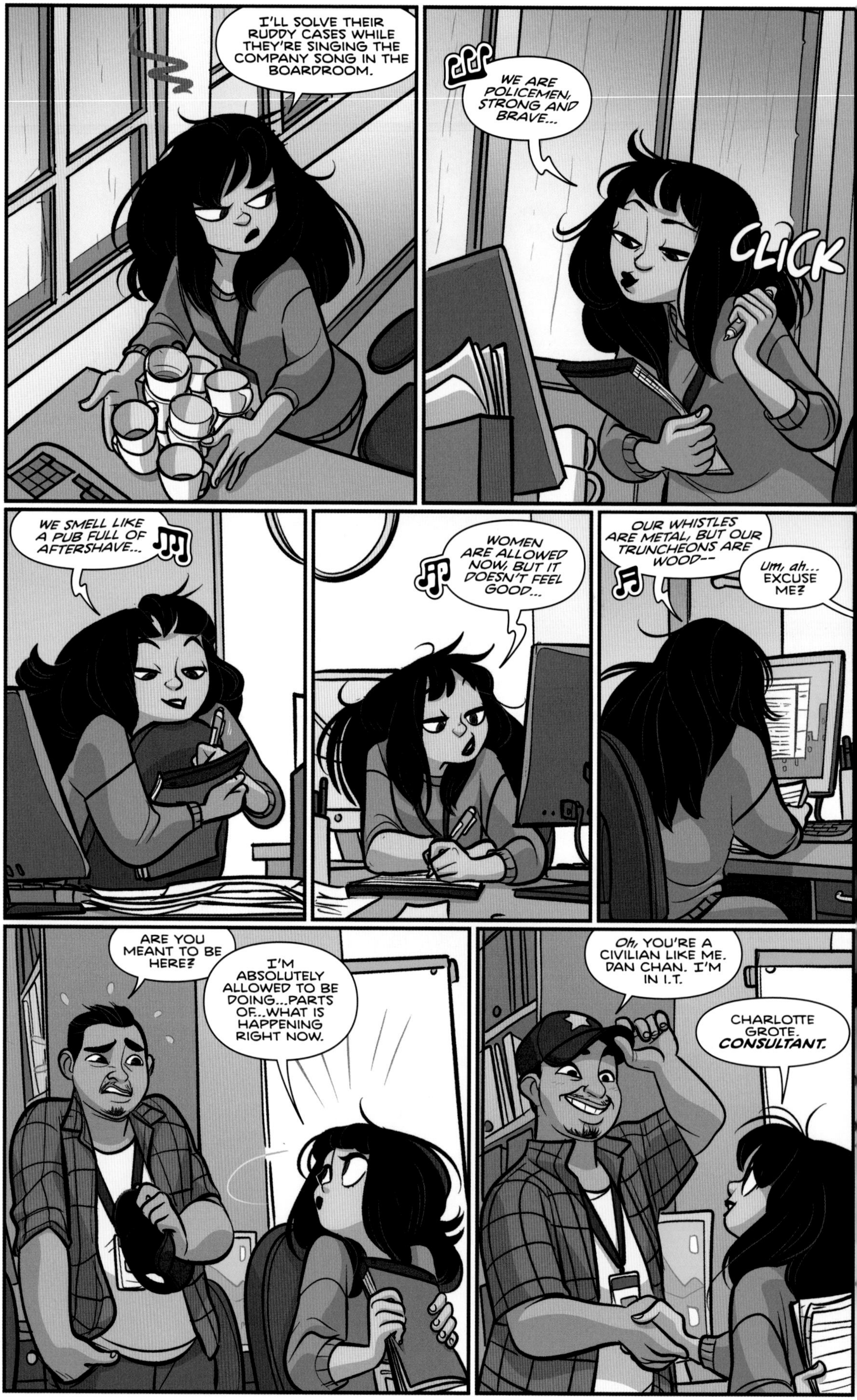

I'LL SOLVE THEIR RUDDY CASES WHILE THEY'RE SINGING THE COMPANY SONG IN THE BOARDROOM.
WE ARE POLICEMEN, STRONG AND BRAVE...
CLICK
WE SMELL LIKE A PUB FULL OF AFTERSHAVE...
WOMEN ARE ALLOWED NOW, BUT IT DOESN'T FEEL GOOD...
OUR WHISTLES ARE METAL, BUT OUR TRUNCHEONS ARE WOOD--
Um, ah... EXCUSE ME?
ARE YOU MEANT TO BE HERE?
I'M ABSOLUTELY ALLOWED TO BE DOING...PARTS OF...WHAT IS HAPPENING RIGHT NOW.
Oh, YOU'RE A CIVILIAN LIKE ME. DAN CHAN. I'M IN I.T.
CHARLOTTE GROTE. CONSULTANT.

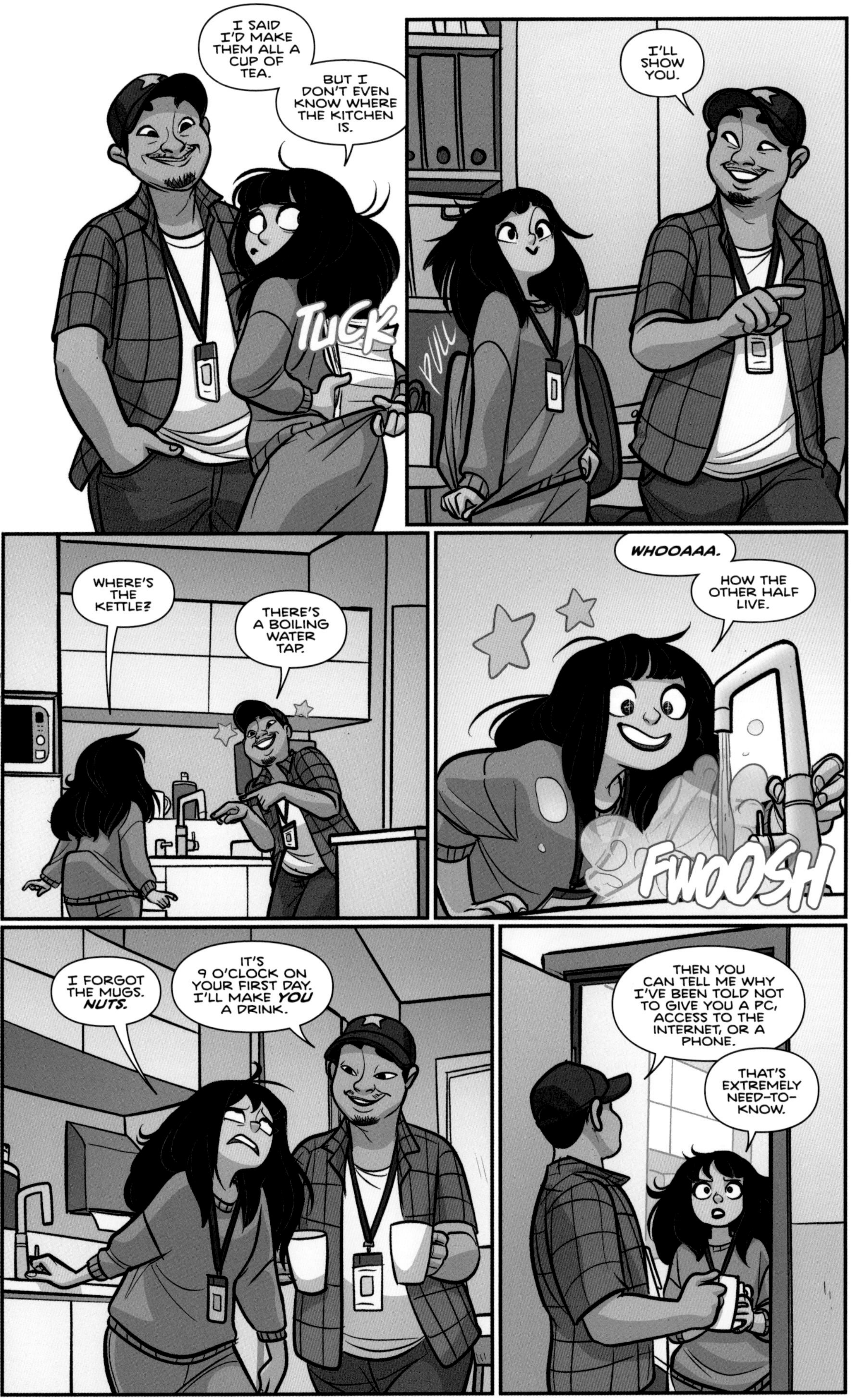

I SAID I'D MAKE THEM ALL A CUP OF TEA.
BUT I DON'T EVEN KNOW WHERE THE KITCHEN IS.
TUCK
I'LL SHOW YOU.
PULL
WHERE'S THE KETTLE?
THERE'S A BOILING WATER TAP.
WHOOAAA.
HOW THE OTHER HALF LIVE.
FWOOSH
I FORGOT THE MUGS. NUTS.
IT'S 9 O'CLOCK ON YOUR FIRST DAY. I'LL MAKE YOU A DRINK.
THEN YOU CAN TELL ME WHY I'VE BEEN TOLD NOT TO GIVE YOU A PC, ACCESS TO THE INTERNET, OR A PHONE.
THAT'S EXTREMELY NEED-TO-KNOW.

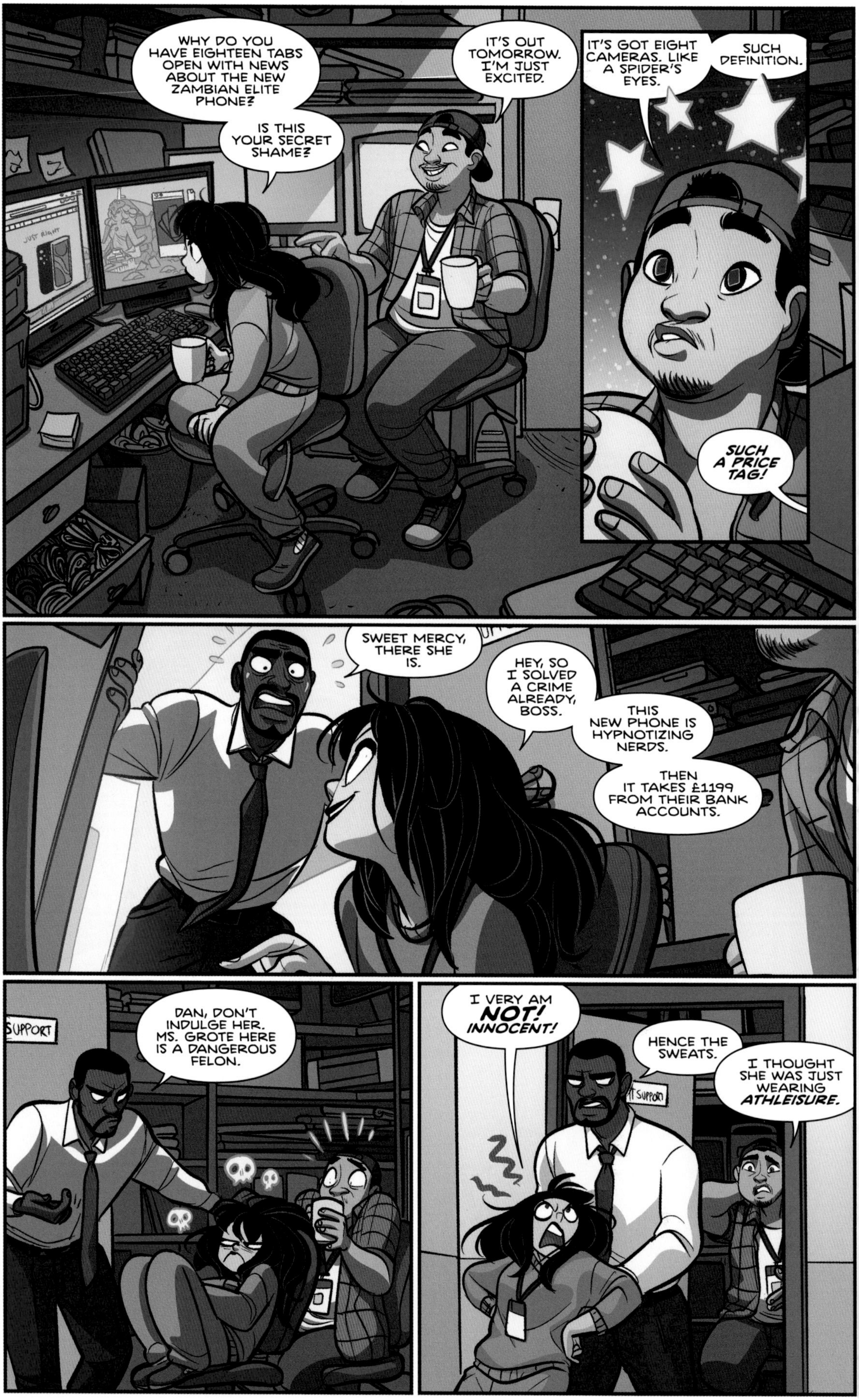
WHY DO YOU HAVE EIGHTEEN TABS OPEN WITH NEWS ABOUT THE NEW ZAMBIAN ELITE PHONE?
IS THIS YOUR SECRET SHAME?
IT'S OUT TOMORROW. I'M JUST EXCITED.
JUST RIGHT
IT'S GOT EIGHT CAMERAS. LIKE A SPIDER'S EYES.
SUCH DEFINITION.
SUCH A PRICE TAG!
SWEET MERCY, THERE SHE IS.
HEY, SO I SOLVED A CRIME ALREADY, BOSS.
THIS NEW PHONE IS HYPNOTIZING NERDS.
THEN IT TAKES £1199 FROM THEIR BANK ACCOUNTS.
SUPPORT
DAN, DON'T INDULGE HER. MS. GROTE HERE IS A DANGEROUS FELON.
I VERY AM NOT! INNOCENT!
HENCE THE SWEATS.
I THOUGHT SHE WAS JUST WEARING ATHLEISURE.
IT SUPPORT

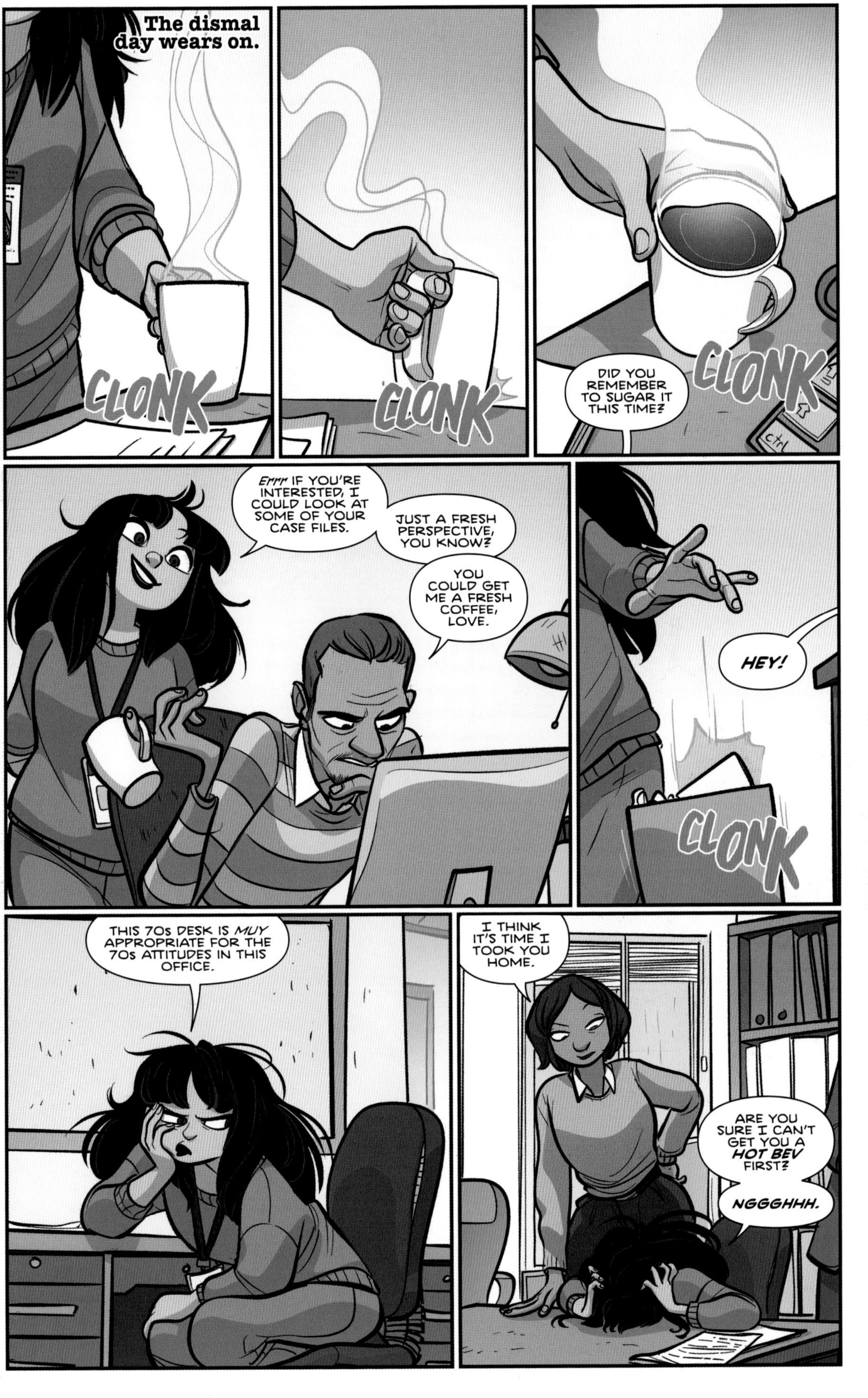
The dismal day wears on.
CLONK
CLONK
DID YOU REMEMBER TO SUGAR IT THIS TIME?
CLONK
ctrl
*Errr* IF YOU'RE INTERESTED, I COULD LOOK AT SOME OF YOUR CASE FILES.
JUST A FRESH PERSPECTIVE, YOU KNOW?
YOU COULD GET ME A FRESH COFFEE, LOVE.
HEY!
CLONK
THIS 70s DESK IS *MUY* APPROPRIATE FOR THE 70s ATTITUDES IN THIS OFFICE.
I THINK IT'S TIME I TOOK YOU HOME.
ARE YOU SURE I CAN'T GET YOU A ***HOT BEV*** FIRST?
***NGGGHHH.***

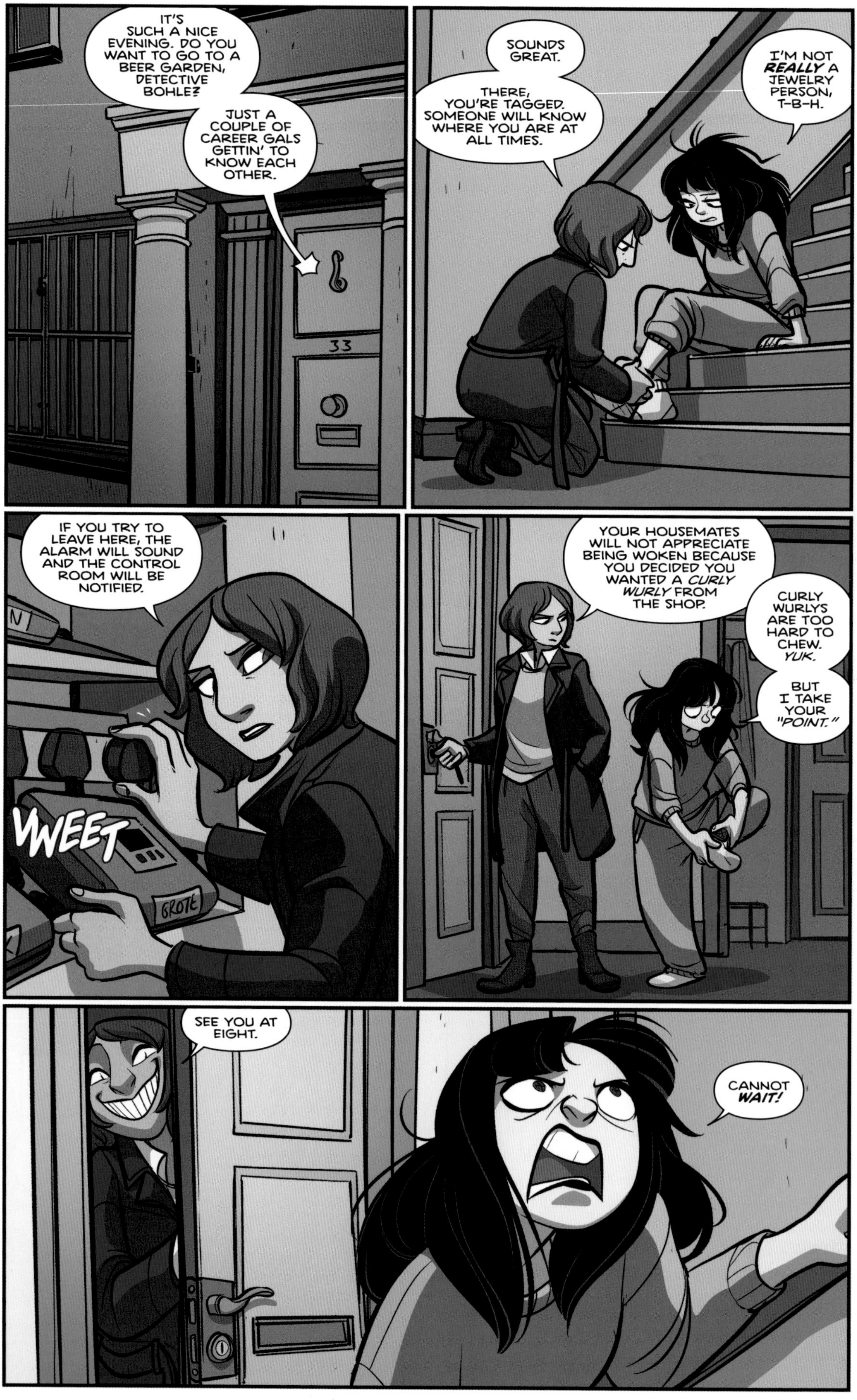
IT'S SUCH A NICE EVENING. DO YOU WANT TO GO TO A BEER GARDEN, DETECTIVE BOHLE?
JUST A COUPLE OF CAREER GALS GETTIN' TO KNOW EACH OTHER.
33
SOUNDS GREAT.
THERE, YOU'RE TAGGED. SOMEONE WILL KNOW WHERE YOU ARE AT ALL TIMES.
I'M NOT REALLY A JEWELRY PERSON, T-B-H.
IF YOU TRY TO LEAVE HERE, THE ALARM WILL SOUND AND THE CONTROL ROOM WILL BE NOTIFIED.
VWEET
GROTE
YOUR HOUSEMATES WILL NOT APPRECIATE BEING WOKEN BECAUSE YOU DECIDED YOU WANTED A CURLY WURLY FROM THE SHOP.
CURLY WURLYS ARE TOO HARD TO CHEW. YUK.
BUT I TAKE YOUR "POINT."
SEE YOU AT EIGHT.
CANNOT WAIT!

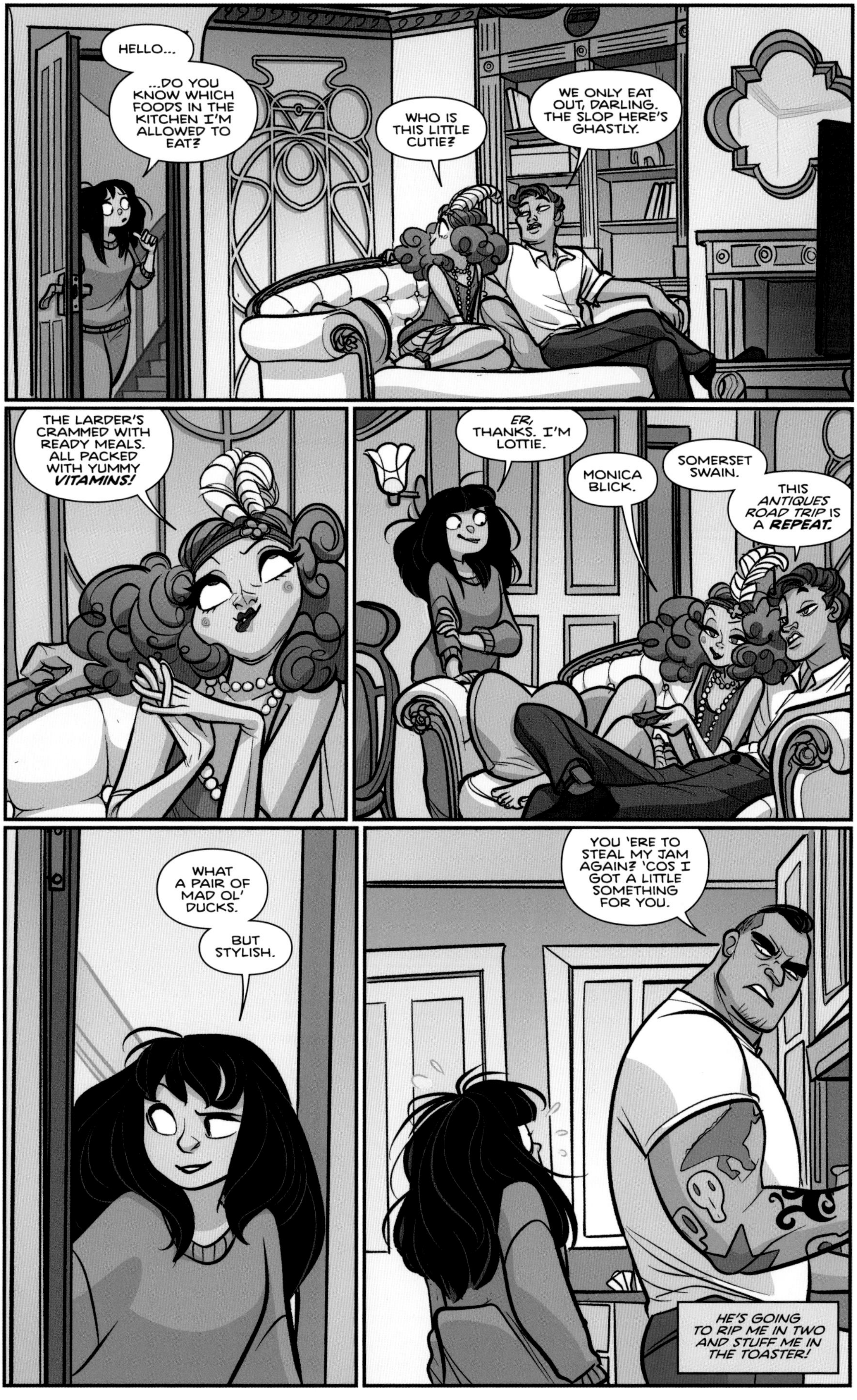
HELLO...
...DO YOU KNOW WHICH FOODS IN THE KITCHEN I'M ALLOWED TO EAT?
WHO IS THIS LITTLE CUTIE?
WE ONLY EAT OUT, DARLING. THE SLOP HERE'S GHASTLY.
THE LARDER'S CRAMMED WITH READY MEALS. ALL PACKED WITH YUMMY *VITAMINS!*
*ER,* THANKS. I'M LOTTIE.
MONICA BLICK.
SOMERSET SWAIN.
THIS *ANTIQUES ROAD TRIP* IS A ***REPEAT.***
WHAT A PAIR OF MAD OL' DUCKS.
BUT STYLISH.
YOU 'ERE TO STEAL MY JAM AGAIN? 'COS I GOT A LITTLE SOMETHING FOR YOU.
*HE'S GOING TO RIP ME IN TWO AND STUFF ME IN THE TOASTER!*

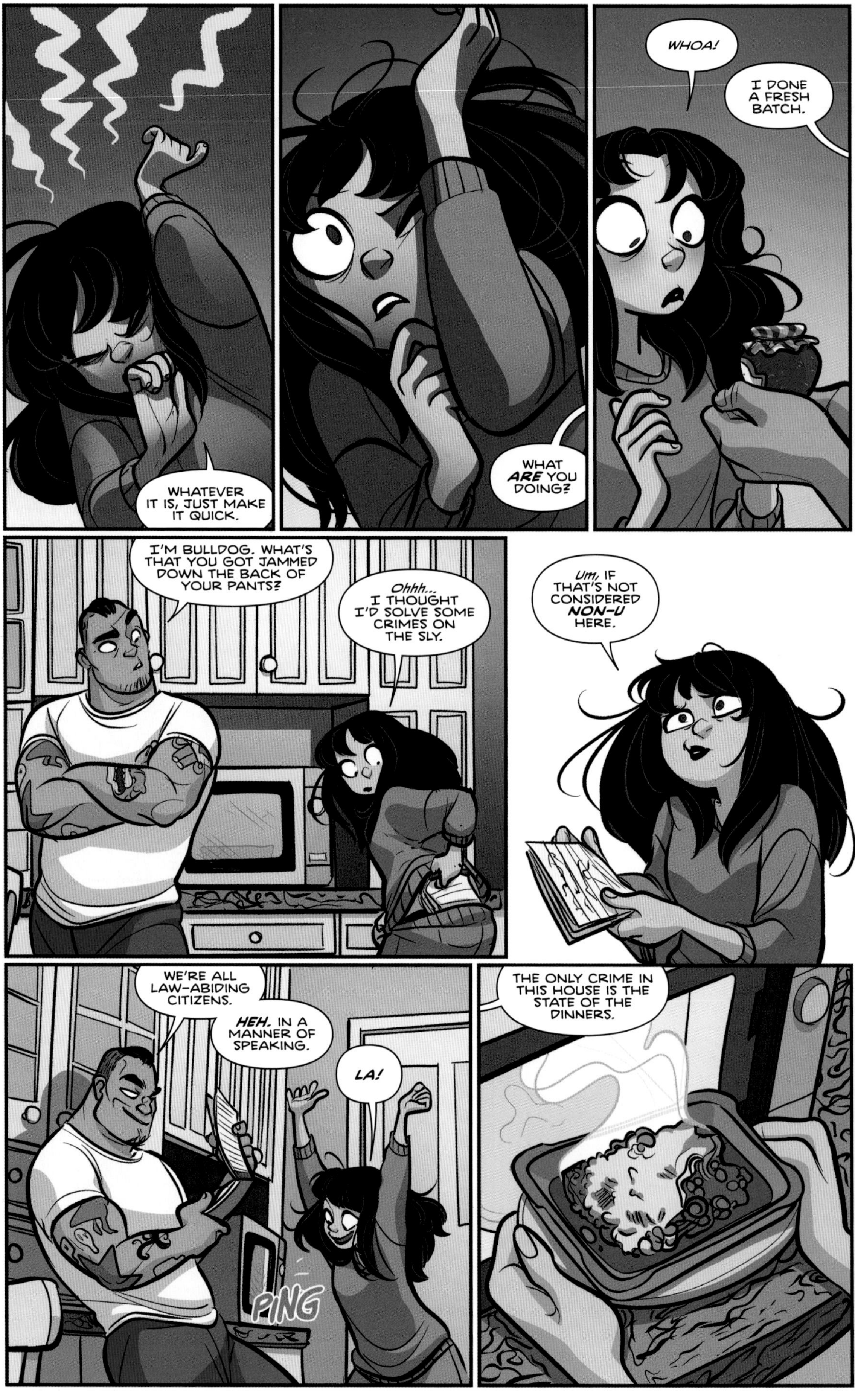
WHATEVER IT IS, JUST MAKE IT QUICK.
WHAT ARE YOU DOING?
WHOA!
I DONE A FRESH BATCH.
I'M BULLDOG. WHAT'S THAT YOU GOT JAMMED DOWN THE BACK OF YOUR PANTS?
Ohhh... I THOUGHT I'D SOLVE SOME CRIMES ON THE SLY.
Um, IF THAT'S NOT CONSIDERED NON-U HERE.
WE'RE ALL LAW-ABIDING CITIZENS.
HEH. IN A MANNER OF SPEAKING.
LA!
PING
THE ONLY CRIME IN THIS HOUSE IS THE STATE OF THE DINNERS.

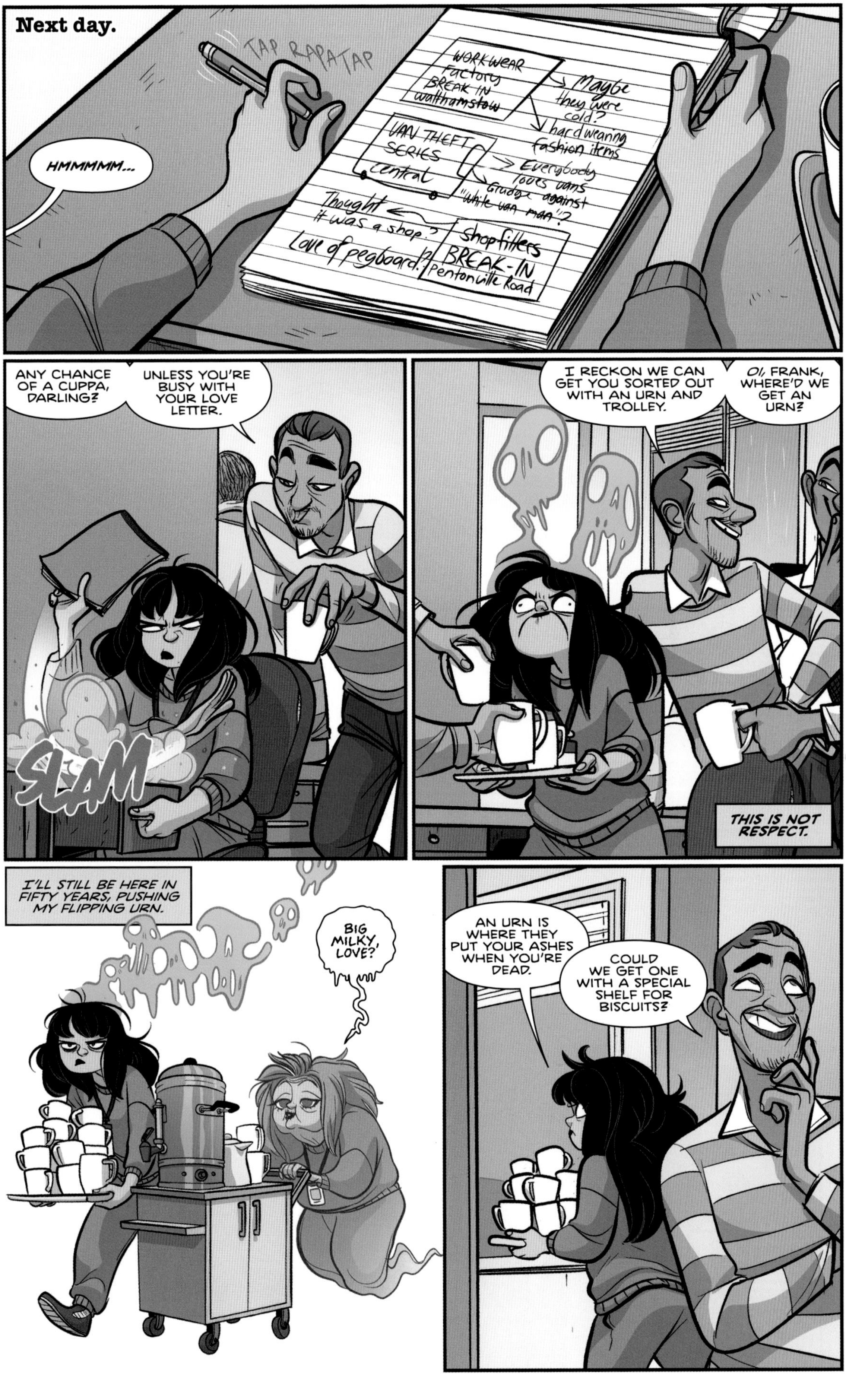
Next day.
TAP RAPATAP
HMMMMM...
WORKWEAR Factory BREAK IN walthamstow
Maybe they were cold?
hardwearing fashion items
VAN THEFT SERIES central
Everybody loves vans
Grudge against "white van man"?
Thought it was a shop?
Love of pegboard!?
Shopfitters BREAK-IN Pentonville Road
ANY CHANCE OF A CUPPA, DARLING?
UNLESS YOU'RE BUSY WITH YOUR LOVE LETTER.
SLAM
I RECKON WE CAN GET YOU SORTED OUT WITH AN URN AND TROLLEY.
OI, FRANK, WHERE'D WE GET AN URN?
THIS IS NOT RESPECT.
I'LL STILL BE HERE IN FIFTY YEARS, PUSHING MY FLIPPING URN.
BIG MILKY, LOVE?'
AN URN IS WHERE THEY PUT YOUR ASHES WHEN YOU'RE DEAD.
COULD WE GET ONE WITH A SPECIAL SHELF FOR BISCUITS?

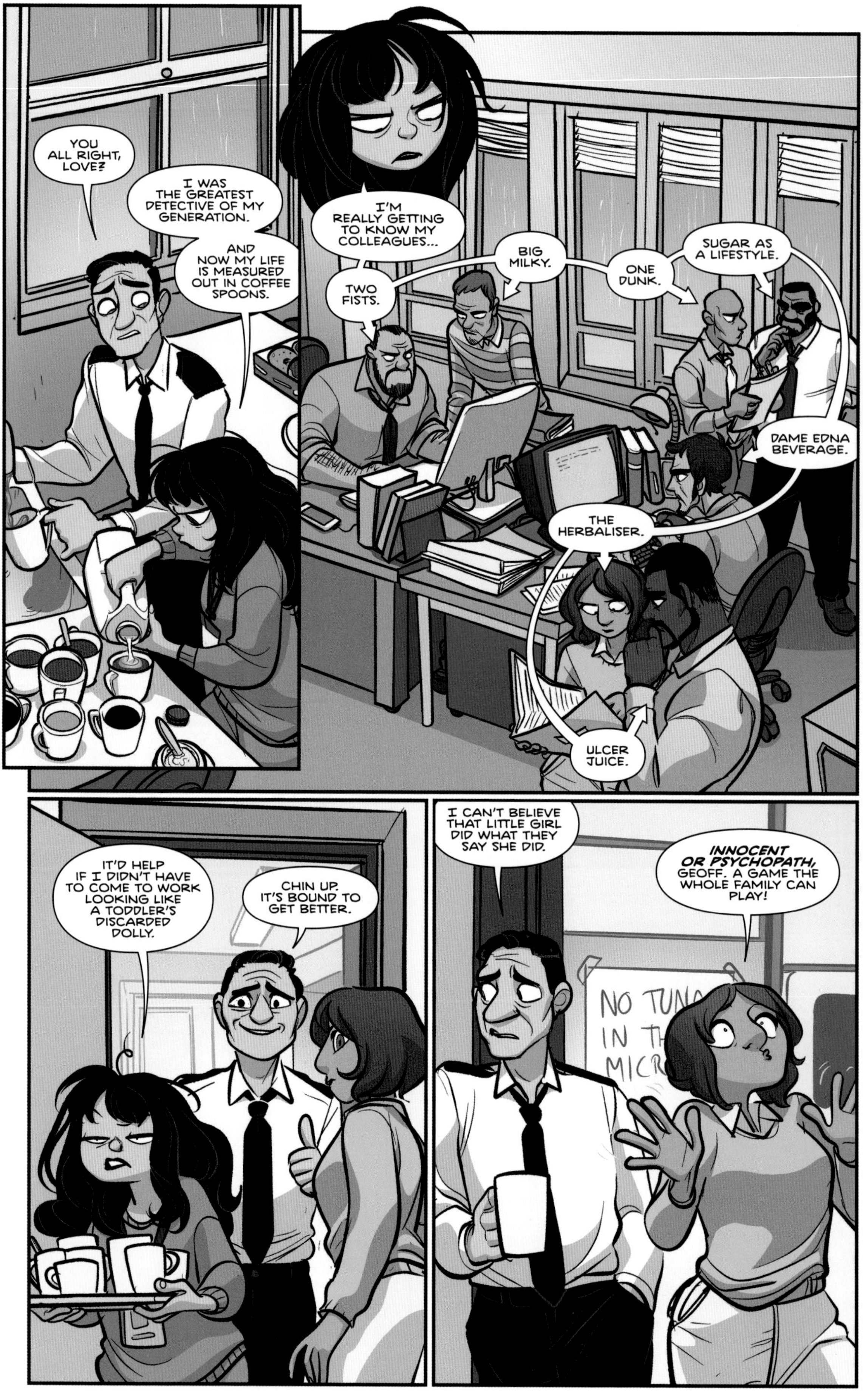
YOU ALL RIGHT, LOVE?
I WAS THE GREATEST DETECTIVE OF MY GENERATION.
AND NOW MY LIFE IS MEASURED OUT IN COFFEE SPOONS.
I'M REALLY GETTING TO KNOW MY COLLEAGUES...
TWO FISTS.
BIG MILKY.
ONE DUNK.
SUGAR AS A LIFESTYLE.
DAME EDNA BEVERAGE.
THE HERBALISER.
ULCER JUICE.
IT'D HELP IF I DIDN'T HAVE TO COME TO WORK LOOKING LIKE A TODDLER'S DISCARDED DOLLY.
CHIN UP. IT'S BOUND TO GET BETTER.
I CAN'T BELIEVE THAT LITTLE GIRL DID WHAT THEY SAY SHE DID.
*INNOCENT OR PSYCHOPATH,* GEOFF. A GAME THE WHOLE FAMILY CAN PLAY!
NO TUN
IN TH
MICR

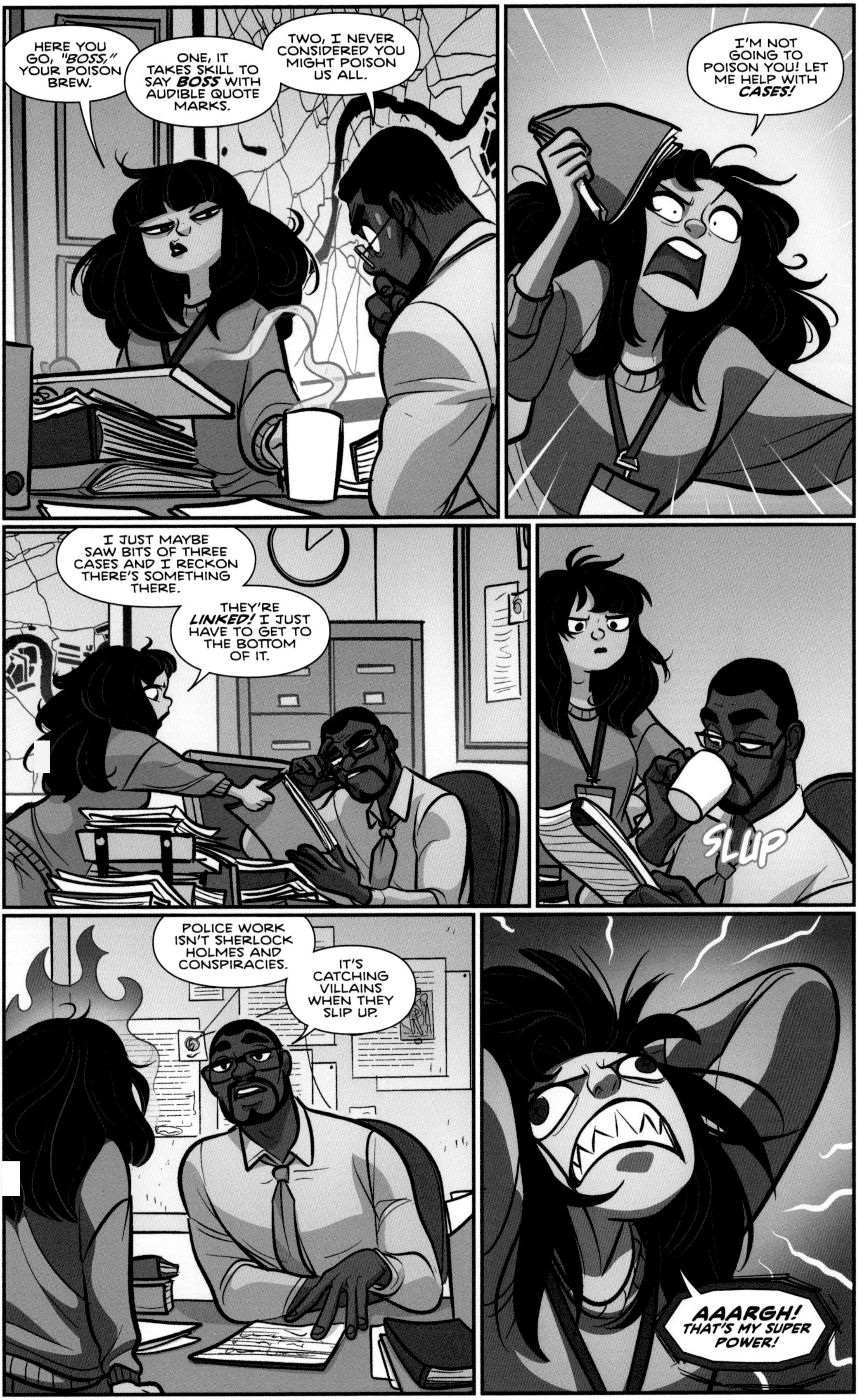
HERE YOU GO, "BOSS," YOUR POISON BREW.
ONE, IT TAKES SKILL TO SAY **BOSS** WITH AUDIBLE QUOTE MARKS.
TWO, I NEVER CONSIDERED YOU MIGHT POISON US ALL.
I'M NOT GOING TO POISON YOU! LET ME HELP WITH ***CASES!***
I JUST MAYBE SAW BITS OF THREE CASES AND I RECKON THERE'S SOMETHING THERE.
THEY'RE ***LINKED!*** I JUST HAVE TO GET TO THE BOTTOM OF IT.
SLUP
POLICE WORK ISN'T SHERLOCK HOLMES AND CONSPIRACIES.
IT'S CATCHING VILLAINS WHEN THEY SLIP UP.
AAARGH! THAT'S MY SUPER POWER!

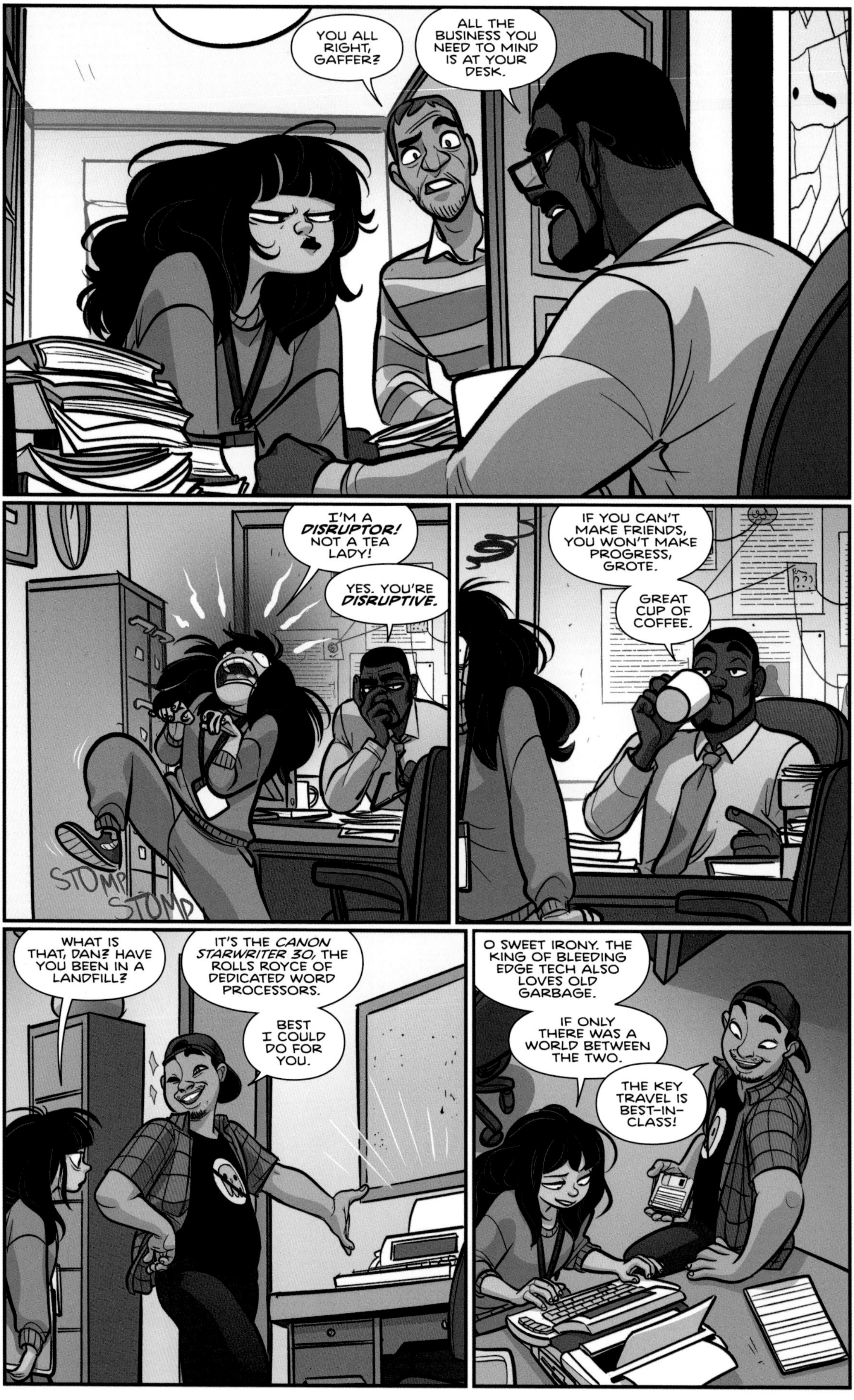
YOU ALL RIGHT, GAFFER?
ALL THE BUSINESS YOU NEED TO MIND IS AT YOUR DESK.
I'M A *DISRUPTOR!* NOT A TEA LADY!
YES. YOU'RE *DISRUPTIVE.*
STOMP STOMP
IF YOU CAN'T MAKE FRIENDS, YOU WON'T MAKE PROGRESS, GROTE.
GREAT CUP OF COFFEE.
WHAT IS THAT, DAN? HAVE YOU BEEN IN A LANDFILL?
IT'S THE *CANON STARWRITER 30,* THE ROLLS ROYCE OF DEDICATED WORD PROCESSORS.
BEST I COULD DO FOR YOU.
O SWEET IRONY. THE KING OF BLEEDING EDGE TECH ALSO LOVES OLD GARBAGE.
IF ONLY THERE WAS A WORLD BETWEEN THE TWO.
THE KEY TRAVEL IS BEST-IN-CLASS!

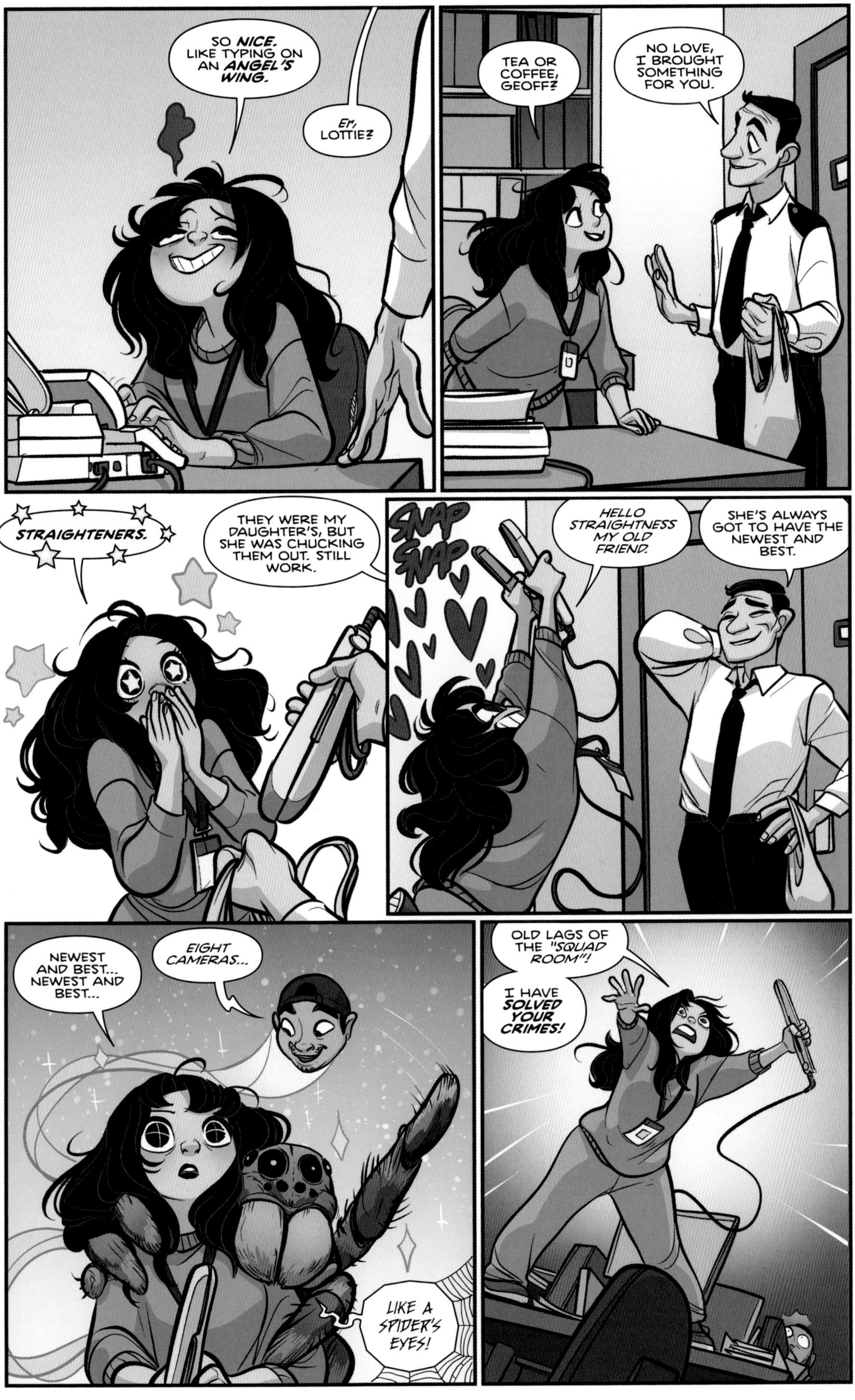
SO NICE. LIKE TYPING ON AN ANGEL'S WING.
EM, LOTTIE?
TEA OR COFFEE, GEOFF?
NO LOVE, I BROUGHT SOMETHING FOR YOU.
STRAIGHTENERS.
THEY WERE MY DAUGHTER'S, BUT SHE WAS CHUCKING THEM OUT. STILL WORK.
SNAP SNAP
HELLO STRAIGHTNESS MY OLD FRIEND.
SHE'S ALWAYS GOT TO HAVE THE NEWEST AND BEST.
NEWEST AND BEST... NEWEST AND BEST...
EIGHT CAMERAS...
LIKE A SPIDER'S EYES!
OLD LAGS OF THE "SQUAD ROOM"!
I HAVE SOLVED YOUR CRIMES!

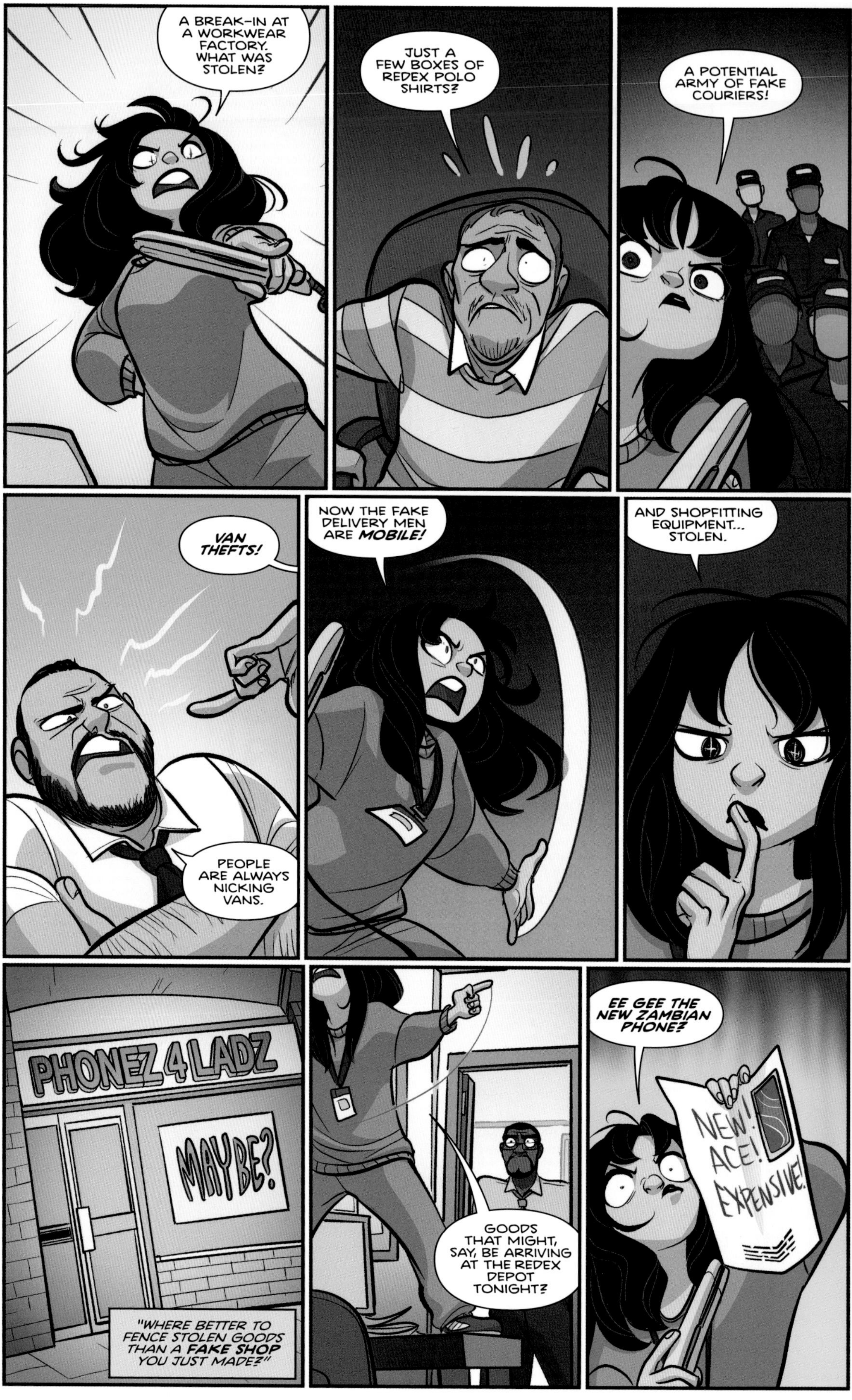
A BREAK-IN AT A WORKWEAR FACTORY. WHAT WAS STOLEN?
JUST A FEW BOXES OF REDEX POLO SHIRTS?
A POTENTIAL ARMY OF FAKE COURIERS!
VAN THEFTS!
PEOPLE ARE ALWAYS NICKING VANS.
NOW THE FAKE DELIVERY MEN ARE MOBILE!
AND SHOPFITTING EQUIPMENT... STOLEN.
PHONEZ 4 LADZ
MAYBE?
"WHERE BETTER TO FENCE STOLEN GOODS THAN A FAKE SHOP YOU JUST MADE?"
GOODS THAT MIGHT, SAY, BE ARRIVING AT THE REDEX DEPOT TONIGHT?
EE GEE THE NEW ZAMBIAN PHONE?
NEW! ACE! EXPENSIVE!

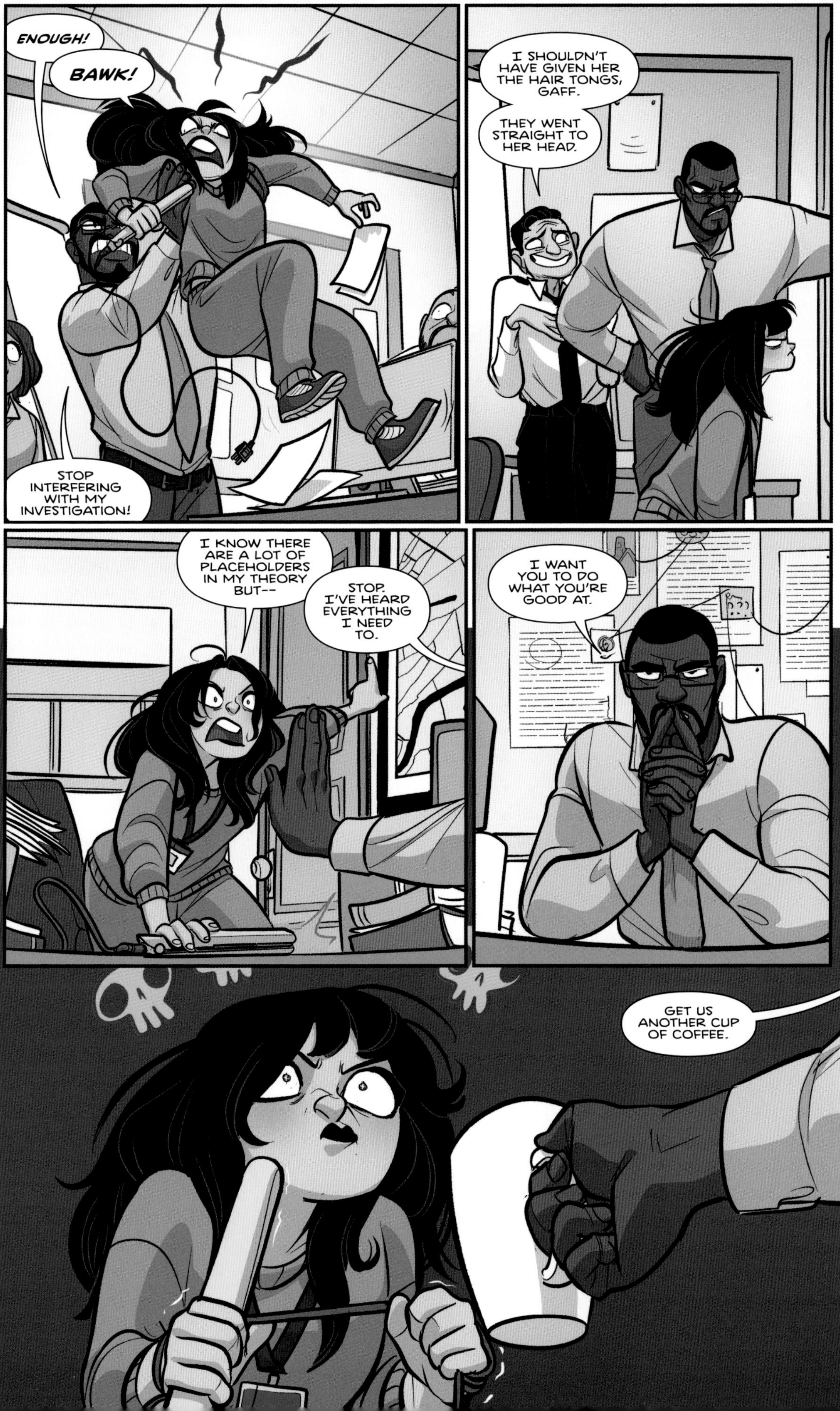
ENOUGH!
BAWK!
STOP INTERFERING WITH MY INVESTIGATION!
I SHOULDN'T HAVE GIVEN HER THE HAIR TONGS, GAFF.
THEY WENT STRAIGHT TO HER HEAD.
I KNOW THERE ARE A LOT OF PLACEHOLDERS IN MY THEORY BUT--
STOP. I'VE HEARD EVERYTHING I NEED TO.
I WANT YOU TO DO WHAT YOU'RE GOOD AT.
GET US ANOTHER CUP OF COFFEE.

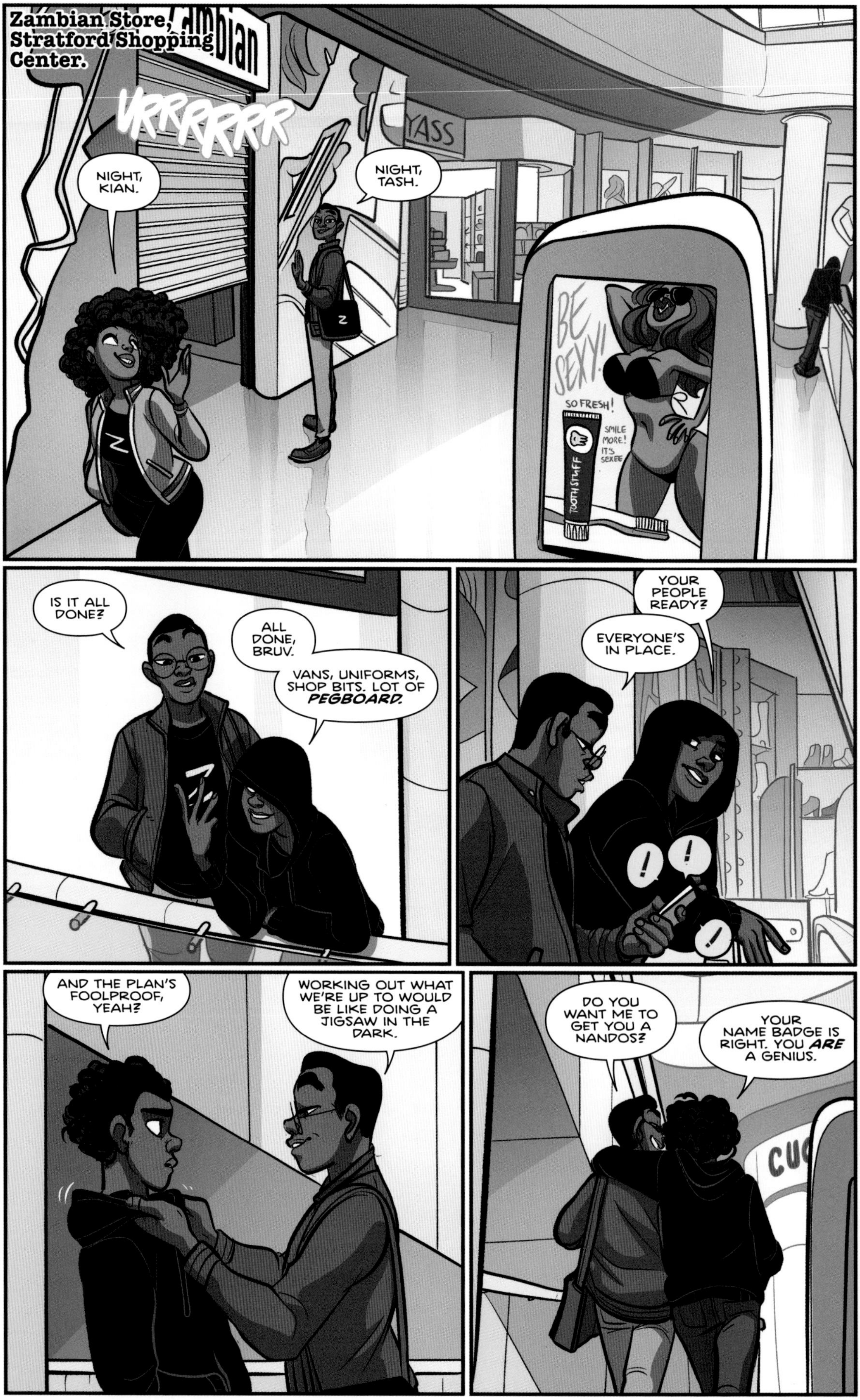
Zambian Store, Stratford Shopping Center.
ZAMBIAN
URRRRRRR
NIGHT, KIAN.
NIGHT, TASH.
YASS
BE SEXY!
SO FRESH!
SMILE MORE! IT'S SEXEE
TOOTH STUFF
IS IT ALL DONE?
ALL DONE, BRUV.
VANS, UNIFORMS, SHOP BITS. LOT OF *PEGBOARD.*
YOUR PEOPLE READY?
EVERYONE'S IN PLACE.
!
!
!
AND THE PLAN'S FOOLPROOF, YEAH?
WORKING OUT WHAT WE'RE UP TO WOULD BE LIKE DOING A JIGSAW IN THE DARK.
DO YOU WANT ME TO GET YOU A NANDOS?
YOUR NAME BADGE IS RIGHT. YOU *ARE* A GENIUS.
CUC

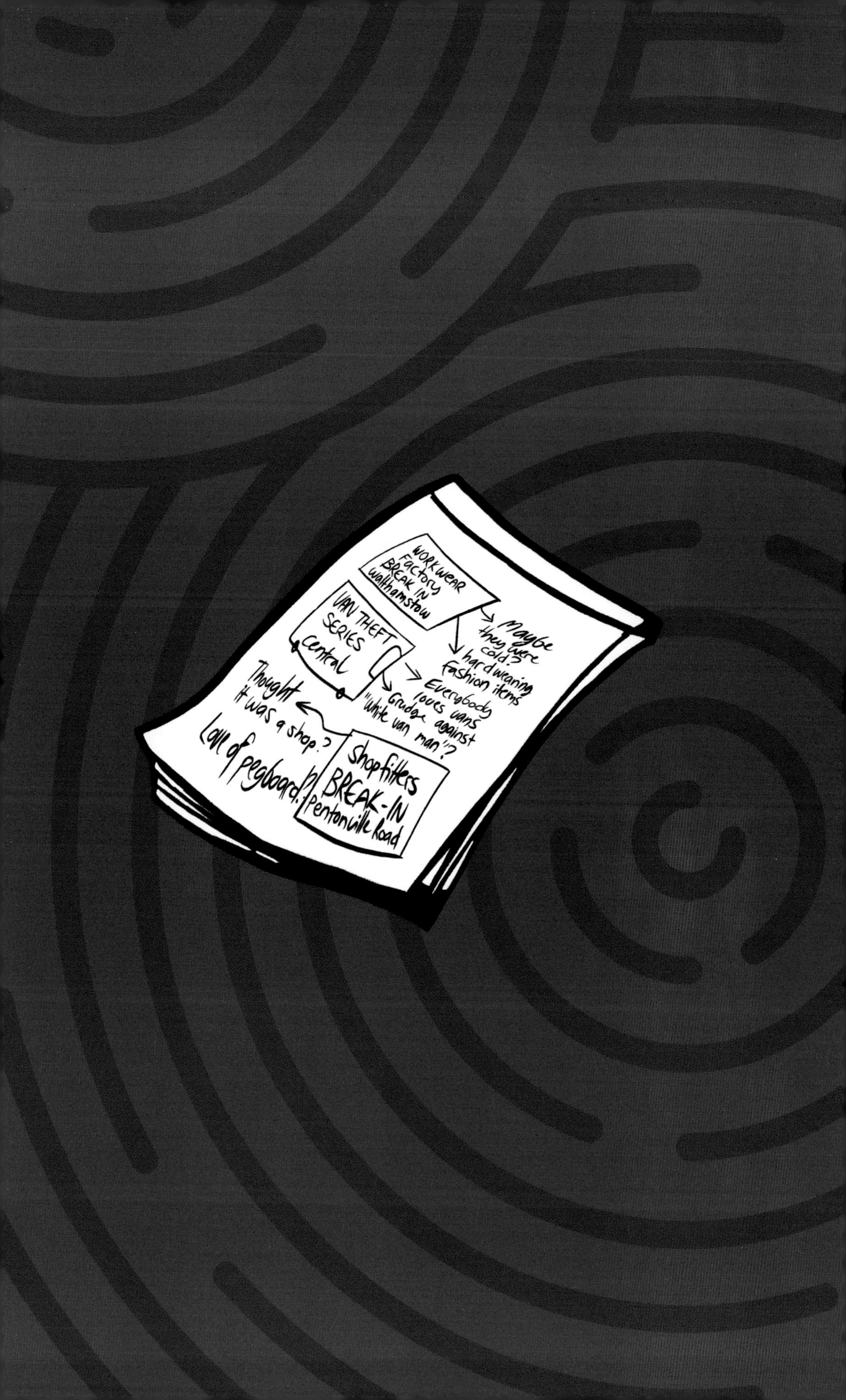
WORKWEAR Factory BREAK IN Walthamstow
Maybe they were cold?
hardwearing fashion items
VAN THEFT SERIES Central
Everybody loves vans
Grudge against "White van man"?
Thought it was a shop?
Love of pegboard?!
Shopfitters BREAK-IN Pentonville Road

# CHAPTER FOUR

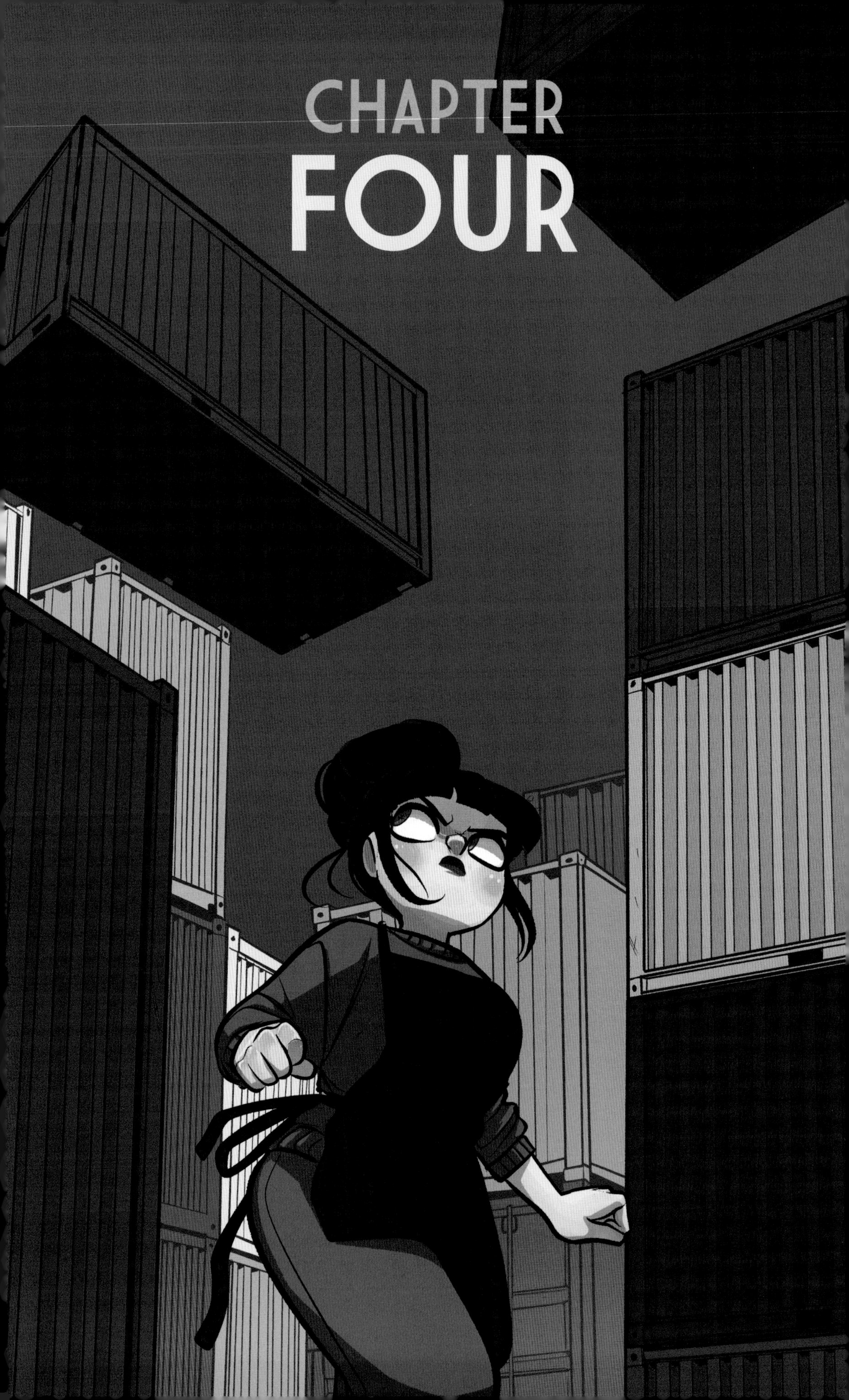

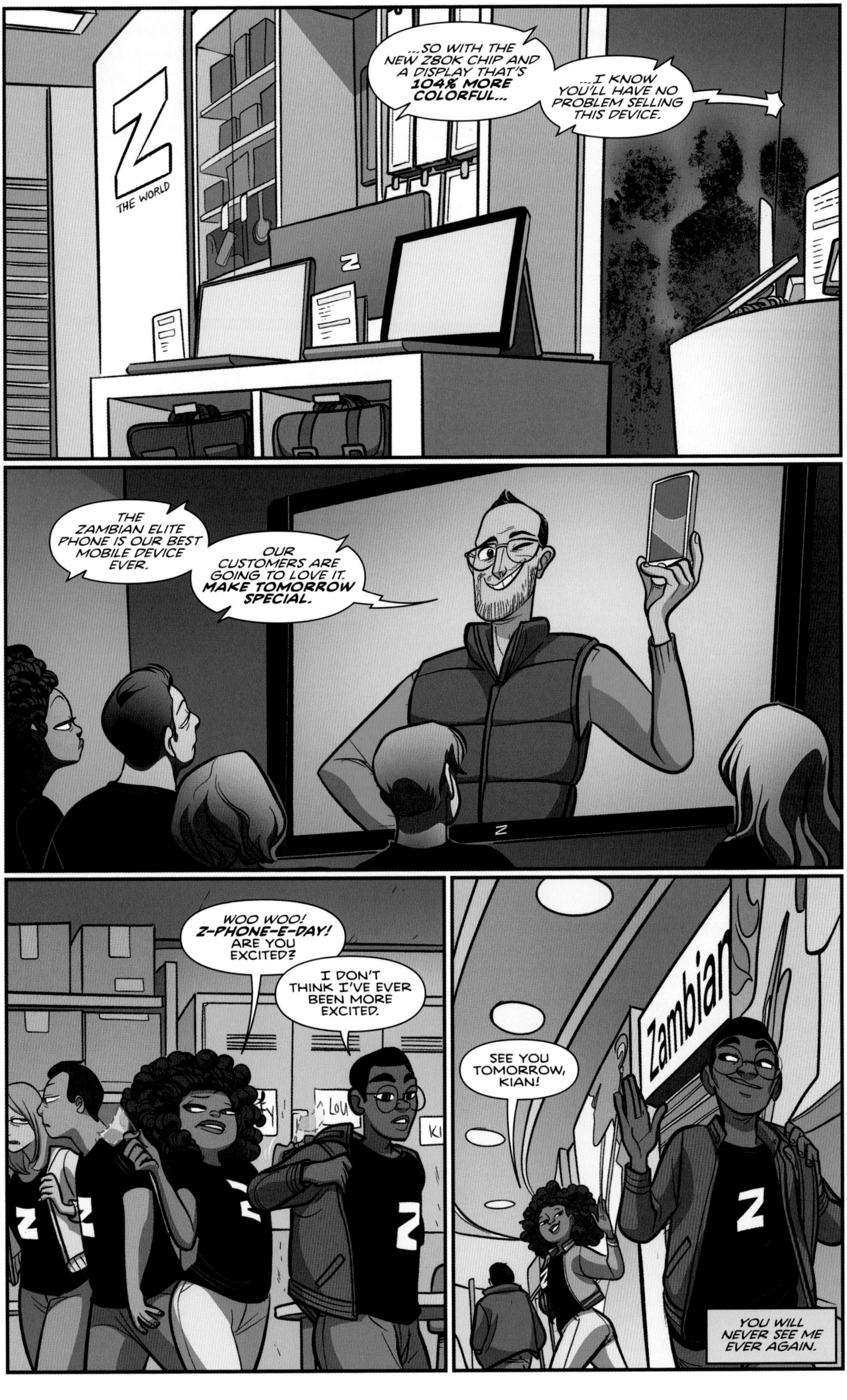

Z THE WORLD
...SO WITH THE NEW Z80K CHIP AND A DISPLAY THAT'S **104% MORE COLORFUL...**
...I KNOW YOU'LL HAVE NO PROBLEM SELLING THIS DEVICE.
THE ZAMBIAN ELITE PHONE IS OUR BEST MOBILE DEVICE EVER.
OUR CUSTOMERS ARE GOING TO LOVE IT. **MAKE TOMORROW SPECIAL.**
WOO WOO! **Z-PHONE-E-DAY!** ARE YOU EXCITED?
I DON'T THINK I'VE EVER BEEN MORE EXCITED.
Zambian
SEE YOU TOMORROW, KIAN!
YOU WILL NEVER SEE ME EVER AGAIN.

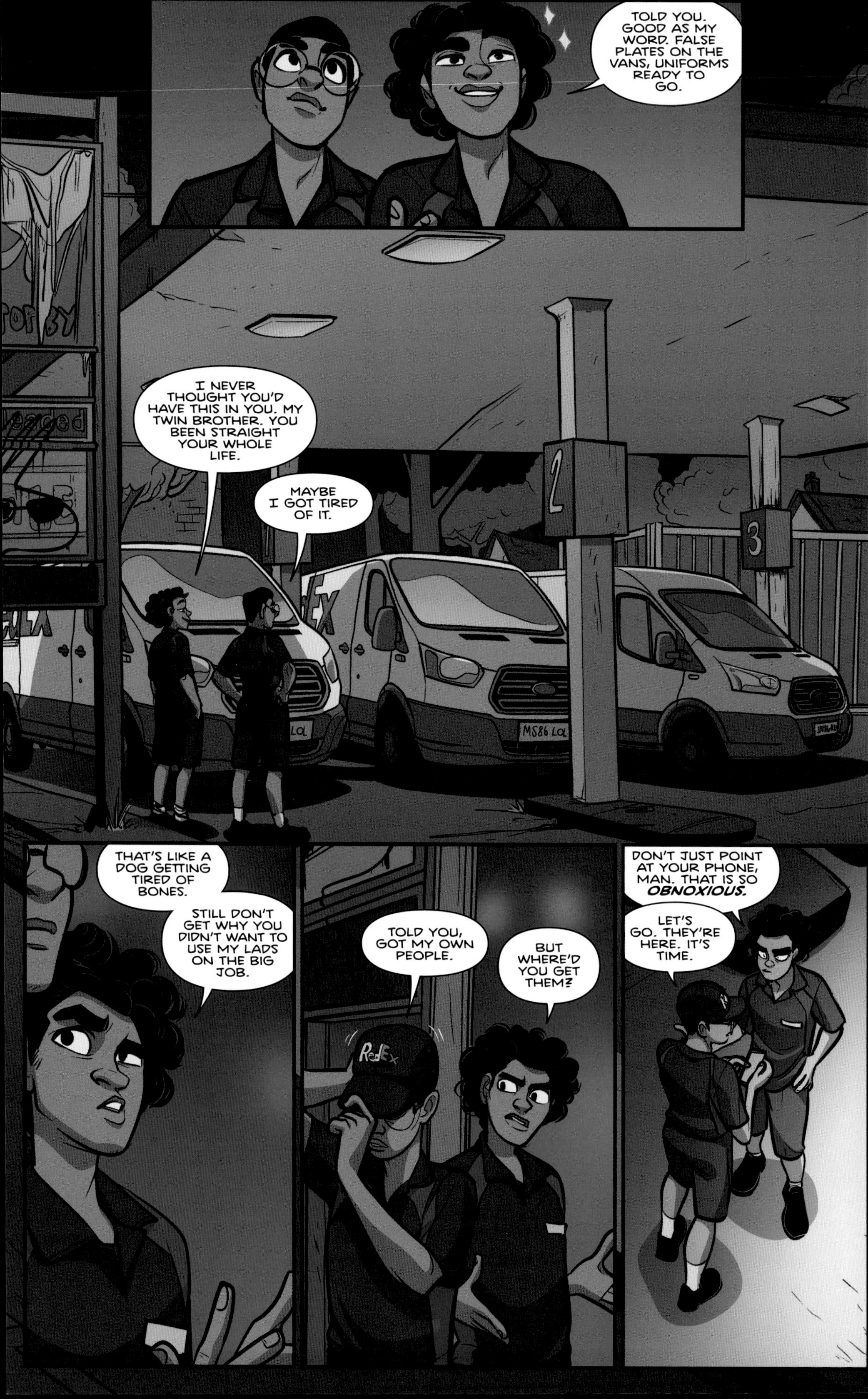
TOLD YOU. GOOD AS MY WORD. FALSE PLATES ON THE VANS, UNIFORMS READY TO GO.
I NEVER THOUGHT YOU'D HAVE THIS IN YOU. MY TWIN BROTHER. YOU BEEN STRAIGHT YOUR WHOLE LIFE.
MAYBE I GOT TIRED OF IT.
THAT'S LIKE A DOG GETTING TIRED OF BONES.
STILL DON'T GET WHY YOU DIDN'T WANT TO USE MY LADS ON THE BIG JOB.
TOLD YOU, GOT MY OWN PEOPLE.
BUT WHERE'D YOU GET THEM?
RedEx
DON'T JUST POINT AT YOUR PHONE, MAN. THAT IS SO ***OBNOXIOUS.***
LET'S GO. THEY'RE HERE. IT'S TIME.

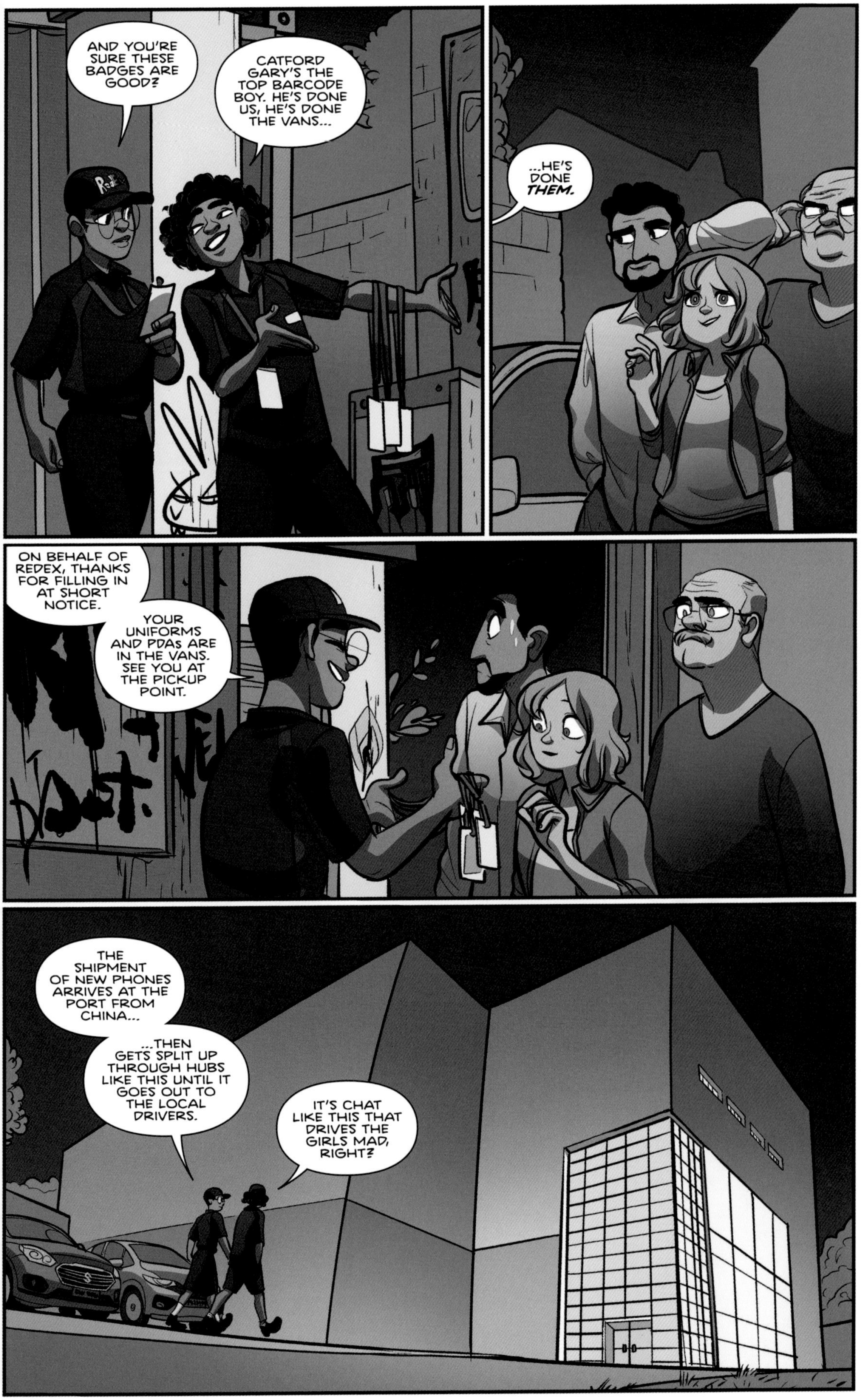
AND YOU'RE SURE THESE BADGES ARE GOOD?
CATFORD GARY'S THE TOP BARCODE BOY. HE'S DONE US, HE'S DONE THE VANS...
...HE'S DONE *THEM.*
ON BEHALF OF REDEX, THANKS FOR FILLING IN AT SHORT NOTICE.
YOUR UNIFORMS AND PDAs ARE IN THE VANS. SEE YOU AT THE PICKUP POINT.
THE SHIPMENT OF NEW PHONES ARRIVES AT THE PORT FROM CHINA...
...THEN GETS SPLIT UP THROUGH HUBS LIKE THIS UNTIL IT GOES OUT TO THE LOCAL DRIVERS.
IT'S CHAT LIKE THIS THAT DRIVES THE GIRLS MAD, RIGHT?

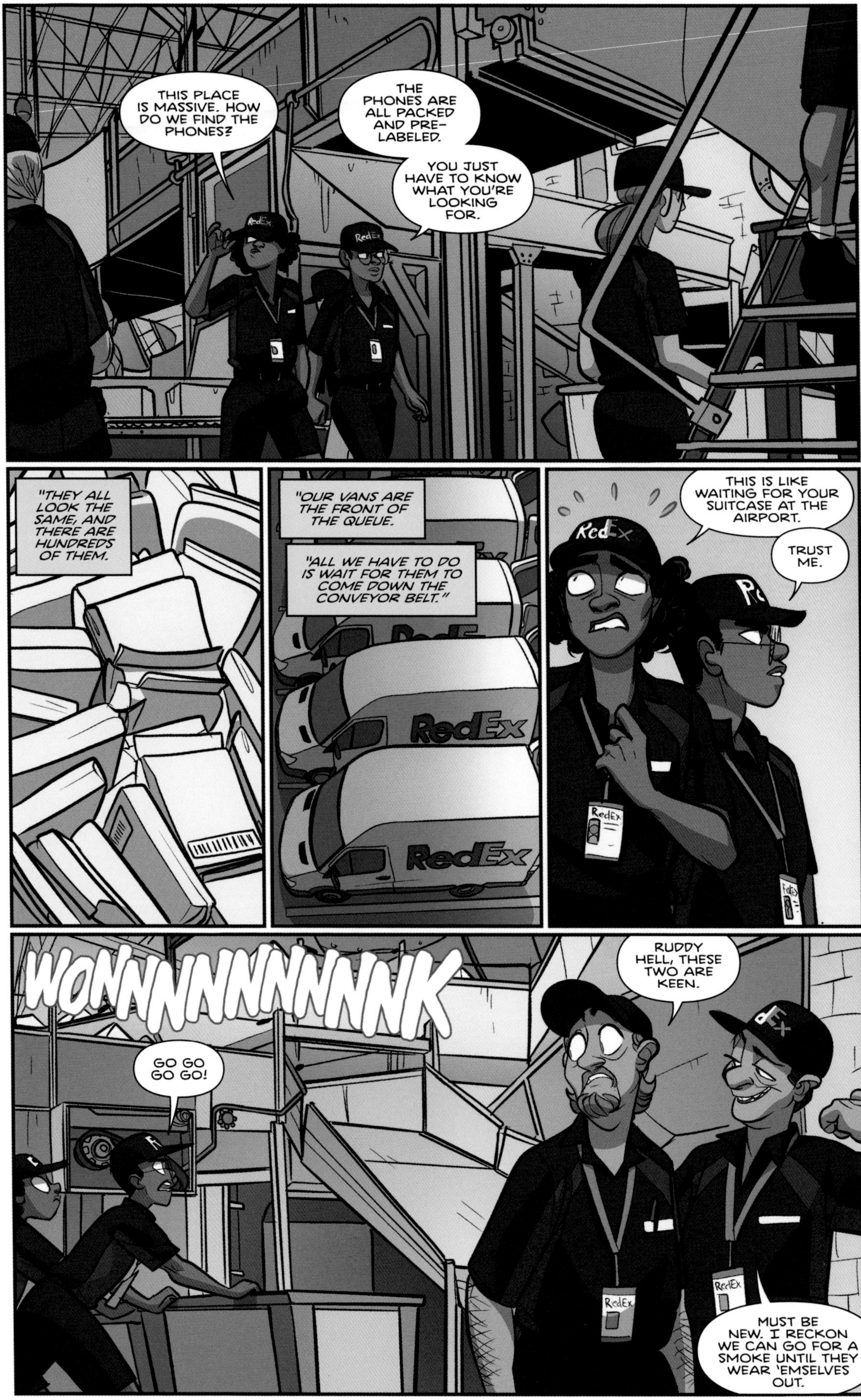
THIS PLACE IS MASSIVE. HOW DO WE FIND THE PHONES?
THE PHONES ARE ALL PACKED AND PRE-LABELED.
YOU JUST HAVE TO KNOW WHAT YOU'RE LOOKING FOR.
"THEY ALL LOOK THE SAME, AND THERE ARE HUNDREDS OF THEM.
"OUR VANS ARE THE FRONT OF THE QUEUE.
"ALL WE HAVE TO DO IS WAIT FOR THEM TO COME DOWN THE CONVEYOR BELT."
RedEx
RedEx
THIS IS LIKE WAITING FOR YOUR SUITCASE AT THE AIRPORT.
TRUST ME.
WONNNNNNNNNNK
GO GO GO GO!
RUDDY HELL, THESE TWO ARE KEEN.
MUST BE NEW. I RECKON WE CAN GO FOR A SMOKE UNTIL THEY WEAR 'EMSELVES OUT.

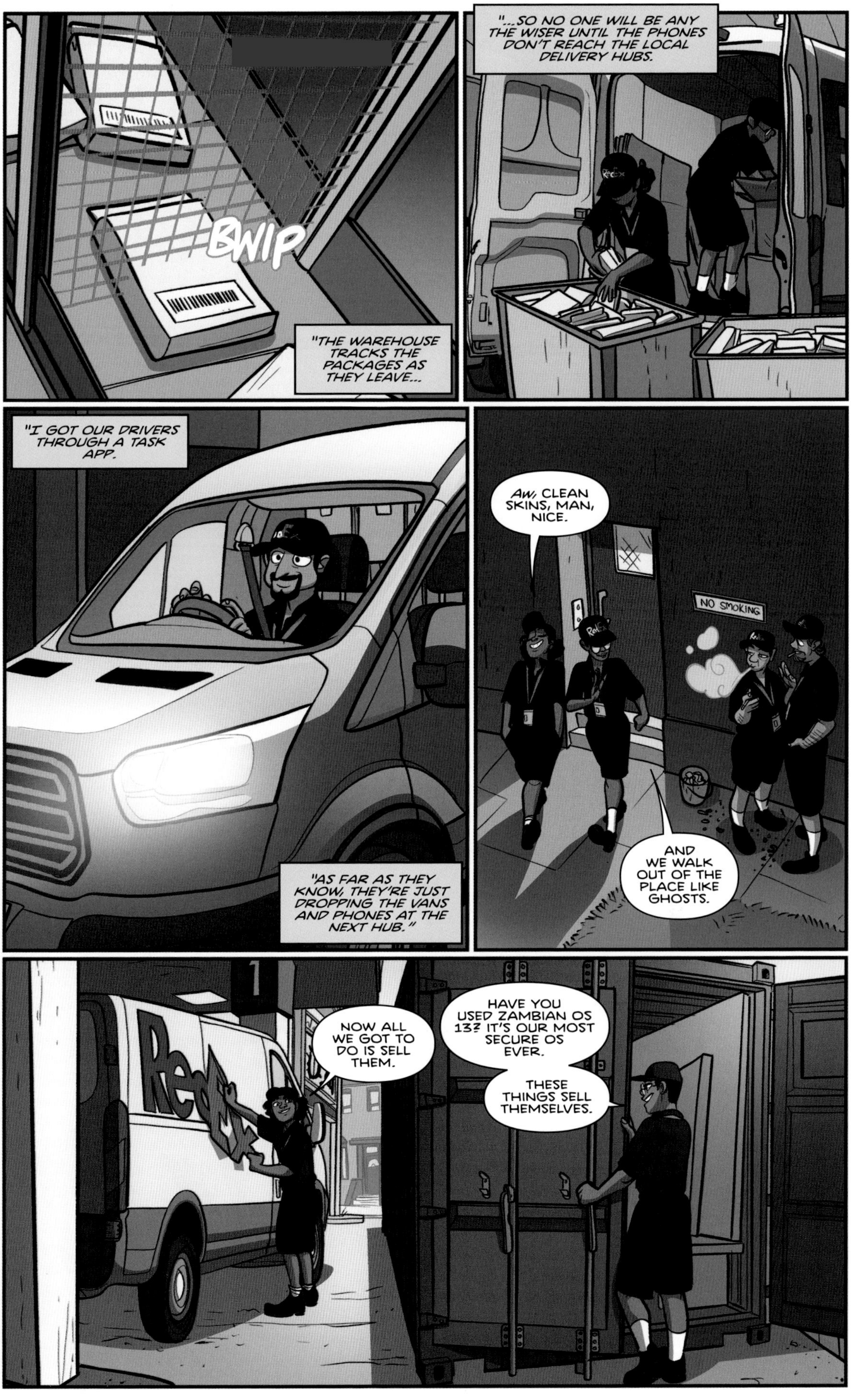
[redacted]
BWIP
"THE WAREHOUSE TRACKS THE PACKAGES AS THEY LEAVE...
"...SO NO ONE WILL BE ANY THE WISER UNTIL THE PHONES DON'T REACH THE LOCAL DELIVERY HUBS.
"I GOT OUR DRIVERS THROUGH A TASK APP.
"AS FAR AS THEY KNOW, THEY'RE JUST DROPPING THE VANS AND PHONES AT THE NEXT HUB."
AW, CLEAN SKINS, MAN, NICE.
NO SMOKING
AND WE WALK OUT OF THE PLACE LIKE GHOSTS.
NOW ALL WE GOT TO DO IS SELL THEM.
HAVE YOU USED ZAMBIAN OS 13? IT'S OUR MOST SECURE OS EVER.
THESE THINGS SELL THEMSELVES.

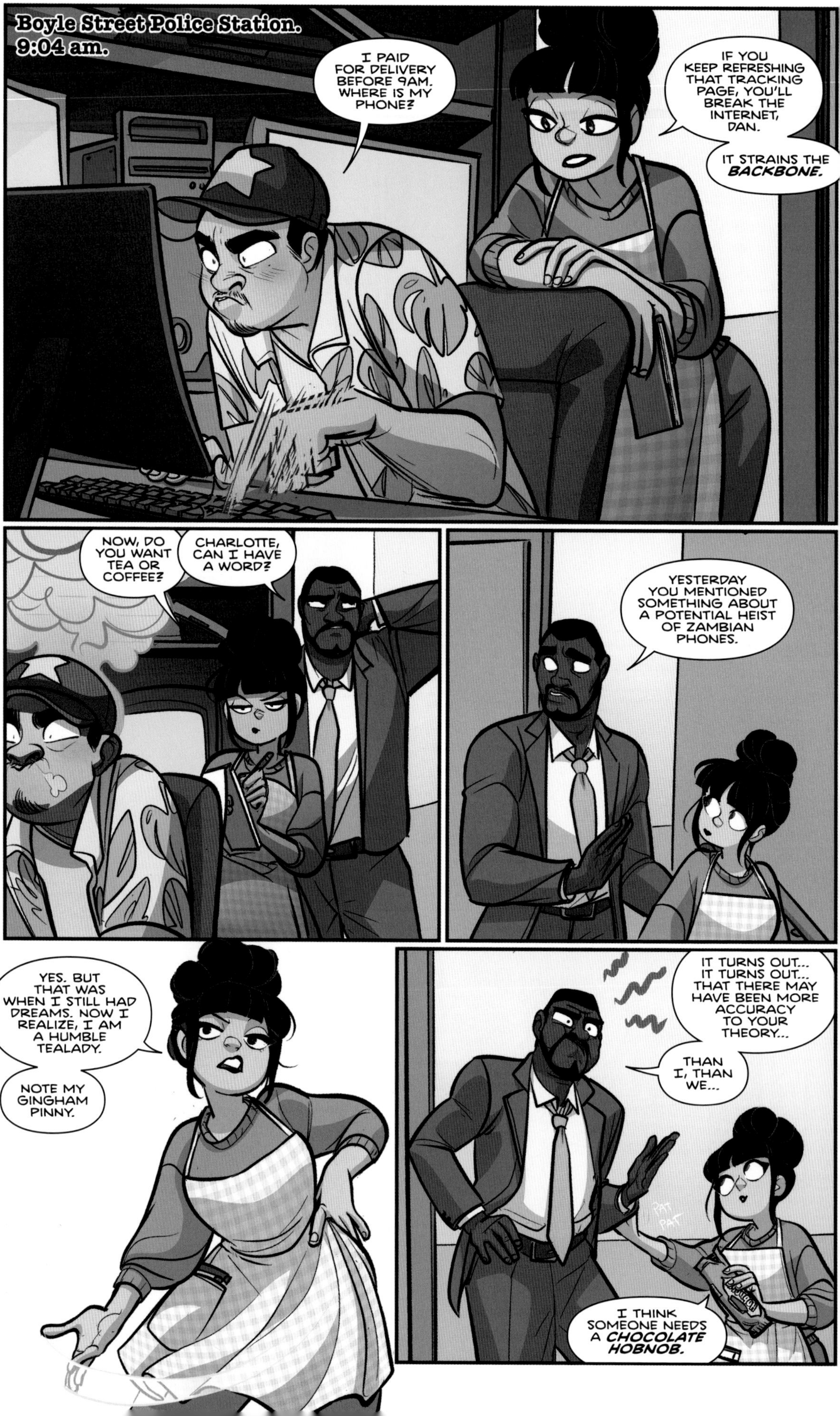
Boyle Street Police Station.
9:04 am.
I PAID FOR DELIVERY BEFORE 9AM. WHERE IS MY PHONE?
IF YOU KEEP REFRESHING THAT TRACKING PAGE, YOU'LL BREAK THE INTERNET, DAN.
IT STRAINS THE BACKBONE.
NOW, DO YOU WANT TEA OR COFFEE?
CHARLOTTE, CAN I HAVE A WORD?
YESTERDAY YOU MENTIONED SOMETHING ABOUT A POTENTIAL HEIST OF ZAMBIAN PHONES.
YES. BUT THAT WAS WHEN I STILL HAD DREAMS. NOW I REALIZE, I AM A HUMBLE TEALADY.
NOTE MY GINGHAM PINNY.
IT TURNS OUT... IT TURNS OUT... THAT THERE MAY HAVE BEEN MORE ACCURACY TO YOUR THEORY...
THAN I, THAN WE...
PAT PAT
I THINK SOMEONE NEEDS A CHOCOLATE HOBNOB.

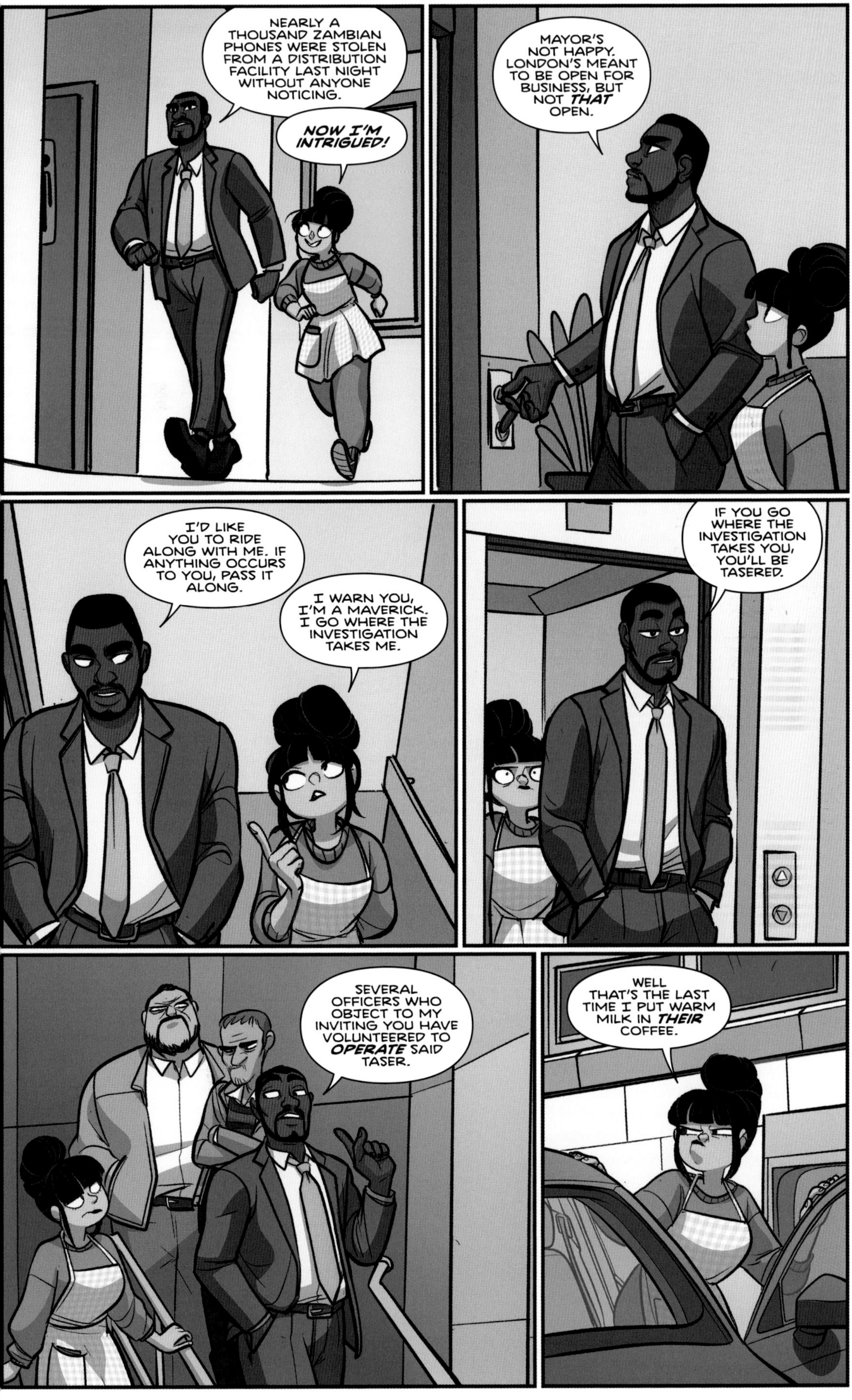

NEARLY A THOUSAND ZAMBIAN PHONES WERE STOLEN FROM A DISTRIBUTION FACILITY LAST NIGHT WITHOUT ANYONE NOTICING.
NOW I'M INTRIGUED!
MAYOR'S NOT HAPPY. LONDON'S MEANT TO BE OPEN FOR BUSINESS, BUT NOT *THAT* OPEN.
I'D LIKE YOU TO RIDE ALONG WITH ME. IF ANYTHING OCCURS TO YOU, PASS IT ALONG.
I WARN YOU, I'M A MAVERICK. I GO WHERE THE INVESTIGATION TAKES ME.
IF YOU GO WHERE THE INVESTIGATION TAKES YOU, YOU'LL BE TASERED.
SEVERAL OFFICERS WHO OBJECT TO MY INVITING YOU HAVE VOLUNTEERED TO *OPERATE* SAID TASER.
WELL THAT'S THE LAST TIME I PUT WARM MILK IN *THEIR* COFFEE.

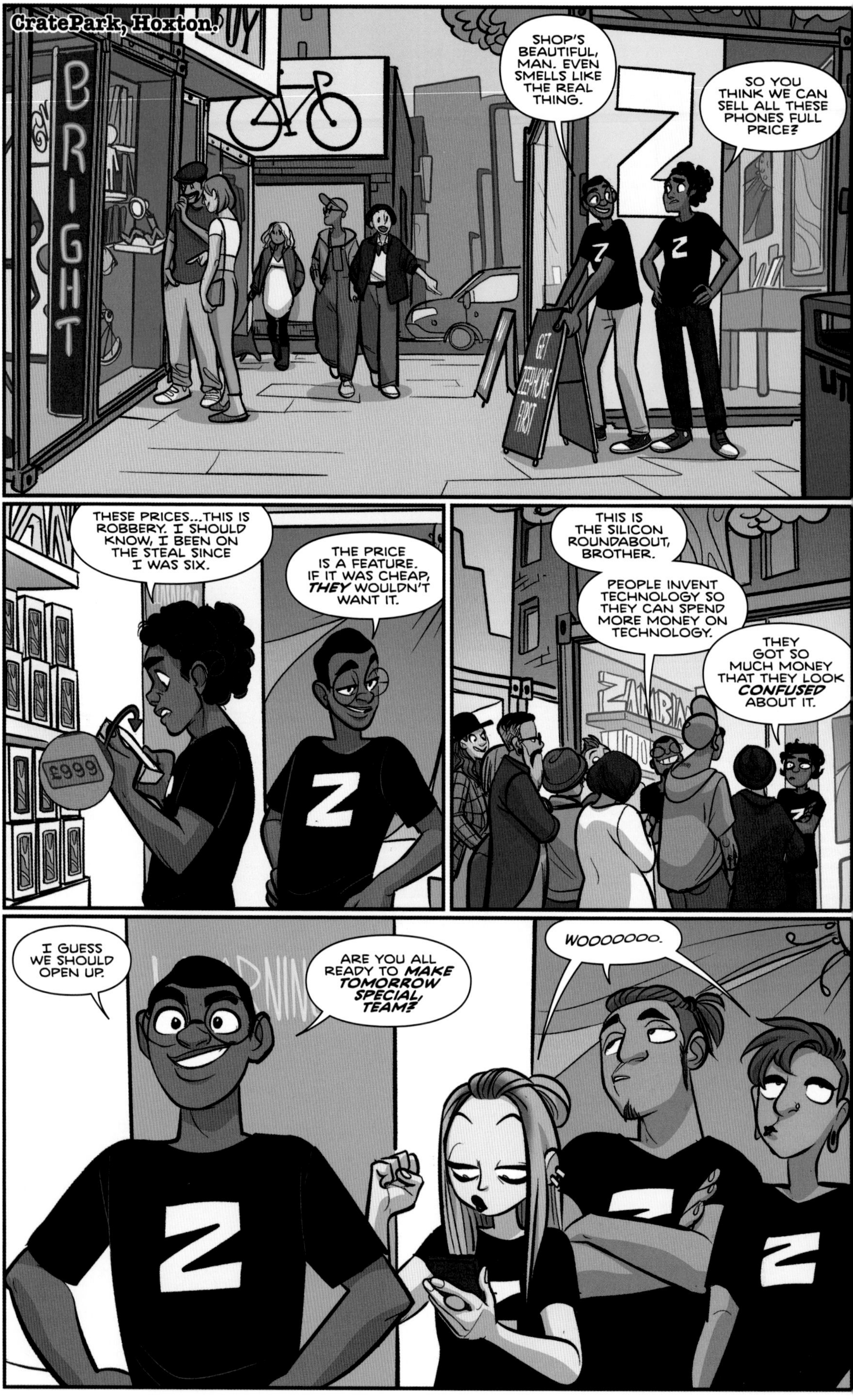
CratePark, Hoxton.
BRIGHT
SHOP'S BEAUTIFUL, MAN. EVEN SMELLS LIKE THE REAL THING.
SO YOU THINK WE CAN SELL ALL THESE PHONES FULL PRICE?
GET ZEEPHONE FIRST
THESE PRICES...THIS IS ROBBERY. I SHOULD KNOW, I BEEN ON THE STEAL SINCE I WAS SIX.
£999
THE PRICE IS A FEATURE. IF IT WAS CHEAP, *THEY* WOULDN'T WANT IT.
THIS IS THE SILICON ROUNDABOUT, BROTHER.
PEOPLE INVENT TECHNOLOGY SO THEY CAN SPEND MORE MONEY ON TECHNOLOGY.
THEY GOT SO MUCH MONEY THAT THEY LOOK *CONFUSED* ABOUT IT.
I GUESS WE SHOULD OPEN UP.
ARE YOU ALL READY TO *MAKE TOMORROW SPECIAL, TEAM?*
WOOOOOOO.

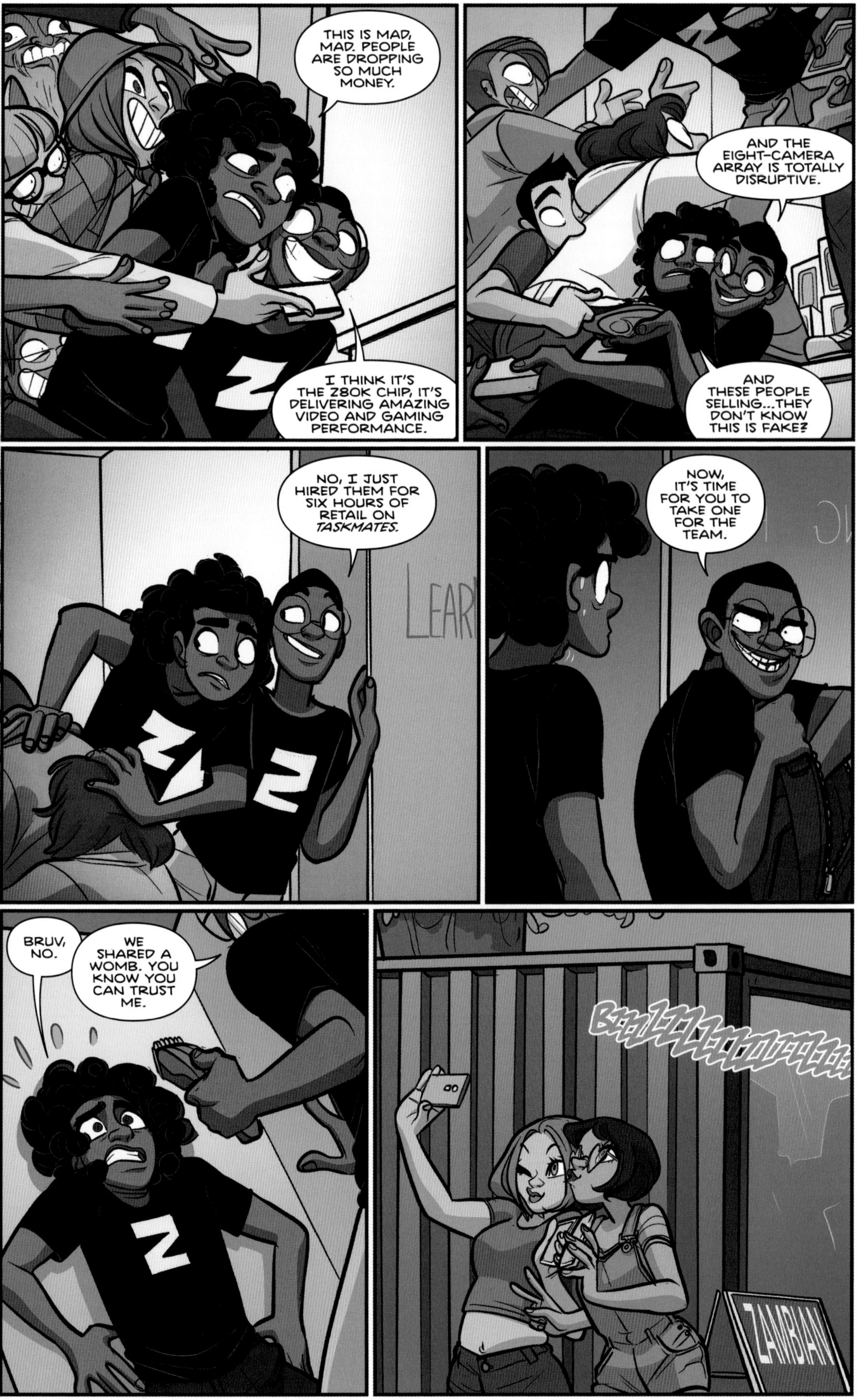
THIS IS MAD, MAD. PEOPLE ARE DROPPING SO MUCH MONEY.
I THINK IT'S THE Z80K CHIP, IT'S DELIVERING AMAZING VIDEO AND GAMING PERFORMANCE.
AND THE EIGHT-CAMERA ARRAY IS TOTALLY DISRUPTIVE.
AND THESE PEOPLE SELLING... THEY DON'T KNOW THIS IS FAKE?
NO, I JUST HIRED THEM FOR SIX HOURS OF RETAIL ON *TASKMATES.*
NOW, IT'S TIME FOR YOU TO TAKE ONE FOR THE TEAM.
BRUV, NO.
WE SHARED A WOMB. YOU KNOW YOU CAN TRUST ME.
ZAMBIAN

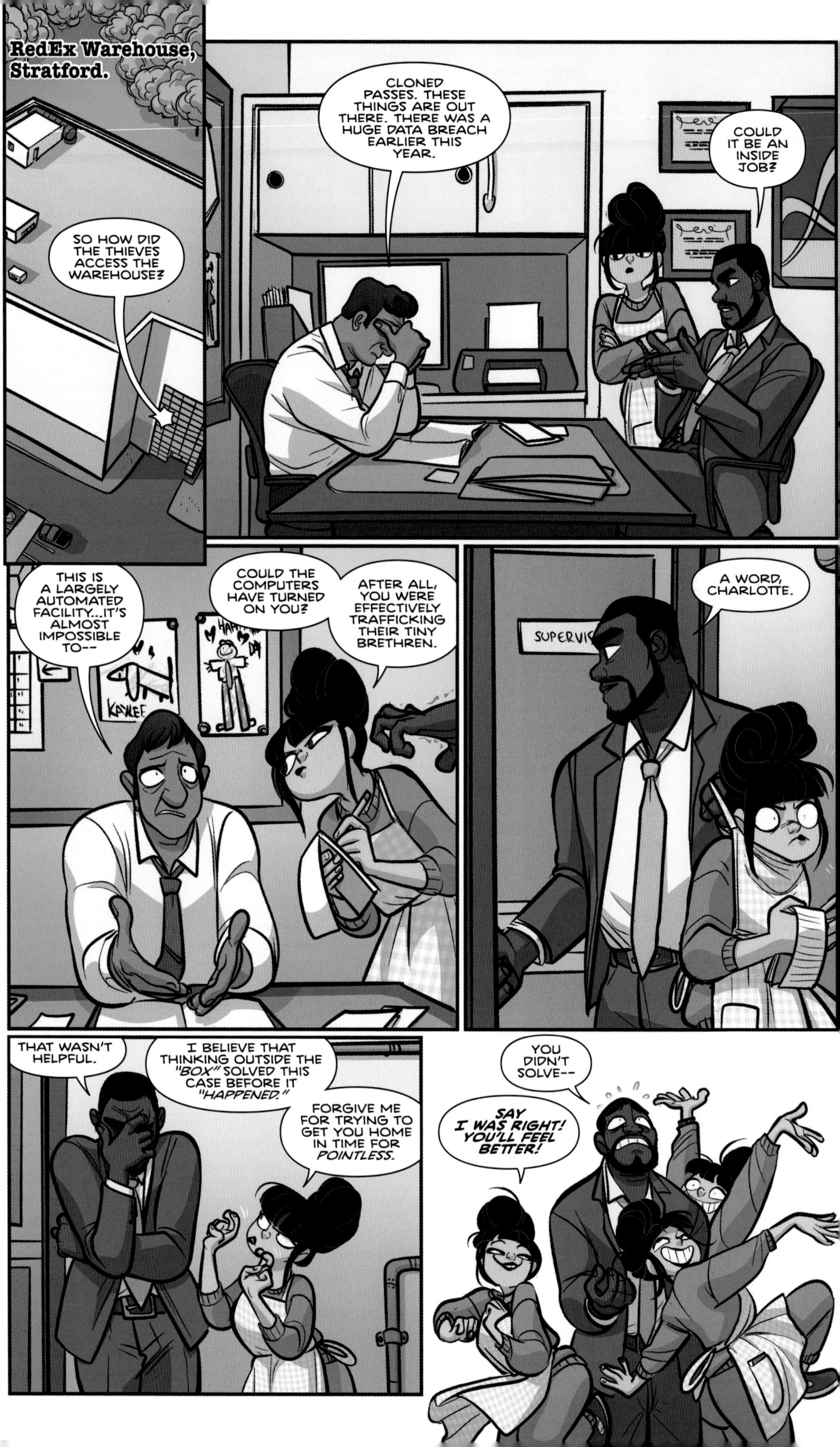
RedEx Warehouse, Stratford.
SO HOW DID THE THIEVES ACCESS THE WAREHOUSE?
CLONED PASSES. THESE THINGS ARE OUT THERE. THERE WAS A HUGE DATA BREACH EARLIER THIS YEAR.
COULD IT BE AN INSIDE JOB?
THIS IS A LARGELY AUTOMATED FACILITY...IT'S ALMOST IMPOSSIBLE TO--
COULD THE COMPUTERS HAVE TURNED ON YOU?
AFTER ALL, YOU WERE EFFECTIVELY TRAFFICKING THEIR TINY BRETHREN.
KAYLEE
SUPERVIS
A WORD, CHARLOTTE.
THAT WASN'T HELPFUL.
I BELIEVE THAT THINKING OUTSIDE THE *"BOX"* SOLVED THIS CASE BEFORE IT *"HAPPENED."*
FORGIVE ME FOR TRYING TO GET YOU HOME IN TIME FOR *POINTLESS.*
YOU DIDN'T SOLVE--
***SAY I WAS RIGHT! YOU'LL FEEL BETTER!***

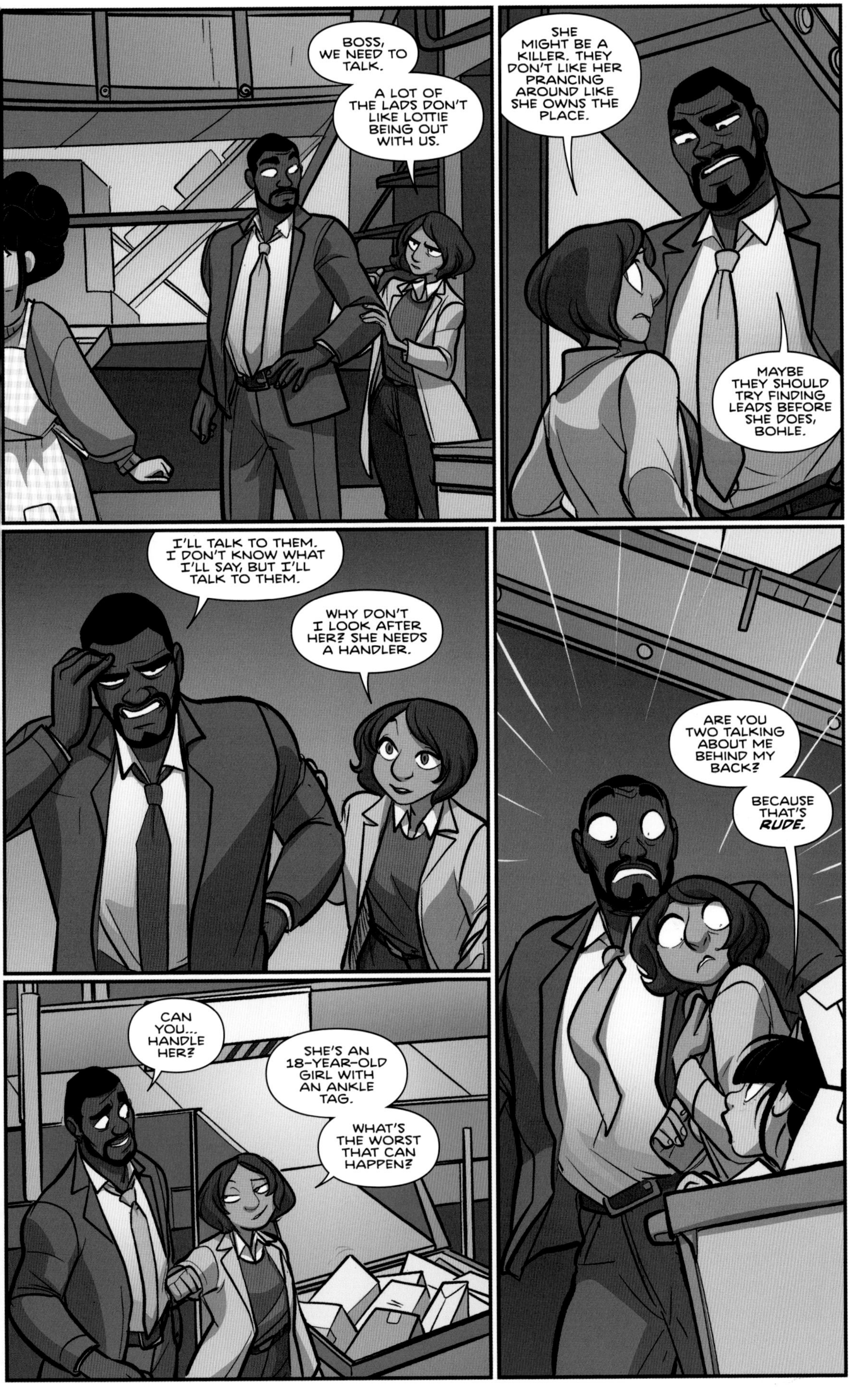
BOSS, WE NEED TO TALK.
A LOT OF THE LADS DON'T LIKE LOTTIE BEING OUT WITH US.
SHE MIGHT BE A KILLER. THEY DON'T LIKE HER PRANCING AROUND LIKE SHE OWNS THE PLACE.
MAYBE THEY SHOULD TRY FINDING LEADS BEFORE SHE DOES, BOHLE.
I'LL TALK TO THEM. I DON'T KNOW WHAT I'LL SAY, BUT I'LL TALK TO THEM.
WHY DON'T I LOOK AFTER HER? SHE NEEDS A HANDLER.
CAN YOU... HANDLE HER?
SHE'S AN 18-YEAR-OLD GIRL WITH AN ANKLE TAG.
WHAT'S THE WORST THAT CAN HAPPEN?
ARE YOU TWO TALKING ABOUT ME BEHIND MY BACK?
BECAUSE THAT'S *RUDE.*

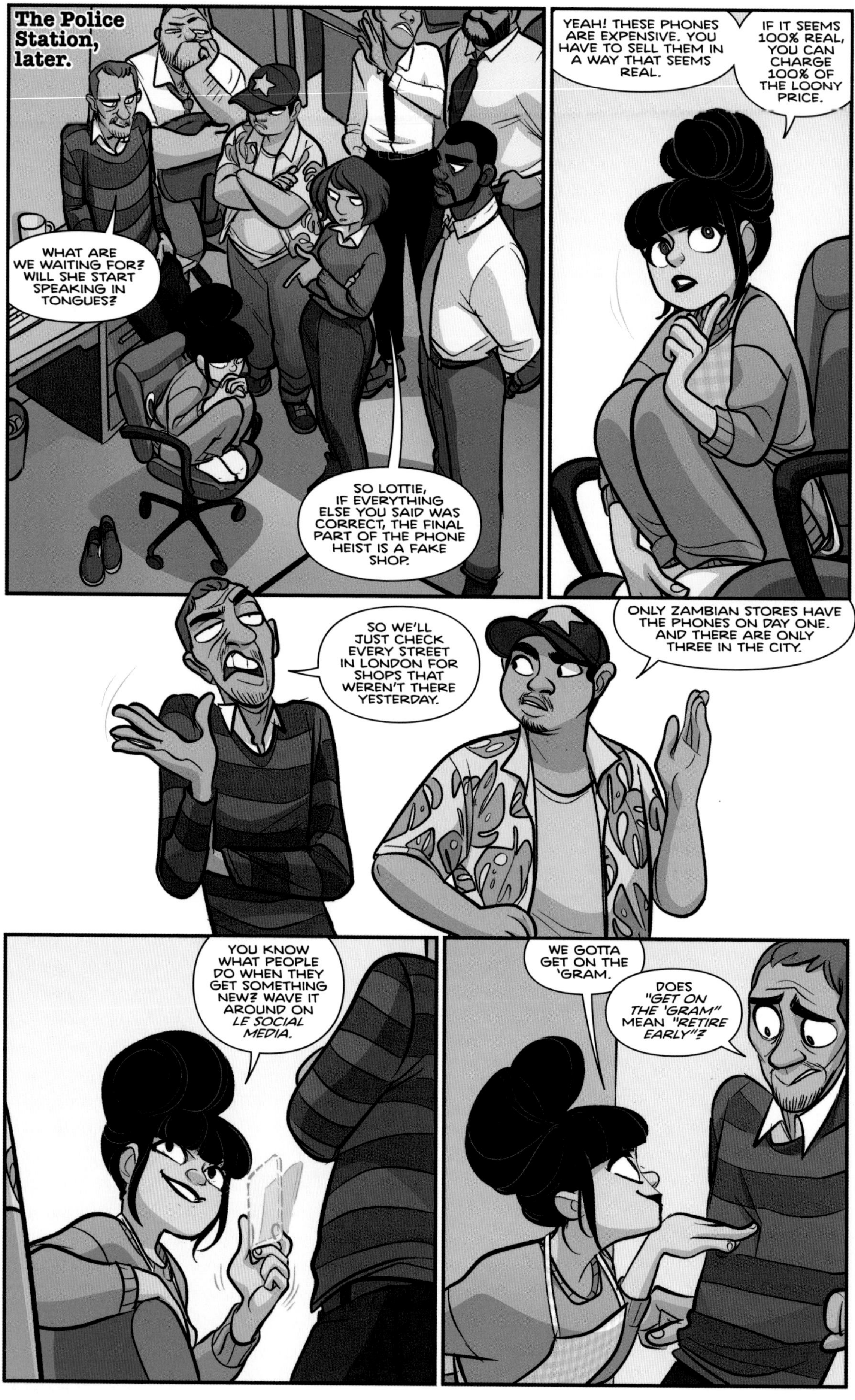
The Police Station, later.
WHAT ARE WE WAITING FOR? WILL SHE START SPEAKING IN TONGUES?
SO LOTTIE, IF EVERYTHING ELSE YOU SAID WAS CORRECT, THE FINAL PART OF THE PHONE HEIST IS A FAKE SHOP.
YEAH! THESE PHONES ARE EXPENSIVE. YOU HAVE TO SELL THEM IN A WAY THAT SEEMS REAL.
IF IT SEEMS 100% REAL, YOU CAN CHARGE 100% OF THE LOONY PRICE.
SO WE'LL JUST CHECK EVERY STREET IN LONDON FOR SHOPS THAT WEREN'T THERE YESTERDAY.
ONLY ZAMBIAN STORES HAVE THE PHONES ON DAY ONE. AND THERE ARE ONLY THREE IN THE CITY.
YOU KNOW WHAT PEOPLE DO WHEN THEY GET SOMETHING NEW? WAVE IT AROUND ON *LE SOCIAL MEDIA*.
WE GOTTA GET ON THE 'GRAM.
DOES *"GET ON THE 'GRAM"* MEAN *"RETIRE EARLY"*?

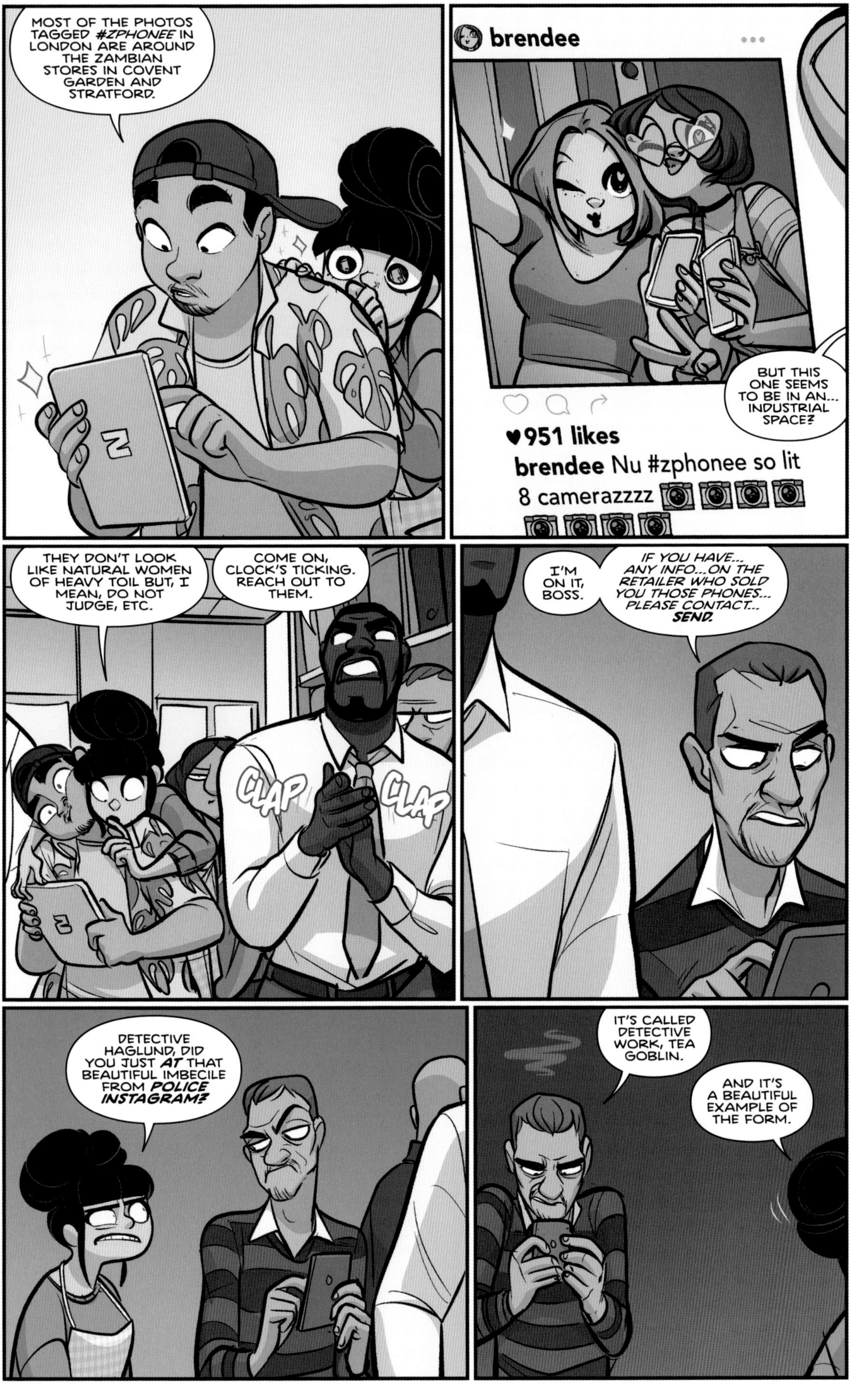
MOST OF THE PHOTOS TAGGED #ZPHONEE IN LONDON ARE AROUND THE ZAMBIAN STORES IN COVENT GARDEN AND STRATFORD.
brendee
BUT THIS ONE SEEMS TO BE IN AN... INDUSTRIAL SPACE?
951 likes
brendee Nu #zphonee so lit 8 camerazzzz
THEY DON'T LOOK LIKE NATURAL WOMEN OF HEAVY TOIL BUT, I MEAN, DO NOT JUDGE, ETC.
COME ON, CLOCK'S TICKING. REACH OUT TO THEM.
CLAP
CLAP
I'M ON IT, BOSS.
IF YOU HAVE... ANY INFO... ON THE RETAILER WHO SOLD YOU THOSE PHONES... PLEASE CONTACT... SEND.
DETECTIVE HAGLUND, DID YOU JUST AT THAT BEAUTIFUL IMBECILE FROM POLICE INSTAGRAM?
IT'S CALLED DETECTIVE WORK, TEA GOBLIN.
AND IT'S A BEAUTIFUL EXAMPLE OF THE FORM.

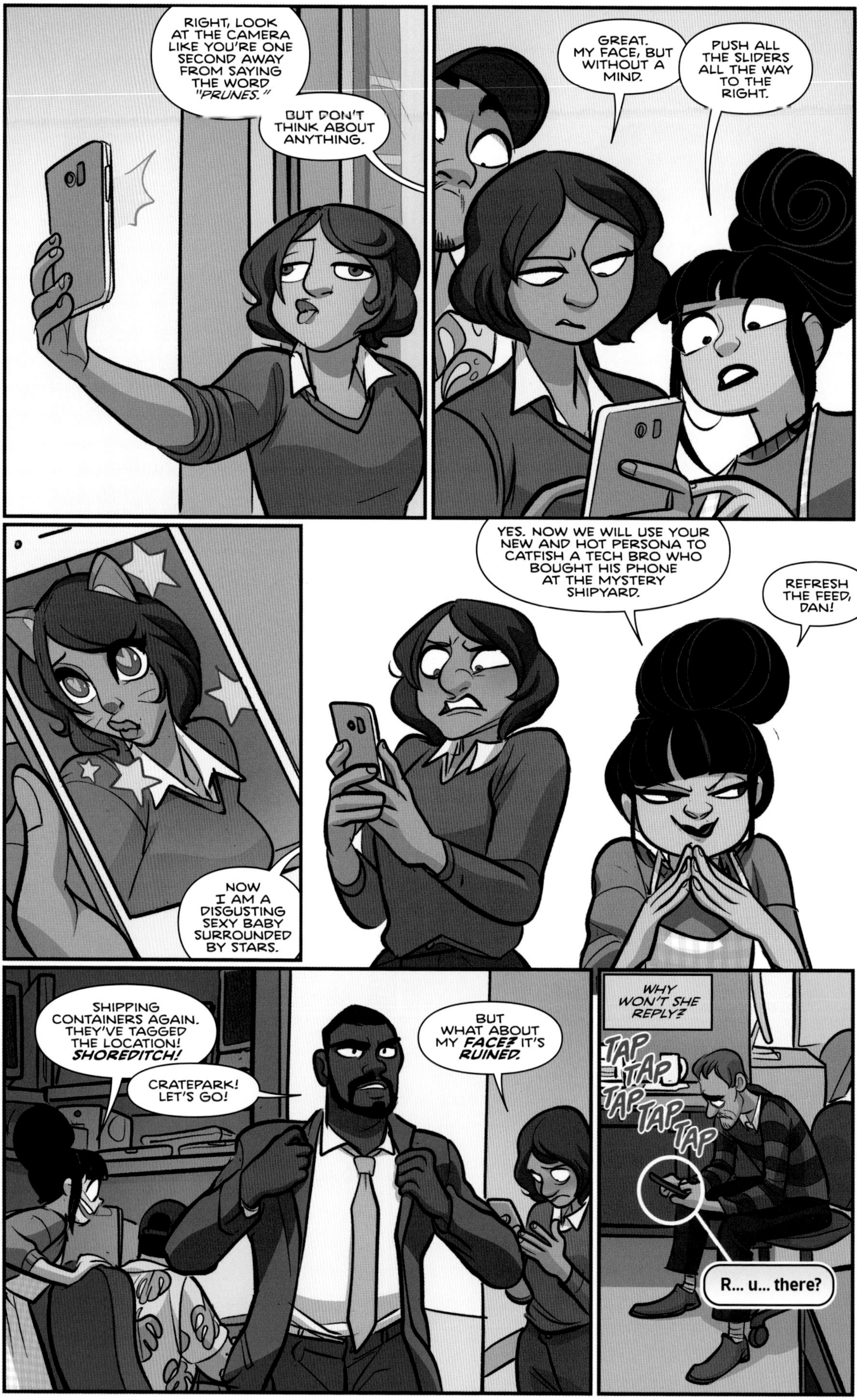
RIGHT, LOOK AT THE CAMERA LIKE YOU'RE ONE SECOND AWAY FROM SAYING THE WORD "PRUNES."
BUT DON'T THINK ABOUT ANYTHING.
GREAT. MY FACE, BUT WITHOUT A MIND.
PUSH ALL THE SLIDERS ALL THE WAY TO THE RIGHT.
NOW I AM A DISGUSTING SEXY BABY SURROUNDED BY STARS.
YES. NOW WE WILL USE YOUR NEW AND HOT PERSONA TO CATFISH A TECH BRO WHO BOUGHT HIS PHONE AT THE MYSTERY SHIPYARD.
REFRESH THE FEED, DAN!
SHIPPING CONTAINERS AGAIN. THEY'VE TAGGED THE LOCATION! SHOREDITCH!
CRATEPARK! LET'S GO!
BUT WHAT ABOUT MY FACE? IT'S RUINED.
WHY WON'T SHE REPLY?
TAP TAP TAP TAP TAP
R... u... there?

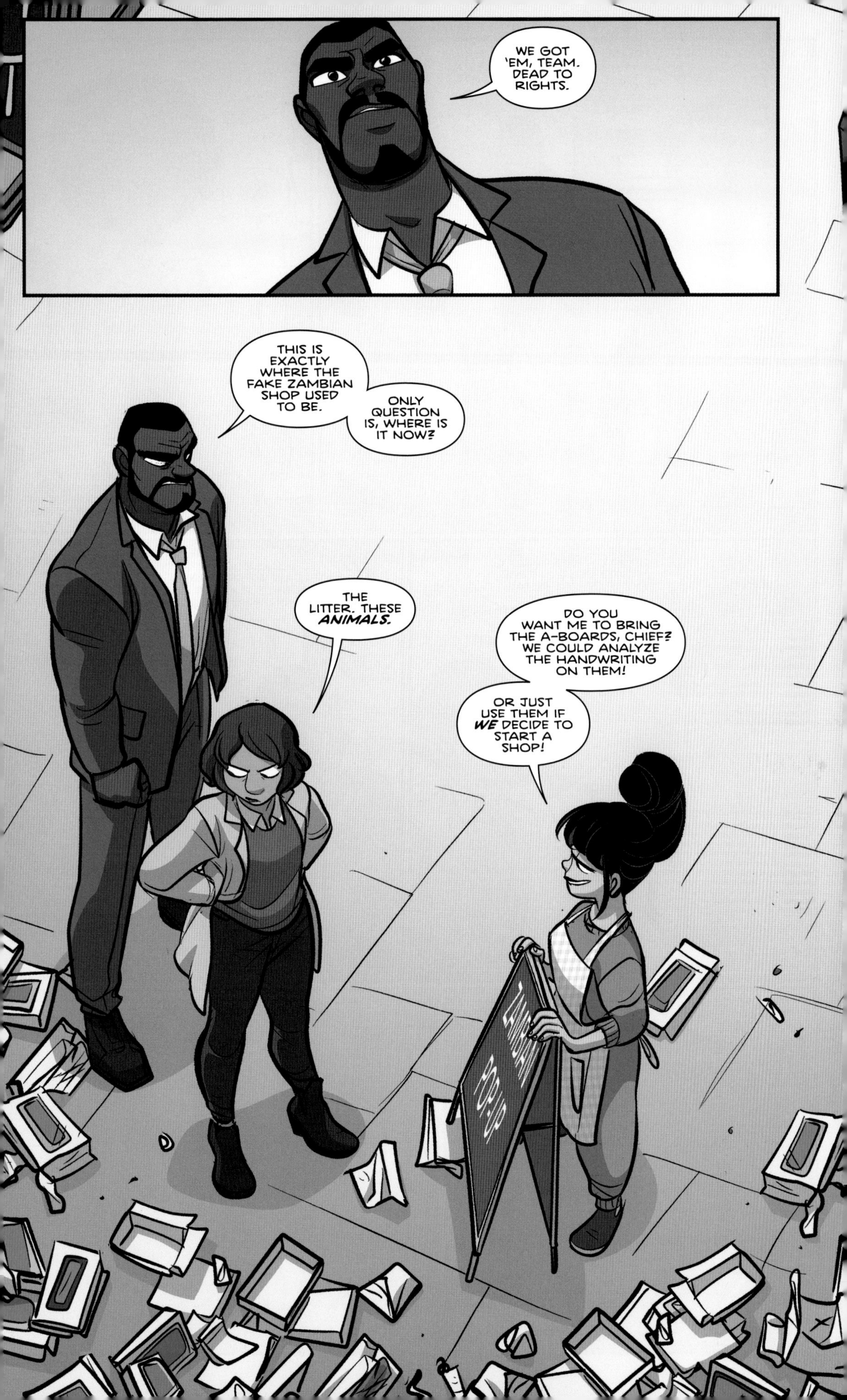
WE GOT 'EM, TEAM. DEAD TO RIGHTS.
THIS IS EXACTLY WHERE THE FAKE ZAMBIAN SHOP USED TO BE.
ONLY QUESTION IS, WHERE IS IT NOW?
THE LITTER. THESE *ANIMALS.*
DO YOU WANT ME TO BRING THE A-BOARDS, CHIEF? WE COULD ANALYZE THE HANDWRITING ON THEM!
OR JUST USE THEM IF *WE* DECIDE TO START A SHOP!

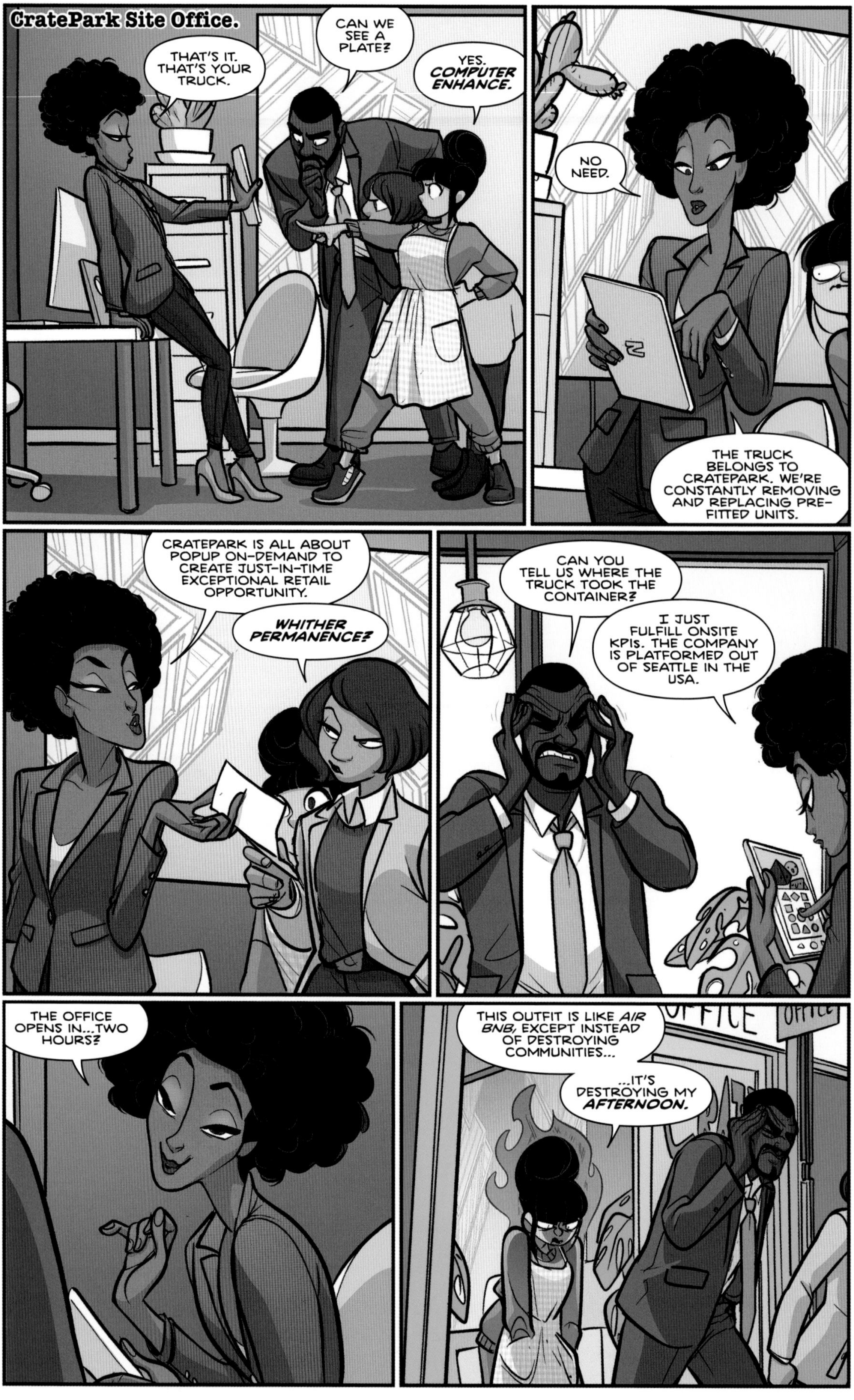
CratePark Site Office.
THAT'S IT. THAT'S YOUR TRUCK.
CAN WE SEE A PLATE?
YES. COMPUTER ENHANCE.
NO NEED.
THE TRUCK BELONGS TO CRATEPARK. WE'RE CONSTANTLY REMOVING AND REPLACING PRE-FITTED UNITS.
CRATEPARK IS ALL ABOUT POPUP ON-DEMAND TO CREATE JUST-IN-TIME EXCEPTIONAL RETAIL OPPORTUNITY.
WHITHER PERMANENCE?
CAN YOU TELL US WHERE THE TRUCK TOOK THE CONTAINER?
I JUST FULFILL ONSITE KPIs. THE COMPANY IS PLATFORMED OUT OF SEATTLE IN THE USA.
THE OFFICE OPENS IN...TWO HOURS?
THIS OUTFIT IS LIKE AIR BNB, EXCEPT INSTEAD OF DESTROYING COMMUNITIES...
...IT'S DESTROYING MY AFTERNOON.

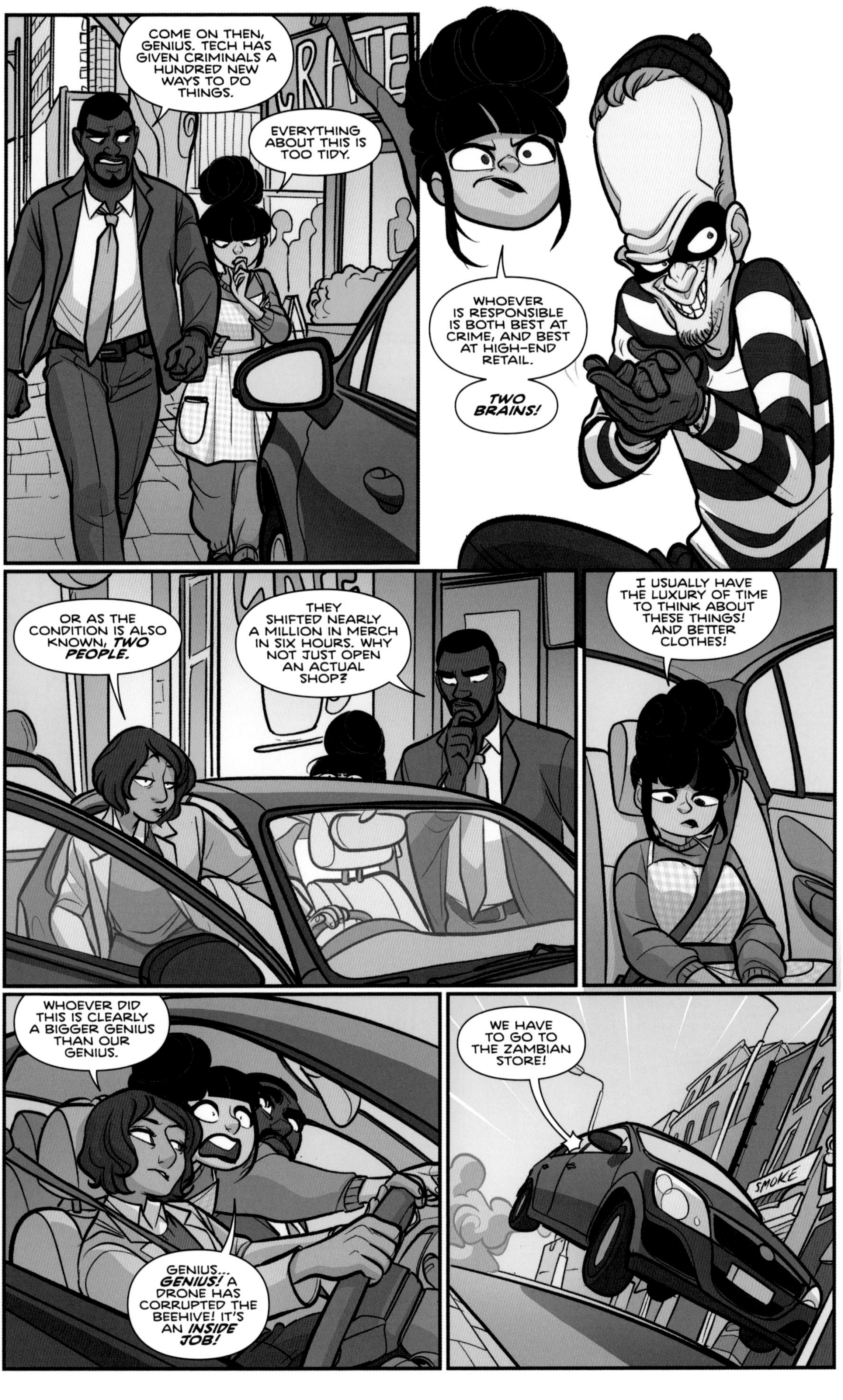
COME ON THEN, GENIUS. TECH HAS GIVEN CRIMINALS A HUNDRED NEW WAYS TO DO THINGS.
EVERYTHING ABOUT THIS IS TOO TIDY.
WHOEVER IS RESPONSIBLE IS BOTH BEST AT CRIME, AND BEST AT HIGH-END RETAIL.
TWO BRAINS!
OR AS THE CONDITION IS ALSO KNOWN, TWO PEOPLE.
THEY SHIFTED NEARLY A MILLION IN MERCH IN SIX HOURS. WHY NOT JUST OPEN AN ACTUAL SHOP?
I USUALLY HAVE THE LUXURY OF TIME TO THINK ABOUT THESE THINGS! AND BETTER CLOTHES!
WHOEVER DID THIS IS CLEARLY A BIGGER GENIUS THAN OUR GENIUS.
GENIUS... GENIUS! A DRONE HAS CORRUPTED THE BEEHIVE! IT'S AN INSIDE JOB!
WE HAVE TO GO TO THE ZAMBIAN STORE!
SMOKE

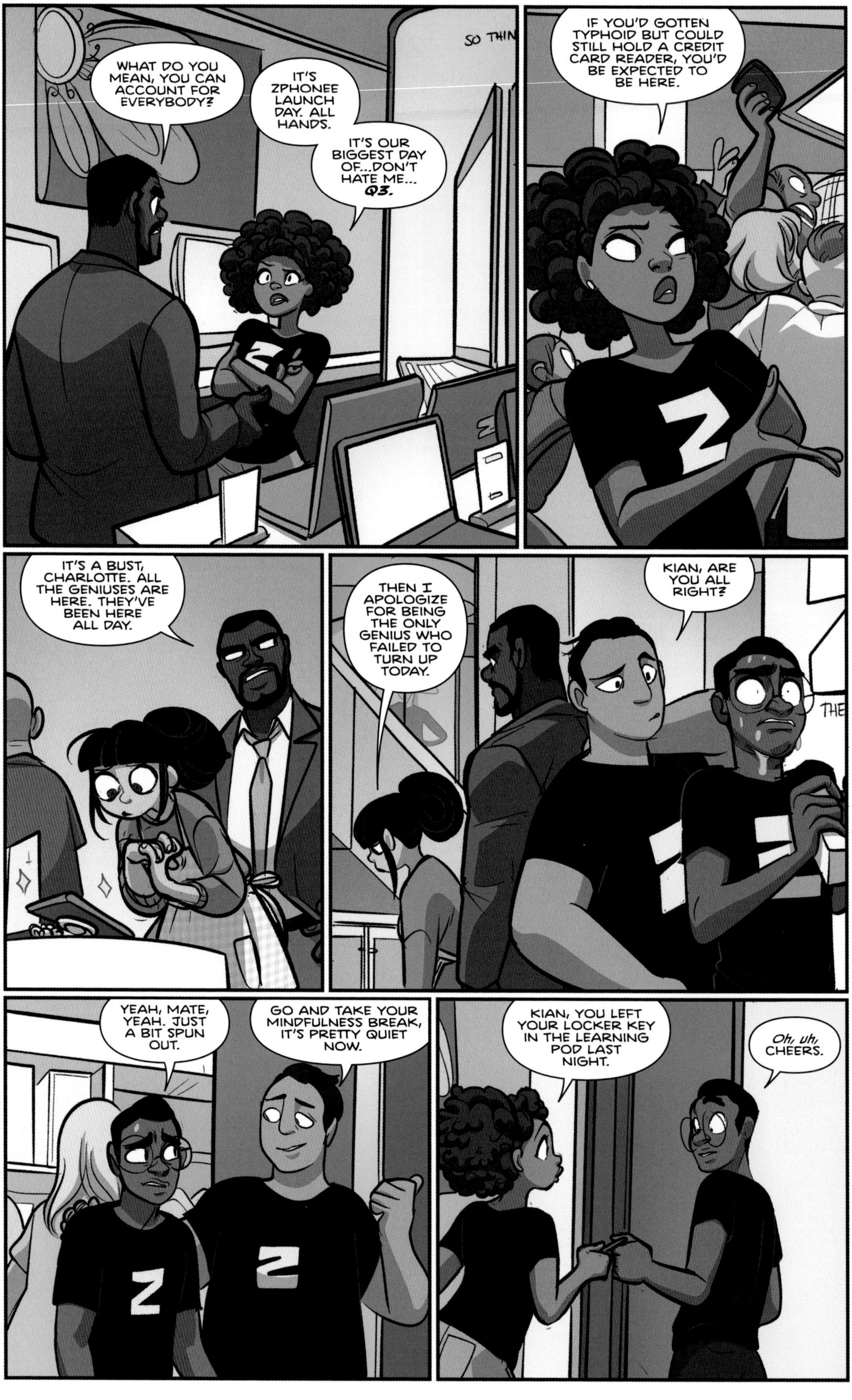
WHAT DO YOU MEAN, YOU CAN ACCOUNT FOR EVERYBODY?
IT'S ZPHONEE LAUNCH DAY. ALL HANDS.
IT'S OUR BIGGEST DAY OF...DON'T HATE ME... Q3.
SO THIN
IF YOU'D GOTTEN TYPHOID BUT COULD STILL HOLD A CREDIT CARD READER, YOU'D BE EXPECTED TO BE HERE.
IT'S A BUST, CHARLOTTE. ALL THE GENIUSES ARE HERE. THEY'VE BEEN HERE ALL DAY.
THEN I APOLOGIZE FOR BEING THE ONLY GENIUS WHO FAILED TO TURN UP TODAY.
KIAN, ARE YOU ALL RIGHT?
THE
YEAH, MATE, YEAH. JUST A BIT SPUN OUT.
GO AND TAKE YOUR MINDFULNESS BREAK, IT'S PRETTY QUIET NOW.
KIAN, YOU LEFT YOUR LOCKER KEY IN THE LEARNING POD LAST NIGHT.
*Oh, uh,* CHEERS.

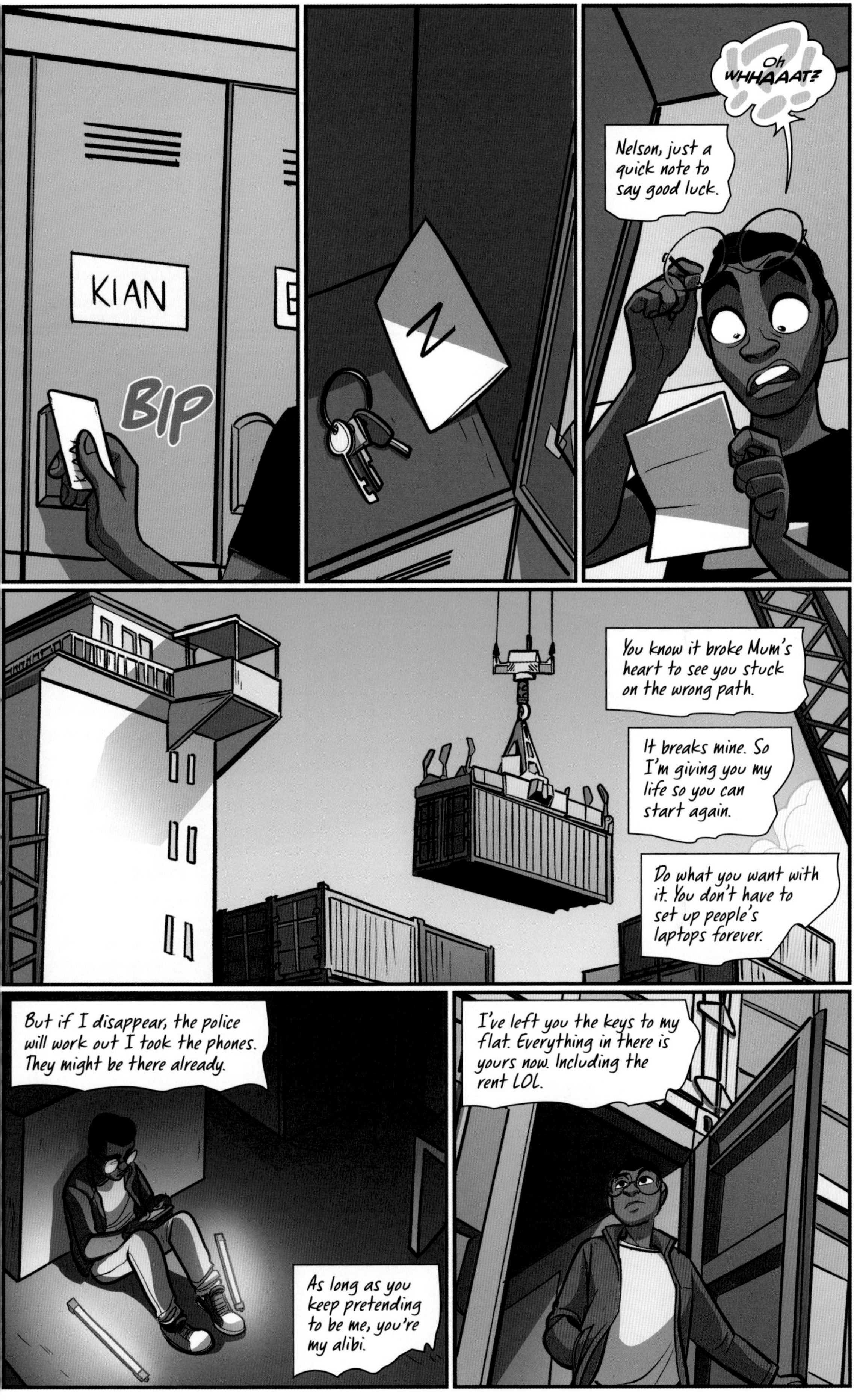
KIAN
BIP
Oh WHHAAAT?
Nelson, just a quick note to say good luck.
You know it broke Mum's heart to see you stuck on the wrong path.
It breaks mine. So I'm giving you my life so you can start again.
Do what you want with it. You don't have to set up people's laptops forever.
But if I disappear, the police will work out I took the phones. They might be there already.
As long as you keep pretending to be me, you're my alibi.
I've left you the keys to my flat. Everything in there is yours now. Including the rent LOL.

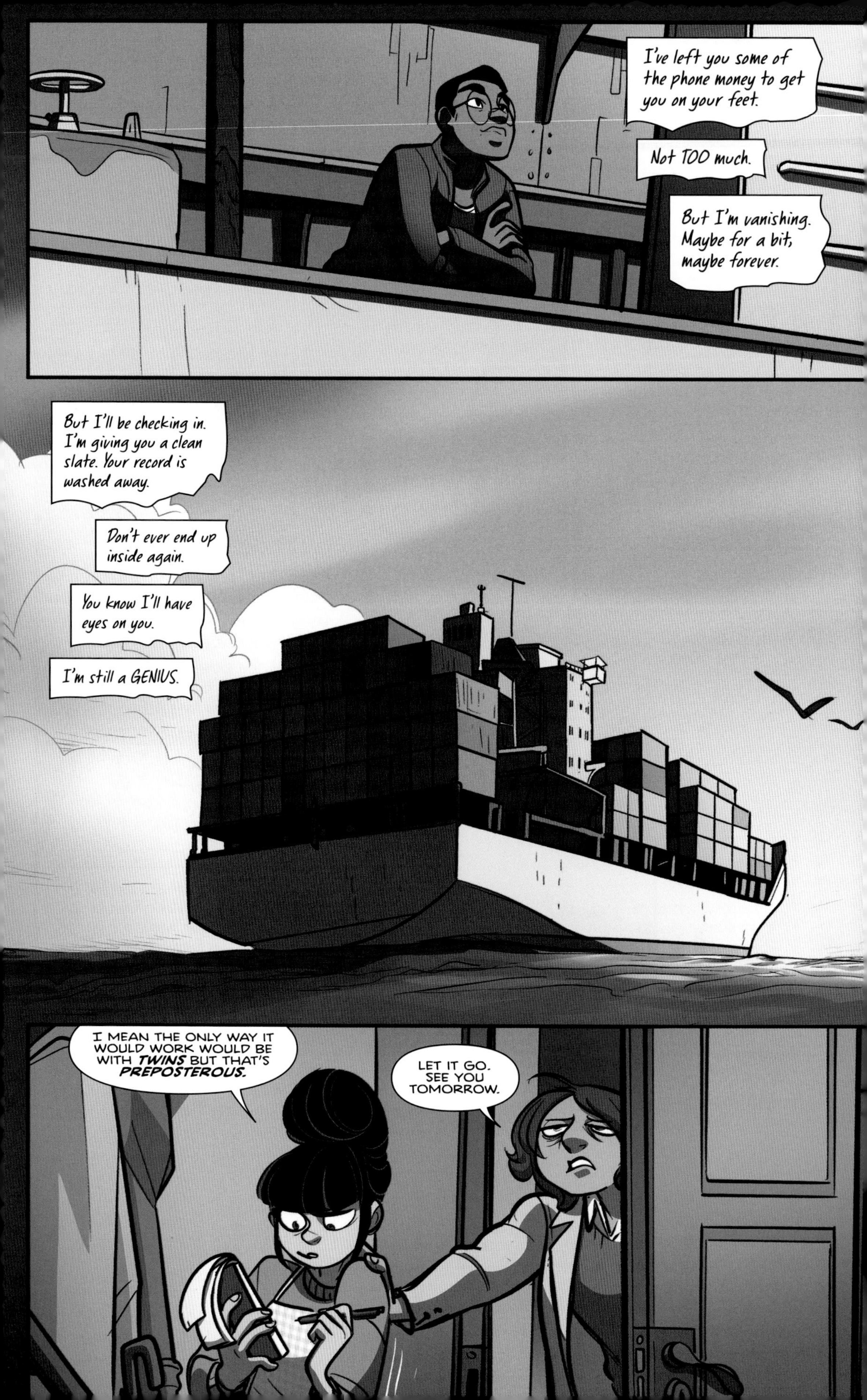
I've left you some of the phone money to get you on your feet.
Not TOO much.
But I'm vanishing. Maybe for a bit, maybe forever.
But I'll be checking in. I'm giving you a clean slate. Your record is washed away.
Don't ever end up inside again.
You know I'll have eyes on you.
I'm still a GENIUS.
I MEAN THE ONLY WAY IT WOULD WORK WOULD BE WITH *TWINS* BUT THAT'S *PREPOSTEROUS.*
LET IT GO. SEE YOU TOMORROW.

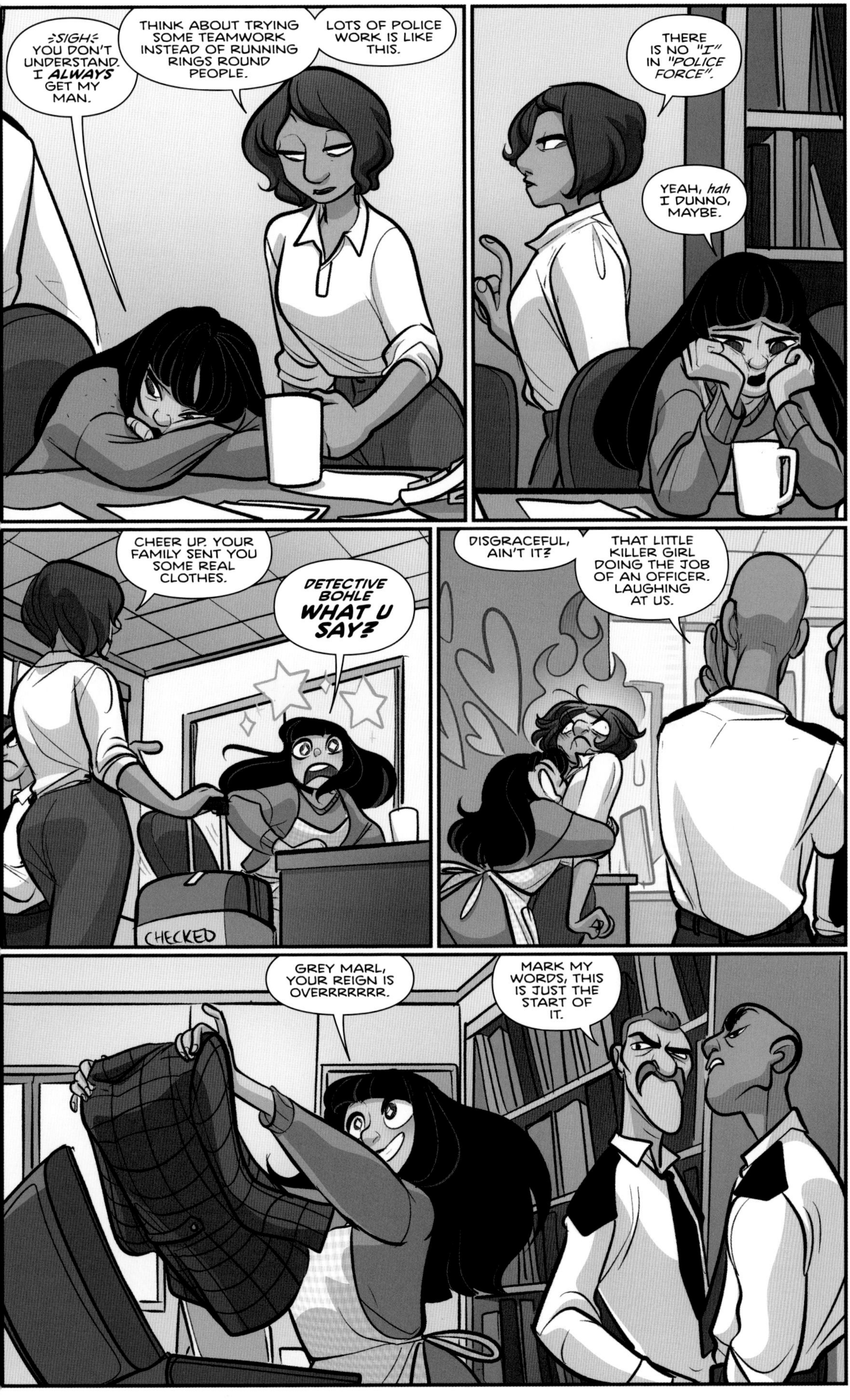
*SIGH* YOU DON'T UNDERSTAND. I **ALWAYS** GET MY MAN.
THINK ABOUT TRYING SOME TEAMWORK INSTEAD OF RUNNING RINGS ROUND PEOPLE.
LOTS OF POLICE WORK IS LIKE THIS.
THERE IS NO *"I"* IN *"POLICE FORCE"*.
YEAH, *hah* I DUNNO, MAYBE.
CHEER UP. YOUR FAMILY SENT YOU SOME REAL CLOTHES.
*DETECTIVE BOHLE* **WHAT U SAY?**
CHECKED
DISGRACEFUL, AIN'T IT?
THAT LITTLE KILLER GIRL DOING THE JOB OF AN OFFICER. LAUGHING AT US.
GREY MARL, YOUR REIGN IS OVERRRRRRR.
MARK MY WORDS, THIS IS JUST THE START OF IT.

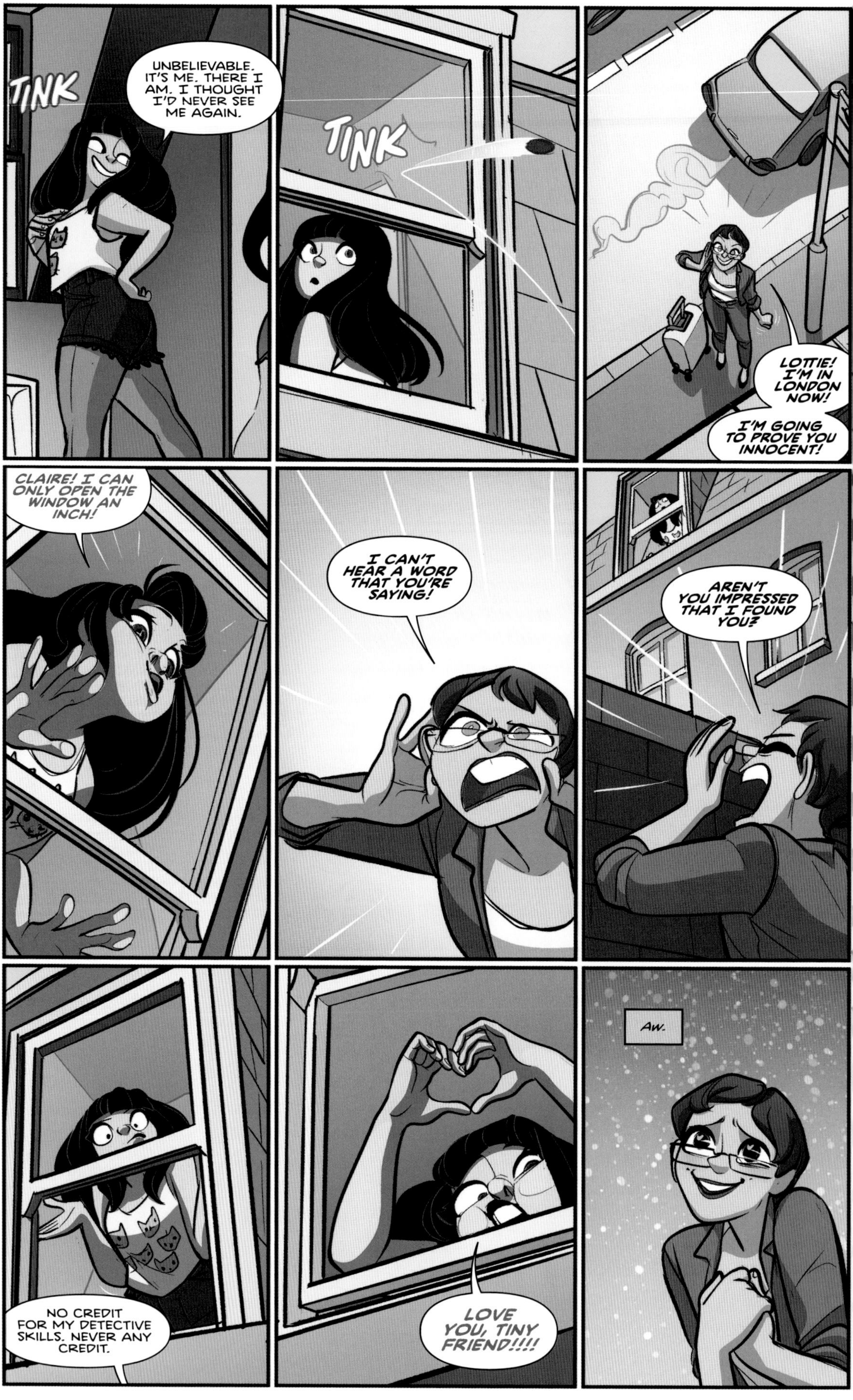
TINK
UNBELIEVABLE. IT'S ME. THERE I AM. I THOUGHT I'D NEVER SEE ME AGAIN.
TINK
LOTTIE! I'M IN LONDON NOW!
I'M GOING TO PROVE YOU INNOCENT!
CLAIRE! I CAN ONLY OPEN THE WINDOW AN INCH!
I CAN'T HEAR A WORD THAT YOU'RE SAYING!
AREN'T YOU IMPRESSED THAT I FOUND YOU?
NO CREDIT FOR MY DETECTIVE SKILLS. NEVER ANY CREDIT.
LOVE YOU, TINY FRIEND!!!!
AW.

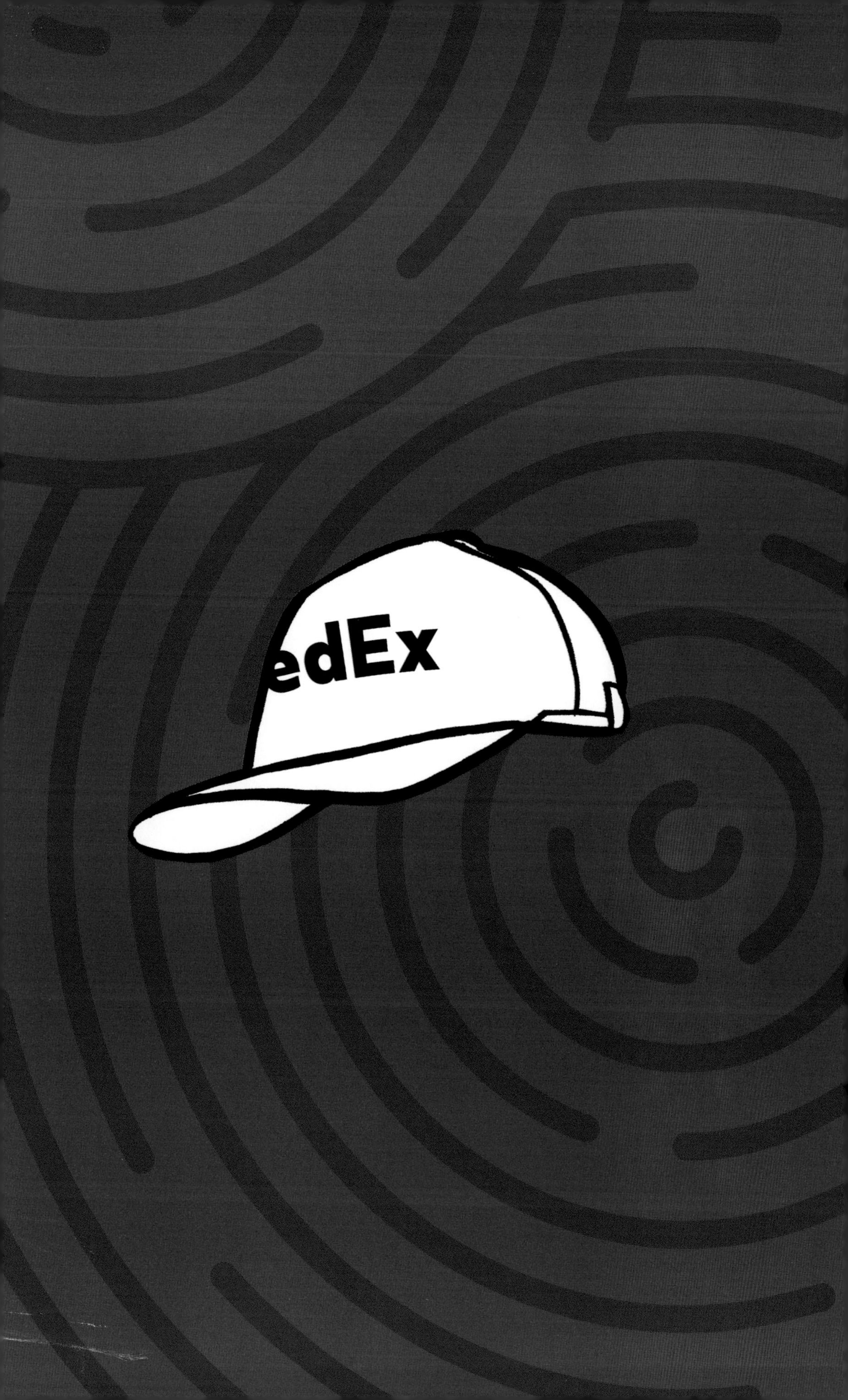
edEx

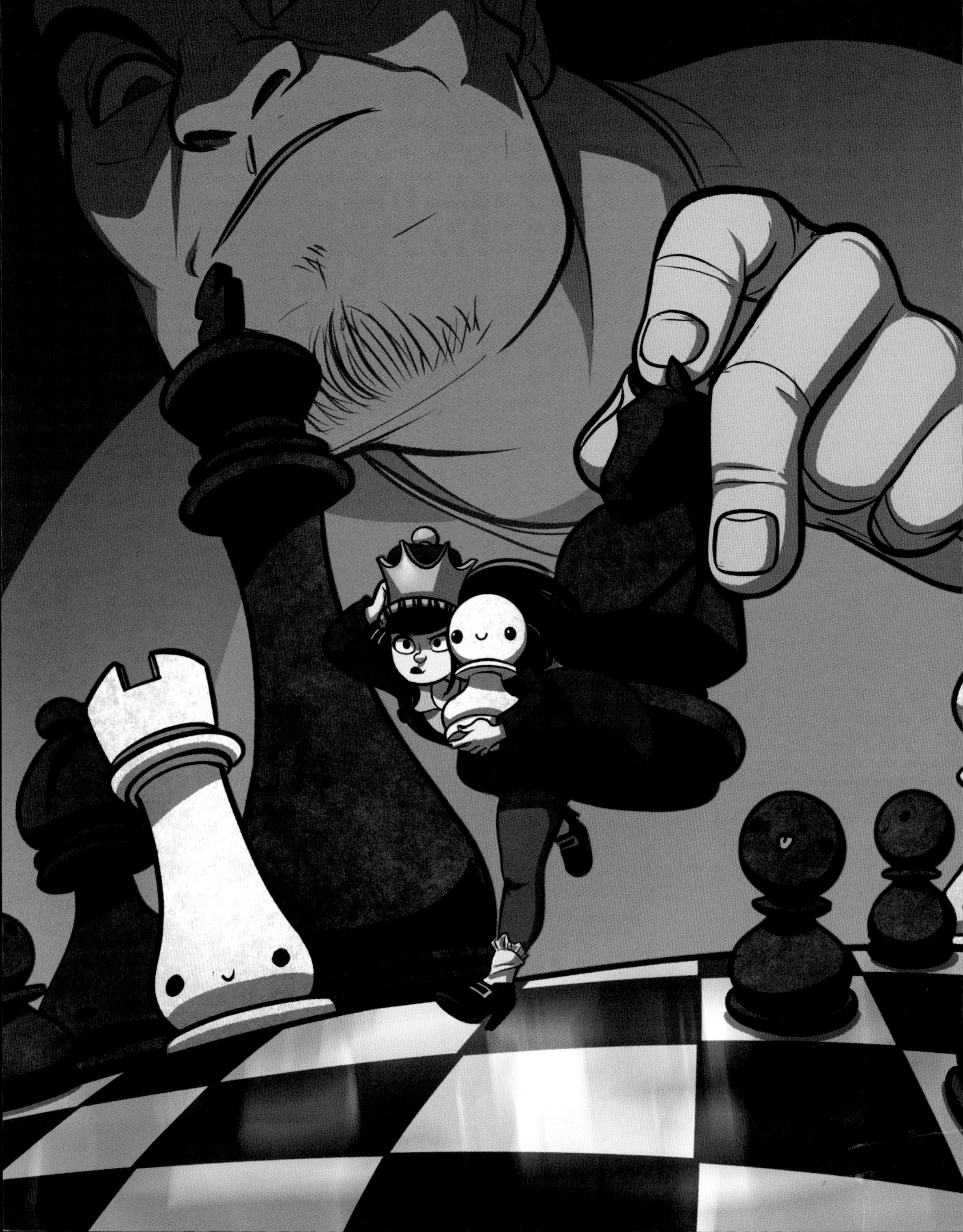

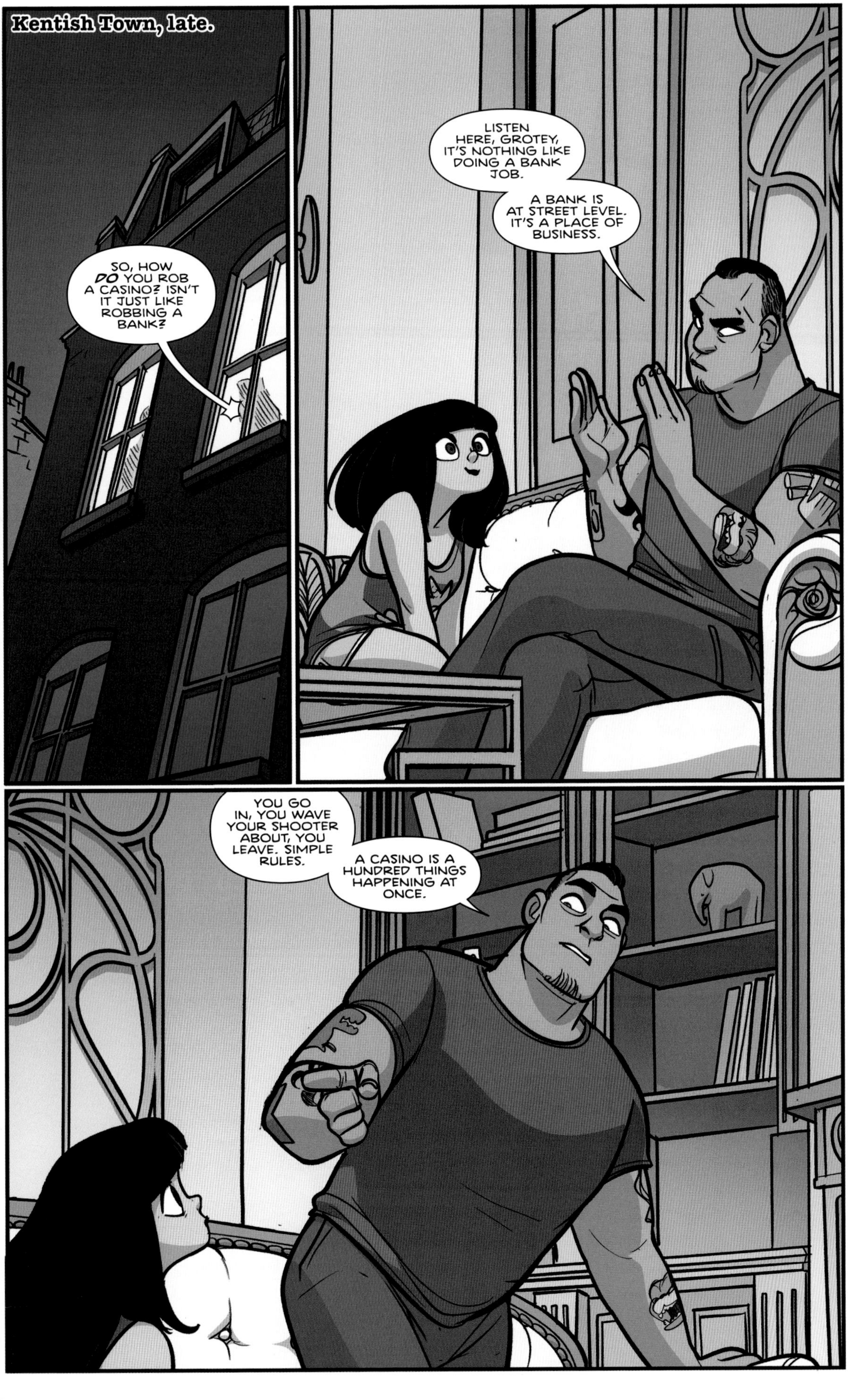
Kentish Town, late.
SO, HOW *DO* YOU ROB A CASINO? ISN'T IT JUST LIKE ROBBING A BANK?
LISTEN HERE, GROTEY, IT'S NOTHING LIKE DOING A BANK JOB.
A BANK IS AT STREET LEVEL. IT'S A PLACE OF BUSINESS.
YOU GO IN, YOU WAVE YOUR SHOOTER ABOUT, YOU LEAVE. SIMPLE RULES.
A CASINO IS A HUNDRED THINGS HAPPENING AT ONCE.

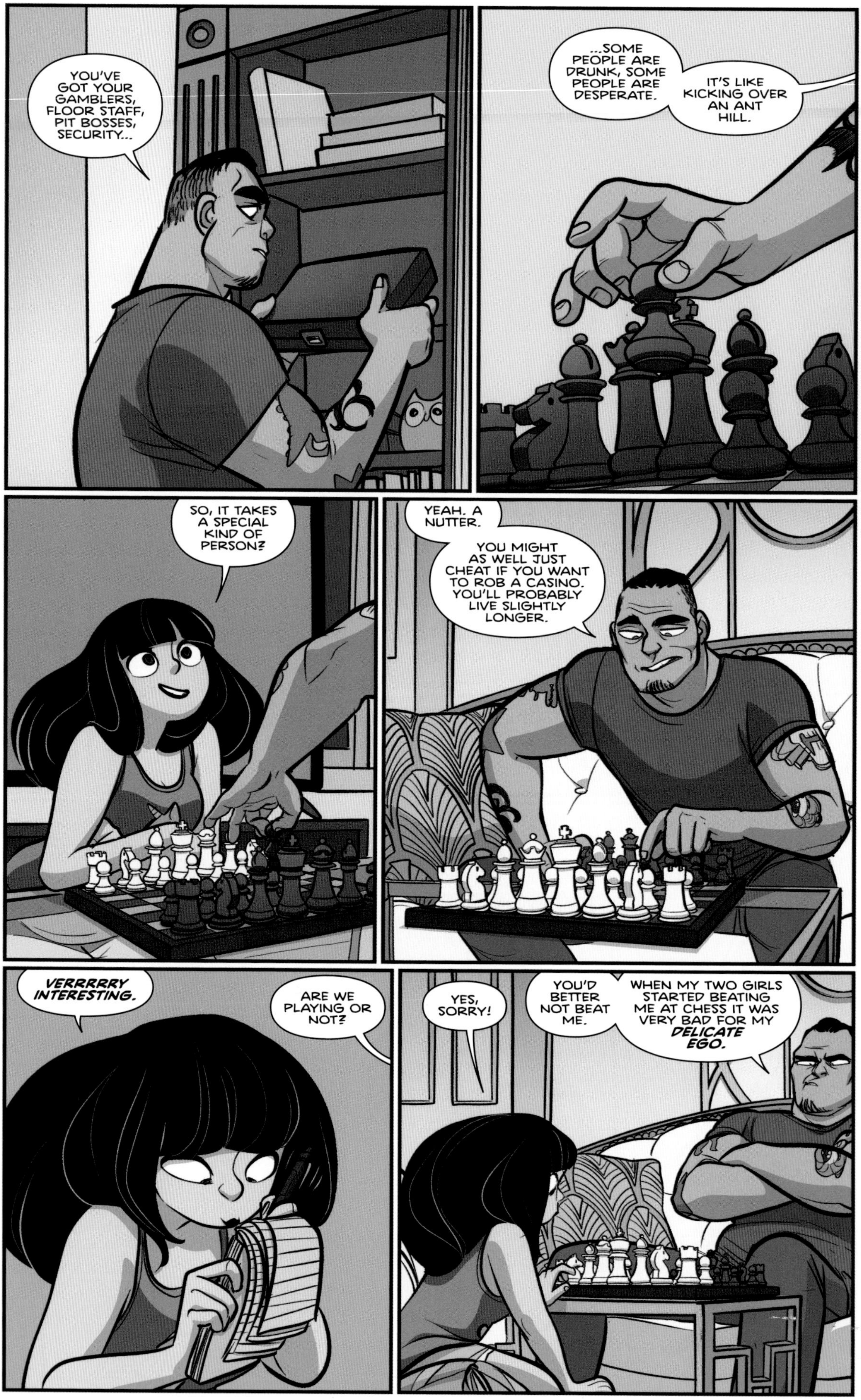
YOU'VE GOT YOUR GAMBLERS, FLOOR STAFF, PIT BOSSES, SECURITY...
...SOME PEOPLE ARE DRUNK, SOME PEOPLE ARE DESPERATE.
IT'S LIKE KICKING OVER AN ANT HILL.
SO, IT TAKES A SPECIAL KIND OF PERSON?
YEAH. A NUTTER.
YOU MIGHT AS WELL JUST CHEAT IF YOU WANT TO ROB A CASINO. YOU'LL PROBABLY LIVE SLIGHTLY LONGER.
VERRRRRY INTERESTING.
ARE WE PLAYING OR NOT?
YES, SORRY!
YOU'D BETTER NOT BEAT ME.
WHEN MY TWO GIRLS STARTED BEATING ME AT CHESS IT WAS VERY BAD FOR MY DELICATE EGO.

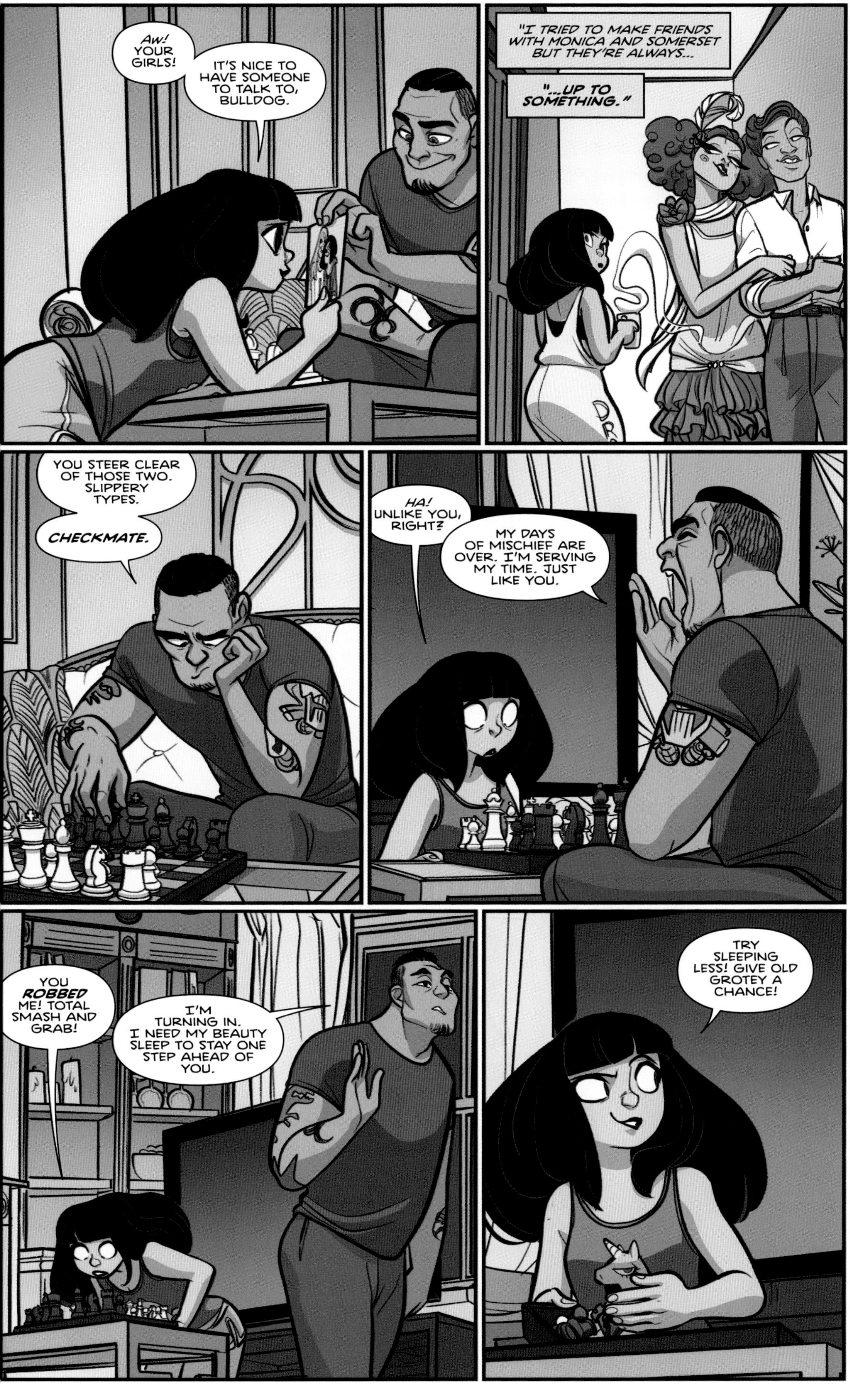
AW! YOUR GIRLS!
IT'S NICE TO HAVE SOMEONE TO TALK TO, BULLDOG.
"I TRIED TO MAKE FRIENDS WITH MONICA AND SOMERSET BUT THEY'RE ALWAYS...
"...UP TO SOMETHING."
YOU STEER CLEAR OF THOSE TWO. SLIPPERY TYPES.
CHECKMATE.
HA! UNLIKE YOU, RIGHT?
MY DAYS OF MISCHIEF ARE OVER. I'M SERVING MY TIME. JUST LIKE YOU.
YOU ROBBED ME! TOTAL SMASH AND GRAB!
I'M TURNING IN. I NEED MY BEAUTY SLEEP TO STAY ONE STEP AHEAD OF YOU.
TRY SLEEPING LESS! GIVE OLD GROTEY A CHANCE!

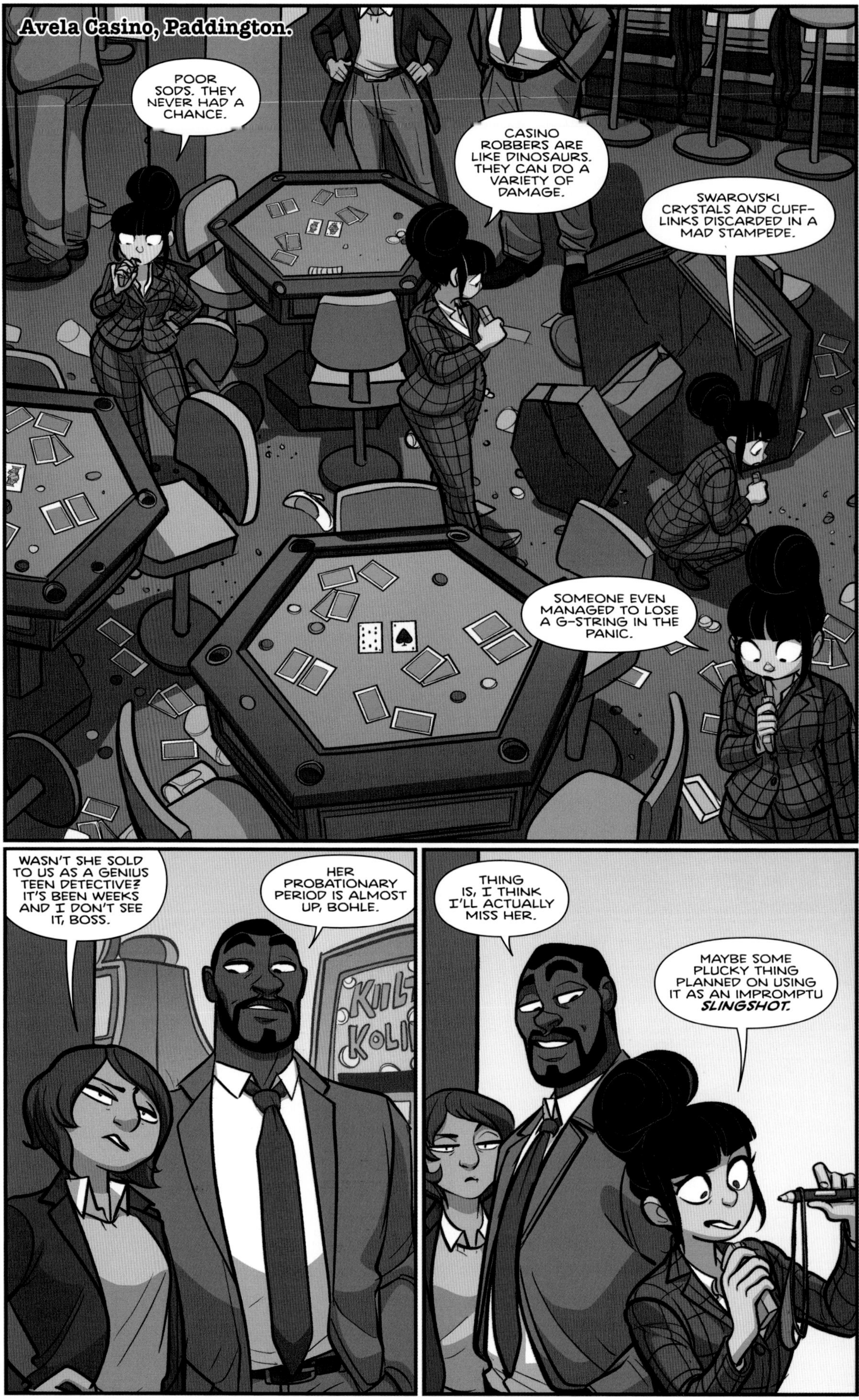
Avela Casino, Paddington.
POOR SODS. THEY NEVER HAD A CHANCE.
CASINO ROBBERS ARE LIKE DINOSAURS. THEY CAN DO A VARIETY OF DAMAGE.
SWAROVSKI CRYSTALS AND CUFF-LINKS DISCARDED IN A MAD STAMPEDE.
SOMEONE EVEN MANAGED TO LOSE A G-STRING IN THE PANIC.
WASN'T SHE SOLD TO US AS A GENIUS TEEN DETECTIVE? IT'S BEEN WEEKS AND I DON'T SEE IT, BOSS.
HER PROBATIONARY PERIOD IS ALMOST UP, BOHLE.
THING IS, I THINK I'LL ACTUALLY MISS HER.
MAYBE SOME PLUCKY THING PLANNED ON USING IT AS AN IMPROMPTU *SLINGSHOT.*

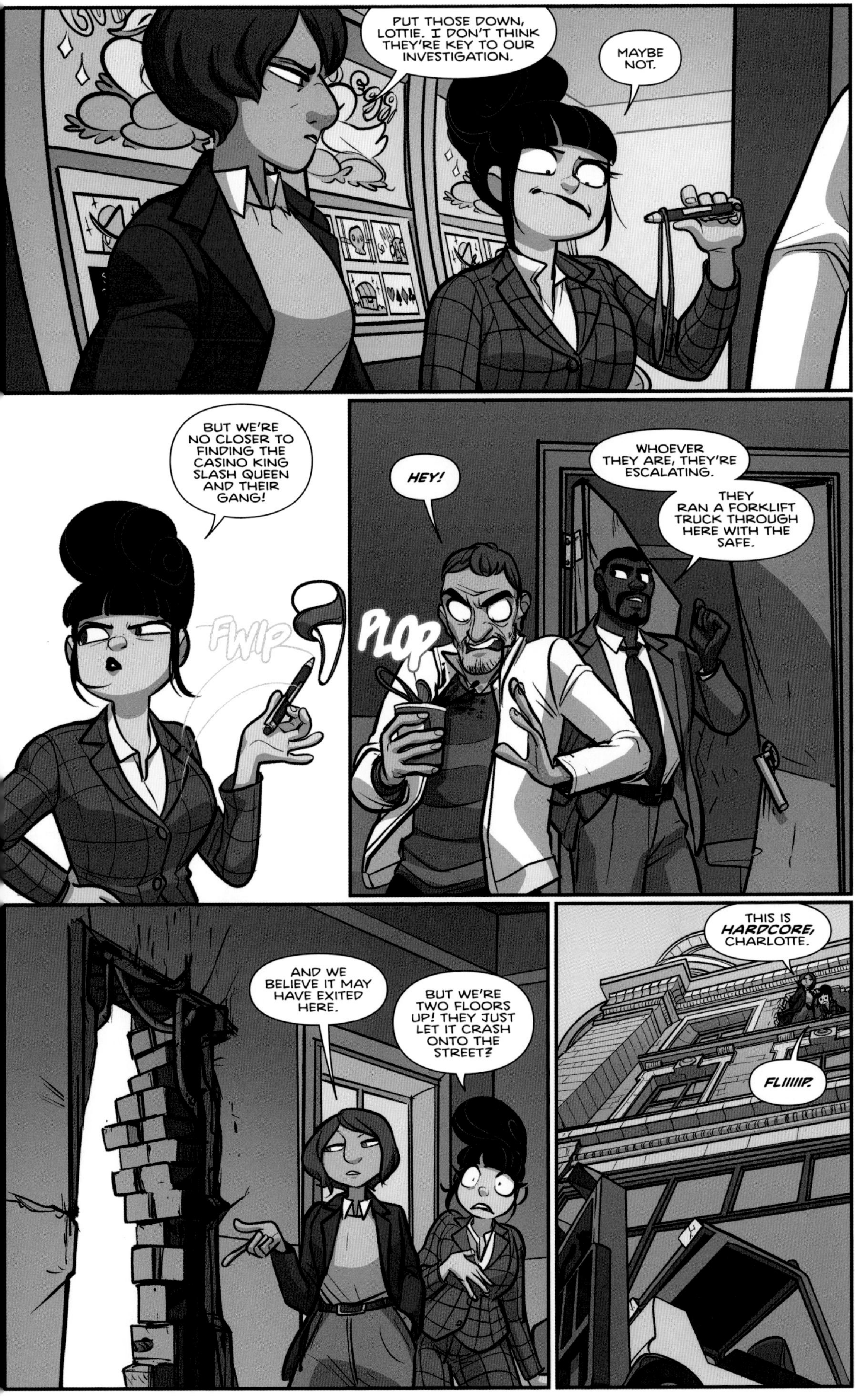

PUT THOSE DOWN, LOTTIE. I DON'T THINK THEY'RE KEY TO OUR INVESTIGATION.
MAYBE NOT.
BUT WE'RE NO CLOSER TO FINDING THE CASINO KING SLASH QUEEN AND THEIR GANG!
FWIP
PLOP
HEY!
WHOEVER THEY ARE, THEY'RE ESCALATING.
THEY RAN A FORKLIFT TRUCK THROUGH HERE WITH THE SAFE.
AND WE BELIEVE IT MAY HAVE EXITED HERE.
BUT WE'RE TWO FLOORS UP! THEY JUST LET IT CRASH ONTO THE STREET?
THIS IS *HARDCORE,* CHARLOTTE.
FLIIIIIP.

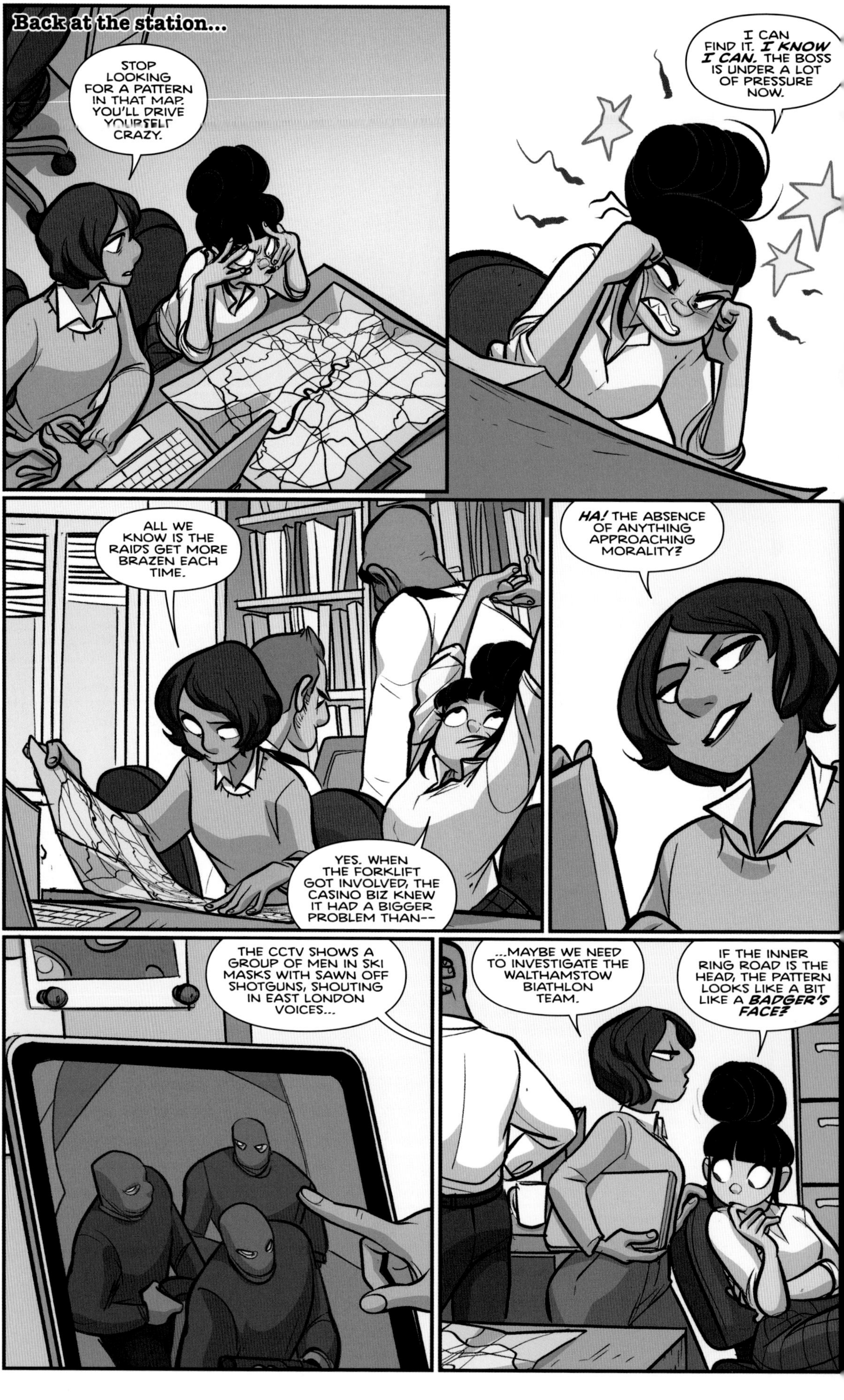
Back at the station...
STOP LOOKING FOR A PATTERN IN THAT MAP. YOU'LL DRIVE YOURSELF CRAZY.
I CAN FIND IT. I KNOW I CAN. THE BOSS IS UNDER A LOT OF PRESSURE NOW.
ALL WE KNOW IS THE RAIDS GET MORE BRAZEN EACH TIME.
YES. WHEN THE FORKLIFT GOT INVOLVED, THE CASINO BIZ KNEW IT HAD A BIGGER PROBLEM THAN--
HA! THE ABSENCE OF ANYTHING APPROACHING MORALITY?
THE CCTV SHOWS A GROUP OF MEN IN SKI MASKS WITH SAWN OFF SHOTGUNS, SHOUTING IN EAST LONDON VOICES...
...MAYBE WE NEED TO INVESTIGATE THE WALTHAMSTOW BIATHLON TEAM.
IF THE INNER RING ROAD IS THE HEAD, THE PATTERN LOOKS LIKE A BIT LIKE A BADGER'S FACE?

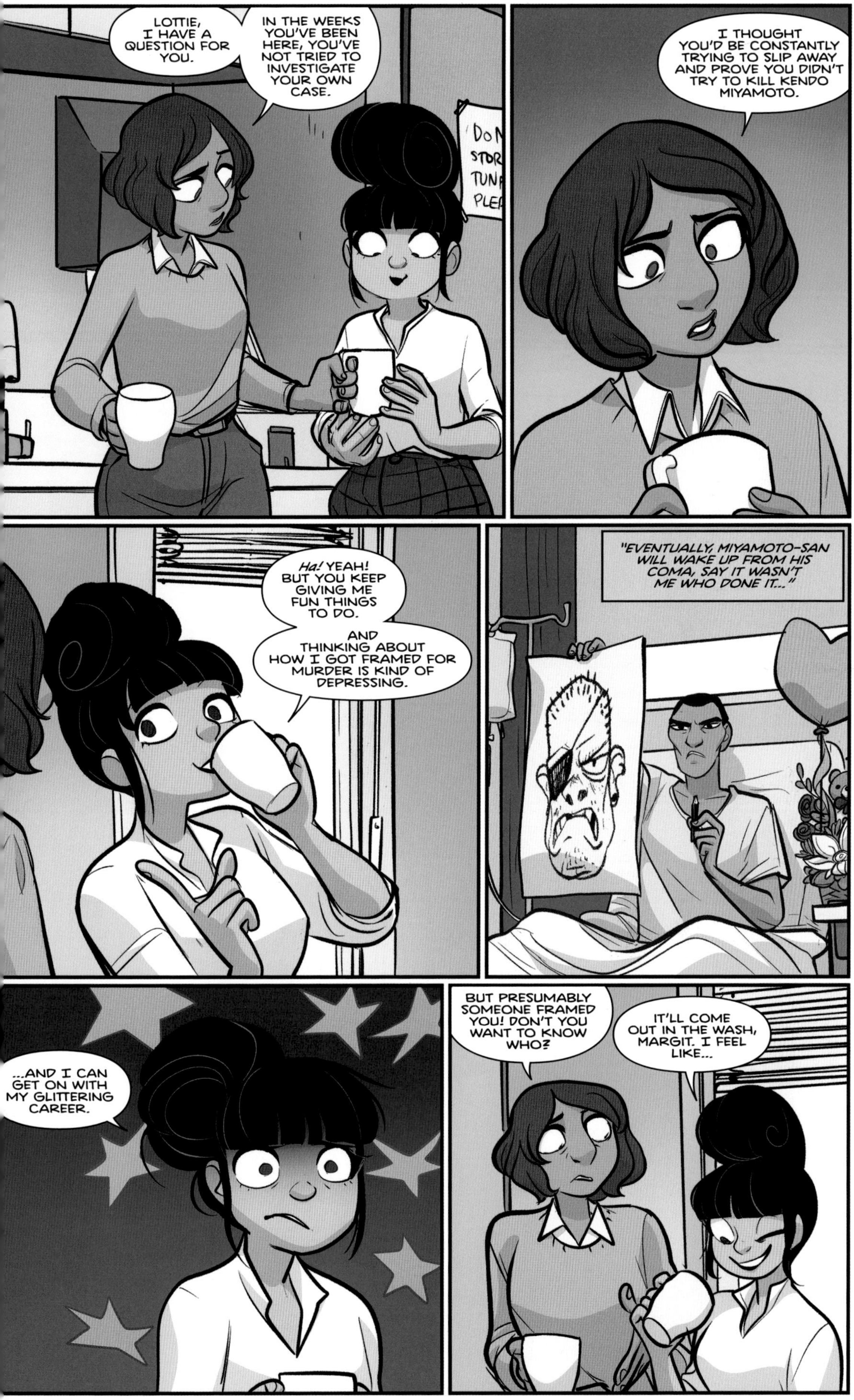
LOTTIE, I HAVE A QUESTION FOR YOU.
IN THE WEEKS YOU'VE BEEN HERE, YOU'VE NOT TRIED TO INVESTIGATE YOUR OWN CASE.
I THOUGHT YOU'D BE CONSTANTLY TRYING TO SLIP AWAY AND PROVE YOU DIDN'T TRY TO KILL KENDO MIYAMOTO.
*Ha!* YEAH! BUT YOU KEEP GIVING ME FUN THINGS TO DO.
AND THINKING ABOUT HOW I GOT FRAMED FOR MURDER IS KIND OF DEPRESSING.
"EVENTUALLY, MIYAMOTO-SAN WILL WAKE UP FROM HIS COMA, SAY IT WASN'T ME WHO DONE IT..."
...AND I CAN GET ON WITH MY GLITTERING CAREER.
BUT PRESUMABLY SOMEONE FRAMED YOU! DON'T YOU WANT TO KNOW WHO?
IT'LL COME OUT IN THE WASH, MARGIT. I FEEL LIKE...

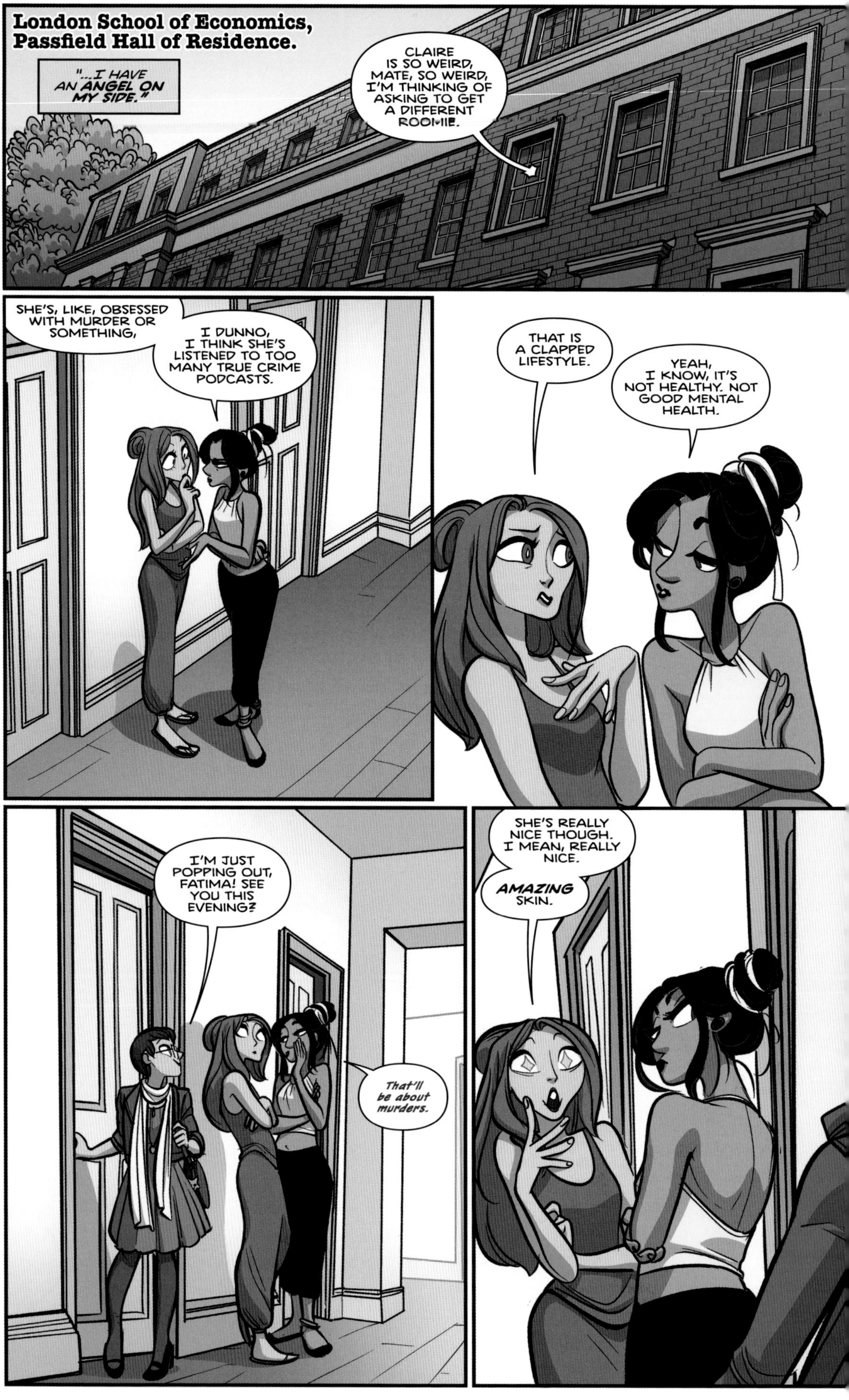
London School of Economics,
Passfield Hall of Residence.
"...I HAVE AN ANGEL ON MY SIDE."
CLAIRE IS SO WEIRD, MATE, SO WEIRD, I'M THINKING OF ASKING TO GET A DIFFERENT ROOMIE.
SHE'S, LIKE, OBSESSED WITH MURDER OR SOMETHING,
I DUNNO, I THINK SHE'S LISTENED TO TOO MANY TRUE CRIME PODCASTS.
THAT IS A CLAPPED LIFESTYLE.
YEAH, I KNOW, IT'S NOT HEALTHY. NOT GOOD MENTAL HEALTH.
I'M JUST POPPING OUT, FATIMA! SEE YOU THIS EVENING?
That'll be about murders.
SHE'S REALLY NICE THOUGH. I MEAN, REALLY NICE.
AMAZING SKIN.

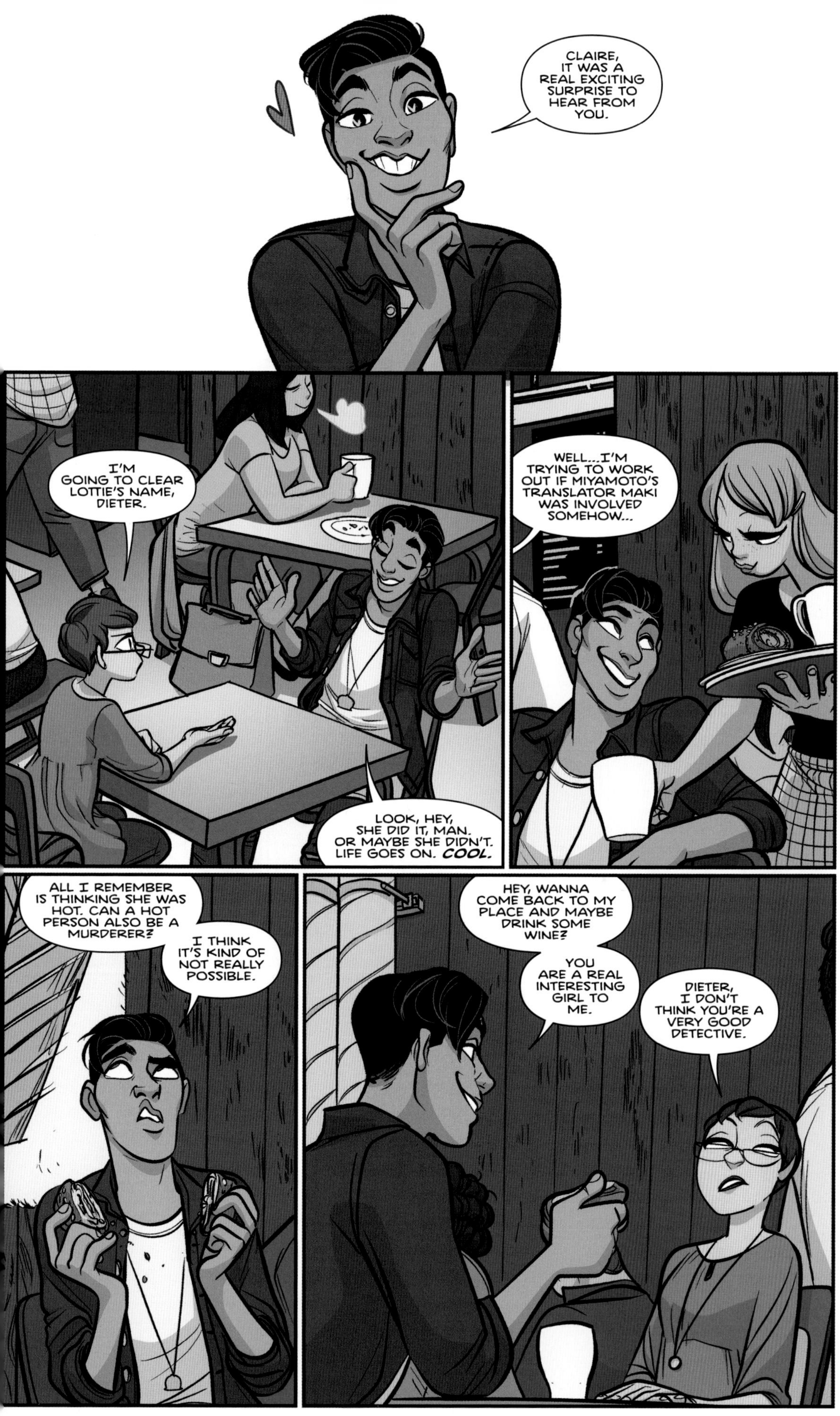
CLAIRE, IT WAS A REAL EXCITING SURPRISE TO HEAR FROM YOU.
I'M GOING TO CLEAR LOTTIE'S NAME, DIETER.
LOOK, HEY, SHE DID IT, MAN. OR MAYBE SHE DIDN'T. LIFE GOES ON. COOL.
WELL...I'M TRYING TO WORK OUT IF MIYAMOTO'S TRANSLATOR MAKI WAS INVOLVED SOMEHOW...
ALL I REMEMBER IS THINKING SHE WAS HOT. CAN A HOT PERSON ALSO BE A MURDERER?
I THINK IT'S KIND OF NOT REALLY POSSIBLE.
HEY, WANNA COME BACK TO MY PLACE AND MAYBE DRINK SOME WINE?
YOU ARE A REAL INTERESTING GIRL TO ME.
DIETER, I DON'T THINK YOU'RE A VERY GOOD DETECTIVE.

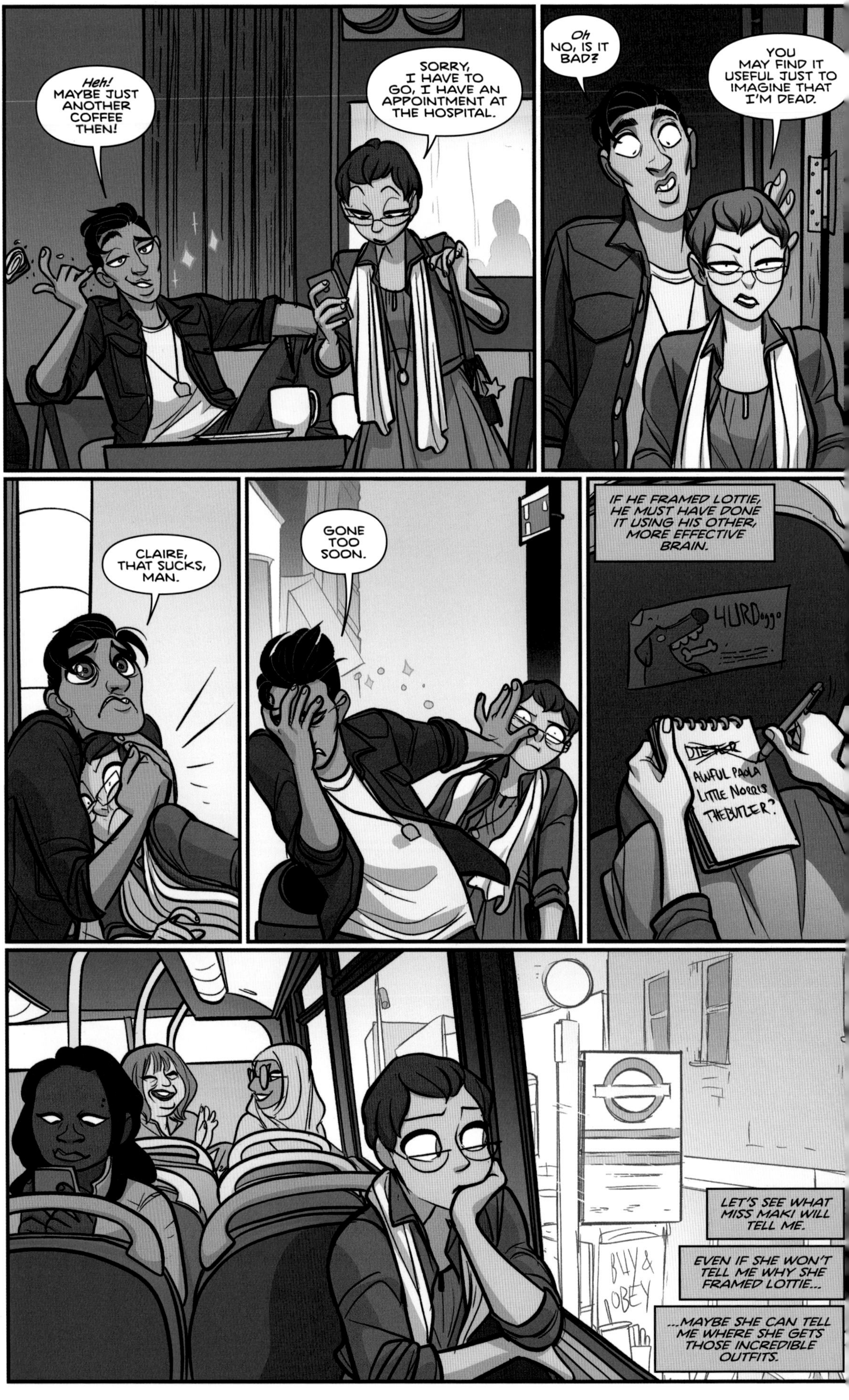
Heh! MAYBE JUST ANOTHER COFFEE THEN!
SORRY, I HAVE TO GO, I HAVE AN APPOINTMENT AT THE HOSPITAL.
Oh NO, IS IT BAD?
YOU MAY FIND IT USEFUL JUST TO IMAGINE THAT I'M DEAD.
CLAIRE, THAT SUCKS, MAN.
GONE TOO SOON.
IF HE FRAMED LOTTIE, HE MUST HAVE DONE IT USING HIS OTHER, MORE EFFECTIVE BRAIN.
AWFUL PAOLA
LITTLE NORRIS
THE BUTLER?
LET'S SEE WHAT MISS MAKI WILL TELL ME.
EVEN IF SHE WON'T TELL ME WHY SHE FRAMED LOTTIE...
...MAYBE SHE CAN TELL ME WHERE SHE GETS THOSE INCREDIBLE OUTFITS.

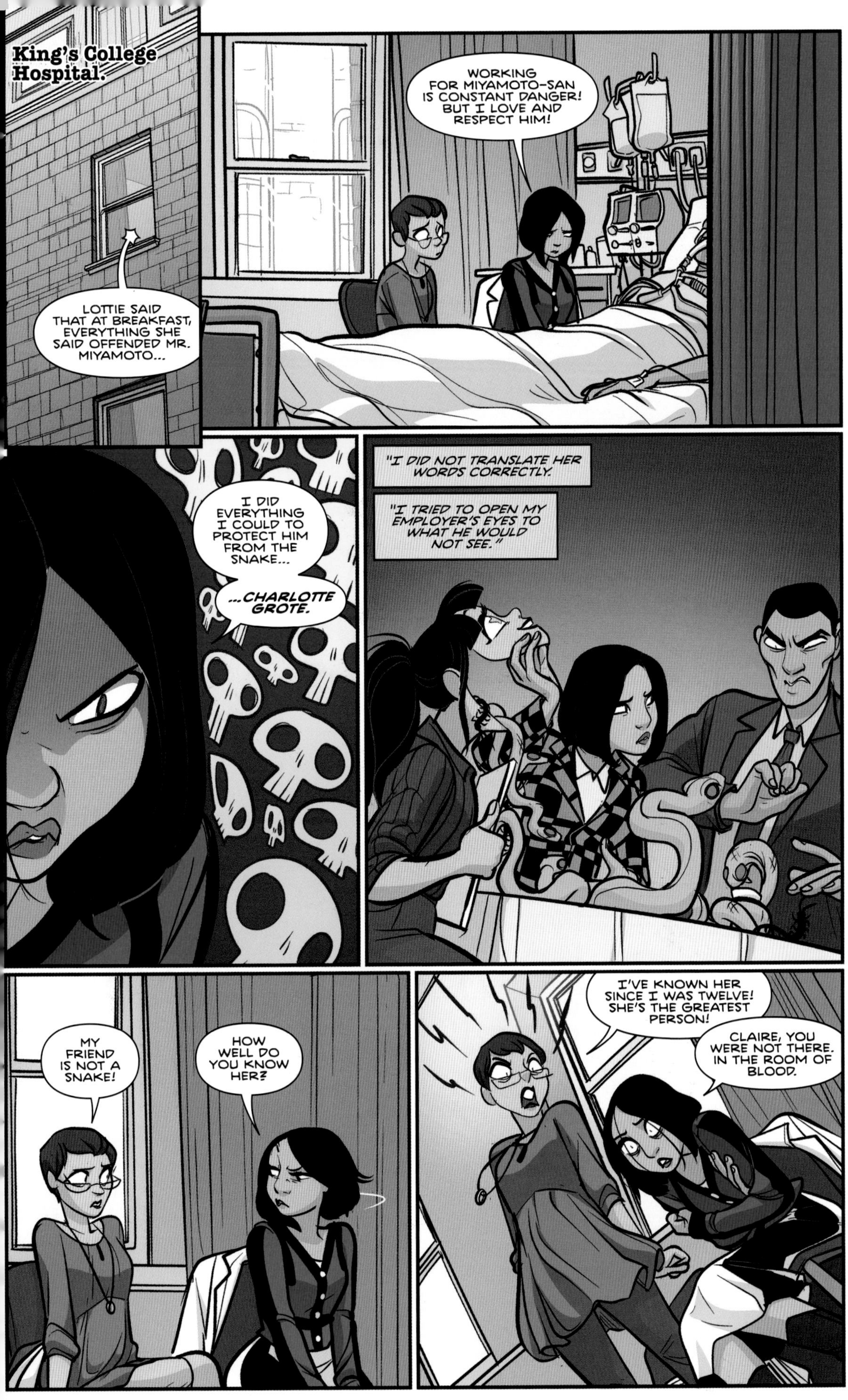
King's College Hospital.
LOTTIE SAID THAT AT BREAKFAST, EVERYTHING SHE SAID OFFENDED MR. MIYAMOTO...
WORKING FOR MIYAMOTO-SAN IS CONSTANT DANGER! BUT I LOVE AND RESPECT HIM!
I DID EVERYTHING I COULD TO PROTECT HIM FROM THE SNAKE...
...CHARLOTTE GROTE.
"I DID NOT TRANSLATE HER WORDS CORRECTLY.
"I TRIED TO OPEN MY EMPLOYER'S EYES TO WHAT HE WOULD NOT SEE."
MY FRIEND IS NOT A SNAKE!
HOW WELL DO YOU KNOW HER?
I'VE KNOWN HER SINCE I WAS TWELVE! SHE'S THE GREATEST PERSON!
CLAIRE, YOU WERE NOT THERE. IN THE ROOM OF BLOOD.

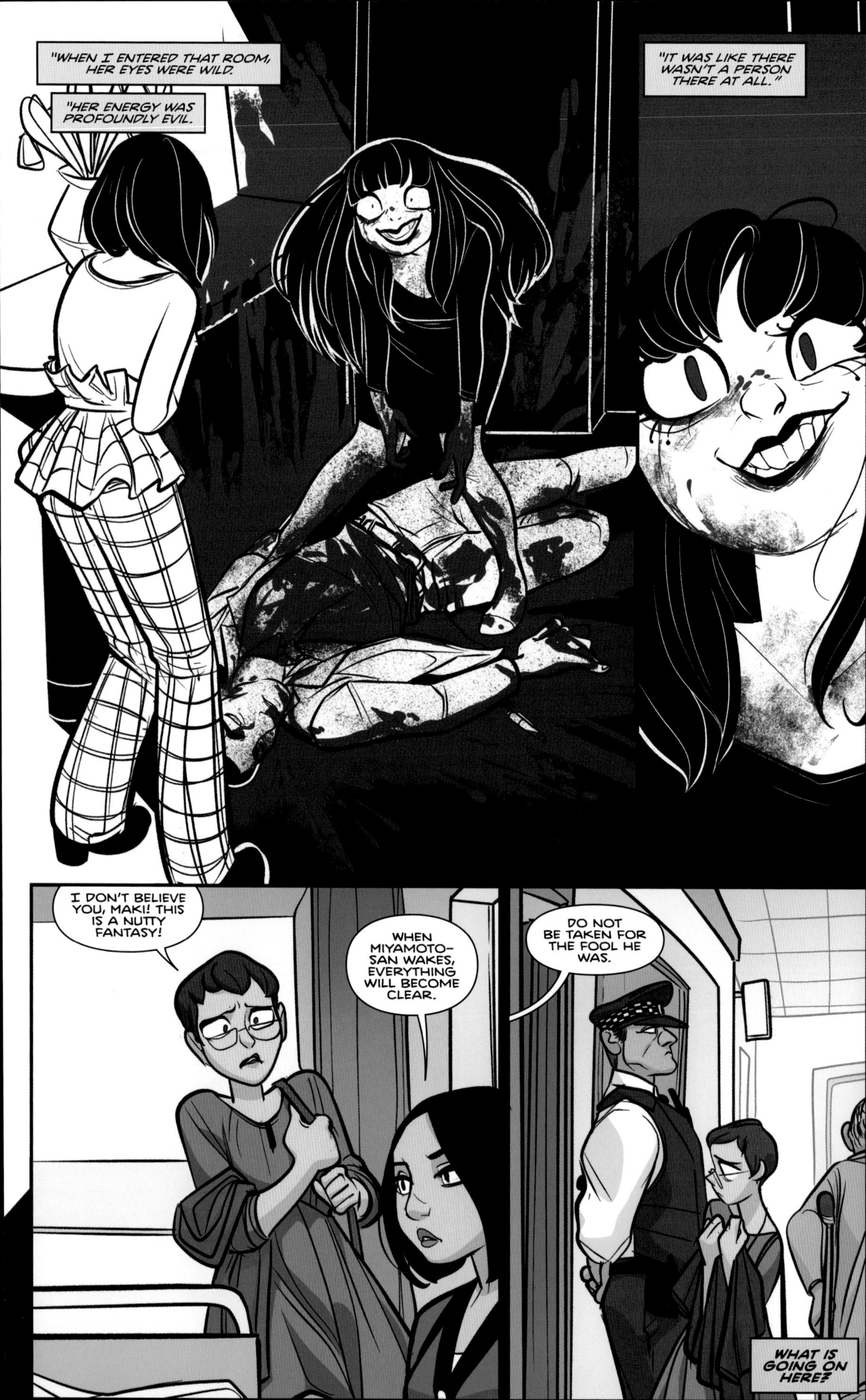
"WHEN I ENTERED THAT ROOM, HER EYES WERE WILD.
"HER ENERGY WAS PROFOUNDLY EVIL.
"IT WAS LIKE THERE WASN'T A PERSON THERE AT ALL."
I DON'T BELIEVE YOU, MAKI! THIS IS A NUTTY FANTASY!
WHEN MIYAMOTO-SAN WAKES, EVERYTHING WILL BECOME CLEAR.
DO NOT BE TAKEN FOR THE FOOL HE WAS.
WHAT IS GOING ON HERE?

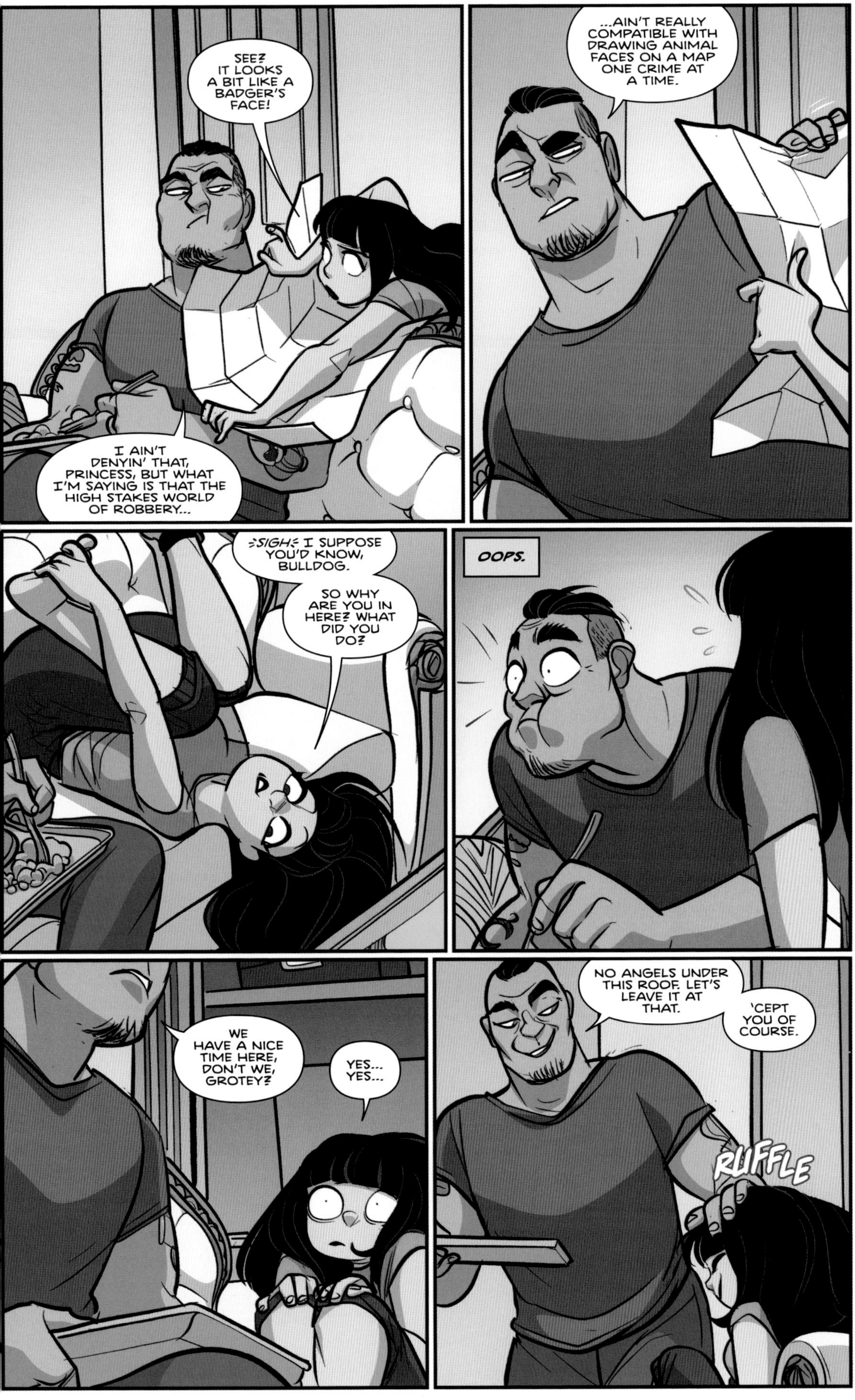
SEE? IT LOOKS A BIT LIKE A BADGER'S FACE!
I AIN'T DENYIN' THAT, PRINCESS, BUT WHAT I'M SAYING IS THAT THE HIGH STAKES WORLD OF ROBBERY...
...AIN'T REALLY COMPATIBLE WITH DRAWING ANIMAL FACES ON A MAP ONE CRIME AT A TIME.
SIGH I SUPPOSE YOU'D KNOW, BULLDOG.
SO WHY ARE YOU IN HERE? WHAT DID YOU DO?
OOPS.
WE HAVE A NICE TIME HERE, DON'T WE, GROTEY?
YES... YES...
NO ANGELS UNDER THIS ROOF. LET'S LEAVE IT AT THAT.
'CEPT YOU OF COURSE.
RUFFLE

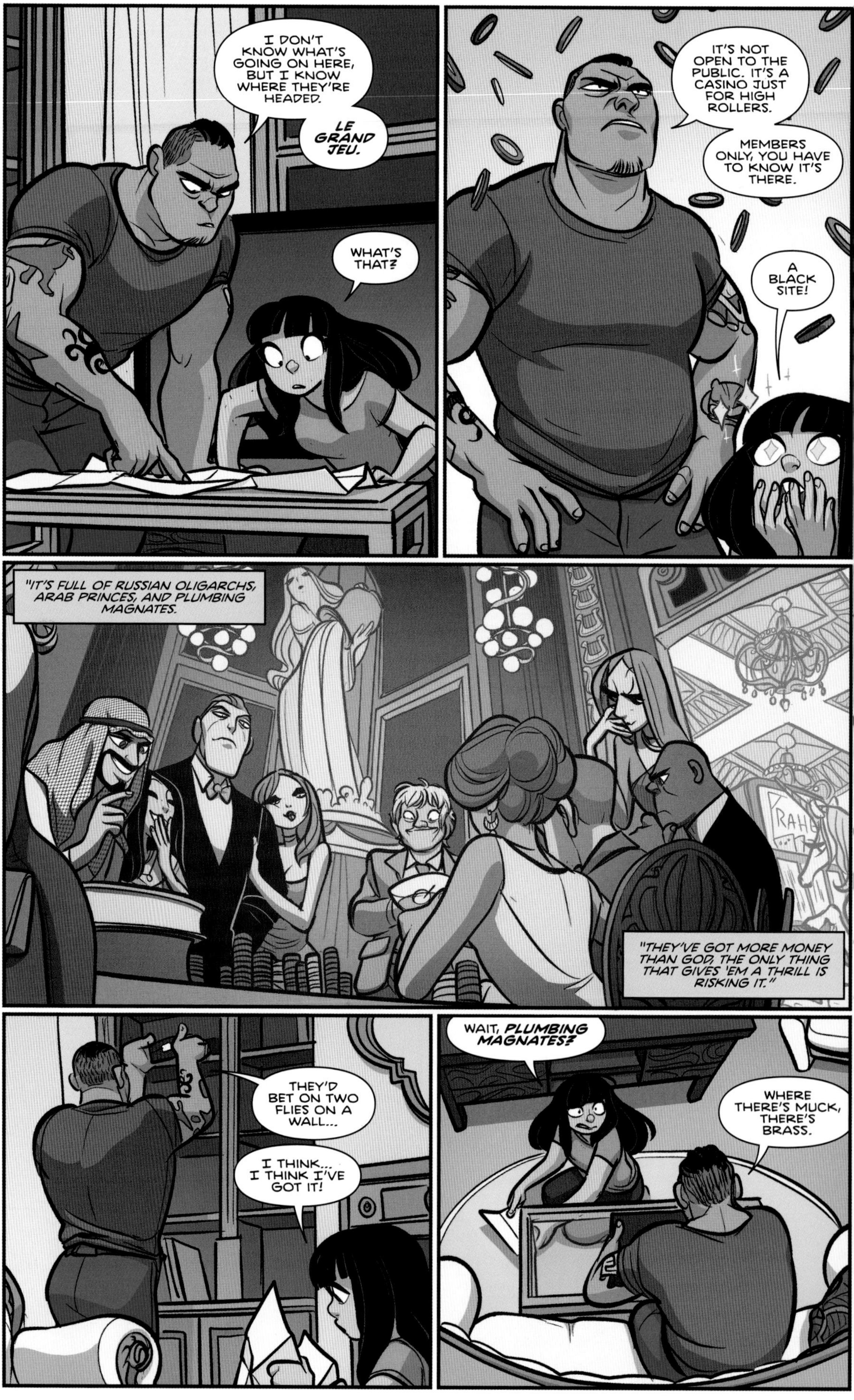
I DON'T KNOW WHAT'S GOING ON HERE, BUT I KNOW WHERE THEY'RE HEADED.
LE GRAND JEU.
WHAT'S THAT?
IT'S NOT OPEN TO THE PUBLIC. IT'S A CASINO JUST FOR HIGH ROLLERS.
MEMBERS ONLY, YOU HAVE TO KNOW IT'S THERE.
A BLACK SITE!
"IT'S FULL OF RUSSIAN OLIGARCHS, ARAB PRINCES, AND PLUMBING MAGNATES.
"THEY'VE GOT MORE MONEY THAN GOD, THE ONLY THING THAT GIVES 'EM A THRILL IS RISKING IT."
THEY'D BET ON TWO FLIES ON A WALL...
I THINK... I THINK I'VE GOT IT!
WAIT, PLUMBING MAGNATES?
WHERE THERE'S MUCK, THERE'S BRASS.

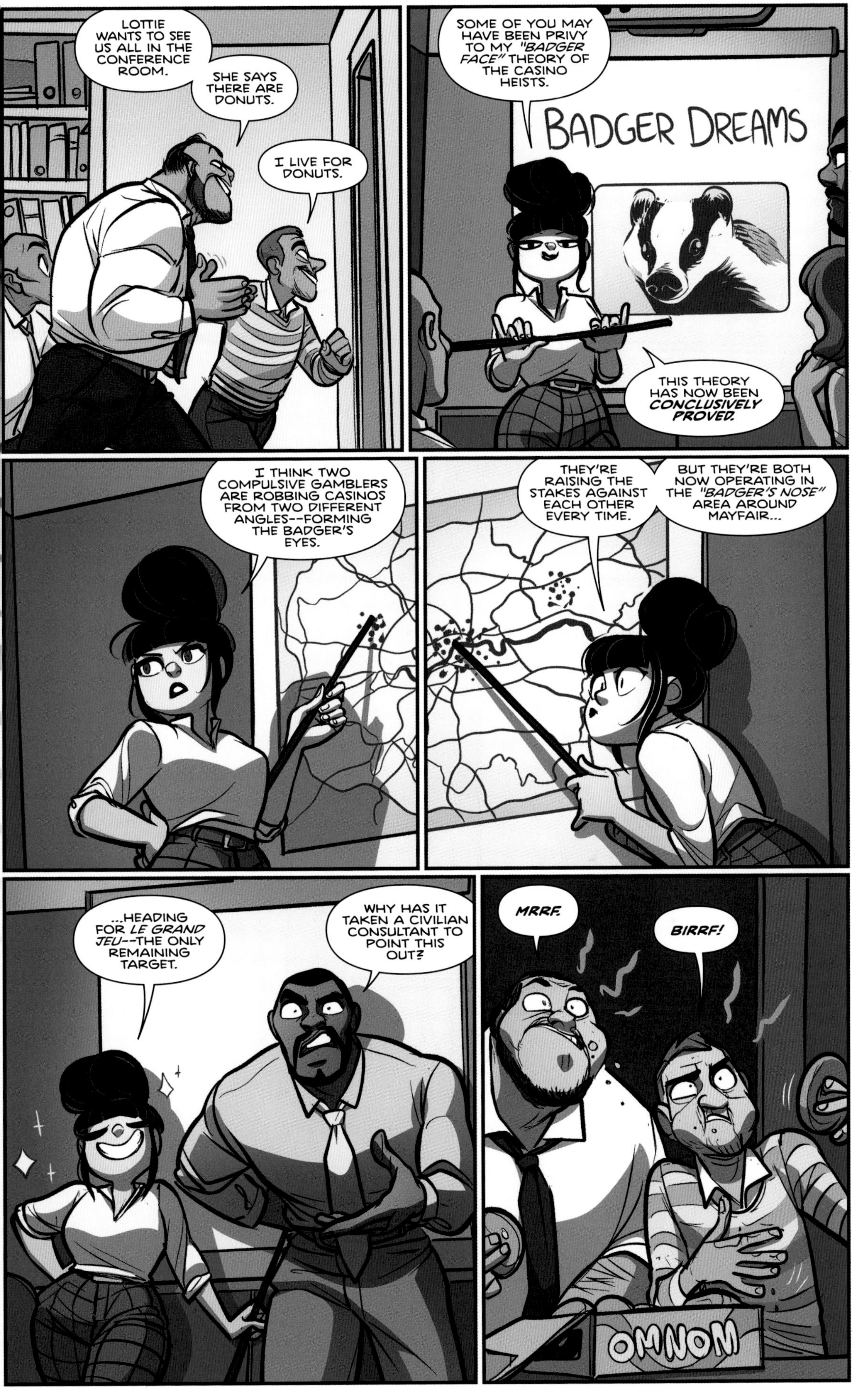
LOTTIE WANTS TO SEE US ALL IN THE CONFERENCE ROOM.
SHE SAYS THERE ARE DONUTS.
I LIVE FOR DONUTS.
SOME OF YOU MAY HAVE BEEN PRIVY TO MY "BADGER FACE" THEORY OF THE CASINO HEISTS.
BADGER DREAMS
THIS THEORY HAS NOW BEEN CONCLUSIVELY PROVED.
I THINK TWO COMPULSIVE GAMBLERS ARE ROBBING CASINOS FROM TWO DIFFERENT ANGLES--FORMING THE BADGER'S EYES.
THEY'RE RAISING THE STAKES AGAINST EACH OTHER EVERY TIME.
BUT THEY'RE BOTH NOW OPERATING IN THE "BADGER'S NOSE" AREA AROUND MAYFAIR...
...HEADING FOR LE GRAND JEU--THE ONLY REMAINING TARGET.
WHY HAS IT TAKEN A CIVILIAN CONSULTANT TO POINT THIS OUT?
MRRF.
BIRRF!
OMNOM

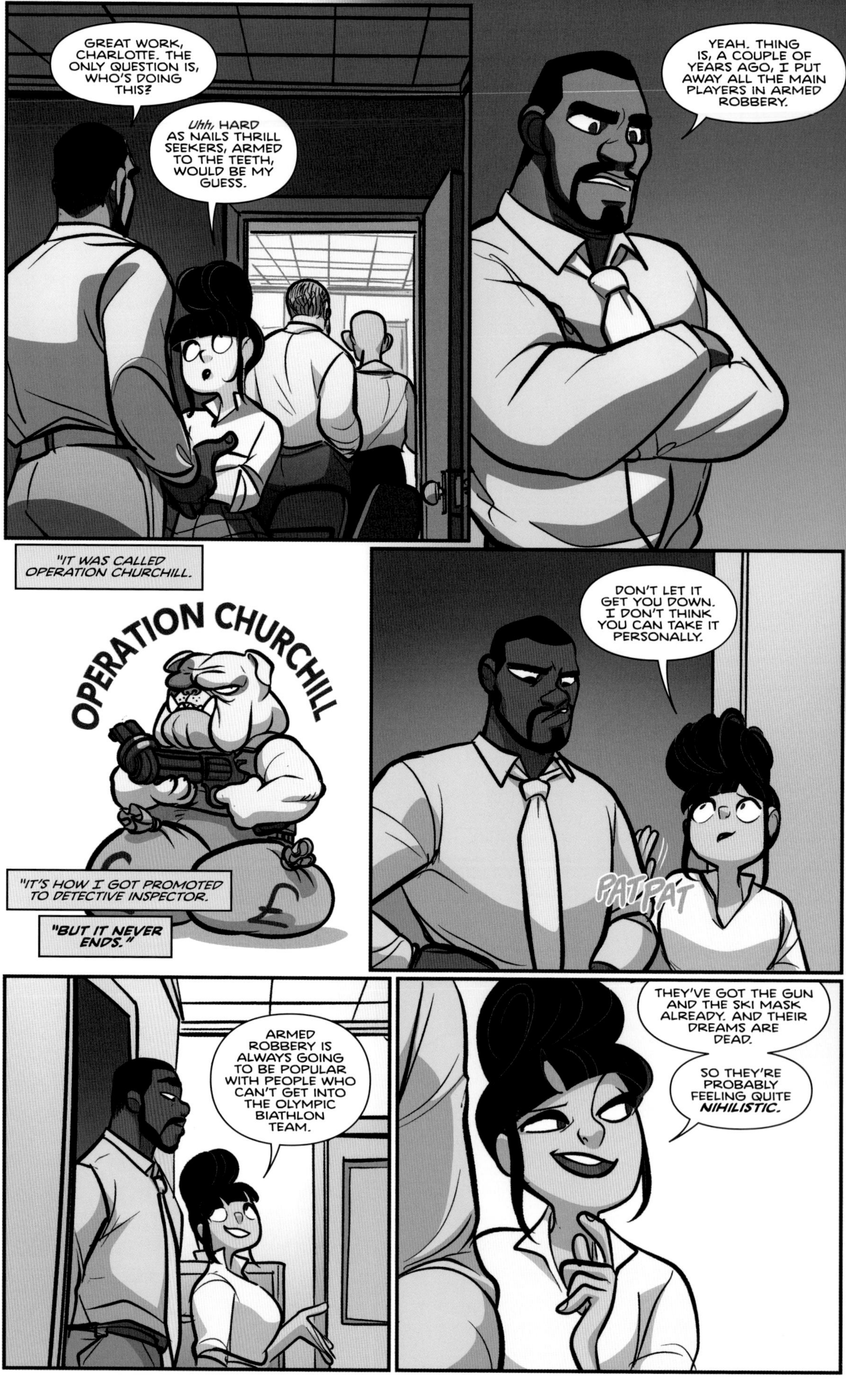
GREAT WORK, CHARLOTTE. THE ONLY QUESTION IS, WHO'S DOING THIS?
*Uhh,* HARD AS NAILS THRILL SEEKERS, ARMED TO THE TEETH, WOULD BE MY GUESS.
YEAH. THING IS, A COUPLE OF YEARS AGO, I PUT AWAY ALL THE MAIN PLAYERS IN ARMED ROBBERY.
"IT WAS CALLED OPERATION CHURCHILL.
OPERATION CHURCHILL
"IT'S HOW I GOT PROMOTED TO DETECTIVE INSPECTOR.
"BUT IT NEVER ENDS."
DON'T LET IT GET YOU DOWN. I DON'T THINK YOU CAN TAKE IT PERSONALLY.
PAT PAT
ARMED ROBBERY IS ALWAYS GOING TO BE POPULAR WITH PEOPLE WHO CAN'T GET INTO THE OLYMPIC BIATHLON TEAM.
THEY'VE GOT THE GUN AND THE SKI MASK ALREADY. AND THEIR DREAMS ARE DEAD.
SO THEY'RE PROBABLY FEELING QUITE ***NIHILISTIC.***

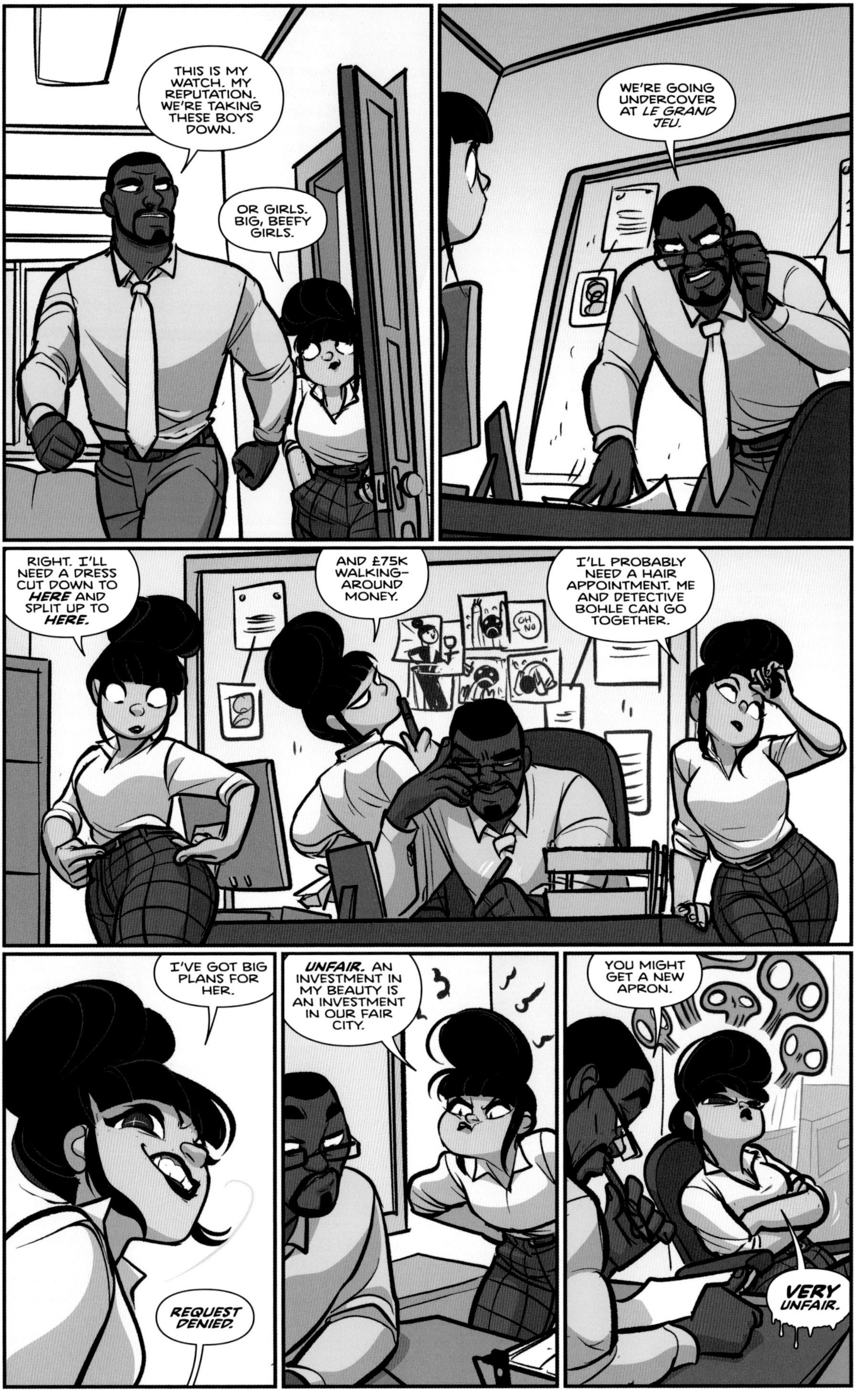
THIS IS MY WATCH. MY REPUTATION. WE'RE TAKING THESE BOYS DOWN.
OR GIRLS. BIG, BEEFY GIRLS.
WE'RE GOING UNDERCOVER AT *LE GRAND JEU.*
RIGHT. I'LL NEED A DRESS CUT DOWN TO **HERE** AND SPLIT UP TO **HERE.**
AND £75K WALKING-AROUND MONEY.
OH NO
I'LL PROBABLY NEED A HAIR APPOINTMENT. ME AND DETECTIVE BOHLE CAN GO TOGETHER.
I'VE GOT BIG PLANS FOR HER.
**REQUEST DENIED.**
***UNFAIR.*** AN INVESTMENT IN MY BEAUTY IS AN INVESTMENT IN OUR FAIR CITY.
YOU MIGHT GET A NEW APRON.
***VERY*** **UNFAIR.**

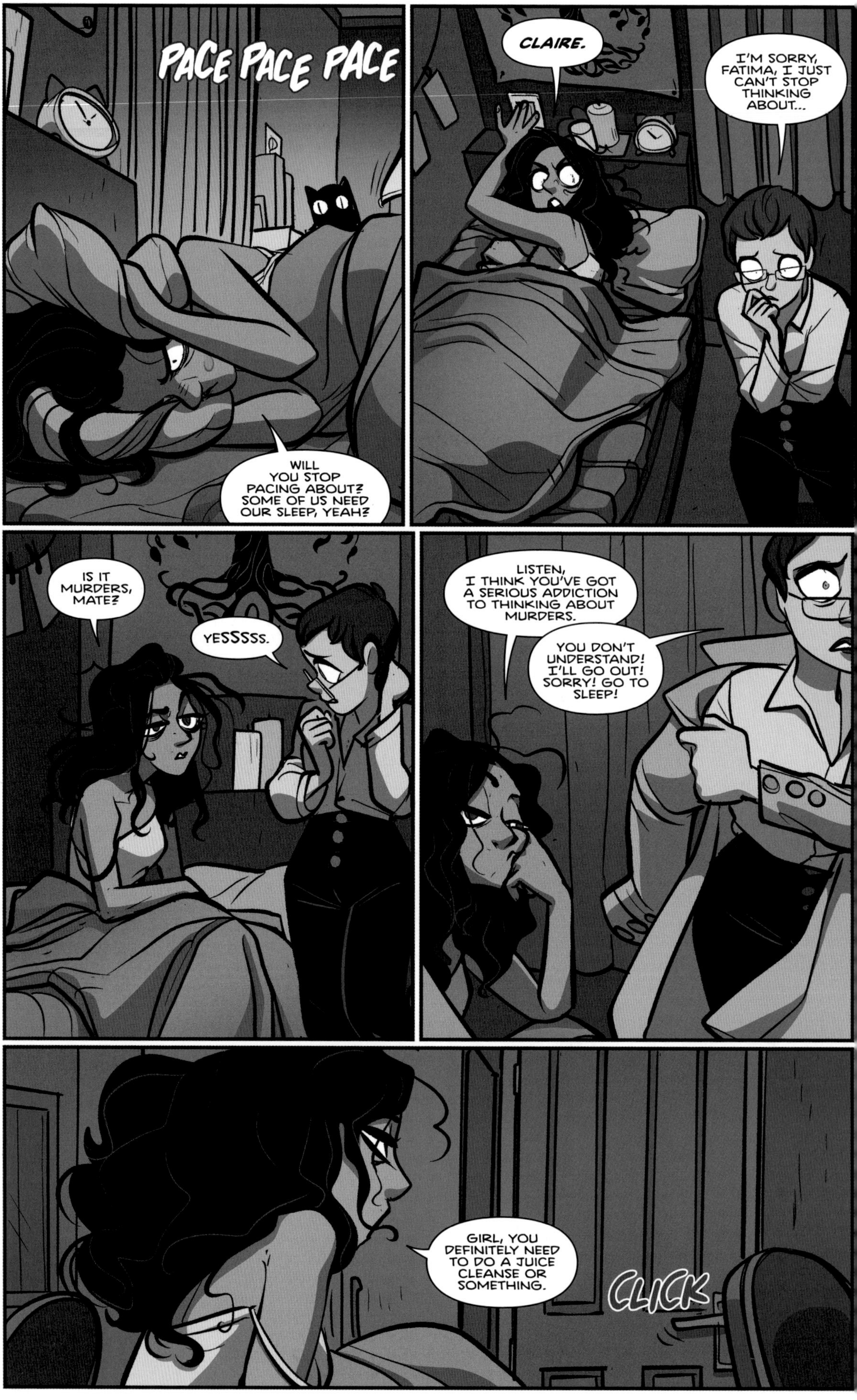
PACE PACE PACE
WILL YOU STOP PACING ABOUT? SOME OF US NEED OUR SLEEP, YEAH?
CLAIRE.
I'M SORRY, FATIMA, I JUST CAN'T STOP THINKING ABOUT...
IS IT MURDERS, MATE?
YESSSSS.
LISTEN, I THINK YOU'VE GOT A SERIOUS ADDICTION TO THINKING ABOUT MURDERS.
YOU DON'T UNDERSTAND! I'LL GO OUT! SORRY! GO TO SLEEP!
GIRL, YOU DEFINITELY NEED TO DO A JUICE CLEANSE OR SOMETHING.
CLICK

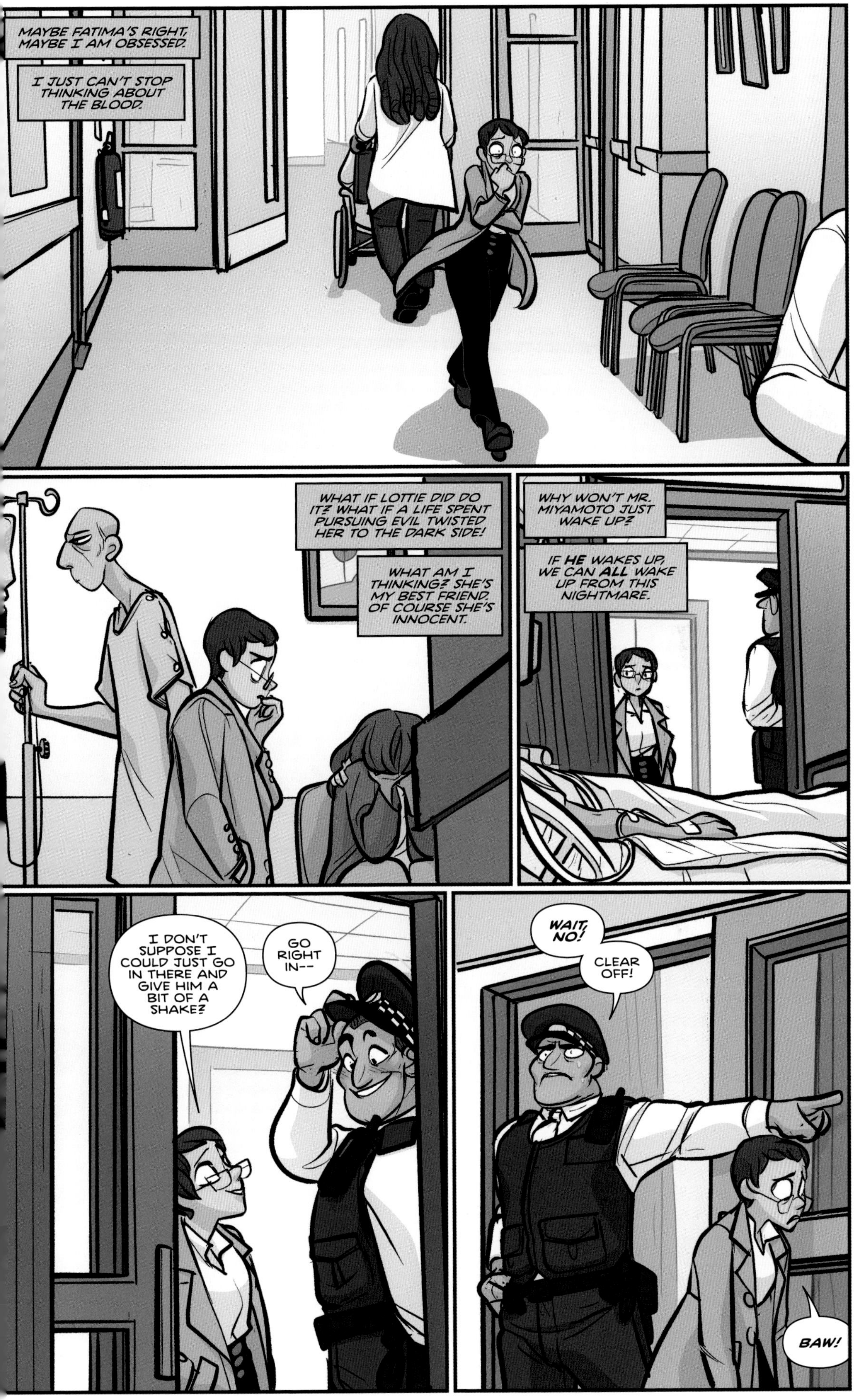
MAYBE FATIMA'S RIGHT, MAYBE I AM OBSESSED.
I JUST CAN'T STOP THINKING ABOUT THE BLOOD.
WHAT IF LOTTIE DID DO IT? WHAT IF A LIFE SPENT PURSUING EVIL TWISTED HER TO THE DARK SIDE!
WHAT AM I THINKING? SHE'S MY BEST FRIEND. OF COURSE SHE'S INNOCENT.
WHY WON'T MR. MIYAMOTO JUST WAKE UP?
IF HE WAKES UP, WE CAN ALL WAKE UP FROM THIS NIGHTMARE.
I DON'T SUPPOSE I COULD JUST GO IN THERE AND GIVE HIM A BIT OF A SHAKE?
GO RIGHT IN--
WAIT, NO!
CLEAR OFF!
BAW!

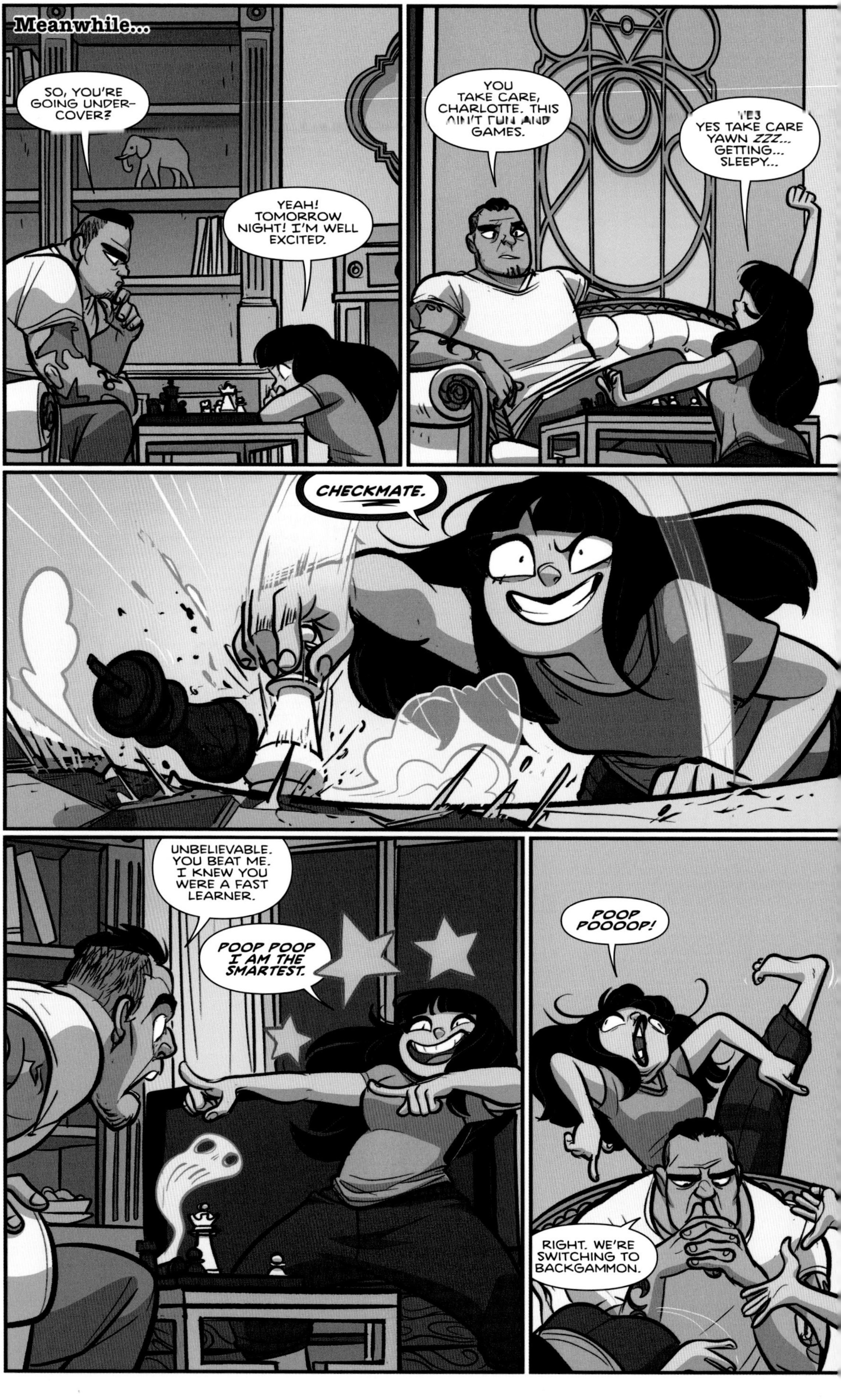
Meanwhile...
SO, YOU'RE GOING UNDER-COVER?
YEAH! TOMORROW NIGHT! I'M WELL EXCITED.
YOU TAKE CARE, CHARLOTTE. THIS AIN'T FUN AND GAMES.
YES TAKE CARE YAWN ZZZ... GETTING... SLEEPY...
CHECKMATE.
UNBELIEVABLE. YOU BEAT ME. I KNEW YOU WERE A FAST LEARNER.
POOP POOP I AM THE SMARTEST.
POOP POOOOP!
RIGHT. WE'RE SWITCHING TO BACKGAMMON.

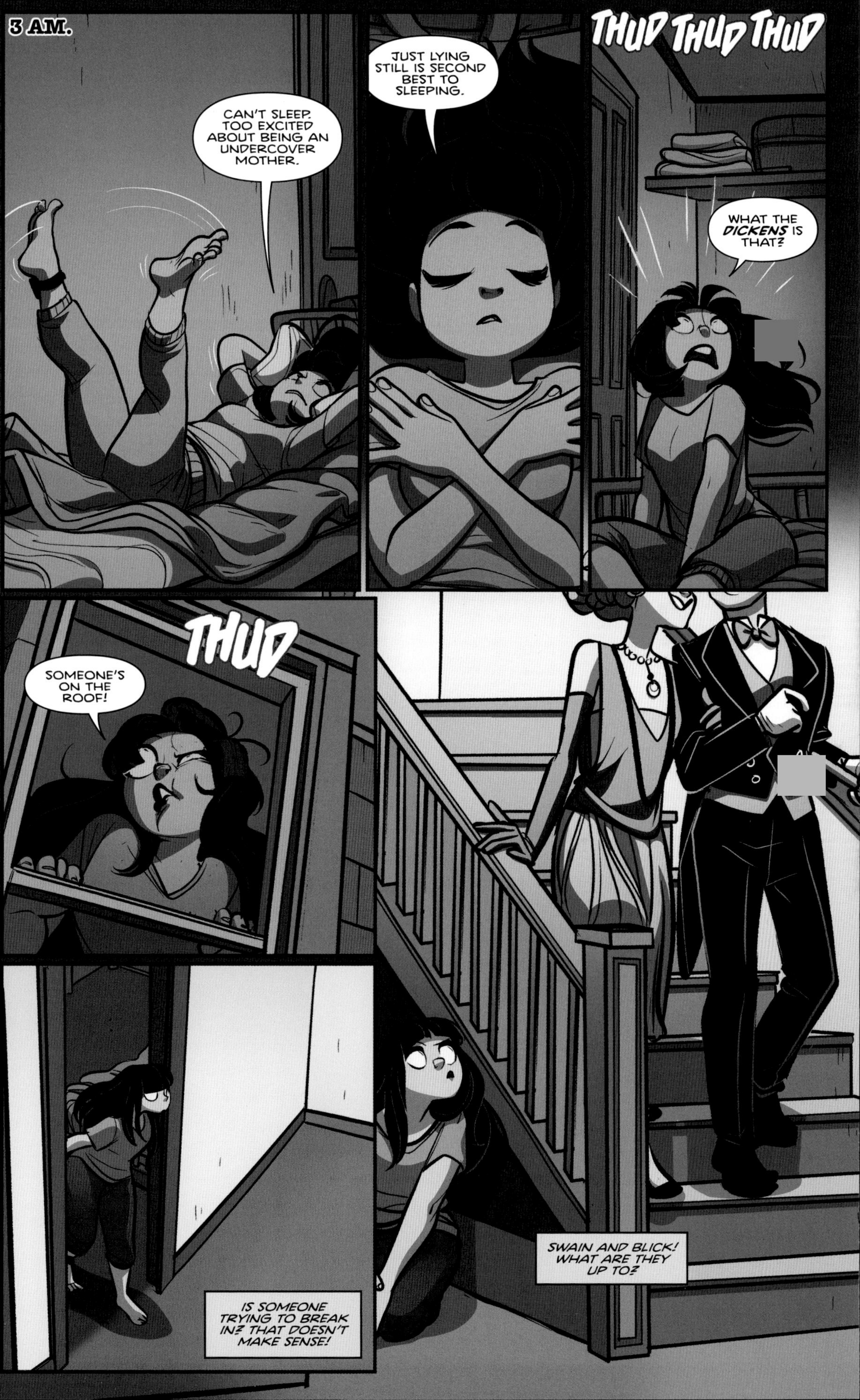
3 A.M.
CAN'T SLEEP. TOO EXCITED ABOUT BEING AN UNDERCOVER MOTHER.
JUST LYING STILL IS SECOND BEST TO SLEEPING.
THUD THUD THUD
WHAT THE DICKENS IS THAT?
THUD
SOMEONE'S ON THE ROOF!
IS SOMEONE TRYING TO BREAK IN? THAT DOESN'T MAKE SENSE!
SWAIN AND BLICK! WHAT ARE THEY UP TO?

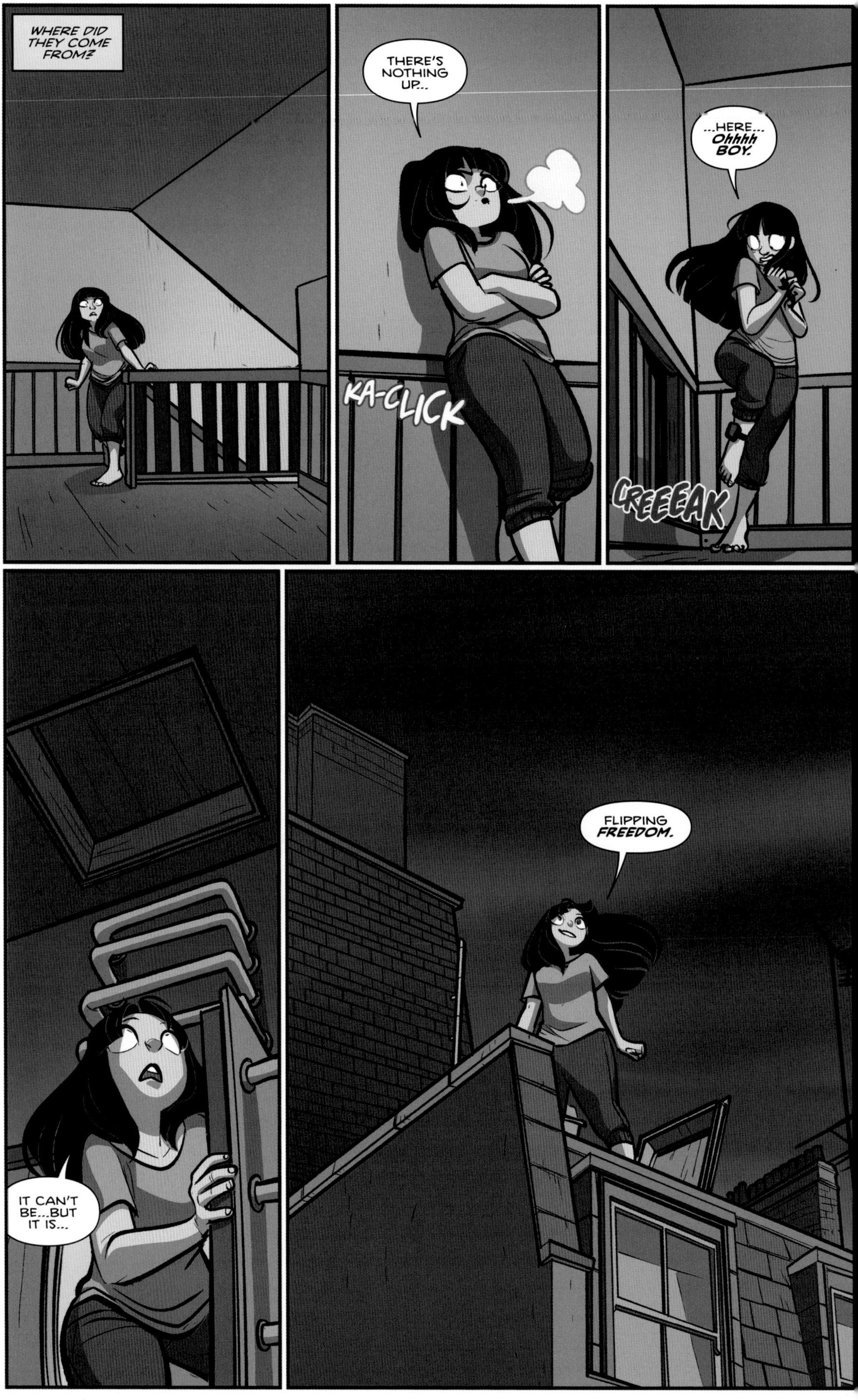
WHERE DID THEY COME FROM?
THERE'S NOTHING UP...
KA-CLICK
...HERE... *Ohhhh* **BOY.**
CREEEAK
IT CAN'T BE...BUT IT IS...
FLIPPING ***FREEDOM.***

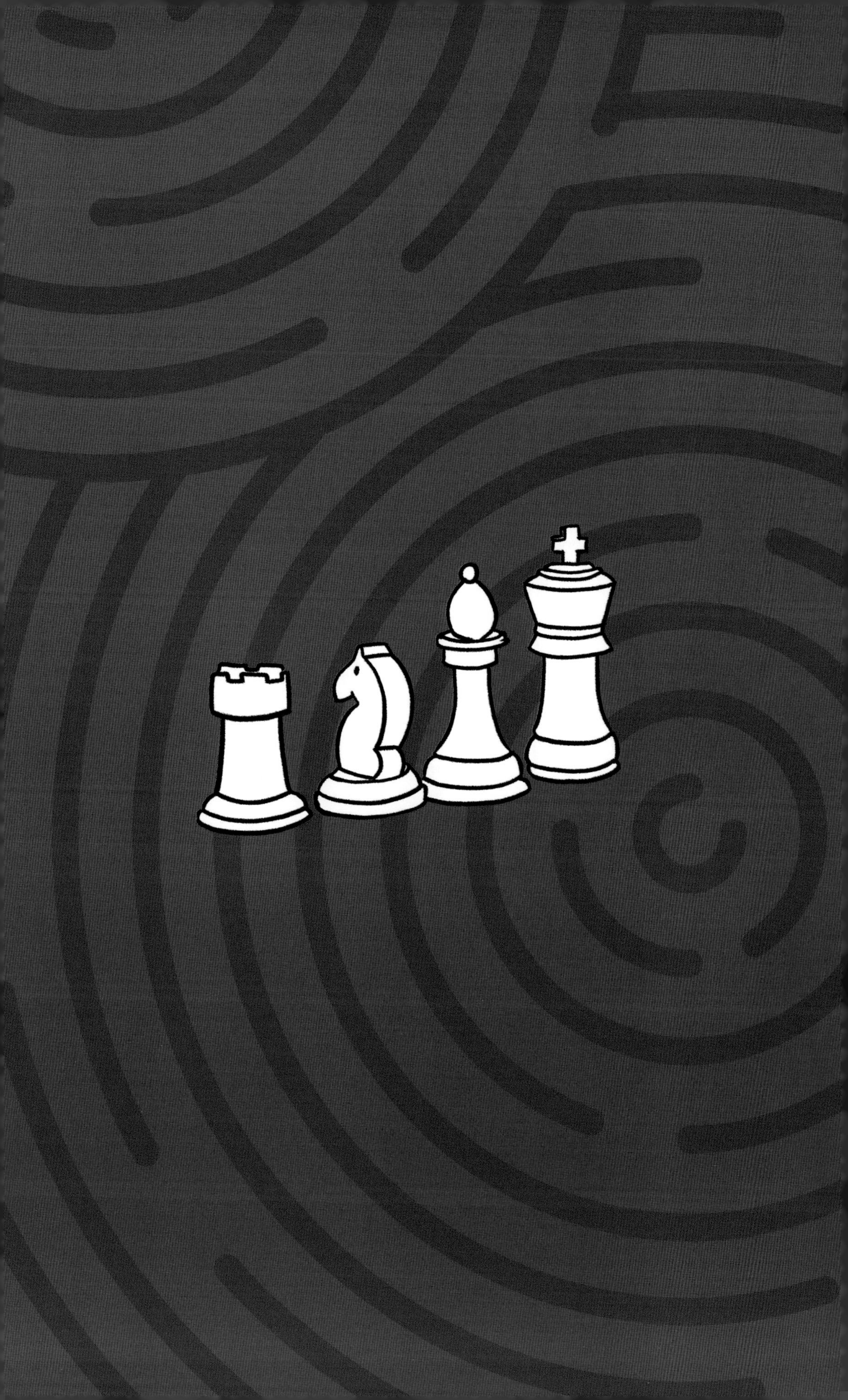

# CHAPTER SIX

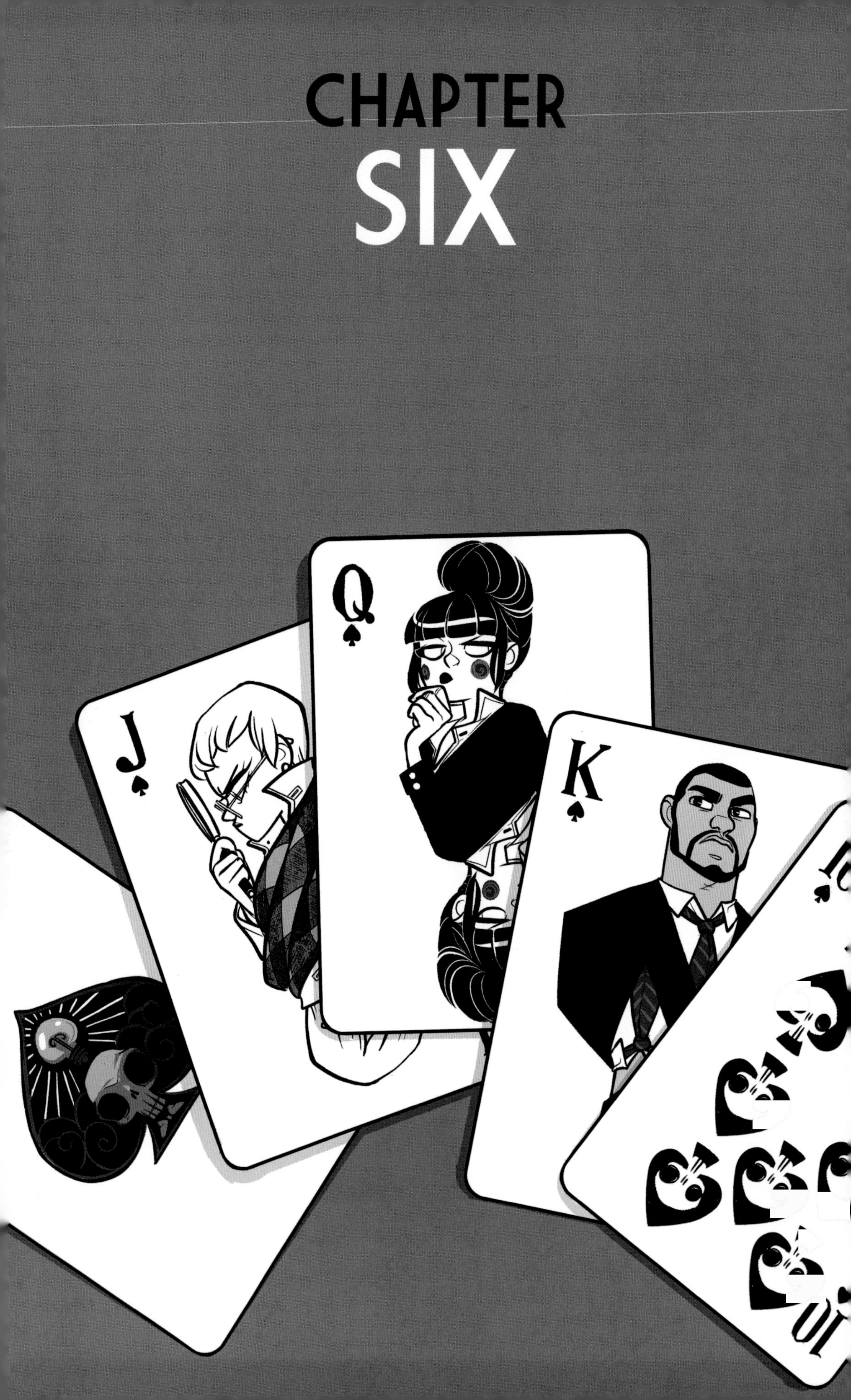

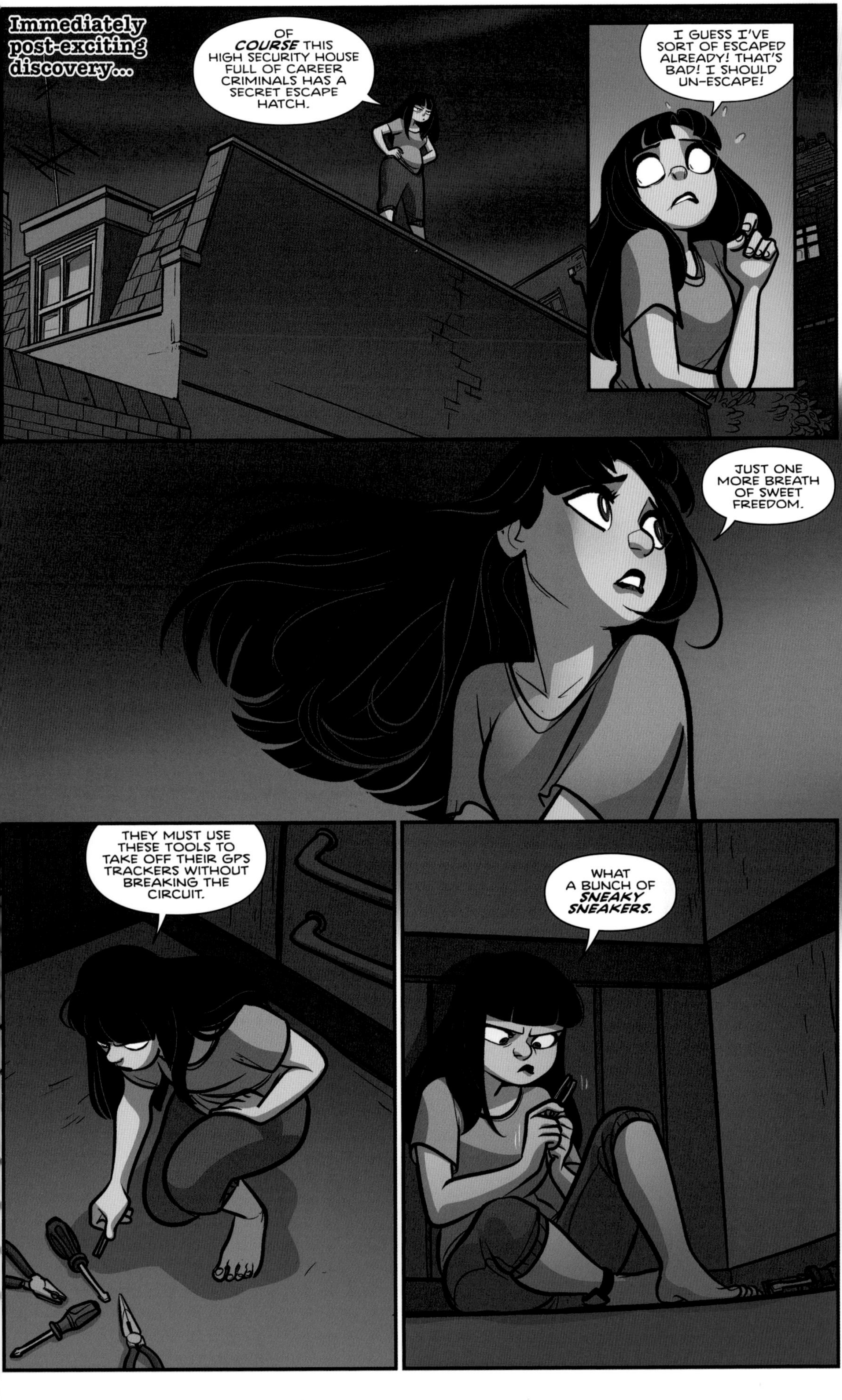
Immediately post-exciting discovery...
OF COURSE THIS HIGH SECURITY HOUSE FULL OF CAREER CRIMINALS HAS A SECRET ESCAPE HATCH.
I GUESS I'VE SORT OF ESCAPED ALREADY! THAT'S BAD! I SHOULD UN-ESCAPE!
JUST ONE MORE BREATH OF SWEET FREEDOM.
THEY MUST USE THESE TOOLS TO TAKE OFF THEIR GPS TRACKERS WITHOUT BREAKING THE CIRCUIT.
WHAT A BUNCH OF SNEAKY SNEAKERS.

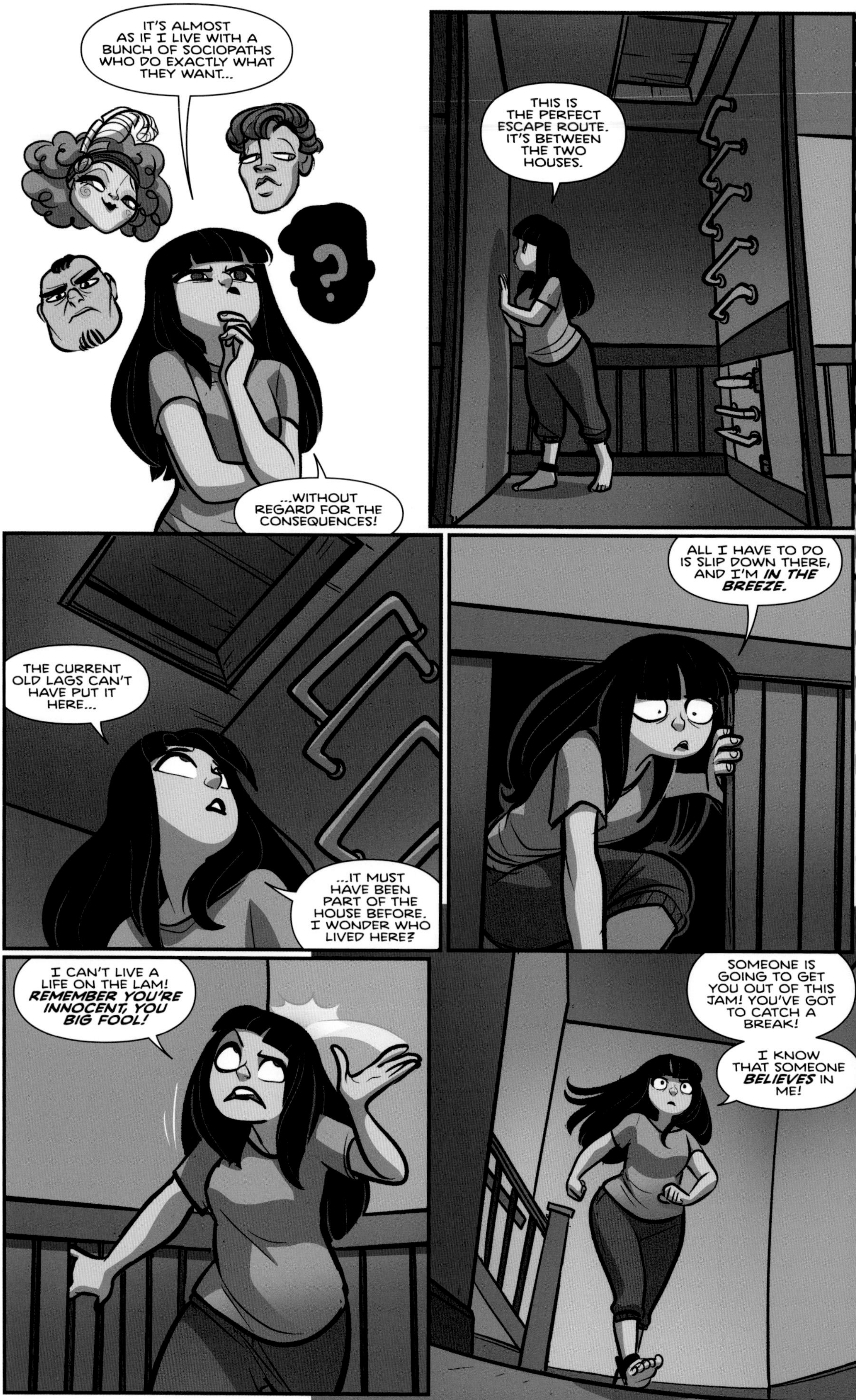
IT'S ALMOST AS IF I LIVE WITH A BUNCH OF SOCIOPATHS WHO DO EXACTLY WHAT THEY WANT...
...WITHOUT REGARD FOR THE CONSEQUENCES!
THIS IS THE PERFECT ESCAPE ROUTE. IT'S BETWEEN THE TWO HOUSES.
THE CURRENT OLD LAGS CAN'T HAVE PUT IT HERE...
...IT MUST HAVE BEEN PART OF THE HOUSE BEFORE. I WONDER WHO LIVED HERE?
ALL I HAVE TO DO IS SLIP DOWN THERE, AND I'M IN THE BREEZE.
I CAN'T LIVE A LIFE ON THE LAM! REMEMBER YOU'RE INNOCENT, YOU BIG FOOL!
SOMEONE IS GOING TO GET YOU OUT OF THIS JAM! YOU'VE GOT TO CATCH A BREAK!
I KNOW THAT SOMEONE BELIEVES IN ME!

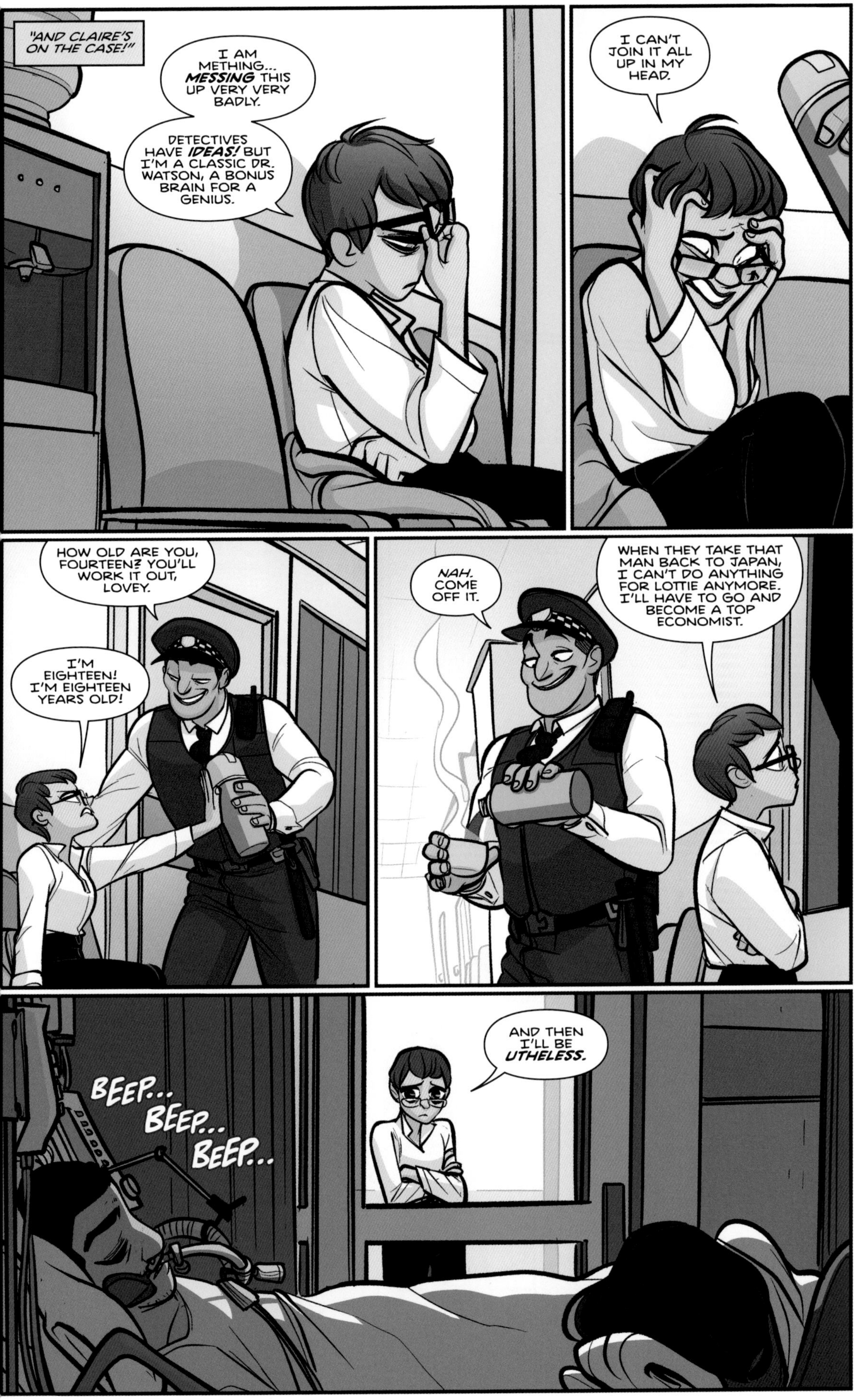
"AND CLAIRE'S ON THE CASE!"
I AM METHING... MESSING THIS UP VERY VERY BADLY.
DETECTIVES HAVE IDEAS! BUT I'M A CLASSIC DR. WATSON, A BONUS BRAIN FOR A GENIUS.
I CAN'T JOIN IT ALL UP IN MY HEAD.
HOW OLD ARE YOU, FOURTEEN? YOU'LL WORK IT OUT, LOVEY.
I'M EIGHTEEN! I'M EIGHTEEN YEARS OLD!
NAH. COME OFF IT.
WHEN THEY TAKE THAT MAN BACK TO JAPAN, I CAN'T DO ANYTHING FOR LOTTIE ANYMORE. I'LL HAVE TO GO AND BECOME A TOP ECONOMIST.
BEEP... BEEP... BEEP...
AND THEN I'LL BE UTHELESS.

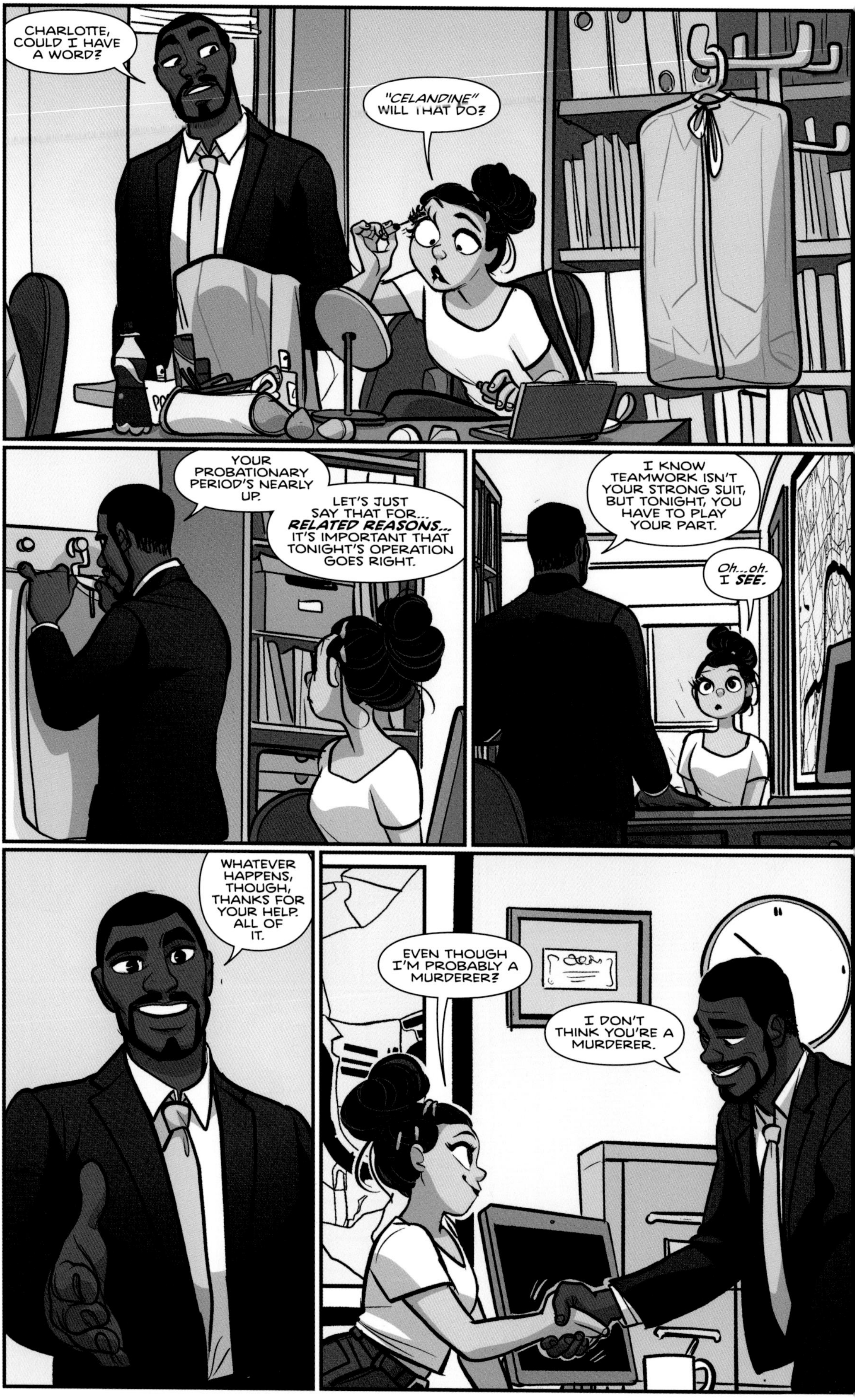
CHARLOTTE, COULD I HAVE A WORD?
"CELANDINE" WILL THAT DO?
YOUR PROBATIONARY PERIOD'S NEARLY UP.
LET'S JUST SAY THAT FOR... RELATED REASONS... IT'S IMPORTANT THAT TONIGHT'S OPERATION GOES RIGHT.
I KNOW TEAMWORK ISN'T YOUR STRONG SUIT, BUT TONIGHT, YOU HAVE TO PLAY YOUR PART.
Oh...oh. I SEE.
WHATEVER HAPPENS, THOUGH, THANKS FOR YOUR HELP. ALL OF IT.
EVEN THOUGH I'M PROBABLY A MURDERER?
I DON'T THINK YOU'RE A MURDERER.

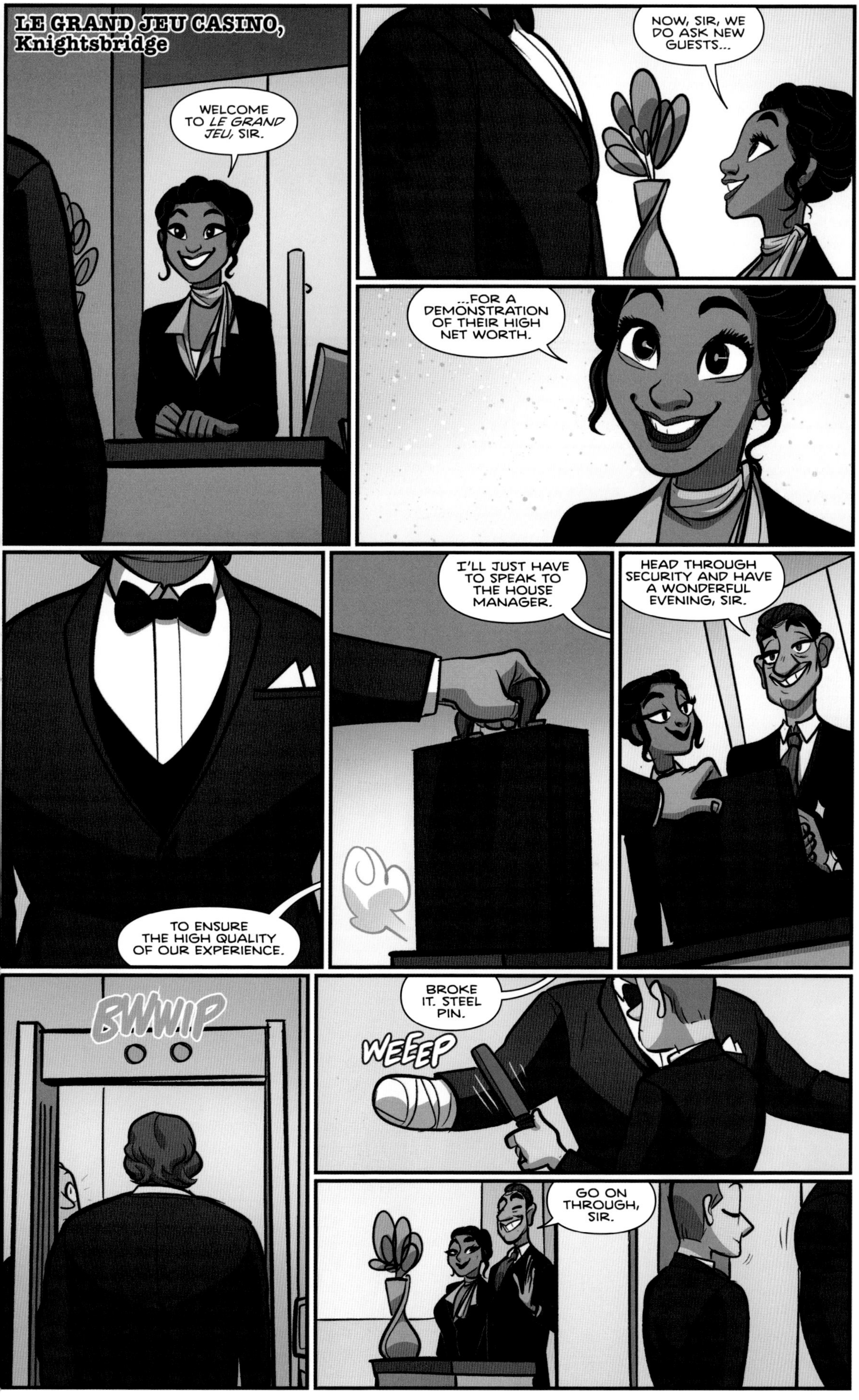
LE GRAND JEU CASINO, Knightsbridge
WELCOME TO LE GRAND JEU, SIR.
NOW, SIR, WE DO ASK NEW GUESTS...
...FOR A DEMONSTRATION OF THEIR HIGH NET WORTH.
TO ENSURE THE HIGH QUALITY OF OUR EXPERIENCE.
I'LL JUST HAVE TO SPEAK TO THE HOUSE MANAGER.
HEAD THROUGH SECURITY AND HAVE A WONDERFUL EVENING, SIR.
BWWIP
BROKE IT. STEEL PIN.
WEEEP
GO ON THROUGH, SIR.

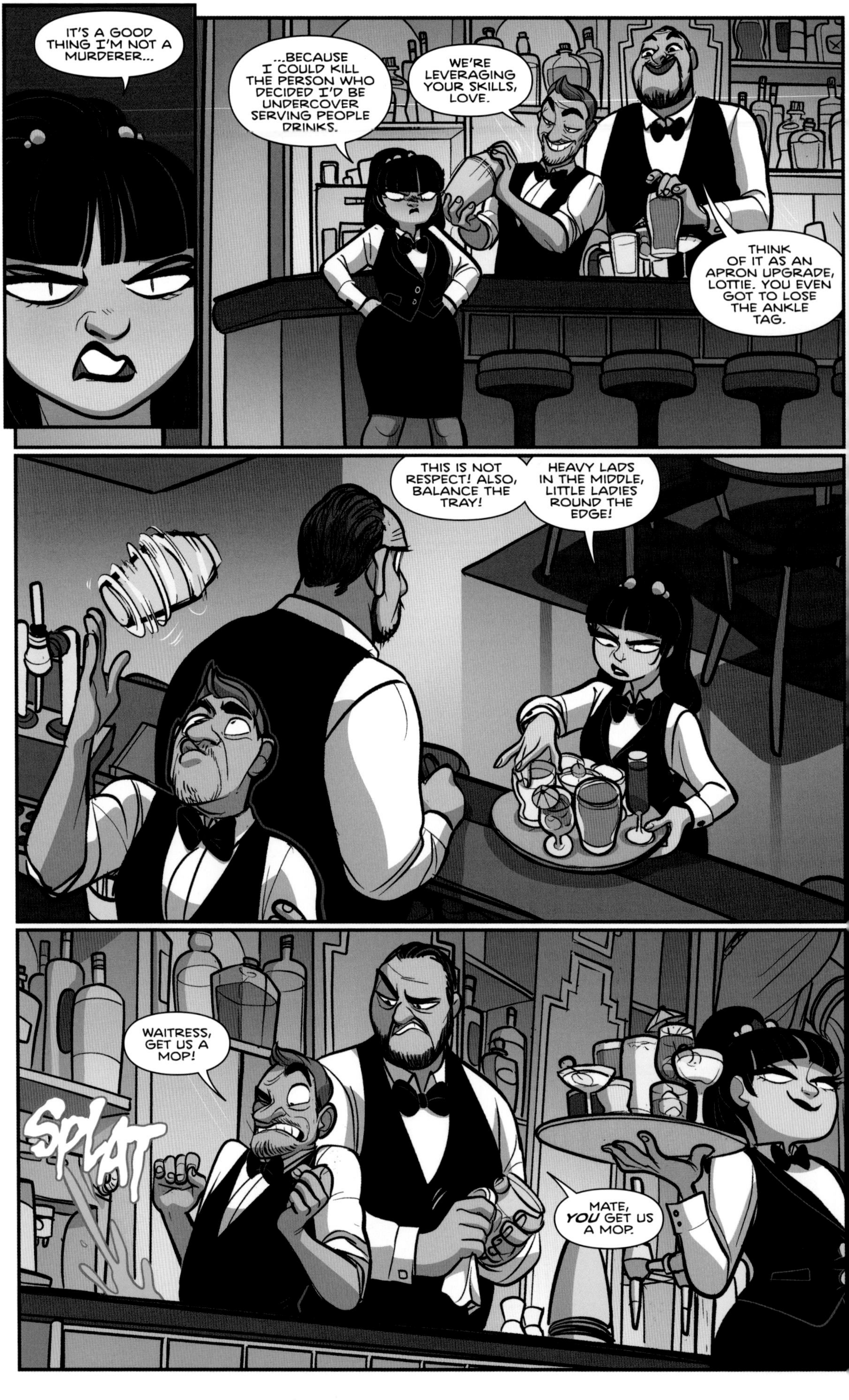
IT'S A GOOD THING I'M NOT A MURDERER...
...BECAUSE I COULD KILL THE PERSON WHO DECIDED I'D BE UNDERCOVER SERVING PEOPLE DRINKS.
WE'RE LEVERAGING YOUR SKILLS, LOVE.
THINK OF IT AS AN APRON UPGRADE, LOTTIE. YOU EVEN GOT TO LOSE THE ANKLE TAG.
THIS IS NOT RESPECT! ALSO, BALANCE THE TRAY!
HEAVY LADS IN THE MIDDLE, LITTLE LADIES ROUND THE EDGE!
WAITRESS, GET US A MOP!
SPLAT
MATE, *YOU* GET US A MOP.

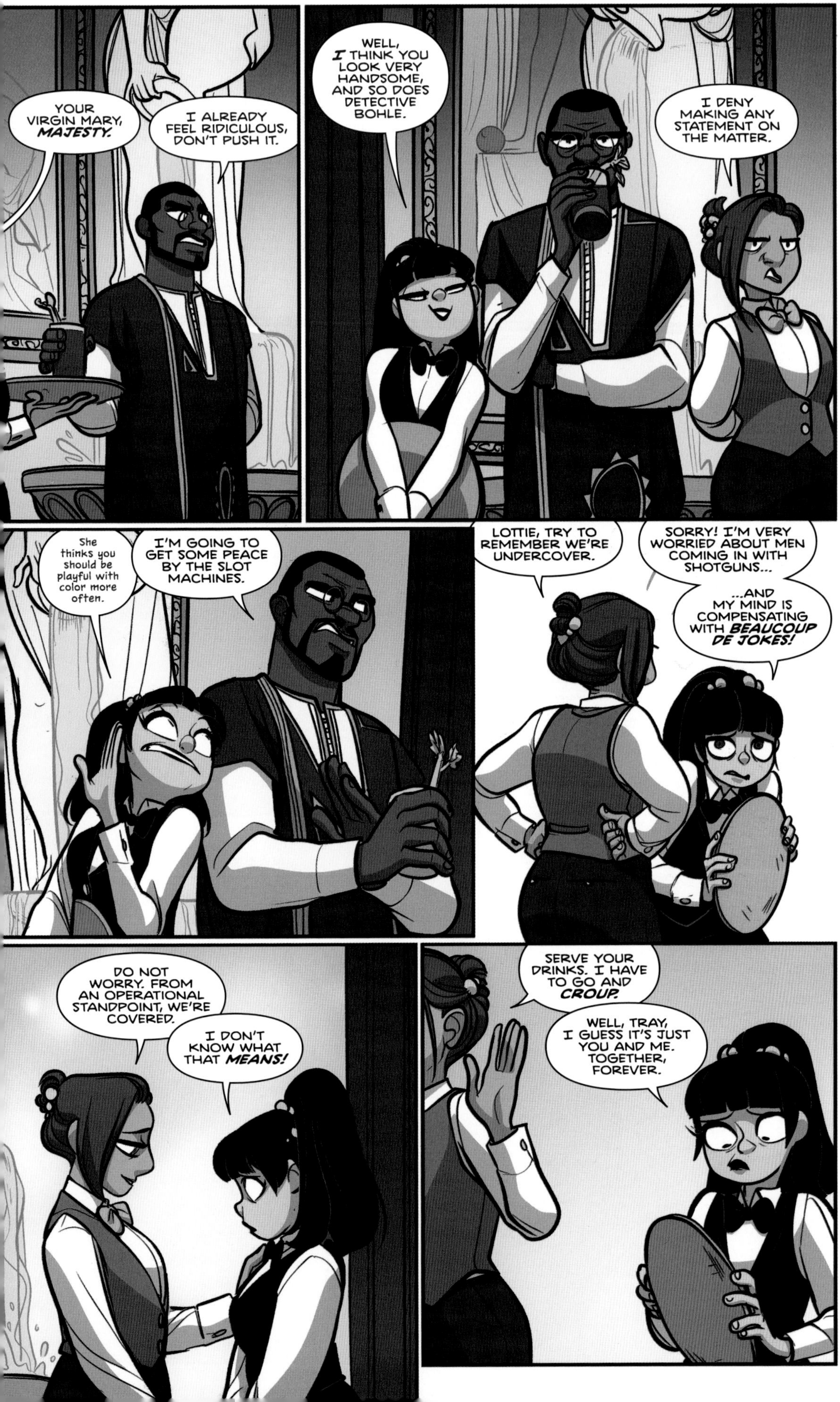
YOUR VIRGIN MARY, MAJESTY.
I ALREADY FEEL RIDICULOUS, DON'T PUSH IT.
WELL, I THINK YOU LOOK VERY HANDSOME, AND SO DOES DETECTIVE BOHLE.
I DENY MAKING ANY STATEMENT ON THE MATTER.
She thinks you should be playful with color more often.
I'M GOING TO GET SOME PEACE BY THE SLOT MACHINES.
LOTTIE, TRY TO REMEMBER WE'RE UNDERCOVER.
SORRY! I'M VERY WORRIED ABOUT MEN COMING IN WITH SHOTGUNS...
...AND MY MIND IS COMPENSATING WITH BEAUCOUP DE JOKES!
DO NOT WORRY. FROM AN OPERATIONAL STANDPOINT, WE'RE COVERED.
I DON'T KNOW WHAT THAT MEANS!
SERVE YOUR DRINKS. I HAVE TO GO AND CROUP.
WELL, TRAY, I GUESS IT'S JUST YOU AND ME. TOGETHER, FOREVER.

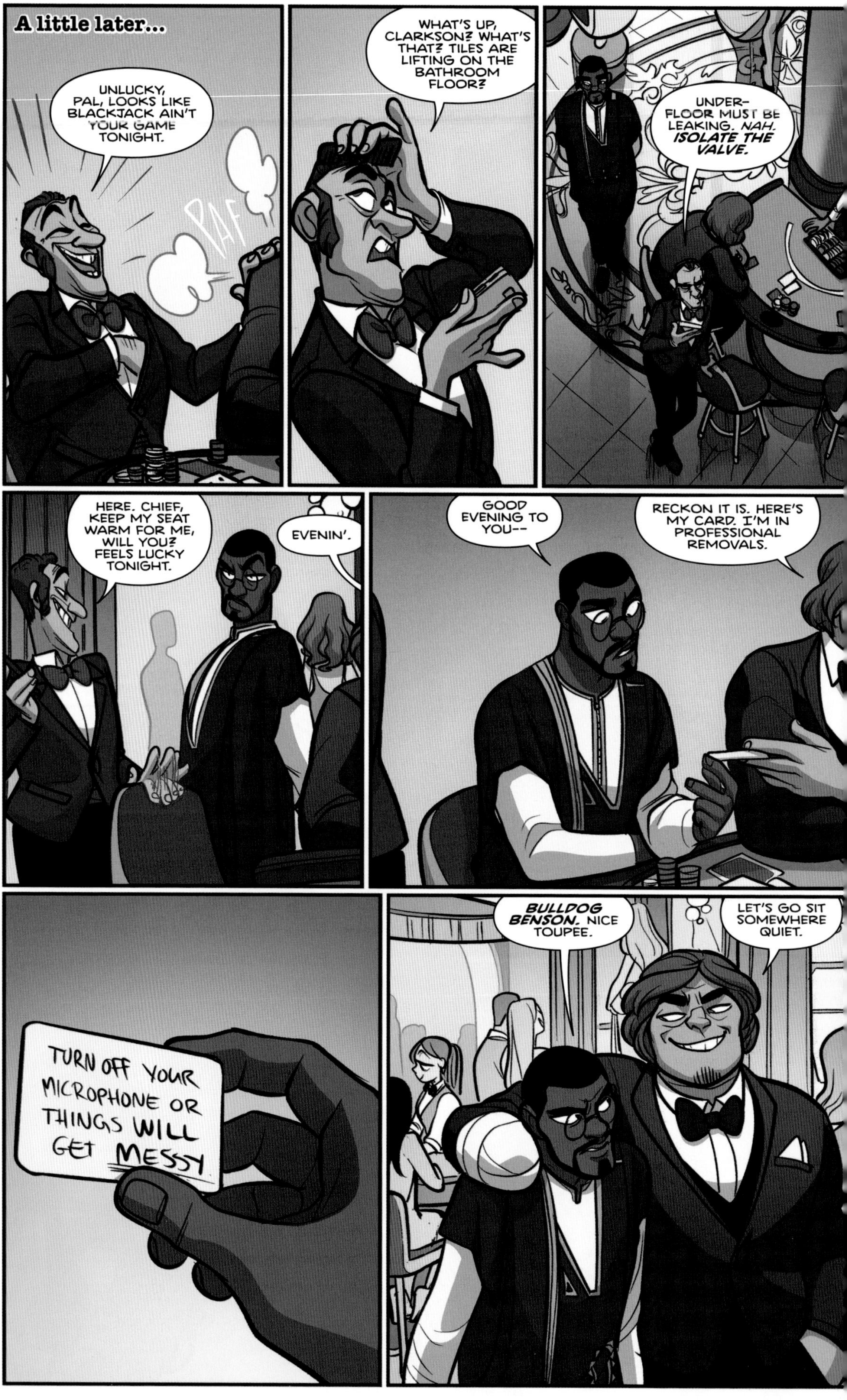
A little later...
UNLUCKY, PAL, LOOKS LIKE BLACKJACK AIN'T YOUR GAME TONIGHT.
PAF
WHAT'S UP, CLARKSON? WHAT'S THAT? TILES ARE LIFTING ON THE BATHROOM FLOOR?
UNDER-FLOOR MUST BE LEAKING. NAH. ISOLATE THE VALVE.
HERE. CHIEF, KEEP MY SEAT WARM FOR ME, WILL YOU? FEELS LUCKY TONIGHT.
EVENIN'.
GOOD EVENING TO YOU--
RECKON IT IS. HERE'S MY CARD. I'M IN PROFESSIONAL REMOVALS.
TURN OFF YOUR MICROPHONE OR THINGS WILL GET MESSY
BULLDOG BENSON. NICE TOUPEE.
LET'S GO SIT SOMEWHERE QUIET.

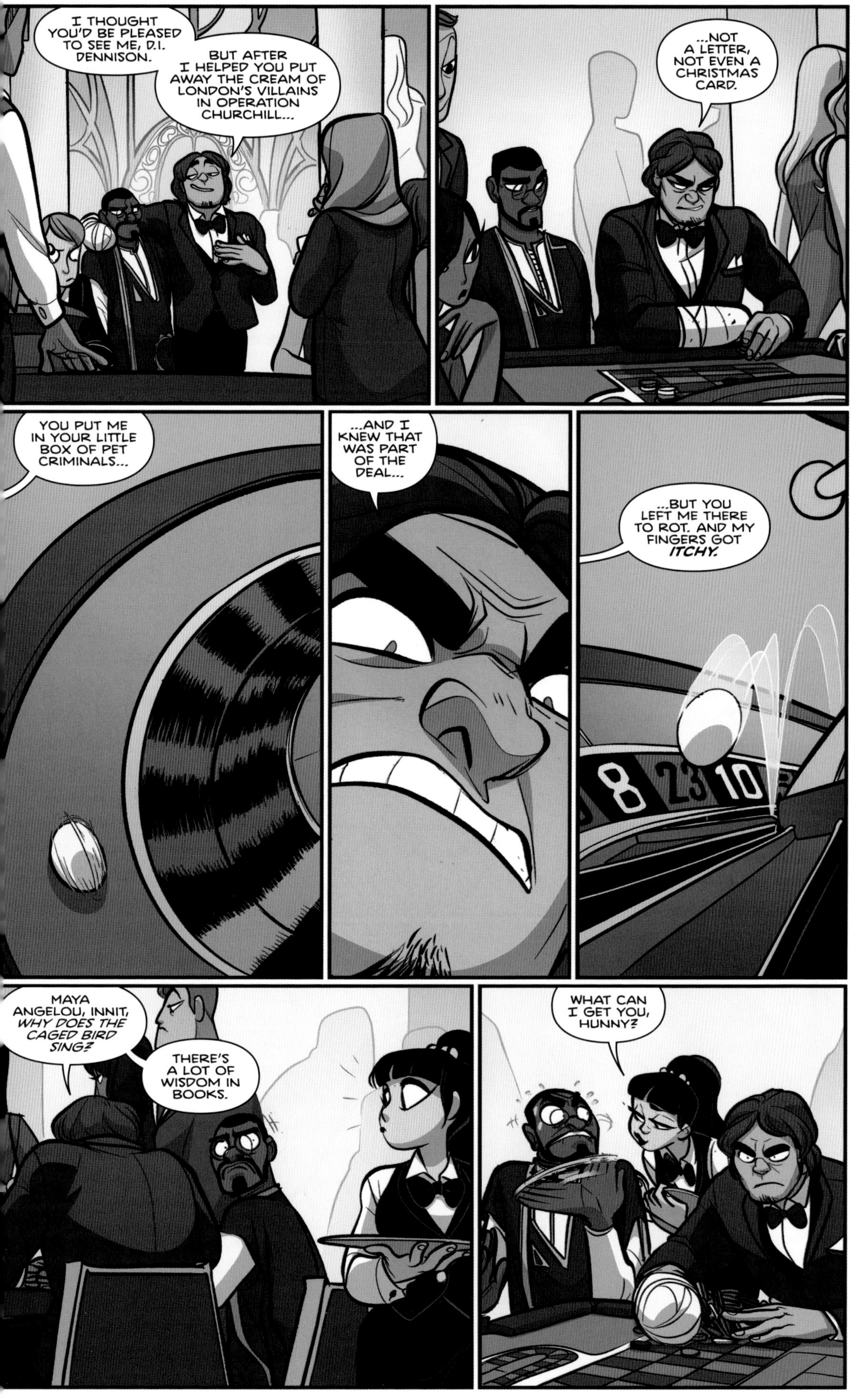
I THOUGHT YOU'D BE PLEASED TO SEE ME, D.I. DENNISON.
BUT AFTER I HELPED YOU PUT AWAY THE CREAM OF LONDON'S VILLAINS IN OPERATION CHURCHILL...
...NOT A LETTER, NOT EVEN A CHRISTMAS CARD.
YOU PUT ME IN YOUR LITTLE BOX OF PET CRIMINALS...
...AND I KNEW THAT WAS PART OF THE DEAL...
...BUT YOU LEFT ME THERE TO ROT. AND MY FINGERS GOT *ITCHY.*
8 23 10
MAYA ANGELOU, INNIT, *WHY DOES THE CAGED BIRD SING?*
THERE'S A LOT OF WISDOM IN BOOKS.
WHAT CAN I GET YOU, HUNNY?

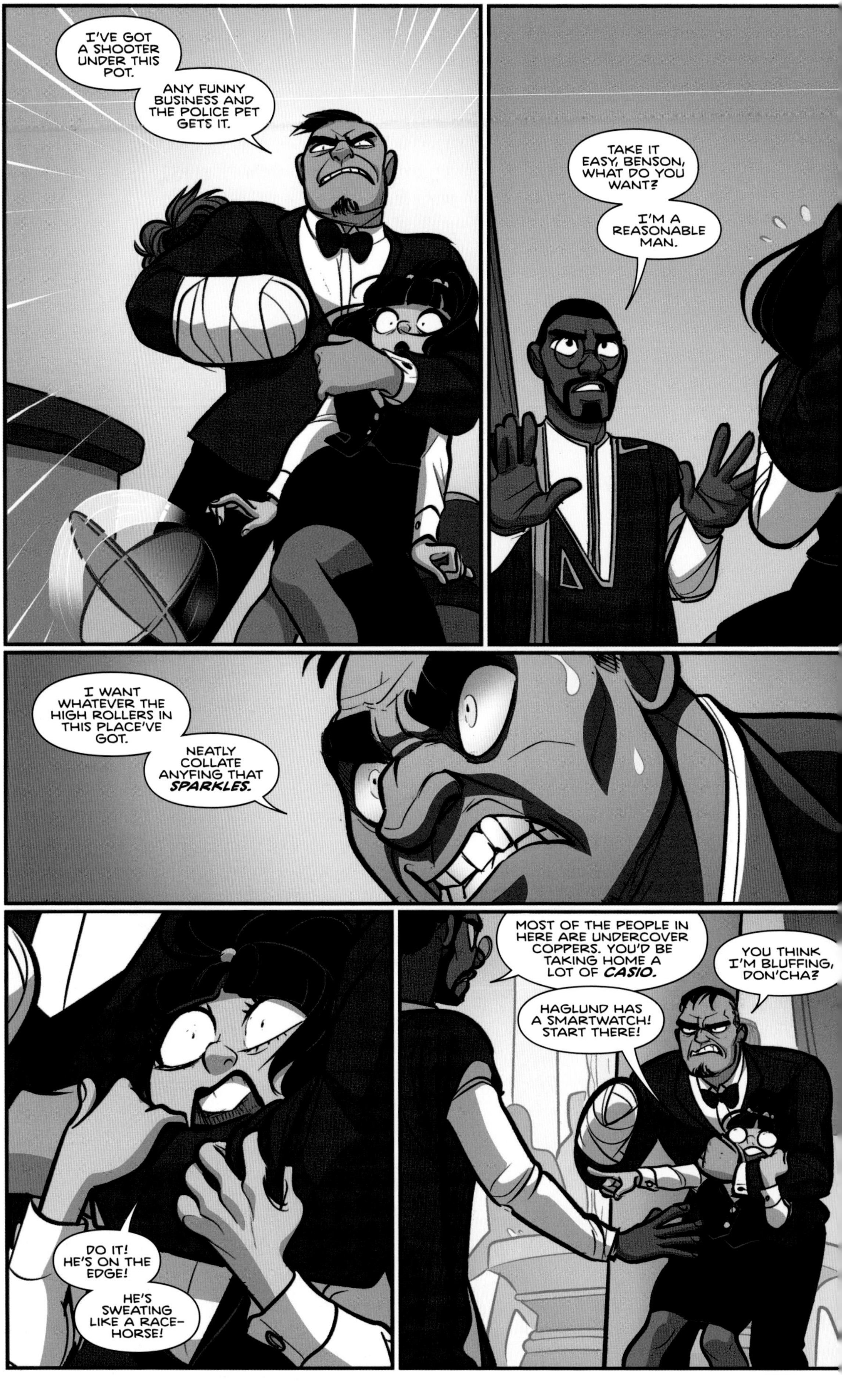

I'VE GOT A SHOOTER UNDER THIS POT.
ANY FUNNY BUSINESS AND THE POLICE PET GETS IT.
TAKE IT EASY, BENSON, WHAT DO YOU WANT?
I'M A REASONABLE MAN.
I WANT WHATEVER THE HIGH ROLLERS IN THIS PLACE'VE GOT.
NEATLY COLLATE ANYFING THAT SPARKLES.
DO IT! HE'S ON THE EDGE!
HE'S SWEATING LIKE A RACE-HORSE!
MOST OF THE PEOPLE IN HERE ARE UNDERCOVER COPPERS. YOU'D BE TAKING HOME A LOT OF CASIO.
HAGLUND HAS A SMARTWATCH! START THERE!
YOU THINK I'M BLUFFING, DON'CHA?

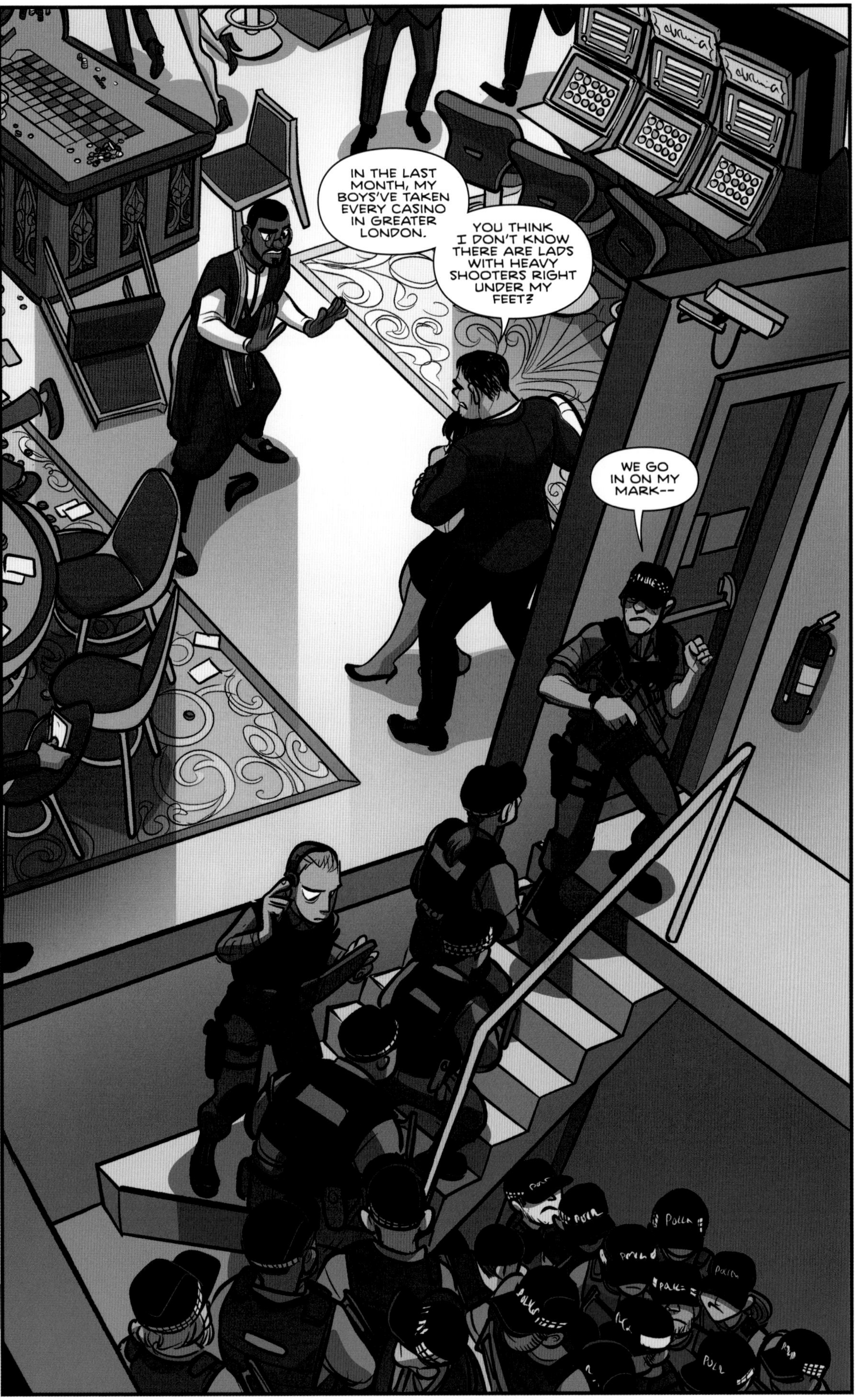
IN THE LAST MONTH, MY BOYS'VE TAKEN EVERY CASINO IN GREATER LONDON.
YOU THINK I DON'T KNOW THERE ARE LADS WITH HEAVY SHOOTERS RIGHT UNDER MY FEET?
WE GO IN ON MY MARK--

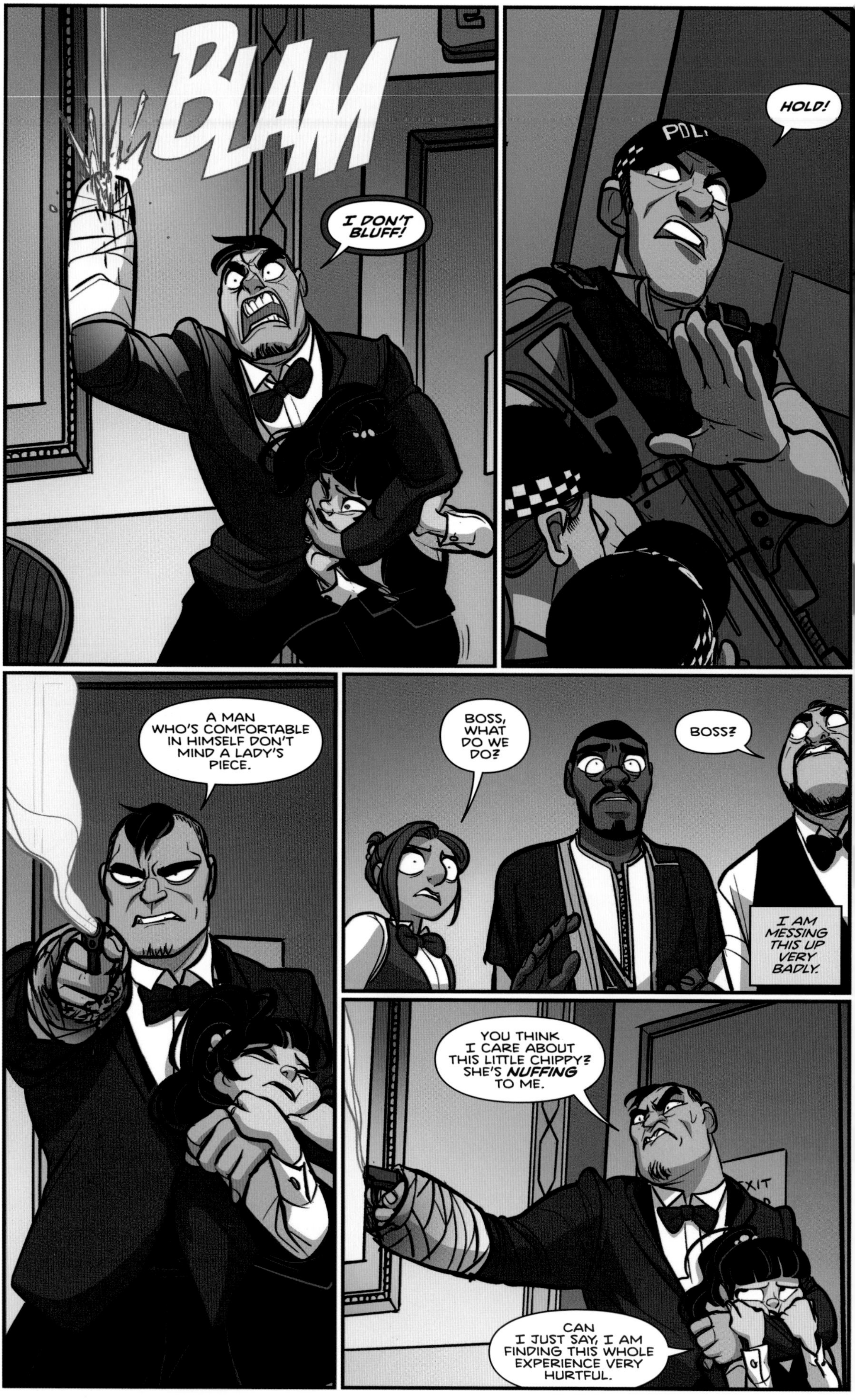
BLAM
I DON'T BLUFF!
HOLD!
POL
A MAN WHO'S COMFORTABLE IN HIMSELF DON'T MIND A LADY'S PIECE.
BOSS, WHAT DO WE DO?
BOSS?
I AM MESSING THIS UP VERY BADLY.
YOU THINK I CARE ABOUT THIS LITTLE CHIPPY? SHE'S *NUFFING* TO ME.
CAN I JUST SAY, I AM FINDING THIS WHOLE EXPERIENCE VERY HURTFUL.

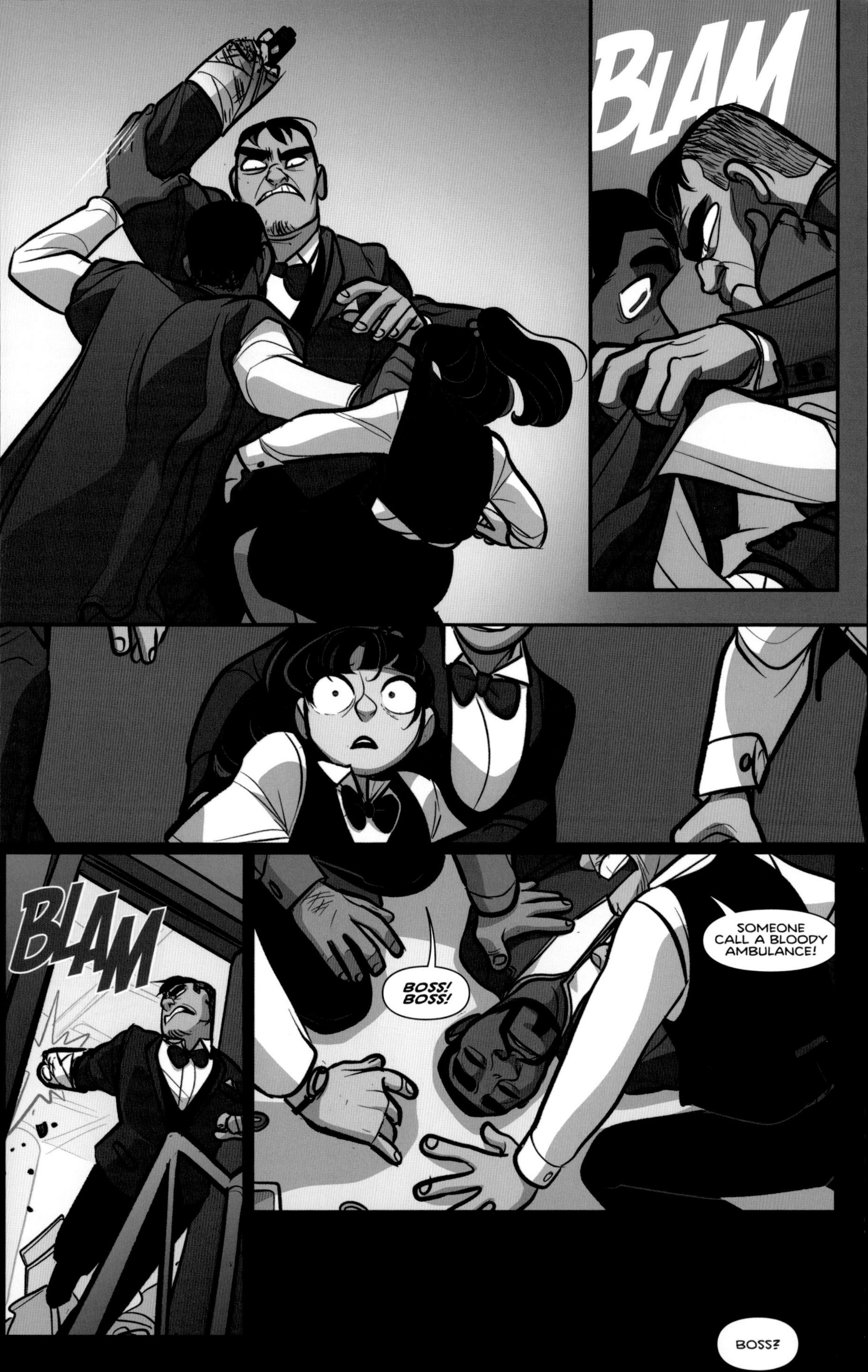
BLAM
BLAM
BOSS! BOSS!
SOMEONE CALL A BLOODY AMBULANCE!
BOSS?

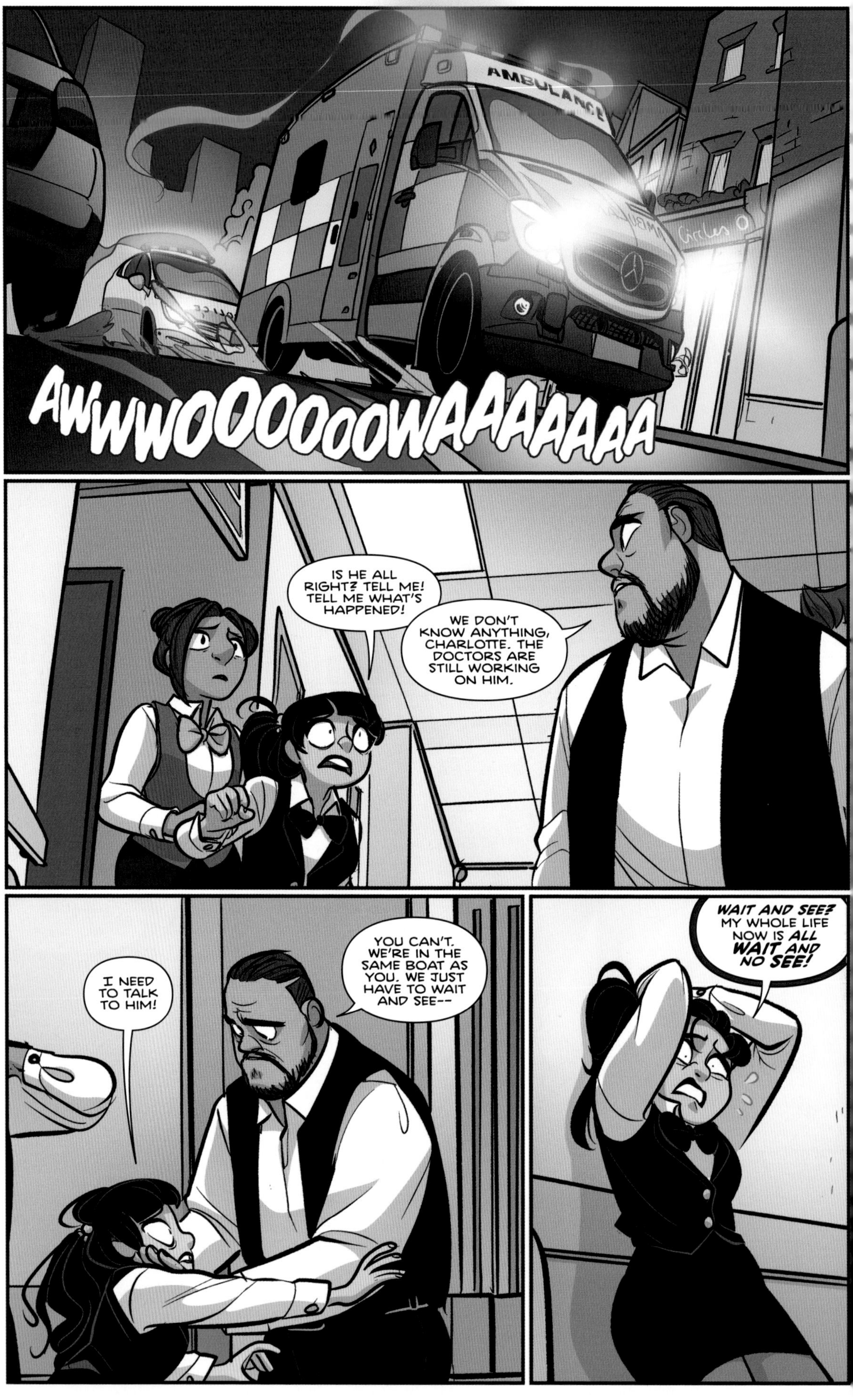
AMBULANCE
Circles
AWWWOOOOOOWAAAAAAA
IS HE ALL RIGHT? TELL ME! TELL ME WHAT'S HAPPENED!
WE DON'T KNOW ANYTHING, CHARLOTTE. THE DOCTORS ARE STILL WORKING ON HIM.
I NEED TO TALK TO HIM!
YOU CAN'T. WE'RE IN THE SAME BOAT AS YOU. WE JUST HAVE TO WAIT AND SEE--
WAIT AND SEE? MY WHOLE LIFE NOW IS ALL WAIT AND NO SEE!

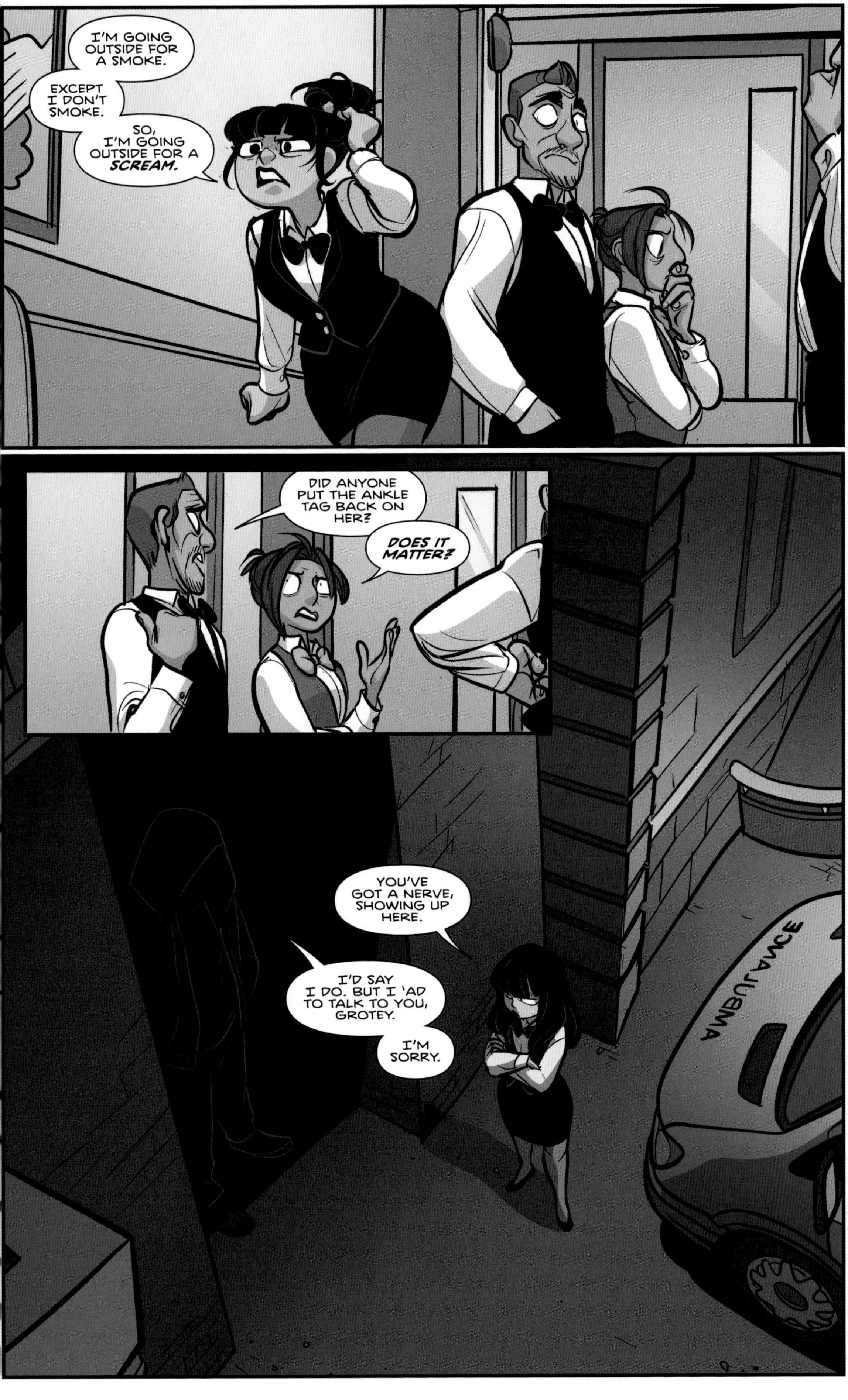
I'M GOING OUTSIDE FOR A SMOKE.
EXCEPT I DON'T SMOKE.
SO, I'M GOING OUTSIDE FOR A *SCREAM.*
DID ANYONE PUT THE ANKLE TAG BACK ON HER?
*DOES IT MATTER?*
YOU'VE GOT A NERVE, SHOWING UP HERE.
I'D SAY I DO. BUT I 'AD TO TALK TO YOU, GROTEY.
I'M SORRY.

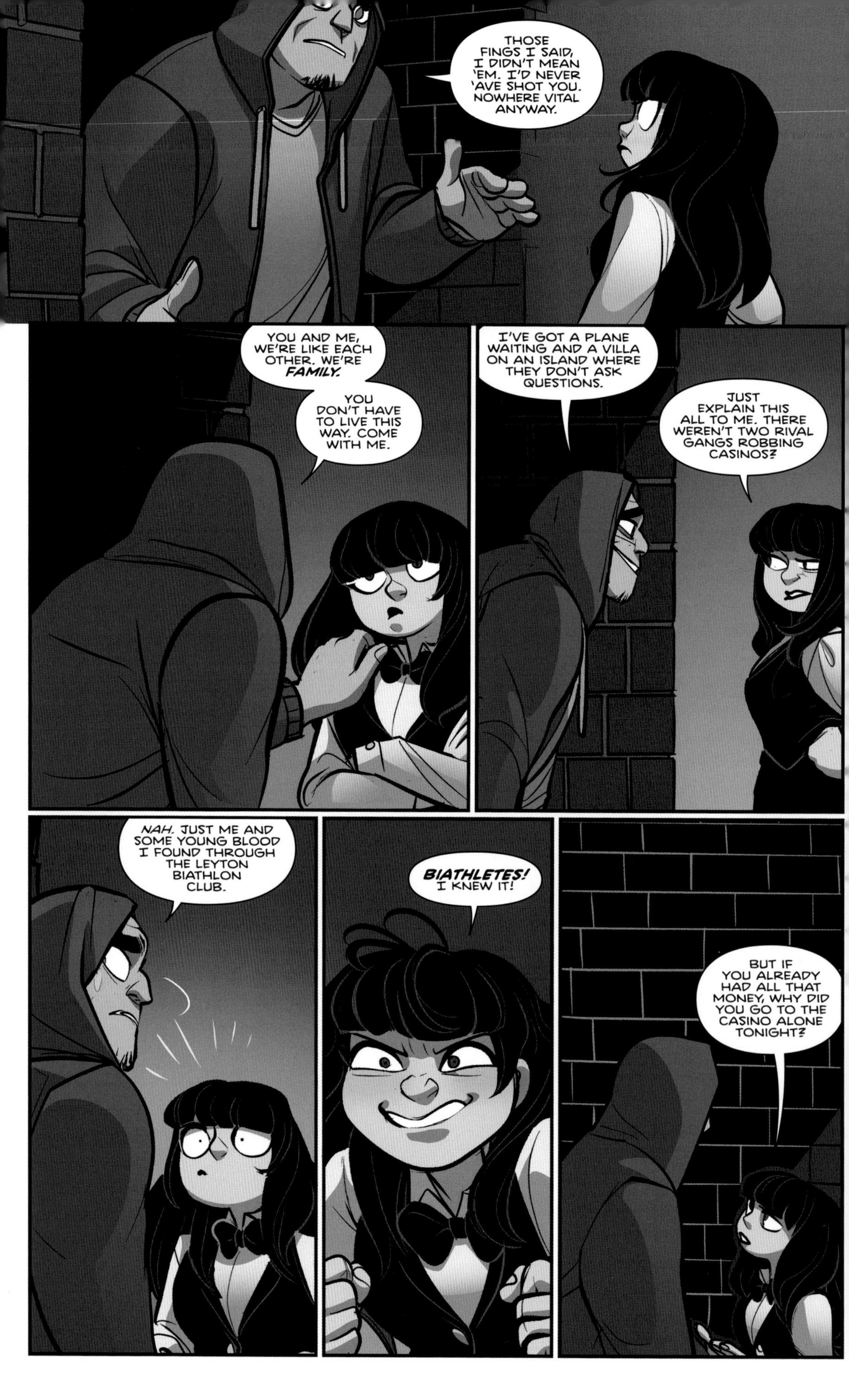
THOSE FINGS I SAID, I DIDN'T MEAN 'EM. I'D NEVER 'AVE SHOT YOU. NOWHERE VITAL ANYWAY.
YOU AND ME, WE'RE LIKE EACH OTHER. WE'RE *FAMILY.*
YOU DON'T HAVE TO LIVE THIS WAY. COME WITH ME.
I'VE GOT A PLANE WAITING AND A VILLA ON AN ISLAND WHERE THEY DON'T ASK QUESTIONS.
JUST EXPLAIN THIS ALL TO ME. THERE WEREN'T TWO RIVAL GANGS ROBBING CASINOS?
*NAH.* JUST ME AND SOME YOUNG BLOOD I FOUND THROUGH THE LEYTON BIATHLON CLUB.
***BIATHLETES!*** I KNEW IT!
BUT IF YOU ALREADY HAD ALL THAT MONEY, WHY DID YOU GO TO THE CASINO ALONE TONIGHT?

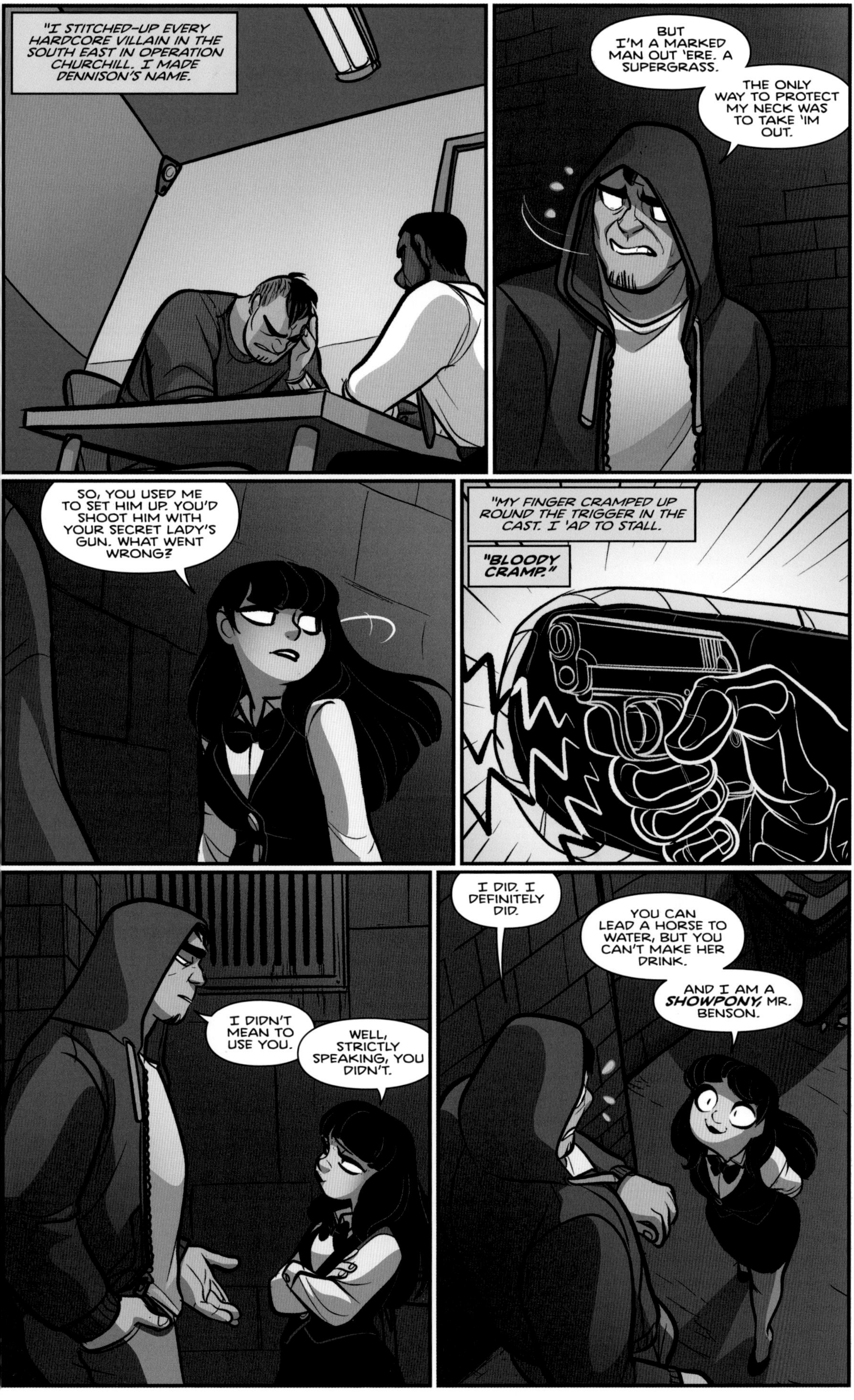
"I STITCHED-UP EVERY HARDCORE VILLAIN IN THE SOUTH EAST IN OPERATION CHURCHILL. I MADE DENNISON'S NAME.
BUT I'M A MARKED MAN OUT 'ERE. A SUPERGRASS.
THE ONLY WAY TO PROTECT MY NECK WAS TO TAKE 'IM OUT.
SO, YOU USED ME TO SET HIM UP. YOU'D SHOOT HIM WITH YOUR SECRET LADY'S GUN. WHAT WENT WRONG?
"MY FINGER CRAMPED UP ROUND THE TRIGGER IN THE CAST. I 'AD TO STALL.
"BLOODY CRAMP."
I DIDN'T MEAN TO USE YOU.
WELL, STRICTLY SPEAKING, YOU DIDN'T.
I DID. I DEFINITELY DID.
YOU CAN LEAD A HORSE TO WATER, BUT YOU CAN'T MAKE HER DRINK.
AND I AM A SHOWPONY, MR. BENSON.

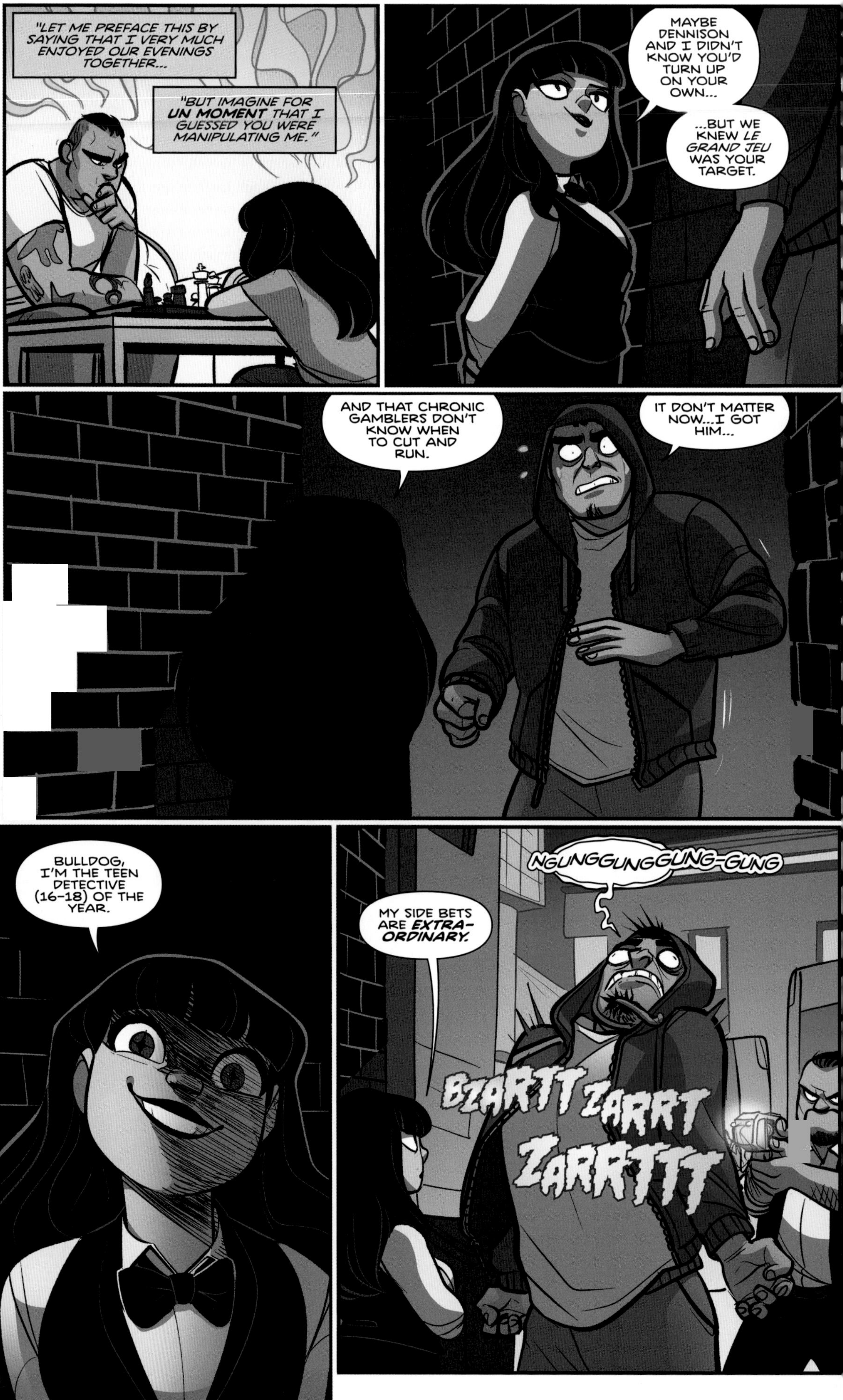
"LET ME PREFACE THIS BY SAYING THAT I VERY MUCH ENJOYED OUR EVENINGS TOGETHER...
"BUT IMAGINE FOR **UN MOMENT** THAT I GUESSED YOU WERE MANIPULATING ME."
MAYBE DENNISON AND I DIDN'T KNOW YOU'D TURN UP ON YOUR OWN...
...BUT WE KNEW *LE GRAND JEU* WAS YOUR TARGET.
AND THAT CHRONIC GAMBLERS DON'T KNOW WHEN TO CUT AND RUN.
IT DON'T MATTER NOW...I GOT HIM...
BULLDOG, I'M THE TEEN DETECTIVE (16-18) OF THE YEAR.
NGUNGGUNGGUNG-GUNG
MY SIDE BETS ARE ***EXTRA-ORDINARY.***
BZARTT ZARRT ZARRTTT

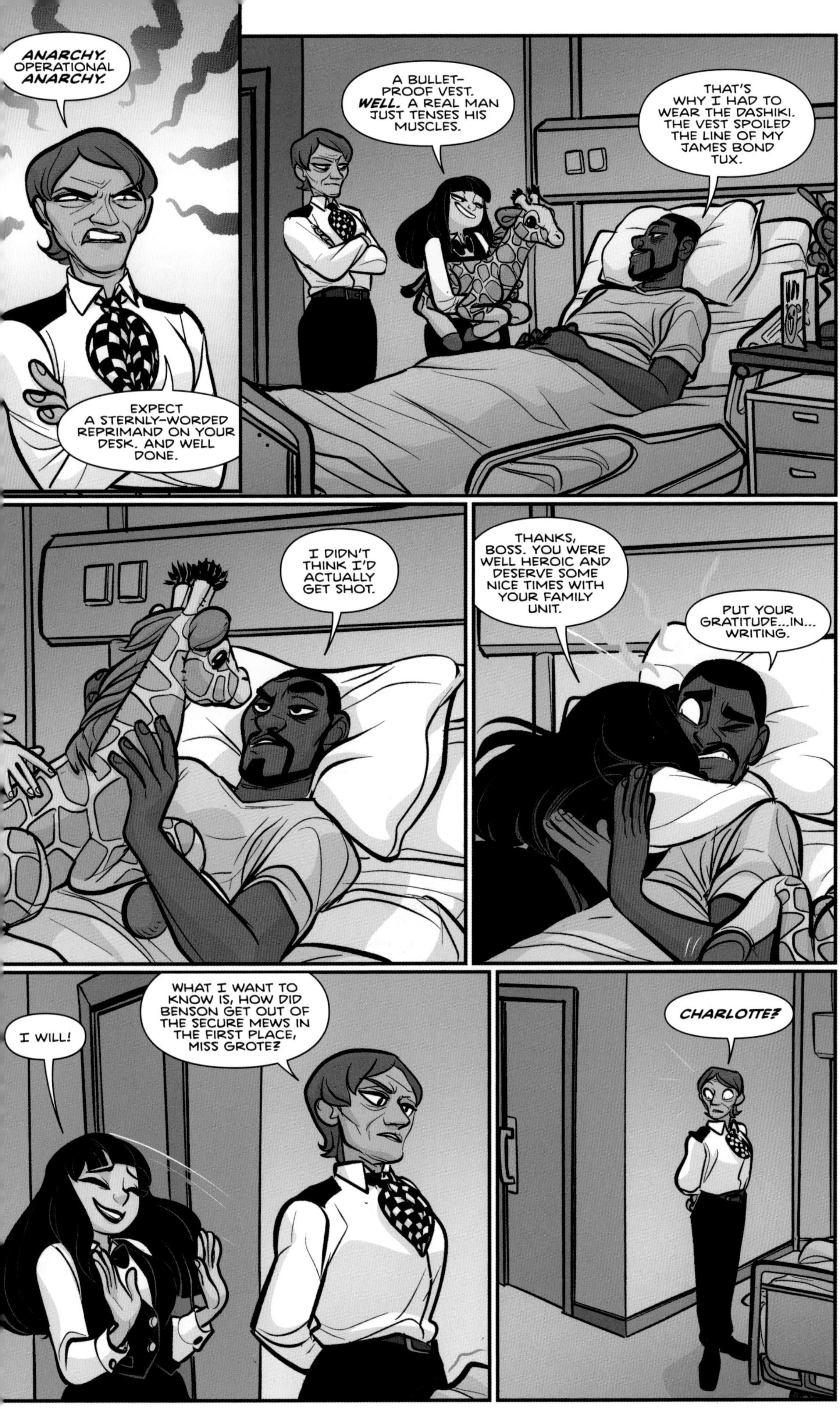
ANARCHY. OPERATIONAL ANARCHY.
EXPECT A STERNLY-WORDED REPRIMAND ON YOUR DESK. AND WELL DONE.
A BULLET-PROOF VEST. WELL. A REAL MAN JUST TENSES HIS MUSCLES.
THAT'S WHY I HAD TO WEAR THE DASHIKI. THE VEST SPOILED THE LINE OF MY JAMES BOND TUX.
I DIDN'T THINK I'D ACTUALLY GET SHOT.
THANKS, BOSS. YOU WERE WELL HEROIC AND DESERVE SOME NICE TIMES WITH YOUR FAMILY UNIT.
PUT YOUR GRATITUDE...IN... WRITING.
I WILL!
WHAT I WANT TO KNOW IS, HOW DID BENSON GET OUT OF THE SECURE MEWS IN THE FIRST PLACE, MISS GROTE?
CHARLOTTE?

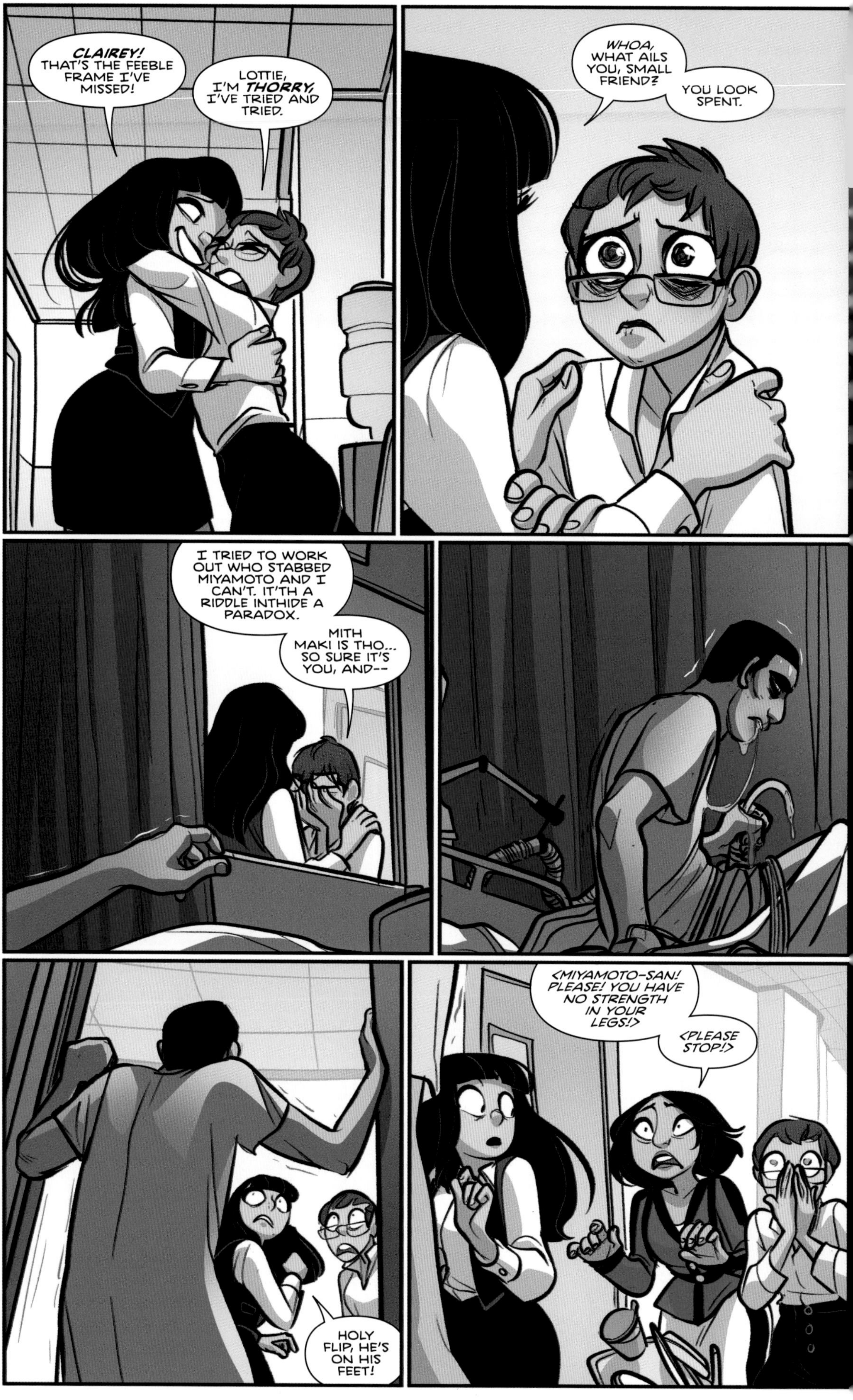
CLAIREY! THAT'S THE FEEBLE FRAME I'VE MISSED!
LOTTIE, I'M THORRY, I'VE TRIED AND TRIED.
WHOA, WHAT AILS YOU, SMALL FRIEND?
YOU LOOK SPENT.
I TRIED TO WORK OUT WHO STABBED MIYAMOTO AND I CAN'T. IT'TH A RIDDLE INTHIDE A PARADOX.
MITH MAKI IS THO... SO SURE IT'S YOU, AND--
HOLY FLIP, HE'S ON HIS FEET!
<MIYAMOTO-SAN! PLEASE! YOU HAVE NO STRENGTH IN YOUR LEGS!>
<PLEASE STOP!>

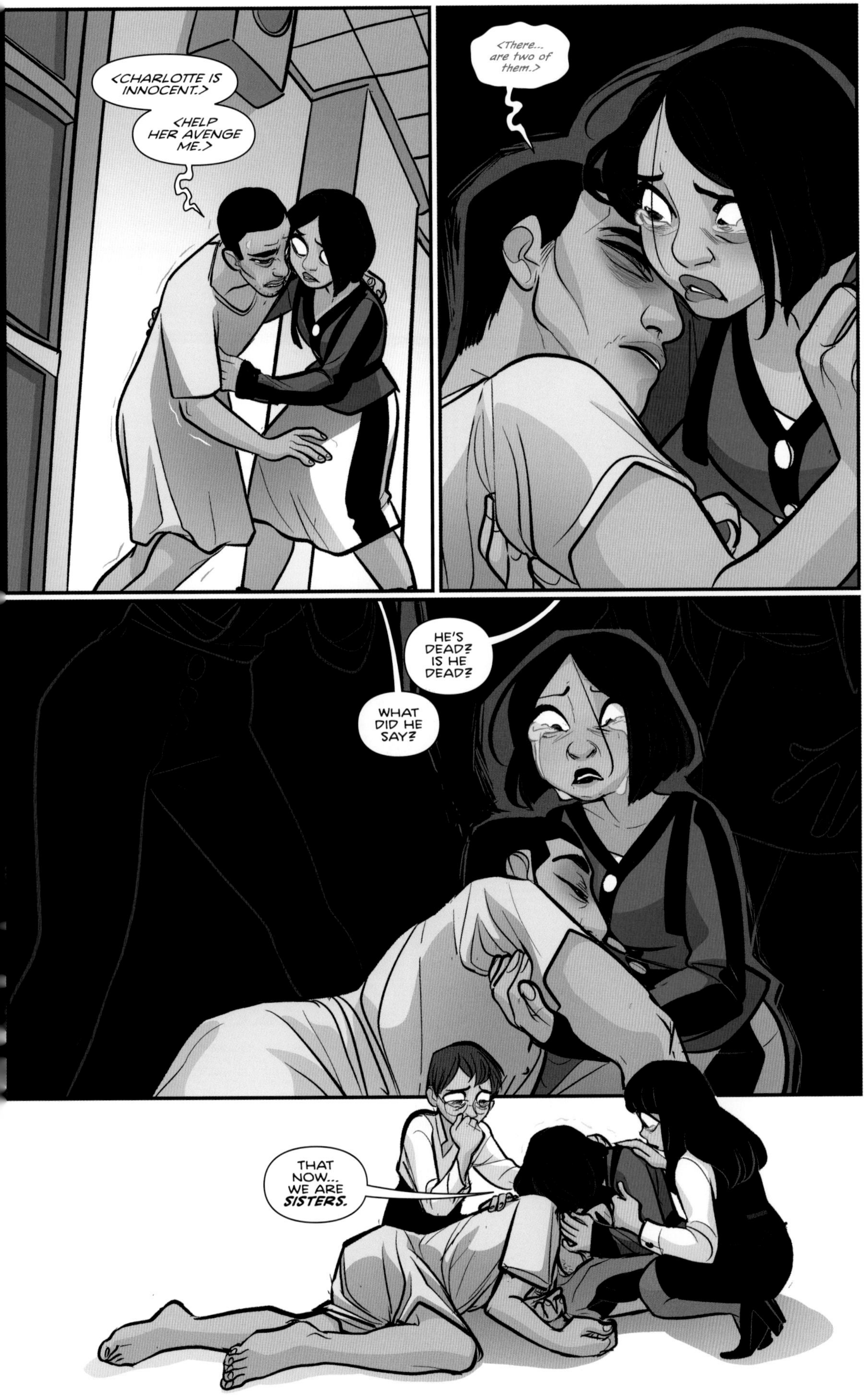

<CHARLOTTE IS INNOCENT.>
<HELP HER AVENGE ME.>
<There... are two of them.>
HE'S DEAD? IS HE DEAD?
WHAT DID HE SAY?
THAT NOW... WE ARE SISTERS.

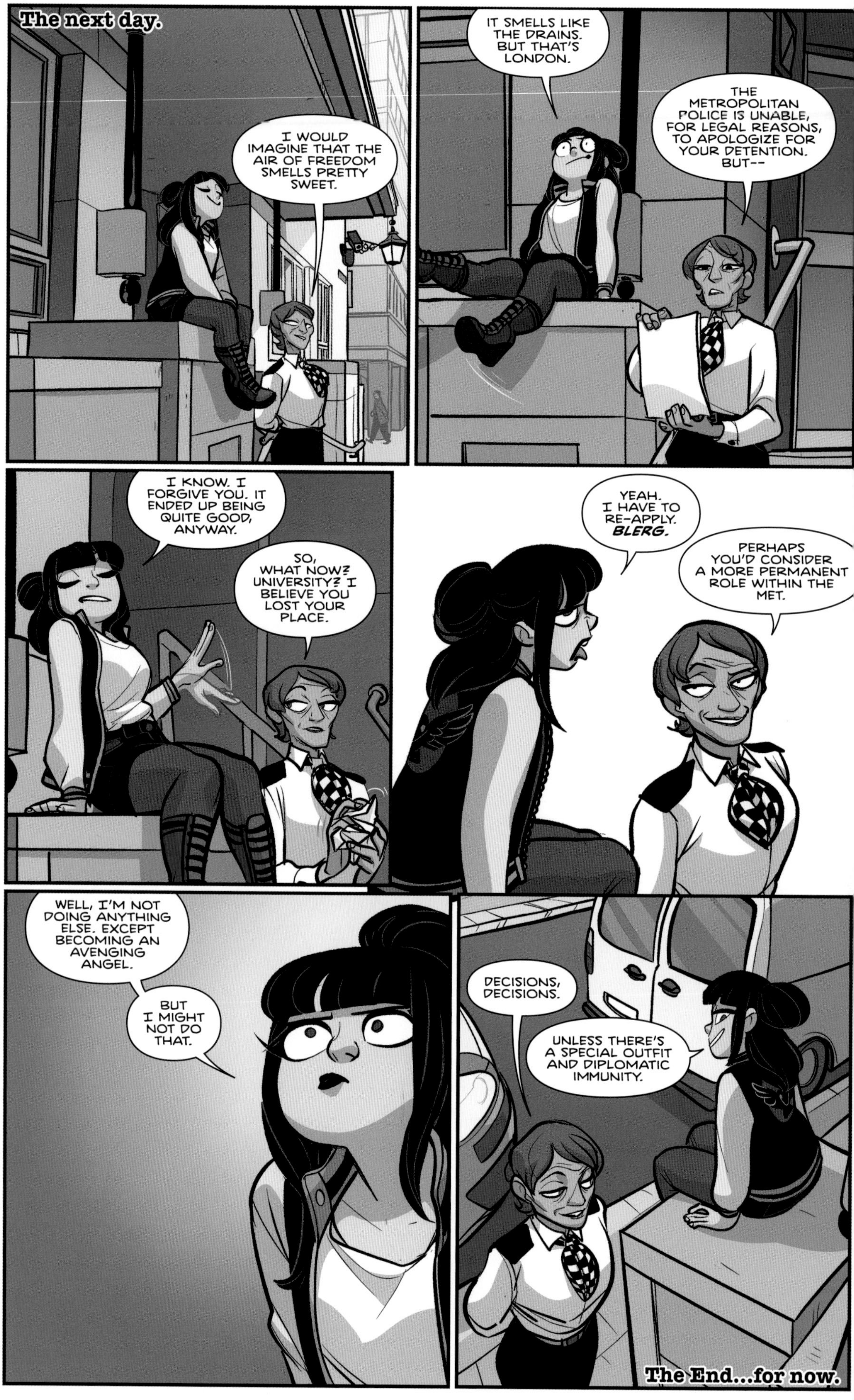
The next day.
I WOULD IMAGINE THAT THE AIR OF FREEDOM SMELLS PRETTY SWEET.
IT SMELLS LIKE THE DRAINS. BUT THAT'S LONDON.
THE METROPOLITAN POLICE IS UNABLE, FOR LEGAL REASONS, TO APOLOGIZE FOR YOUR DETENTION. BUT--
I KNOW. I FORGIVE YOU. IT ENDED UP BEING QUITE GOOD, ANYWAY.
SO, WHAT NOW? UNIVERSITY? I BELIEVE YOU LOST YOUR PLACE.
YEAH. I HAVE TO RE-APPLY. BLERG.
PERHAPS YOU'D CONSIDER A MORE PERMANENT ROLE WITHIN THE MET.
WELL, I'M NOT DOING ANYTHING ELSE. EXCEPT BECOMING AN AVENGING ANGEL.
BUT I MIGHT NOT DO THAT.
DECISIONS, DECISIONS.
UNLESS THERE'S A SPECIAL OUTFIT AND DIPLOMATIC IMMUNITY.
The End...for now.

# COVER GALLERY

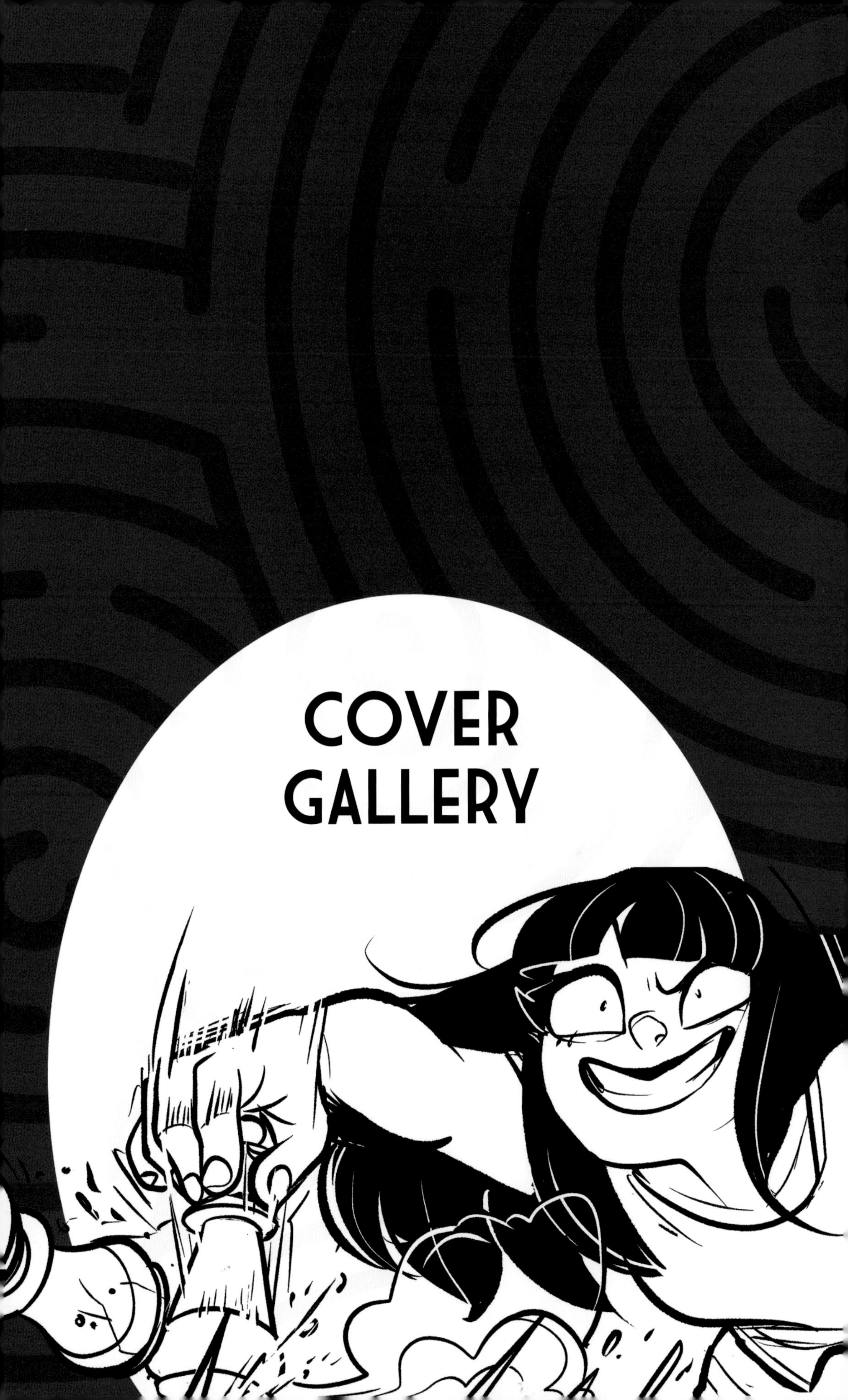

#1 VARIANT COVER BY
**JOHN ALLISON**

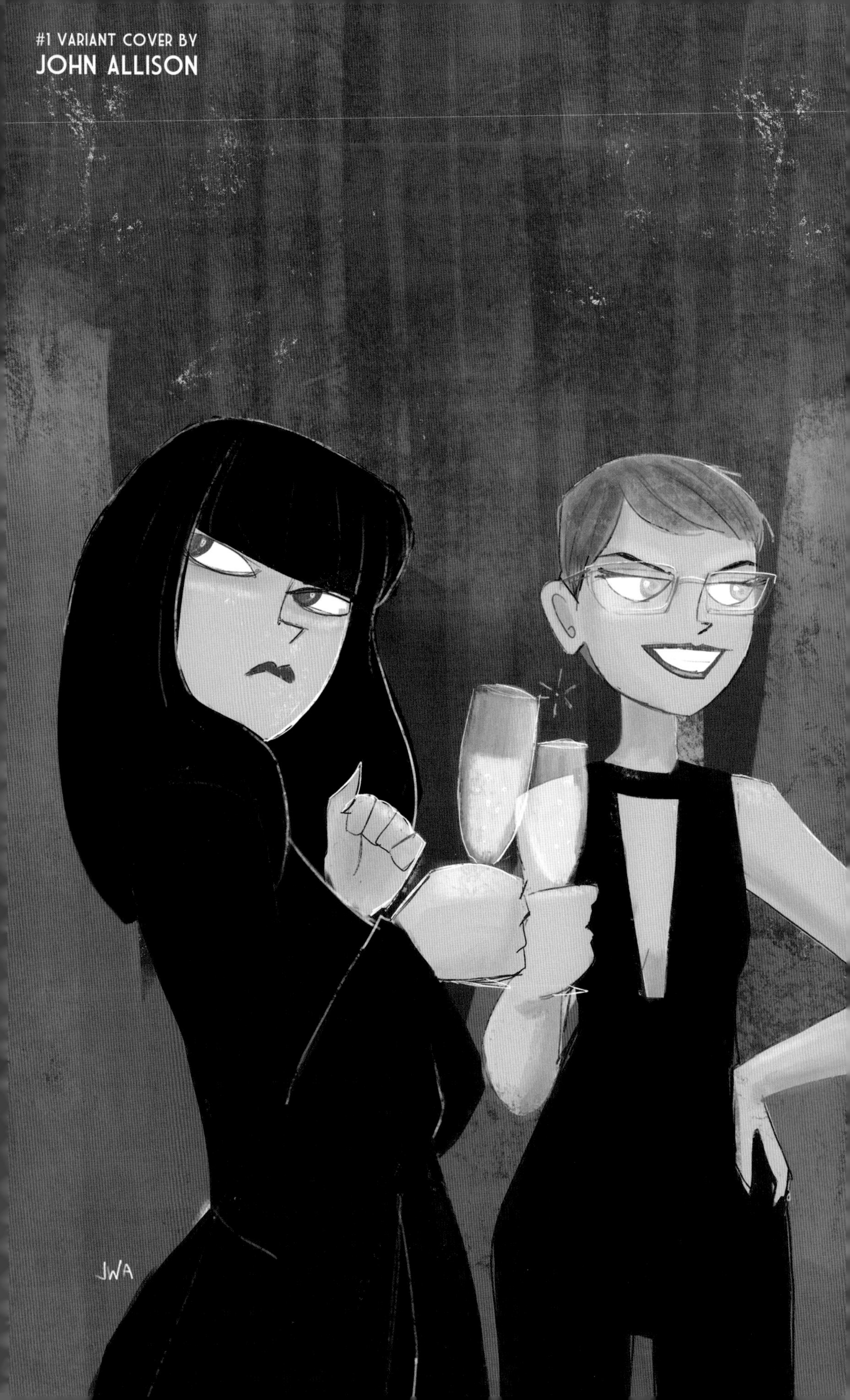

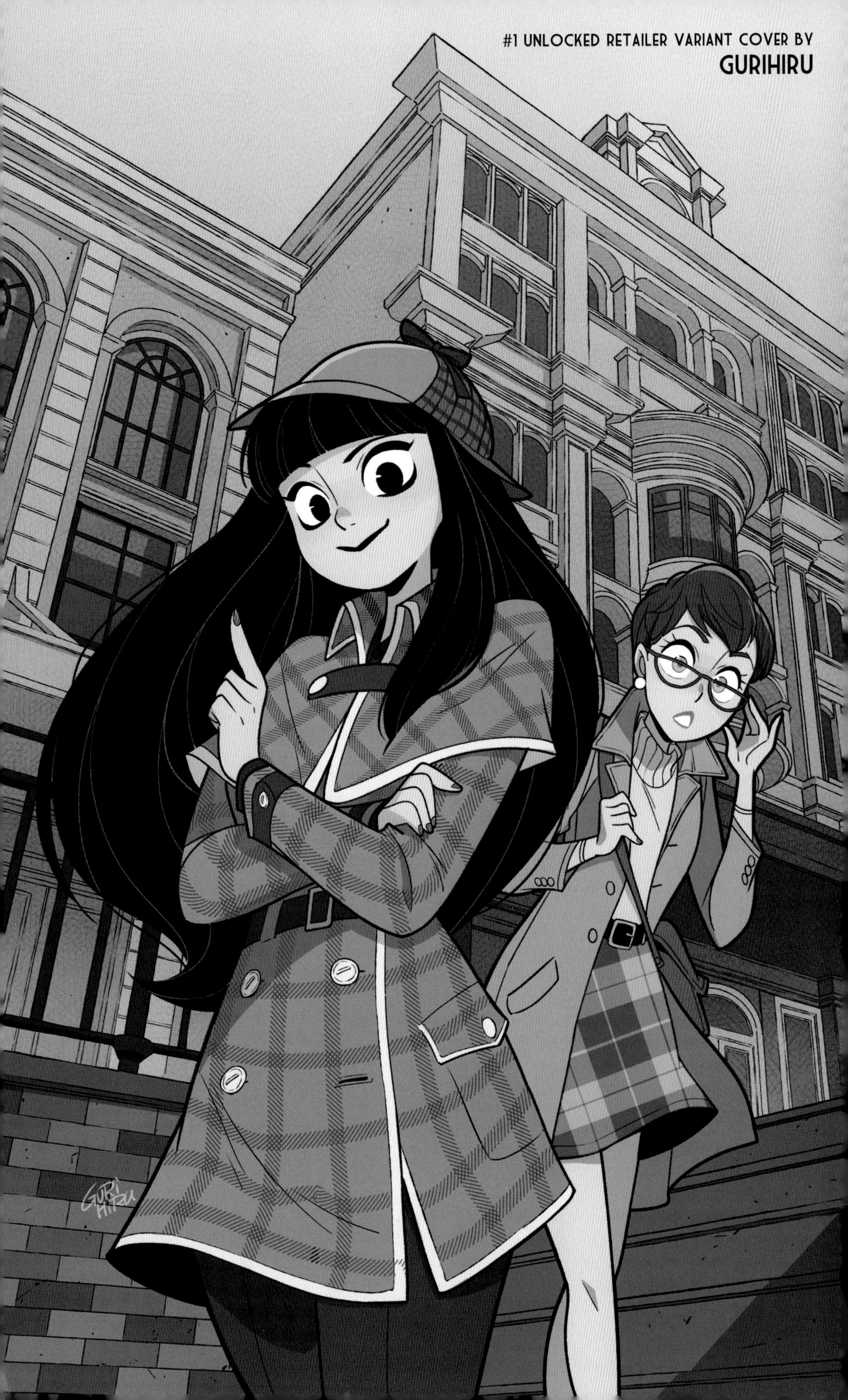
GURI HIRU

#1 UNLOCKED RETAILER VARIANT COVER BY
**GURIHIRU**

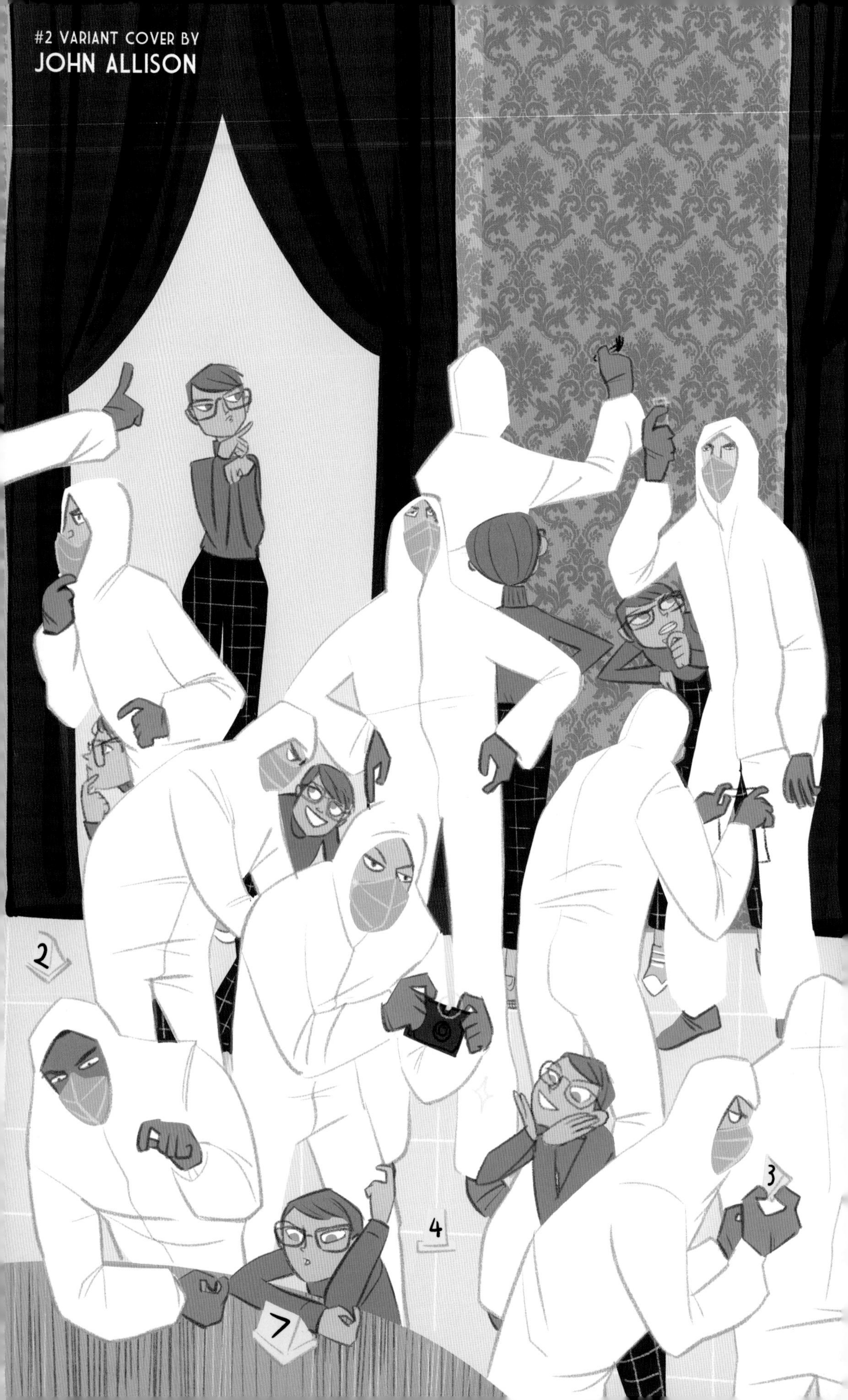
2
4
3
7

#2 VARIANT COVER BY
JOHN ALLISON

#2 UNLOCKED RETAILER VARIANT COVER BY
VERONICA FISH

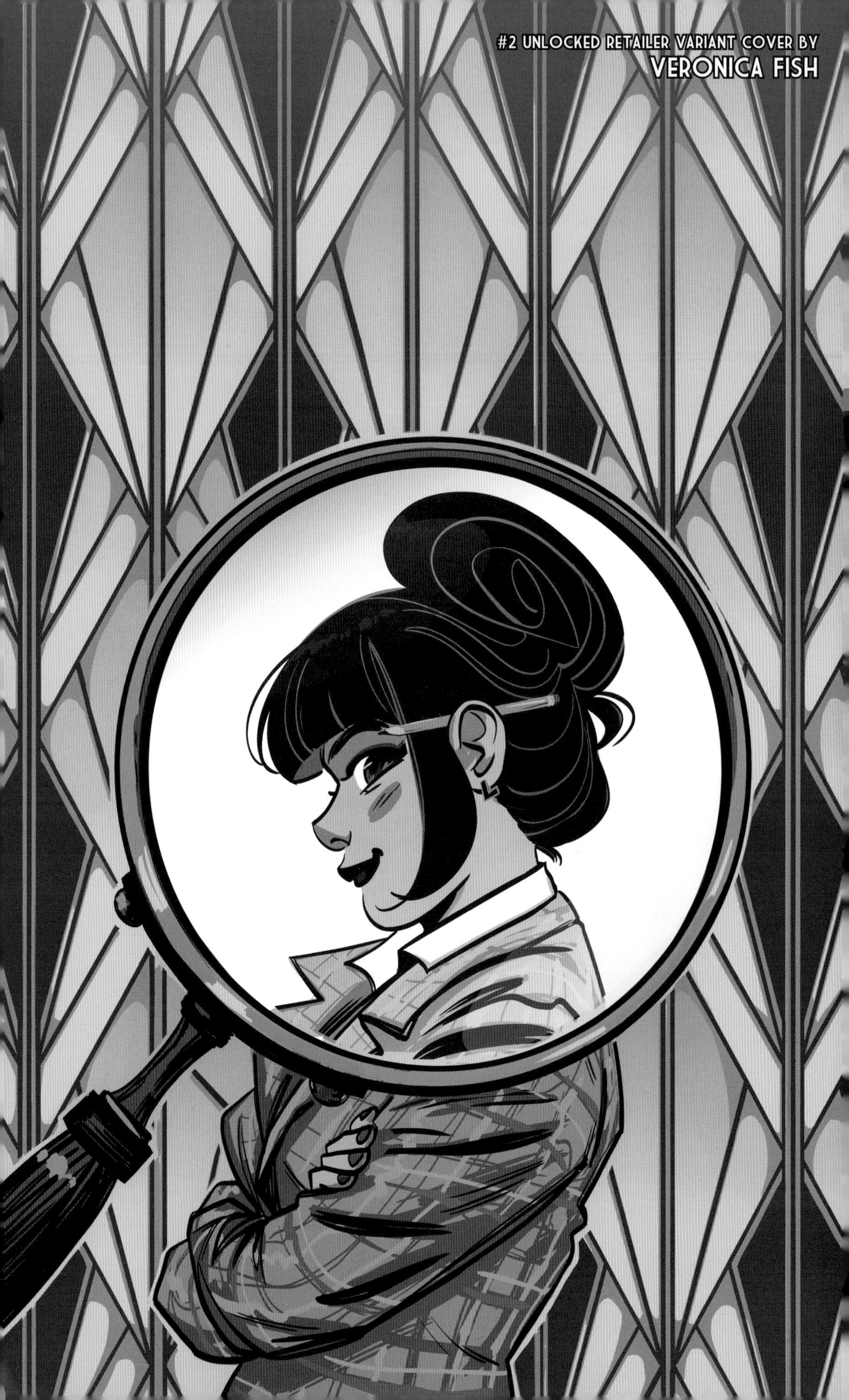

#3 VARIANT COVER BY
JOHN ALLISON

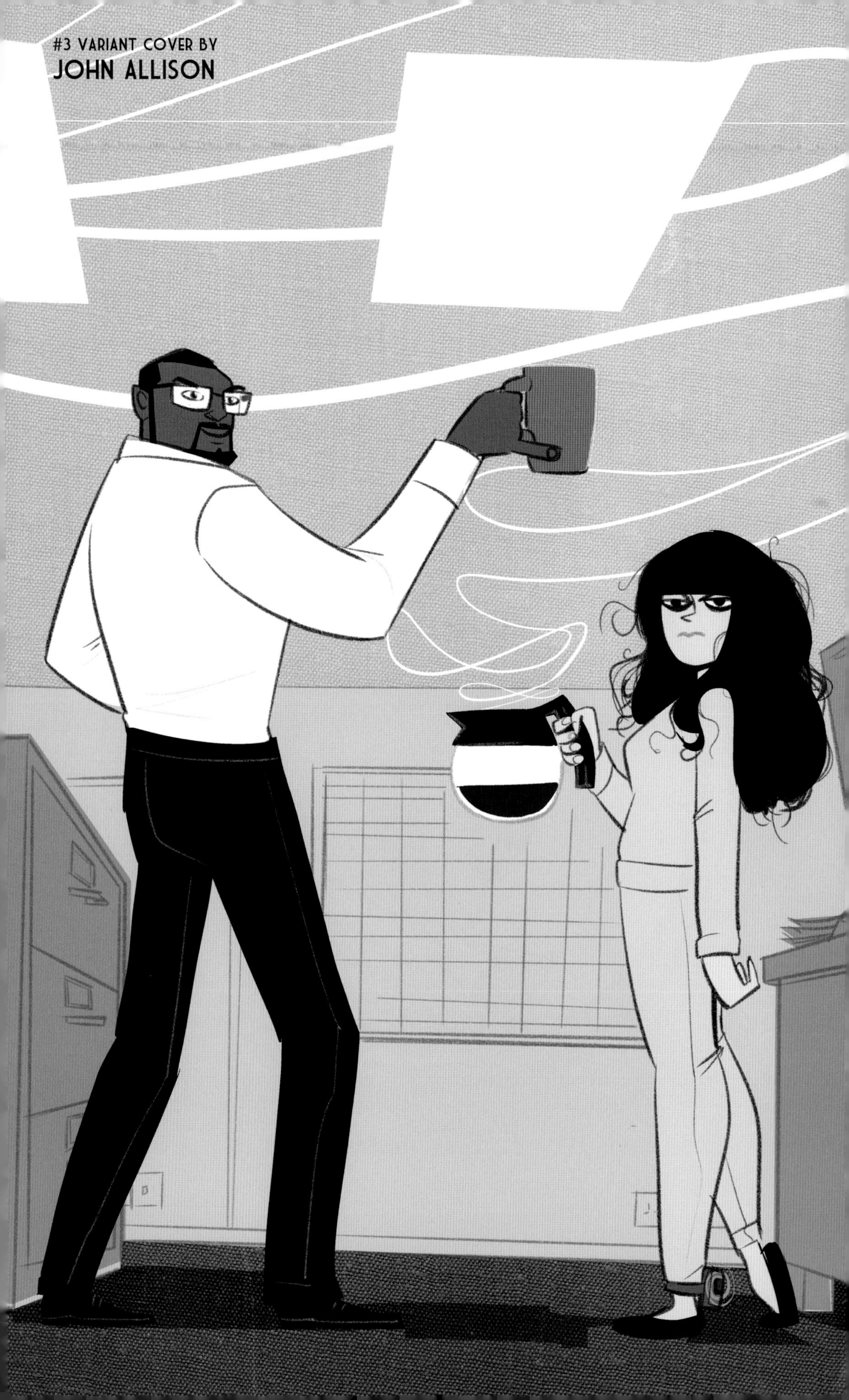

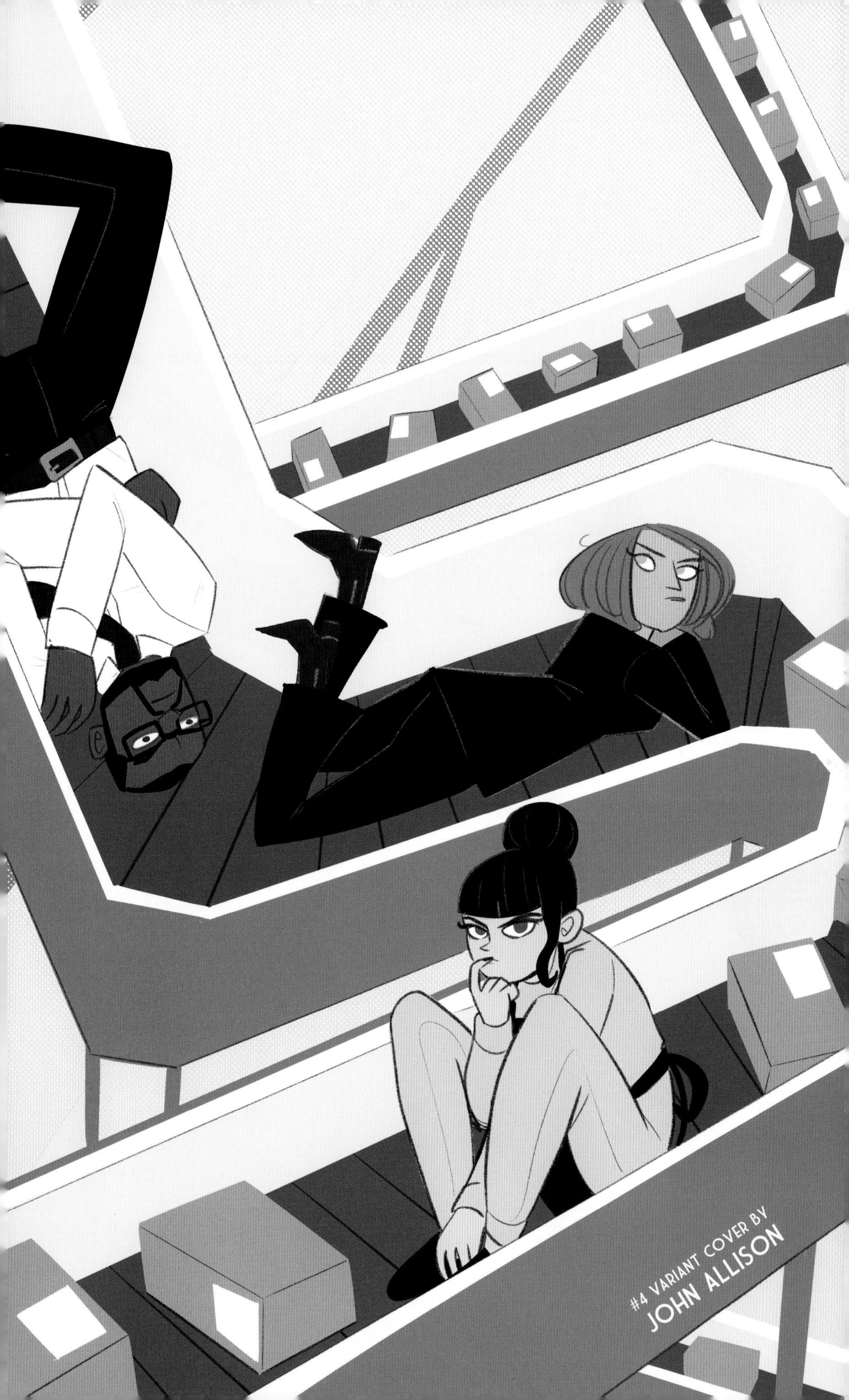
#4 VARIANT COVER BY
JOHN ALLISON

#5 VARIANT COVER BY
JOHN ALLISON

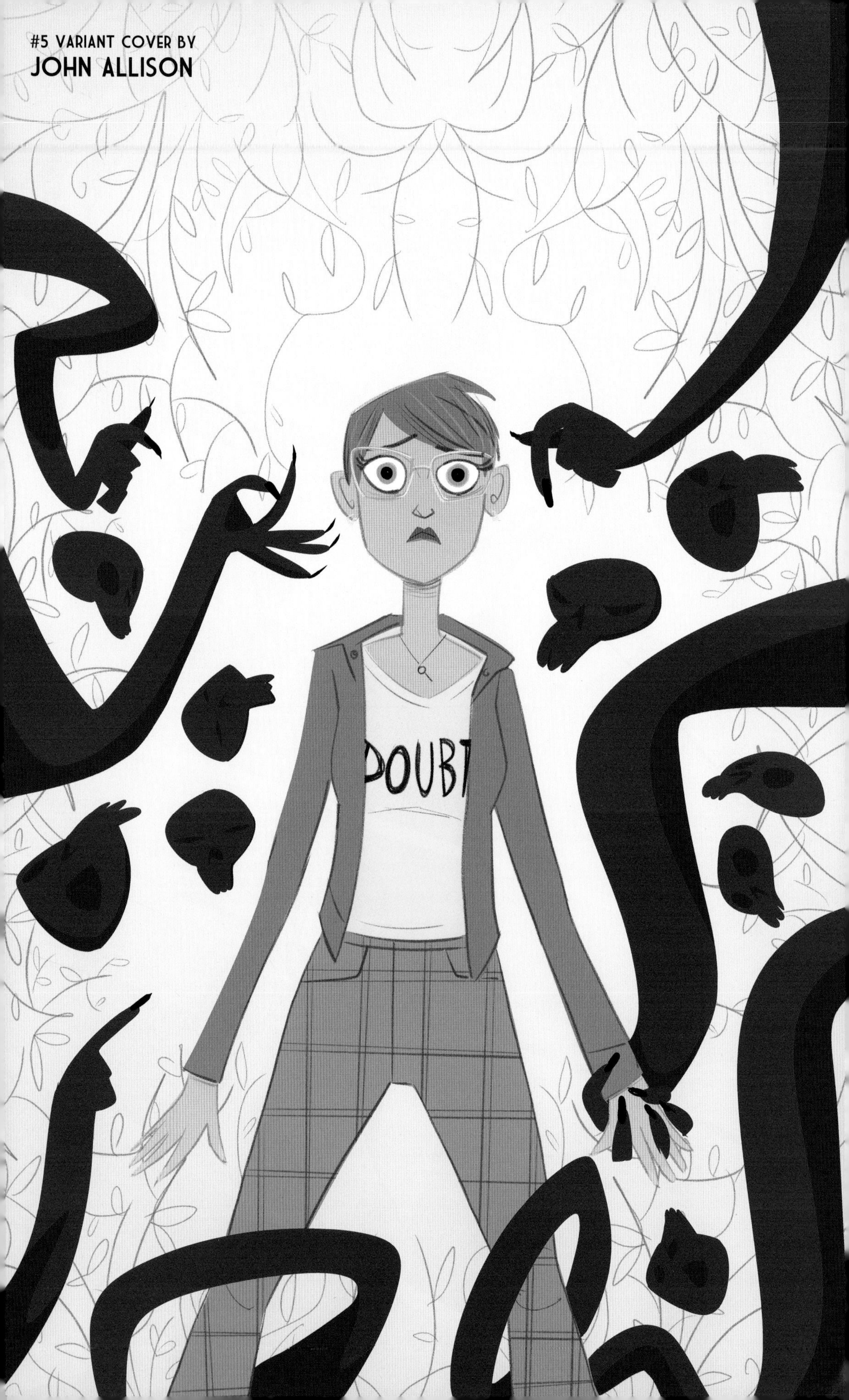
DOUBT

#6 VARIANT COVER BY
JOHN ALLISON

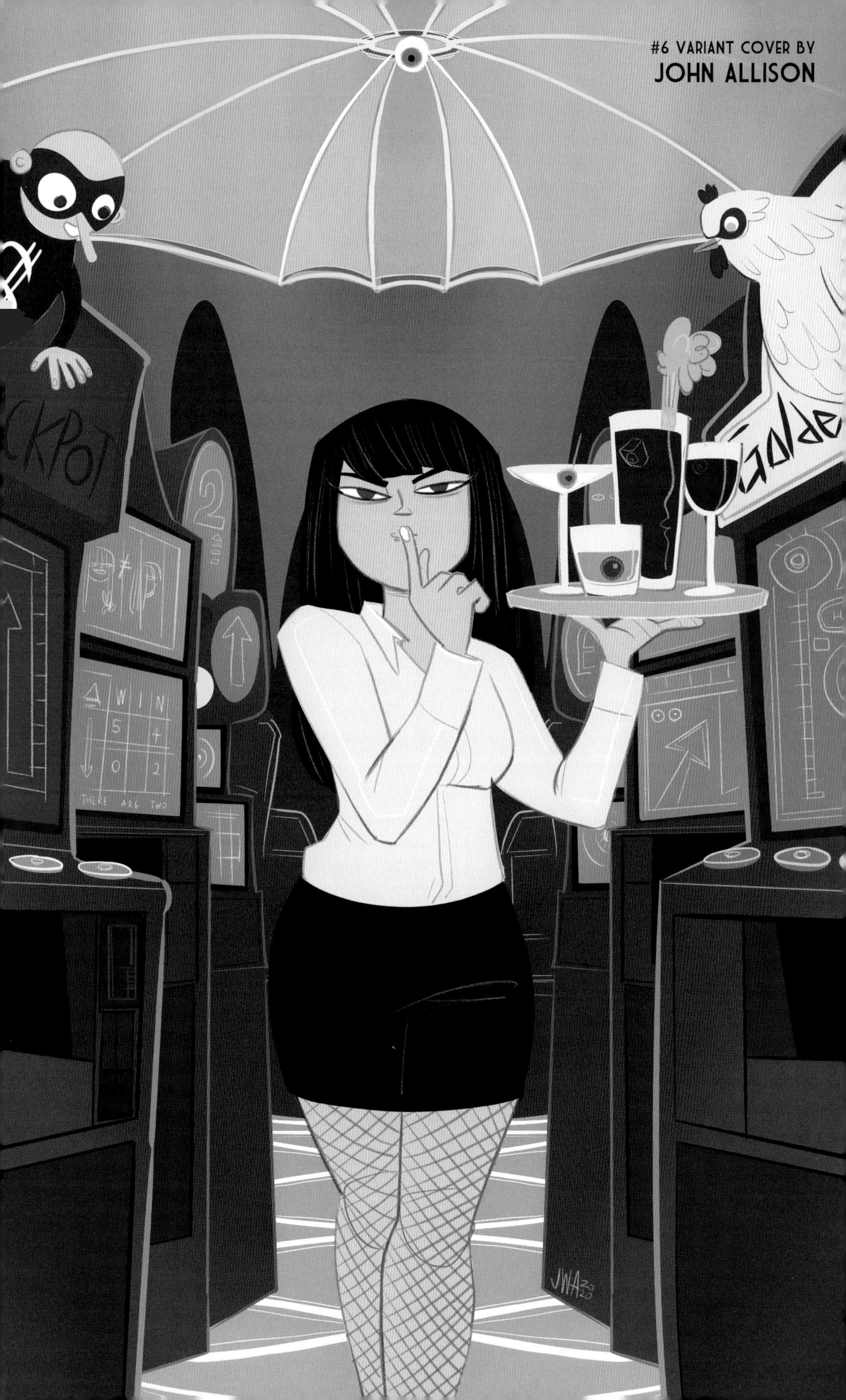
CKPOT
WIN
THERE ARE TWO
JWA 2020

SKETCHES AND SAMPLE PAGE BY

# JOHN ALLISON

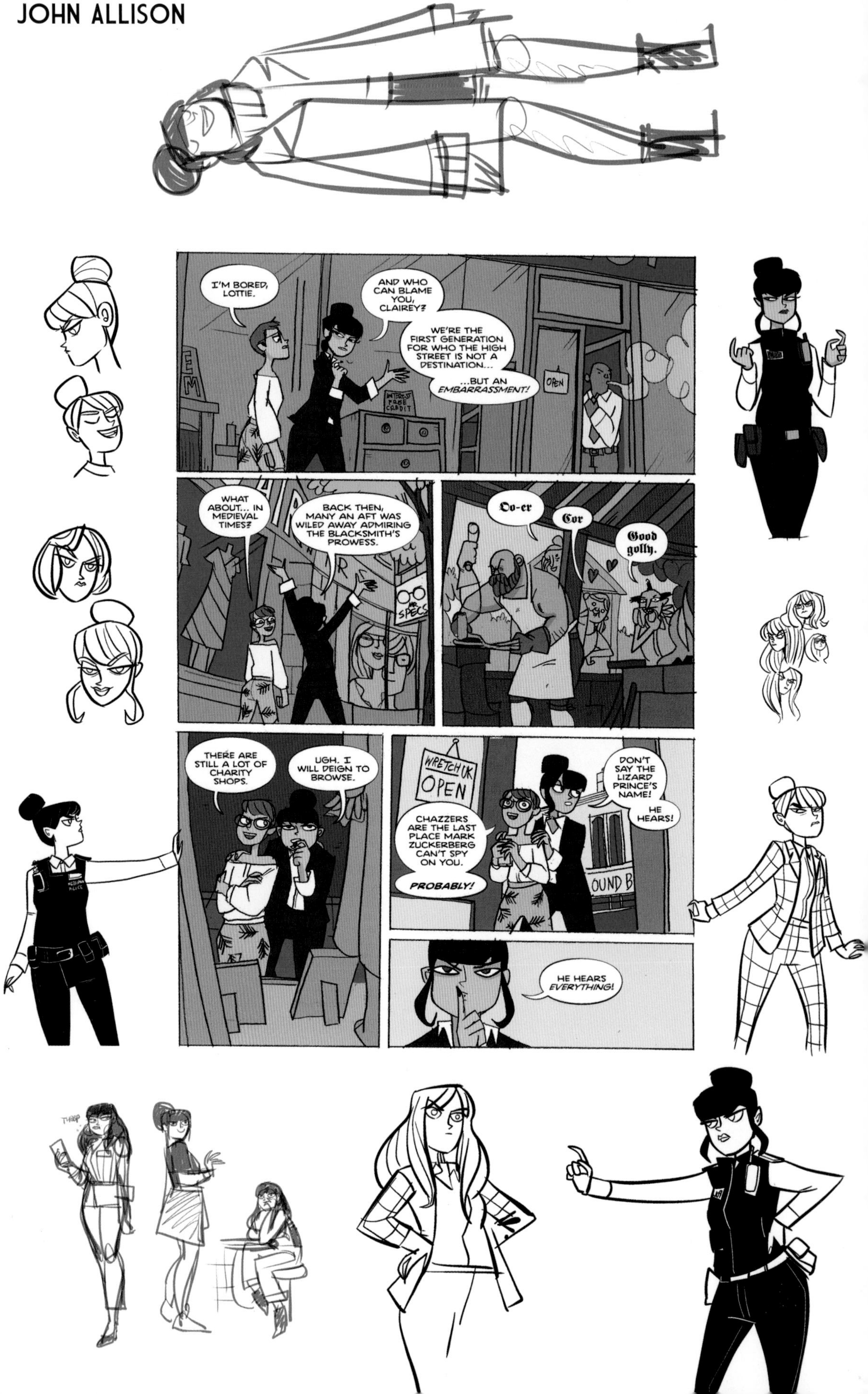
I'M BORED, LOTTIE.
AND WHO CAN BLAME YOU, CLAIREY?
WE'RE THE FIRST GENERATION FOR WHO THE HIGH STREET IS NOT A DESTINATION...
...BUT AN *EMBARRASSMENT!*
INTEREST FREE CREDIT
OPEN
WHAT ABOUT... IN MEDIEVAL TIMES?
BACK THEN, MANY AN AFT WAS WILED AWAY ADMIRING THE BLACKSMITH'S PROWESS.
MR SPECS
Oo-er
Cor
Good golly.
THERE ARE STILL A LOT OF CHARITY SHOPS.
UGH. I WILL DEIGN TO BROWSE.
WRETCH UK OPEN
CHAZZERS ARE THE LAST PLACE MARK ZUCKERBERG CAN'T SPY ON YOU.
**PROBABLY!**
DON'T SAY THE LIZARD PRINCE'S NAME!
HE HEARS!
OUND B
HE HEARS *EVERYTHING!*
THRRP